the
Sorcerer
of
Sainte Felice

the Sorcerer
of
Sainte Felice

ANN FINNIN

flux™
Woodbury, Minnesota

First Edition
First Printing, 2010

Cover design and photo illustration by Kevin R. Brown
Cover images: boy © iStockphoto.com/Sascha Burkard;
    parchment © iStockphoto.com/Anastasiya Maksymenko;
    monastery © iStockphoto.com/Tomasz Parys;
    monk © iStockphoto.com/Roberto A. Sanchez
Map on p. vi © Jared Blando

Flux, an imprint of Llewellyn Worldwide Ltd.

Library of Congress Cataloging-in-Publication Data
Finnin, Ann.
  The sorcerer of Sainte Felice / Ann Finnin.—1st ed.
     p. cm.
  Summary: In fifteenth-century France, fifteen-year-old Michael de Lorraine is saved from execution by Abbot Francis and granted refuge at the Benedictine monastery of Sainte Felice, where he tries to use his powers to save his new friends and mentors from the Inquisition.
  ISBN: 978-0-7387-2070-8
  [1. Magic—Fiction. 2. Wizards—Fiction. 3. Monasteries—Fiction. 4. Inquisition—Fiction. 5. France—History—15th Century—Fiction.] I. Title.
  PZ7.F49842Sor 2010
  [Fic]—dc22

                                                        2010002352

                                Flux
                    Llewellyn Worldwide Ltd.
                      2143 Wooddale Drive
                    Woodbury, MN 55125-2989
                        www.fluxnow.com

            Printed in the United States of America

For Dave

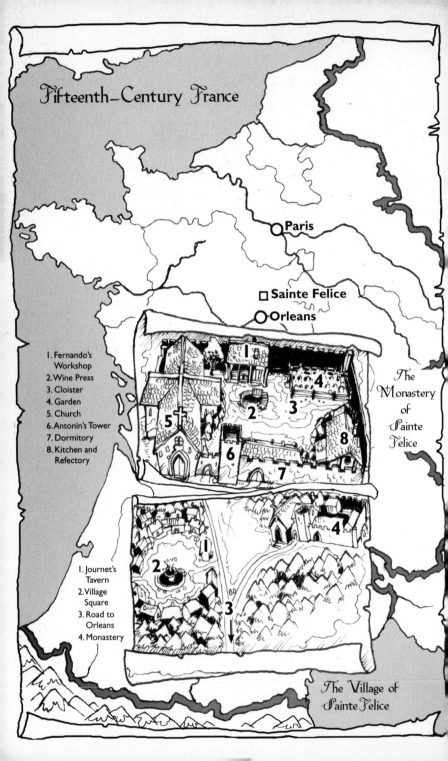

Fifteenth–Century France

Paris

□ Sainte Felice

Orleans

1. Fernando's
   Workshop
2. Wine Press
3. Cloister
4. Garden
5. Church
6. Antonin's Tower
7. Dormitory
8. Kitchen and
   Refectory

The
Monastery
of
Sainte
Felice

1. Journet's
   Tavern
2. Village
   Square
3. Road to
   Orleans
4. Monastery

The Village of
Sainte Felice

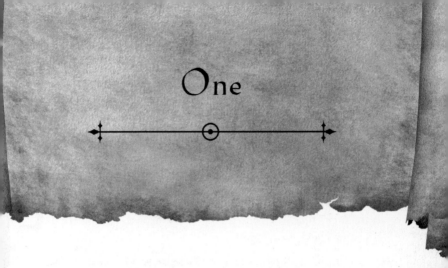

One

I was only an apprentice. I swear it. By all the angels in heaven.

"Michael de Lorraine," the magistrate below me bellowed in a voice like a death knell. A soldier thrust a burning torch into the pile of straw and sticks around my feet. "By the order of His Most Catholic Majesty Louis, King of France, you are hereby condemned to be burnt at the stake in the city of Orleans for the crime of sorcery on this the twenty-second day of August in the year of our Lord, 1480."

I struggled against the rope that bound me to the stake in the center of the pyre. My wrists ached, but the rope held me fast. God, this couldn't be happening. Was I, after only fifteen years in this world, doomed to perish in these cruel flames?

"No!" I screamed as the flames tossed billows of smoke into my face. "No, you can't do this. You can't!"

"Let the sentence be carried out according to the king's law," the magistrate continued in an implacable voice. "And may God have mercy on your soul."

The people gathered in the town square gawked at me as though I were nothing but a freak in a traveling caravan. A cry rose from one throat in the crowd: "Sorcerer!" It soon became a chorus. "Heretic!"

Something hit me in the face. It squished in my hair and smelled rotten. My stomach lurched. Smoke filled my lungs and I choked for breath.

In despair, I cast my gaze up to the darkening sky— more to turn my face away from the billowing smoke than to beseech a God who had abandoned me thus. Summoning all the air left in my lungs, I screamed one final time, hoping that somewhere, somehow, someone might hear me.

My cry was swallowed up by the shouts and commotion that suddenly emerged from the crowd. I squinted my eyes against the smoke and peered through the shimmering heat to see what was happening. My heart rose in my throat. Had my heartfelt cry been heard? Was someone coming to rescue me?

A priest, clad in the black habit of the Benedictine order, pushed his way through the crowd towards me. The magistrate blocked his path, but the priest shoved him aside. Heedless of the flames, he scrambled up onto the pyre beside me.

My heart sank to my toes. I was only going to be shriven, not rescued. What else would a Benedictine priest want with me, save to hear an apprentice sorcerer's last confession?

Then my mouth dropped open in astonishment. Ignoring me completely, the priest lifted one hand to heaven while clutching a golden cross on his breast with the other. Over the deepening roar of the flames, I heard him shout bits of Latin. I didn't quite catch all of what he said. But what I did catch sent a chill down my spine in spite of the flames.

"Gaze down upon the tortured soul, O Archangel Gabriel," he bellowed. "And let the blessed tears of Heaven pour forth from your eyes and rain down upon him. By the power of Almighty God, who spake and it was done."

I shook my head as despair overwhelmed me once more. He was mad. That was why he was here. Hot tears ran down my cheeks. The flames weren't cruel enough. They had to send a madman to torment my final moments on this earth.

I glanced up at a sudden crack of thunder. More water ran down my face, and the drops came not from my eyes but from the blessed heavens. The sprinkle turned into a downpour that squelched the tongues of fire that licked my feet. Steam and ash blew up into my face, blinding me and setting me to coughing. To my amazement, the strange priest's strong fingers unravelled the rope that bound my hands and feet, and he pulled me down from the heap of wood.

"Behold, the judgment of Almighty God!" The priest's

booming voice tolled like a church bell, echoing back from the distant hills. "Blessed be God the Compassionate who has shown mercy on the sinner."

Mercy? I rubbed the smoke from my eyes until I could see more clearly. What was this about mercy? But I had no opportunity to ask. Holding my arm in a tight grip, the priest dragged me through the crowd. The spectators fell back at his approach as wheat before the scythe. Many crossed themselves and bowed their heads. A few even knelt, reaching out their hands to touch the hem of his habit.

Only the magistrate, a thin sparrowhawk of a man named Montaigne, stood in our way. "Go no further, Abbot Duchienne." He crossed his arms across his chest. "You will not get away with this flagrant disregard of the king's justice."

"And God's justice? What of that? God has tendered His divine judgment." The priest waved his hand in the direction of the departing thunderclouds. "Do the very elements themselves have to box your ears to get you to take heed? Now stand aside."

The crowd began to rumble dangerously. The magistrate's tiny eyes flickered from side to side as the people moved in closer. The scowls on their faces told me they weren't pleased with how he was treating my rescuer. Would there be a riot?

"This is only one of your damnable tricks," he hissed. But he stood aside and allowed us to pass unmolested. Excited babble and shouts followed us as we left the town square. The words "truly a miracle" wafted towards me. I felt a shiver down my spine.

Was that what had just happened? A miracle?

The priest led the way towards a rickety cart drawn up at the edge of the square. As we approached, a gaunt mule pulled at its harness and glared at me with a baleful eye. I hesitated for a moment, but the priest grabbed me and pushed me up onto the seat. He vaulted up beside me and gathered up the reins. With a shout, he flicked the reins across the mule's bony rump and we lurched away from the town square.

I glanced over at him discreetly as he maneuvered the mule past the last of the houses towards the road out of town. In spite of his clerical demeanor, I could not help but detect a certain air of smug satisfaction at having defied the magistrate. He was tall and imposing, and his strong chin and aquiline nose made him an arresting figure indeed. He looked as though he had weathered at least forty-five winters and his black hair was streaked with silver. But his eyes were as clear a blue as the summer sky, and looked as though they could darken to winter chill when he was crossed. I knew only that I shouldn't wish to cross him.

I tried to ask him what he planned to do with me, but my throat still felt raw and seared by the burning smoke. We were well down the road before I found my voice.

"Where are you taking me?" I rasped.

"To the monastery near the village of Sainte Felice. You will be safe there."

I felt my stomach drop. God's blood! A monastery? "What if I don't wish to go to a monastery?"

"Then you don't have to," he replied, with a nonchalant shrug. "But it's either that or burn. The choice is yours."

"I see," I muttered in annoyance. "Then, I have no choice. Do I?"

He glanced over at me and raised an eyebrow. "My, aren't you the suspicious one. We offer you sanctuary from the secular authorities who were trying to roast you. Do you fear us as well?"

I swallowed hard. "I fear that if you knew my crime, you would not hesitate to turn me back over to the magistrate."

"Try me."

I glanced over at him, then turned away, biting my lip. "My name is Michael de Lorraine," I began. "And I…"

"Have been tried and convicted by the Holy Office of the Inquisition for the crime of sorcery and turned over to the secular arm to be burnt," he finished. "We already know. I fear you'll have to do better than that."

"You knew?" My eyes grew wide with astonishment. "And still you rescued me from the pyre?"

"Indeed, so. And that is precisely why I am taking you to my monastery." He chuckled softly. "I strongly suggest that you stay with us, or you will be taken again by the magistrate. And I can't guarantee that tomorrow or the next day will bring quite a convenient rainstorm to douse your pyre."

I stared at him, my mind refusing to accept the conclusion I had reached. There hadn't been a cloud in the sky when they had tied me to the stake. No sooner had this mysterious priest mounted the pyre than the clouds had gathered. Had he actually caused the rainstorm?

And if so, how?

"Who *are* you?" I demanded, too suspicious to be polite.

"I am Father Francis Duchienne," he replied. "Abbot of the Monastery of Sainte Felice."

"But how..." My question was interrupted by a group of children who emerged from a cluster of whitewashed cottages and swarmed around the cart. So distracted was I with the abbot's conversation, I had not noticed that the cart had clattered into the square of a tiny village.

"This is Sainte Felice." He encompassed the entire square with a wave of his hand.

"Good day to you, Father Francis." An old man with a haystack of white hair and a bushy mustache waved from the doorway of a tavern. "God keep you."

The abbot waved back. "And God keep you, Emil."

Several old women washing their clothes in the fountain looked up at us and pointed. They left their washing and ran towards us. Braving the hooves of the mule, they grasped at the hem of the abbot's habit with their gnarled hands. The children ran behind the cart, giggling and squealing, until we had passed through the square.

After leaving the village behind, I noticed that there was nothing but bare countryside on either side of the road. Frowning in puzzlement, I craned my neck and looked around. "But where is your monastery?"

"Up there." He pointed up to the top of a small hill.

I don't know just what I had been expecting. Maybe one of the opulent abbeys of Paris. But my heart sank as I gazed up at the cracked façade of the tiny rectangular building. A tower rose from one end overlooking battlements that appeared as though they had definitely seen more successful battles than the present one against the wind and rain. A row of windows looked out over a rusty gate that presumably led into a cloister, and tendrils of ivy crawled over the crumbling stones of the wall that encircled it.

All in all, it looked rather like a home for bats, not black-robed monks.

The abbot urged the mule up a small path that led away from the main road, and I had to hold on to the edge of the seat to keep from falling over. As we neared the gate, I noticed another monk scurrying about amid some twisted grapevines that spanned the hillside behind the building. He looked up at our approach and waved enthusiastically.

Abbot Francis waved back. As we climbed down from the cart, the other monk picked up the hem of his habit and scrambled down the hillside towards us.

"Ah, Francis." He pushed his dark hair away from his brow. He turned to me, his mouth arranging itself in a grin beneath the beak of a nose that dominated his face. "I see your rescue effort was successful."

"Allow me to present Brother Fernando Marcelli," Abbot Francis said, patting the monk's shoulder. "Florentine scholar, alchemist, and advisor to His Holiness himself in happier days…until he ran afoul of agents of the Roman Curia and he was forced to flee Italy."

My mouth dropped open. "He rescued you, too?"

Brother Fernando laughed. "Absolutely. He rescued all of us, one way or another." He took the reins of the mule and led the way to the front gate. "So tell me, Francis. Just how did you manage it this time?"

"A fortuitous storm, Fernando." The abbot allowed himself a soft chuckle. "Which just happened to darken the skies of Orleans and douse the burning pyre. Poor Montaigne. I fear it quite ruined his *auto-da-fe*."

Fernando gave the abbot a reproving look. "Francis, you didn't."

"It was the will of God." The abbot smiled beatifically and crossed himself.

"Will of God indeed!" Fernando snorted. "Francis, sometimes your theatrics worry even me. Now, go on inside. John should have supper ready by now. I'll put the mule in the barn."

The abbot nodded and pushed the iron gate open with a creak. I followed him into the cloister, frowning in puzzlement. Alchemist? It seemed I wasn't the only practitioner of the forbidden arts that the abbot had rescued. There was at least one more. I should have found the revelation reassuring, but it only increased my unease.

Why was this strange priest rescuing sorcerers in the first place?

Abbot Francis led the way along a flagstone path that

wound between plots of earth filled with a variety of colorful herbs. A black mound rose up from the middle of one of the beds. Picking up the hem of his habit, the abbot stepped into the bed, stopped beside the mound, and pointedly cleared his throat. "Marcel?"

The mound moved, and I realized with a start that it was actually another monk crouched on hands and knees in the black earth. He was heavyset, with wide features. He rose to his feet and brushed his hands on his habit, glowering at me from beneath brows knit together in a perpetual frown.

"So, you got him, eh?" His voice was low and gruff.

"Of course." Abbot Francis smiled and turned to me. "This is Brother Marcel de Fontanges, a cunning man and herbalist who has greatly enriched our garden. He was supposed to have been hanged by a superstitious lot of Anjou peasants, but I performed the last rites myself and they buried a coffin full of stones."

Marcel grunted. "I'll bet Montaigne isn't happy about all this."

"Hardly," the abbot sniffed. "But that isn't important. Come into the refectory. It's nearly supper time."

"In a minute." Marcel knelt down in the dirt once again. "I have to finish here before this damned verbena takes over the entire bed."

The abbot nodded his assent and stepped onto the path again. I snuck a backward glance at Brother Marcel—another sorcerer snatched from the jaws of death—calmly clipping a leafy bush with a pair of shears. I swallowed hard, then scrambled to catch up with Abbot Francis as he headed towards a small door at the back of the monastery.

He opened the door and the aroma of freshly baked bread caressed my nostrils. My stomach rumbled, reminding me that I hadn't eaten in at least a day. An older monk, small in stature with a dreamy expression on his face, stood at a wooden table wielding a carving knife. His mousy brown hair was surrounded by a halo of white flour.

"Here we have Brother John Moore," the abbot said as he pointed to the flour-dusted monk. "English poet and seer. His heretical verse was bad enough. But when he foretold the murder of the English king and the victory of the White Rose at Tewksbury, he was condemned to the gibbet for treason as well as witchcraft."

Brother John turned to me and brushed the flour from his hands. "Welcome," he said with a smile so kindly that it warmed my heart. "I trust you are staying for supper."

"Oh, I hope so," I breathed.

"Indeed, so." The abbot chuckled. "Are we ready to eat?"

"Nearly." Brother John grabbed a towel and opened the oven door. He extracted a loaf of herb bread and set it down on the table. It smelled so good I nearly fainted from hunger. "The others are waiting for you in the refectory. And please remind Fernando that it is his turn to serve this week."

"I can't imagine that you would let him forget." The abbot raised an eyebrow. "But I will mention it to him."

I followed the abbot through a doorway into a large

room dominated by a long table lined with benches. A lectern stood in the corner and a sideboard along the wall held a large pitcher of wine, along with wooden trenchers and several earthenware goblets.

"Antonin." Abbot Francis nudged a youngish looking monk with delicate features, yellow hair, and blue eyes who was sitting at the table. He was surrounded by star maps, and leatherbound volumes filled with columns of numbers were piled up beside him. "Do put those away. It's nearly time for supper."

"You've returned already?" The yellow-haired monk glanced up and closed his book. "My, that was quick. You had no trouble from Montaigne, I take it."

"None worth mentioning." Abbot Francis turned to me. "Michael, this is Brother Antonin LeFevre, our Flemish physician and astrologer. He fled from the rotting court of the Holy Roman Emperor and found refuge with us. He has turned his cell into quite an observatory."

Brother Antonin studied me as though I were some rare species of butterfly. "So, this is the latest object of the affections of the Holy Office."

"Let us hope the Holy Office proves a fickle lover and forgets her ardor quickly," muttered another monk sitting at the table. He was the only one sporting a dark mustache.

"And finally we have Juan-José de Saveñera." The abbot indicated the monk with the mustache. "Castilian nobleman and soldier who came to us with the fires of the Spanish Inquisition hot on his heels. It seems they didn't approve of his Moorish mother and his interest in Arabic mysticism."

As the abbot spoke, Brother Fernando and Brother Marcel came through the refectory door and took their places at the table. Brother John stood in the doorway, wiping his hands on a towel. I waited for a moment for any more to arrive. But there appeared to be only five monks in the whole place.

"Is this ... all of you?" I asked, feeling rather foolish.

"Not a large company, I will grant you. But although we are small in numbers, we have accomplished much since we have been here." He turned to the assembled monks. "My brothers, allow me to present Michael de Lorraine. He has chosen to seek sanctuary with us for awhile."

"I still don't understand." I shook my head in confusion. "If you are all fleeing from the persecution of the Church, why do you crouch here in Her very bosom?"

"My son, do you not think this would be the ideal place to hide? The Holy Office will not be seeking sorcerers here in a Benedictine monastery." The abbot eased himself into a large, ornately carved chair by the hearth. He motioned me to a bench beside him. "We have everything here to meet our simple needs. But above all, I have provided a place which is peaceful, quiet, secluded, and safe, perfect for study, contemplation, and the practice of magical arts. As long as we maintain our façade of sanctity, we are secure."

I sat poised on the edge of my seat while all the monks turned their attention to me. It made me squirm on the hard wood of the bench. Would I be subjected to yet another Inquisition?

"But how came you to the stake?" Brother Juan-José leaned towards me with a piercing look. "Such a punishment is seldom meted out to one so young."

"I am fifteen," I retorted, annoyed at being reminded yet again that I look younger than my years. "That's old enough, I assure you. But your abbot appears to know all about me already."

"Not entirely," Abbot Francis said. "All I heard in the village was that a certain Michael de Lorraine was about to be burnt at the stake in Orleans for sorcery. I was hoping you would enlighten me as to how you came by such a fate. Are you indeed a sorcerer?"

I remained silent for a moment, not sure how to answer. All five pairs of eyes were on me, the eyes of men who would know far better than that fool of a magistrate whether or not I was lying. I thought of Abbot Francis standing on my pyre, commanding the rain and having it obey. I decided that the truth was called for.

"No," I finally replied. "Only an apprentice. My master is ... was ... Alphonse, Count de Sainte Jacques. You must have heard of him. He was reputed at one time to be the most gifted necromancer that ever served at the court of the Duke of Normandy."

"His Grace was ever the patron of the arcane arts," Abbot Francis commented noncommittally. "Or so I've heard."

"My master served him well for many years. But then

the Duke was defeated by King Louis, and my master fled to Paris. I was a student there at the University when I met him. I served him for almost two years ... that is, until about a month ago."

"What happened then?" the abbot prompted gently.

"The King's Royal Highwaymen burst into our house at dawn to arrest my master." My voice grew hoarse. As if I could ever forget that dreadful night. "The Inquisition claimed that he had attempted to murder King Louis by magical art while in the service of the Duke."

"My, my." The abbot lifted an eyebrow. "That is quite an accusation. Was it true?"

"I ... I don't know. If he had done such a thing, I had no part in it. They dragged him from his bed and he beseeched me to run to save my own life. I did so, with great reluctance."

"Still, you made it all the way to Orleans," the abbot said. "That is no mean feat. What did you hope to find there?"

"I had hoped to try to get a ship to England, where my master has friends." I clenched my fists in helpless rage. "I swore that I would return and rescue him. But he perished in prison before I could."

"And it was when you inquired after him that you were arrested yourself, I take it."

I nodded. "The magistrate of Orleans had orders to arrest me. I was an 'unrepentant heretic,' and I was to be turned over to the king's justice and the king's fire." I gazed furiously at the black-robed company before me. "I tell you,

I have harmed no one. My only crime, if crime it be, is to reject the pious platitudes of fat churchmen who will promise me salvation for the gold in my pocket—gold with which they adorn their mistresses and furnish their tables. I do not need such as these to steer me to heaven."

"Calm your fury, my young friend." The abbot laid a comforting hand on my shoulder. "You preach to the converted, here. Remember that we have all run afoul of those who seek worldly riches and power in the name of the Kingdom of Heaven."

"And yet," I retorted, "I have heard that many abbeys grow rich by selling indulgences like apples in the marketplace."

I immediately regretted my hasty words, thinking that the abbot would surely be offended. Instead, he leaned back with a secretive smile. "I think you will find us somewhat unusual in that respect. Instead of selling indulgences, we sell wine."

"Wine?" I echoed.

"Fernando, I see our young friend is still skeptical. Perhaps a goblet of your latest batch will convince him."

With a grin, Fernando headed to the sideboard and grabbed the pitcher and several goblets. He poured the blood-colored liquid into one of the goblets and handed it to me.

I took a swallow and let my breath out in a slow sigh. God Almighty, but it was good. Full-bodied and sweet, it warmed my vitals like a maiden's kiss, leaving me with a tingling feeling nearly down to my feet. Never had I tasted anything like it before.

"Well!" I breathed, as my head began to spin.

Abbot Francis leaned forward with a satisfied look. "Now, do you not think that selling such an elixir is far more profitable than selling indulgences?"

"I suppose so." I took another drink and savored the taste that lingered on my tongue. I hated to admit it, but the abbot was right about the wine. I found myself wondering just how it was made.

"So, will you stay with us?"

I mused into my goblet for a moment, trying to sort out my conflicting feelings. I still did not fancy being in a monastery, no matter how congenial it seemed to be. I wasn't suited for monastic life. I wanted to be a scholar. Surely, there must be somewhere else I could go, something else I could do with myself. But I couldn't think of anything just then.

A heavy sigh rose in my breast. God, I was weary. Maybe tomorrow something would occur to me. But for now, all I craved was the comfort of food and bed.

"I'll stay until morning, since you have been so kind as to offer," I finally said, hoping the quaver in my voice wouldn't be noticed. "After that, I really can't say."

"Fair enough." Abbot Francis rose to his feet. "We shall leave it at that. In the meantime, I think that supper is in order. John, what do you have for us this evening?"

I had forgotten how good even simple fare tastes when one is really hungry. Brother John carved up slices of the warm bread and Brother Fernando set a platter of tangy cheese on the table. A heaping trencher of this bread and cheese, washed down with yet another goblet of the excellent wine, lifted my spirits considerably. As I ate, I listened carefully to the monks' conversation. I soon realized that I was among kindred spirits.

"You're pressing your luck with Montaigne, Francis," Brother Juan-José said, scowling into his wine cup. "Defying his authority in public will not be something he will tolerate for long."

"And what will he do, pray tell?" Abbot Francis made no attempt to conceal his contempt. "Run squealing to the bishop? Sorel thinks less of him than I do."

"Still, I hope that you aren't relying overly much upon the bishop's continued goodwill, even if he did ordain you," Antonin commented, resting his chin on his clasped hands with a thoughtful frown. "After all, he has to put up with Montaigne far more than you do. There is only so much annoyance that a man like Sorel can endure."

"No wonder he drinks so much of our wine," Brother Fernando commented. He took a long swallow from his goblet.

"Believe me, Antonin, I harbor no illusions about Sorel," the abbot replied in a serious tone. "But if I can keep Montaigne and the bishop snarling at each other like two curs over a table scrap, they might leave us alone."

"I don't like it, I tell you." Brother Marcel fiddled with the bread on his plate. His swarthy brows were knit in a frown. "Using sorcery to save a sorcerer, in the middle of the town square. Somebody is sure to say something about that sooner or later."

The abbot brushed the comment aside briskly. "No one observed any sorcery. Several hundred God-fearing, church-going, tax-paying citizens of Orleans will attest to the fact that it was a miracle wrought by angels in answer to my fervent prayer. Not even the Archbishop of Paris would have the nerve to dispute it."

Brother Marcel glared at the abbot and pushed his plate away. "I just hope that you know what you're doing. There will be hell to pay if you don't." He rose to his feet. "Now, I must return to my verbena before it grows dark."

"God help the verbena," Juan-José muttered.

Marcel shot him a withering look, then stalked out the door.

"I, too, must go." Antonin got to his feet and gathered up his books and charts. "Venus is rising tonight."

Fernando grinned. "Have a care she does not cast her spell upon you."

"Brazen hussy," Juan-José snorted. "She wouldn't dare."

Antonin paused at the threshold and turned to gaze down his delicate nose at the swarthy Spaniard. "Tut, tut. That's no way to speak of a lady. However, I shall give her your regards anyway." He smiled mischievously and vanished out the door.

Dusk began to throw shadows across the refectory floor. I stifled a yawn, suddenly so weary I could no longer keep my eyes open.

Abbot Francis rose to his feet. "I see that it is time that

we all retire for the night." He raised his hand in benediction. "God grant you all good rest."

Gratefully, I followed Brother John up the stone stairs to what was to be my room for the night. Although it was no larger than my dungeon cell, it was clean and smelled fresh. The bed, fashioned of wooden slats, stood up off the floor by about a foot and held a mattress stuffed with straw and sweet herbs. That, and a stool and a table that held little more than a candleholder, seemed to be the only furnishings. But the bed looked inviting anyway, and I sank down onto it with a heavy sigh.

"I trust that this will do for you." Brother John set the candle on the bedstand. "The straw should not need to be changed for several months yet."

"Thank you, Brother John," I said, watching him bustle about the tiny room. "But I hardly expect to be staying that long."

"We shall see." He glanced over his shoulder at me with a secretive smile, as though he knew something that I didn't. "But for now, rest well."

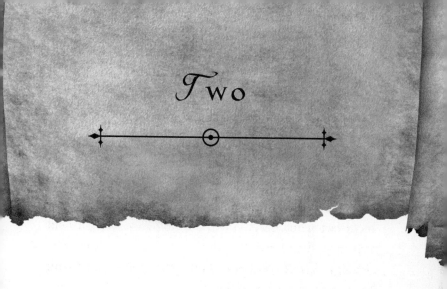

Two

I awoke suddenly in a cold sweat, frightening dreams vanishing in the soft darkness. For a moment, I thought I was still in the filthy dungeon that had been my bedchamber for many nights. Then I saw the smiling face of Lady Luna peeking into the window above my bed, shining her silvery light on the wooden floor. I lay back against the pillow with a heartfelt sigh of relief.

My mind roamed through the strange events of the past day in wonder. I was in a monastery, of all places. And a monastery for refugee wizards, magicians, and heretics. That fact was difficult enough to grasp. But who was their mysterious abbot? For all of his evasion, I knew that it was he who had caused the convenient rainstorm that had doused my funeral pyre. But how would an ordinary priest be invested with such power, as well as the wit to use it?

My mind awhirl, I rose and pulled on my doublet. My

old master had taught me to trust my intuition and it now directed me to the abbey library. With only the light of a candle stump to guide me, I made my way down the staircase and along the corridor.

I soon came to an archway that led into the tower. For a moment, I thought to go up the twisting stairs. But I noticed a light shining from the room just below the battlements; someone was up there and would see me. I decided to try another route.

Passing the archway, I discovered another doorway leading off the corridor. I thrust my head in—right into the jaws of an enormous beast. I jumped back with a shriek and stood in the corridor, trying to calm my pounding heart and hoping against hope that nobody had heard me. Holding the candle above my head, I peeked in the doorway again, and heaved a sigh of relief. The light played off of the surface of two stone gargoyles that flanked the inner entrance. Past the gargoyles, I could see bookshelves.

With a satisfied smile, I tiptoed into the library. The stone eyes of the gargoyles were carved so that they appeared to follow anyone moving past them through the door. The effect was eerie, causing the hair on the back of my neck to prickle in alarm. Swallowing hard, I told myself firmly that they were only made of stone, and pushed the door fully open.

Holding my candle next to my face, I examined the shelves. There was Ptolemy, Albertus Magnus, and the Thrice Greatest Hermes. Even a copy of the book by the mad Arab called Picatrix. I smiled. They were exactly the sort of books that wizard monks would have in their library.

One volume caught my gaze. I put the candleholder on the shelf and took down the large, loosely bound collection of manuscript pages. It was a copy of the Grimoire of Light, very possibly my master's most revered book. It had been written by a magician known only as Seratois, the Wizard of Alceste, whom my master the count had actually met in Rome.

He must have told me the story a hundred times—and each time I was eager to hear him tell me, again, how the celebrated French sorcerer had been the Grand Master of the Fratres Illuminati, a magical order that had included some of the major figures involved in the shady politics of the Papal States. A rival for the sorcerer's title (and, some had whispered, for the affections of a lady) had slipped a drug into Seratois' wine cup, and summoned the Holy Office like jackals to a fresh kill.

So the great Seratois was hauled off to prison in chains. After a trial, rumored to be the scandal of Rome, he was sentenced to burn at the stake. But one of the wheels broke on the cart carrying him to the Piazza, throwing him into the Tiber, where he drowned … or so it was said.

Like my master, I knew the book well. Seratois had been famous for his invocations of the Holy Archangels for aid in commanding the four elements—fire, earth, wind, and rain. His power was rumored to have come from his practice of angelic conjuration, a strange and hidden art by which he could summon angels to visible appearance and beseech their aid. I had read his powerful words over and over, so many times that I felt I could recite them in my sleep. I had mused about how grand it must be to be able to command the very forces of nature herself.

But as my eye now scanned the pages, something struck me as decidedly odd. The entire book was written in a distinctive, florid hand, flowing and ornate with bold ascending and descending strokes. But I noticed that on certain pages, entire passages had been crossed out—passages that I didn't recognize—and others that I did recognize were substituted for them.

I leafed through the rest of the manuscript and found numerous other pages treated thus. I realized with a bit of a shock that I must be holding in my hands not merely a copy of the Grimoire of Light, but the original manuscript. I knew of no copyist who would scratch out a paragraph he had so painstakingly copied and then insert another, not once but several times, unless he was not merely copying, but composing, the paragraphs that he penned.

No, this was the original manuscript. I was certain of it. Somehow one of the monks must have obtained it after the death of its author and brought it to this monastery, presumably for safekeeping. I found myself stroking the soft parchment pages, as if the skin still shrouded the living animal. I could not dismiss the unmistakable feeling that the book lived and breathed, and was almost surprised that it did not purr under my caressing fingers.

Oddly intrigued, I decided that I would bide my time and take advantage of the proffered sanctuary and hospitality of these mysterious monks for as long as they would put up with me. That is, until I could discover what other strange and arcane secrets they possessed.

—◊—

At dawn the next morning, my first restful sleep in days was shattered by the thunder of hoofbeats. Alarmed, I jumped out of bed and ran to the window. My heart hammering with terror as a dozen soldiers rode up the hill towards the monastery.

Throwing on my doublet, I raced down the stairs to the parlor. Brother Fernando, his head thrust out the door, was keeping a watchful eye on the approaching soldiers. After a moment, he turned to the abbot. "They have reached the gate, Francis."

"How many of them are there?" Juan-José fingered a very unmonastic sword at his hip and looked as though he would cheerfully take them all on single-handed.

"Ten," Fernando replied. "They are under the command of that constable from Orleans. You know, the one that the villagers had such trouble with last fall."

"Montaigne's faithful hound," muttered Marcel.

"Well, we must not keep him waiting at the gate," Abbot Francis said, almost cheerfully. "It would be quite inhospitable. I will go and speak with him. The rest of you stay here in case things become unpleasant."

"Francis." Brother John caught at the abbot's sleeve. "Have a care."

Abbot Francis patted John's shoulder and gave him a reassuring smile. "Don't worry, John. I know what I'm doing."

Brother John still looked dubious as Abbot Francis went out the parlor door and headed for the iron gate. I decided to follow at a discreet distance. Trying my best to keep well out of sight behind the wall of the cloister, I watched as the abbot stood at the gate, resting one hand on the iron grillwork and fingering the cross on his breast with the other.

It was the same gesture I had seen when he stood on my burning pyre.

The soldiers rode up to the gate and reined in their mounts. The constable slowly dismounted from his horse. He limped towards the gate, favoring a leg that had probably seen the blade of a sword more than once. I shuddered. He didn't look like the sort of man who would be easily intimidated by earthly threats, much less heavenly ones.

"My lord Abbot," he began, obviously discomfited by the abbot's implacable gaze. "I have come to recapture the fugitive heretic, Michael de Lorraine. Is he here?"

"He is," the abbot replied simply.

I caught my breath in alarm. He wasn't giving me away, was he? Had I been wrong about him? I inched closer, not wanting to miss a single word.

"Then I demand that you surrender him up to the king's justice."

"I fear that you are too late, my lord constable." The abbot crossed his arms over his breast with deceptive calm.

"Young Monsieur de Lorraine has been granted sanctuary within these holy precincts. He is now out of your jurisdiction."

The constable heaved a long suffering sigh. "My Lord Abbot, I pray you, don't be difficult. My orders from the magistrate are to arrest him."

"And my orders from God are that holy sanctuary is not to be violated," Abbot Francis returned firmly. "And, God willing, these hallowed walls will prove to be more conducive to his repentance than the dungeons of Orleans. And now, my good constable, God grant you a good day."

The constable, however, was not to be dismissed so lightly. "I had hoped that it would not come to this, but you leave me no choice. Abbot Duchienne, for the last time, I demand that you surrender the heretic to me at once."

Abbot Francis shook his head. "I'm sorry."

With a scowl, the constable drew the sword that was hanging from his saddle. I clutched at the ivy with trembling hands as the mounted soldiers drew theirs as well. God's death, would they actually cut down the abbot in front of his own monastery?

Abbot Francis seemed unconcerned, save only for his tightened grip on the golden cross. "It is truly a shame that the magistrate should place the immortal souls of his soldiers in such jeopardy." His gaze swept over the arrayed soldiers. "Invading a monastery, with naked steel no less, in order to violate holy sanctuary constitutes the mortal sin of sacrilege. Is extracting one young man from this place worth risking hellfire?"

The soldiers glanced at each other in uncertainty for a moment. It was evident that the abbot's words had not fallen upon deaf ears.

The constable did not waiver. "We'll take our chances," he said. "Now, stand aside."

"I strongly advise you to refrain." The abbot's tone chilled and his expression hardened to determined lines.

Then, beneath my feet, the earth lurched and thumped as though some unseen giant was stomping towards us—first far away, then closer and closer. I clutched the vines in terror. The horses whinnied and fidgeted, and several nervous soldiers dropped their swords on the ground to keep from being thrown from their saddles. Thunder rumbled louder and louder, from deep within the bowels of the mountain. Bits of rock and clods of dirt danced beneath the horses' hooves. Several horses reared and bolted, galloping wildly back down the road towards the village.

The constable turned on the abbot with alarm. "What the devil is going on?"

"All of God's creatures fear His wrath," Abbot Francis intoned solemnly. "Save for man."

"We will leave him here, then." The constable clung to the reins of his own wide-eyed mount. "I swear it. Now, for God's sake, make it stop!"

Abbot Francis smiled. With a sweeping gesture, he made the sign of the cross. Almost immediately, the earth ceased its rumbling.

It took a moment for the soldiers to realize that the ground had stopped moving. Finally, the shaken constable dismounted, retrieved his sword, and stuffed it back into the scabbard. Looking up, he fixed the abbot with a look that was both suspicious and awe-inspired. "So it is true what they say about you."

Abbot Francis only beamed in saintly beatitude. "*Pax vobiscum*," he intoned, raising his hand in benediction. "Peace be with you."

Watching the abbot carefully out of the corner of his eye, the constable remounted his skittish horse and galloped away down the hill. His soldiers needed no encouragement to follow him. Soon the hoofbeats faded into the distance.

I leaned against the door frame, my knees suddenly weak. I could doubt my own eyes no longer. At the foot of my pyre, this man had commanded the element of water to obey him, saving my life in a blessed downpour. Now, the very earth itself had rumbled obediently at the command of this same man. I followed him wordlessly back into the parlor, noting again the self-satisfied air that he couldn't quite hide.

Whatever he was, he was like no priest I had ever met before.

"Well." Abbot Francis settled himself back in his chair. "We have upheld Christian virtues yet again, God be praised. I don't think they will molest us or our young friend here any more for a while. At least, as long as he remains here with us."

"Where else would he go?" Juan-José asked bluntly. "He could hardly return to Orleans, could he? And Paris?"

I couldn't refrain from a derisive laugh. "The soldiers would be on the lookout for me there too, I am sure."

"Then, why not return to your home?" Antonin cocked an inquisitive eyebrow at me. "You do have a family, don't you?"

Staring down at my folded hands, I shuddered as an image flashed in my mind's eye of my widowed mother and three sisters crammed into two rooms above my uncle's cobbler's shop. The last thing she needed would be another mouth to feed. Besides, I could just imagine what my pious mother would think if she found out that her only son had been condemned to the stake for sorcery.

"I don't dare," I whispered.

"Where else, then? England?"

"Yes, I suppose there is still England," I replied, although how I was going to get there with no money and only the singed clothes on my back was beyond me. And even though the count had friends there, would they be willing to take me in? I had to admit, that thought had never occurred to me before. I suddenly felt irked that while I believed I had made a choice to stay at the monastery, there actually was no choice to make.

Abbot Francis dismissed the entire subject with a wave of his hand. "Well, until you find another place to go, you had best stay here with us."

"Thank you," I murmured, feeling extremely chastened. Brother John caught my gaze and winked.

"So, what tasks do we set our young friend to, eh?" Juan-José scrutinized me for a moment, rubbing his chin. I felt a hot flush creep up into my cheeks. Since I was to stay here, even if it was only a temporary arrangement, it was only reasonable that I pull my own weight as part of the community. But I could not help feeling like some odd bit of furniture that needed to be put to some use in order to justify its continued existence. Especially since I was beginning to realize that I didn't know as much about magic as I thought I did.

"Fernando, couldn't you use some help with the wine?" Abbot Francis suggested. "You have several casks that are nearly ready."

"I certainly could," Fernando replied. "Journet wants at least four casks from the first harvest this year. I could only sell him three last year."

"He'll water it down anyway," Marcel put in. "No matter how many casks he gets."

Fernando looked offended. "He only does that for the children."

"They are the only ones who will let him," Antonin observed.

"Then I suggest that we allow Brother Fernando and his new assistant to get on with it," the abbot said pointedly. "Or we shall have to water our wine as well."

I had to trot like a pony to keep up with Brother Fernando's brisk footsteps as he led the way across the garden. I stumbled several times on the flagstones. I finally had to catch at the hem of his habit to keep from falling headlong on my face.

"Not so fast, please," I begged as Brother Fernando turned to me with a smile. "These stones are wet and my shoes are slipping."

"Very well." He reached down and offered me a hand. "We cannot have you falling into the herbs. Marcel would never forgive us."

Picking my way more carefully, I followed Fernando to a stone hut on the far side of the garden. Smoke coiled from a brick chimney nestled in the freshly thatched roof—I thought for a moment that someone might be living there. Sitting in the yard, looking for all the world like a large wash tub, was a wooden wine press freshly stained with purple juice. A dozen or so large casks rested on their sides, one row atop the other, beneath a canopy made of wooden slats.

I remembered the vines clustered on the hillside. "Did you plant the grapes as well?"

Fernando shook his head. "They were already here, as was the press and the casks. Francis says that this used to be a prosperous monastery, some fifty years ago. There were at least twenty monks living here."

"What happened to it?" I asked.

"The English ravaged it during the war." Fernando shrugged. "Probably to get rid of the considerable source of income for the area. Whatever the reason, they succeeded. By the time we arrived, the vines were sadly overgrown and needed pruning badly. It took two years, but I repaired the press and we gathered in our first crop. Now we have at least three crops a year. Sometimes four, if we have a warm fall."

Fernando picked up a metal cup from a nail in the crosspiece of the wine press and drew a little wine from the nearest cask. He sipped it thoughtfully and then handed the cup to me. "I believe it is ready."

I drained the cup, and my face fell. The wine was tasty, sweet, and full-flavored with a hint of some herb or another. But something was missing.

"Is there something wrong?" Fernando asked, noting my expression. "You don't find it sour, do you?"

I shook my head. "No, it isn't that. But the glass you gave me last night was ... different somehow."

"Of course it was," he said lightly. "This batch has not been blessed yet."

My mouth dropped open. "Blessed?"

He pushed open the door of the stone hut, and I gazed with utter astonishment into a miniature but well appointed alchemical laboratory. A long wooden table, littered with copper tubing and assorted glassware, bisected the little room. Bottles of herbs stoppered with cork lined up like soldiers on several small shelves. And instead of an ordinary hearth, a huge brick furnace dominated the far wall. It was the roaring fire contained therein which produced the billows of smoke that curled up the chimney. A glass vessel shaped like a teardrop sat atop the furnace, its swan neck thrust into a series of copper tubing that coiled around itself like a stem from one of the grapevines. The tube emptied into yet another teardrop vessel, propped up on a metal stand on the stone floor.

"The wine must be infused with the Spirit of God," Brother Fernando explained as I followed him into the hut. "By the alchemical process, I have managed to distill the Elixir Vitae, the very essence of life itself. When added to the wine, it produces a liquor of extraordinary healing properties. It truly blesses the vintage."

I examined the apparatus closely. Excitement tingled up my spine. It was so like the drawings I had seen in my master's books. "This was not here when you arrived, was it?"

Fernando laughed brightly. "Hardly. The vessels and the athanor I brought with me from Florence. The furnace I built with bricks from the ruined chimney. I first learned the art in my student days, and gradually refined it over the years until I can produce the Elixir at will."

"Does it also transmute lead into gold?"

"No," Fernando replied bluntly. "That is not the purpose of the art. I wish I had a ducat for every time I've had to explain that to someone."

"Forgive me." I lowered my gaze as a flush of embarrassment flooded my face." I didn't know."

"Of course you didn't." Fernando's tone softened. "But I once had to remind one who very well ought to have known better. And it nearly cost me my life."

"Who could that possibly have been?" I glanced up at him, sensing an interesting story.

He studied me for a moment, then heaved a sigh. "You might as well know. His Holiness himself requested that task of me. It appears he wished to stock the Vatican coffers with gold that couldn't be accounted for by any other means. When I declined to provide the service, the Holy Office appeared miraculously at my door."

I blinked in astonishment. "But I don't understand. If the Pope knew all along that you practiced alchemy, why did the Holy Office not arrest you before that?"

"The Holy Office is only concerned with the practice of alchemy when you fail." Fernando let out a derisive snort. "If you succeed, they take their place in line with the rest of the greedy princelings demanding that you fill their coffers as well. Here." He handed me a pair of leather bellows. "You can blow up the coals in the athanor while I fill the aludel."

I stared down at the bellows in my hand. "You mean we are going to distill the Elixir? Now?"

"No better time." Fernando reached into a coal scuttle and grabbed a small metal scoop. "Antonin assures me that the Moon is finally waxing and that the Sun has entered into the sign of Virgo. Besides..." He grinned at me. "If we wait any longer, the wine will sour." He scooped a pile of coal into the furnace. Sparks flew up from the fire, and soon a tiny tongue of flame licked at the black coals.

"Now, blow on the coals." Fernando took the bellows from my hands and knelt on the ground before the furnace. "Gently, gently... don't blow the fire out, but give it plenty of air. Fire is a living thing, you know. It must have air even as we do or it will die. Now, you try."

Coal dust rose in a black puff as I pumped the bellows,

first slightly, then harder and harder. A ruby glow emerged from the edges of the coals and quickly spread over the entire pile. Fernando watched for a moment, then nodded his approval. "Good, good." He clapped me on the shoulder. "Keep it up. I shall return in a moment."

I continued to pump until he returned, rolling a cask of wine across the floor. He propped it up near the wall and drew about half of the wine into an earthenware pitcher. Then he reached up atop the furnace and poured the purple wine into the swan-necked spout, where it descended into the belly of the aludel. He attached the copper tubing and stepped back, surveying the arrangement with a satisfied grin.

Then Fernando knelt beside me, before the open furnace, as I raised the bellows once more. But he reached over and stayed my hand, shaking his head gently.

"Leave off for just a moment," he said softly, and bowed his head over his clasped hands. I stared at him, dumbfounded. What on earth was he doing? Some meaningless ritual from a church he had risked his life to flee?

I watched him in silence for a long moment while he knelt motionless on the floor, his black habit dusty from the hard-packed earth. Sunlight drifted in from the partially shuttered window, glinting off his dark hair and framing his singular profile with a halo that made him look like a saint in a Florentine fresco.

I suddenly felt a shiver of guilt for being so surprised at his actions. Had I become so cynical that I failed to remember the devotions required by the practice of alchemy? It was an art, a sacred art. Fernando was only paying the art its due. Humility overwhelmed me until I, too, clasped my hands and lowered my head.

Before I could think of anything to say, Fernando quickly crossed himself and vaulted to his feet. "Blow, little brother," he commanded gaily. "Pump the bellows for all you're worth. These coals must become hotter than the back gates of Hell."

I fumbled with the cumbersome bellows for a minute, but soon I was able to pump again with long, smooth strokes. Sparks flew into the air; I feared they should alight in my hair or doublet. But I continued to pump, pump, and pump still more.

"Faster," Fernando cajoled. "You're doing well. Keep it up."

It wasn't long before my arms began to ache and the drops of sweat on my brow trickled down into my eyes. God's blood, this was hard work.

"How much longer?" I beseeched him.

"Just a little longer." He knelt once again beside me. His face glowed with excitement as well as perspiration, and his enthusiasm was infectious. "When you can see the salamanders dance amid the coals, then the Elixir begins to form."

I kept pumping, the ache in my arms fading into numbness. My breathing had quickened, and several times the coal dust had set me coughing, but I dared not stop the bellows even for a moment. The heat enveloped me like a blanket, making me giddy. I dimly heard Fernando chanting in Latin from somewhere beside me.

Finally, he pointed. "Look, little brother. Look there. The salamanders have appeared."

I stopped pumping and stared. Little figures of flame, so translucent they could barely be seen, fluttered and writhed among the coals. They had a vague lizard-like form, but moved so quickly it was difficult to determine just what their shape was. I could barely contain my excitement.

"I see them!" I cried. "By God, there they are. I see them, Brother Fernando, just as I see you."

Then Fernando, his black eyes gleaming like the coals, pointed upwards to the athanor. "And there is the Elixir."

I watched in elation as crystal-clear droplets formed at the neck of the vessel, disappearing into the coils of the tubing as if devoured by some copper serpent. But then they reappeared, first drop by drop, then in a trickle, pouring into the smaller vessel placed to capture them.

Heedless of the ache in my arms, I picked up the bellows again, but Fernando shook his head. "No more, little brother. Too much heat is as harmful as not enough."

Heaving a sigh of relief, I sat back on my heels as the purple wine continued to bubble in the athanor, releasing its crystal spirit into the waiting vessel. Fernando, rubbing his chin, watched the process with an experienced eye. After several long moments, he rose to his feet and raised his arms in benediction. "It is finished." Taking a rag from the table, he yanked the aludel from its perch and poured the still-steaming wine onto the ground.

"And here we have it, the Elixir, the spiritual essence of the wine." He disengaged the smaller vessel, now nearly full of clear liquid, and corked it firmly. "If we blend this with the wine already in the barrel, then we will have the blessed vintage so thoroughly enjoyed by the people of Sainte Felice."

I took the vessel from him and examined it closely. The liquid resembled very clear, but very ordinary, water. "May I open it?"

"If you wish," he replied. "Only have a care not to spill any."

I worked the cork free from the vessel and promptly corked it again as the pungent odor assailed my nostrils. "Whew!" I exclaimed. "That's strong."

Fernando nodded sagely. "The glory of God is too bright for mortal eyes to bear."

"Have you ever tried to drink this undiluted?"

"Once." He grimaced. "And I can assure you that I will never do so again."

"What happened?" I leaned forward eagerly.

"Well, it felt as though my entire inner being had burst into flame. Then, I fell senseless upon the ground and knew no more until the next morning. I awakened and … well, the plague itself could not make a man more ill than I was that day."

"Still," I persisted, "when it is diluted in the wine, it comforts body and soul."

"Indeed, but the proportions must be exactly right. Here, help me tilt this cask up onto its end."

He poured the contents of the flask into the barrel and bunged it up again, sealing the wooden stopper with yellow wax from a candle. We blessed three more casks in the same fashion and stacked them against the far wall. Then the peal of a bell rang out above the roar of the furnace.

Fernando glanced up and brushed the dust off his habit. "That will be the bell for dinner. Come." He waved to me. "We can finish the other casks later. I'm hungry."

I was more than hungry. I was truly famished, and the aroma from the platters that John brought into the refectory tormented me until the abbot had finished saying grace.

"We have three casks blessed," Fernando said while I tucked away a tasty meal of roast fowl and vegetables. "And the other two can be blessed this afternoon."

"Excellent!" The abbot clasped his hands together. "And not one day too soon. I expect Journet to pound upon our door at any moment."

"Well, we should be able to deliver the wine tomorrow," Fernando went on. "That should stave him off for a while."

"Five casks." Antonin frowned. "That is quite a load. You may need one of us to go with you. Marcel, I believe it's your turn."

"I don't want to go into the village." Marcel scowled into his soup bowl.

Juan-José rolled his eyes. "They're not going to burn you, Marcel."

"Doesn't matter." Marcel pushed himself to his feet abruptly. "I still don't trust them. Get somebody else."

He stomped out the door and Juan-José heaved a long-suffering sigh. "I suppose it's me again, blast it."

"Perhaps your new assistant could go," Antonin said, turning to Fernando. "He may enjoy a ride to the village."

I glanced up, a piece of bread halfway to my mouth.

"Journet will no doubt be dying to meet him after all the stories he's heard." Juan-José sat back in his chair with a grin. "It must be the talk of the village by now."

I swallowed hard and lowered my gaze to the table. I hadn't considered how the news of my rescue would spread. What must the villagers think of me?

"Do you wish to go, Michael?" Abbot Francis finally asked.

"I don't know." I felt my stomach drop to my feet. I could almost see Montaigne prowling around the monastery's protective walls, waiting for me like a cat waiting for the mouse to emerge from its hole. "Do you think it safe?"

"Oh, I suspect so," Abbot Francis replied. "While you are with Fernando, at any rate. The villagers consider the king's law as oppressive as we do. *They* certainly won't turn you over to Montaigne."

I considered this for a moment. Maybe the trip would be useful after all. The villagers might be able to give me more clues as to the abbot's identity. If so, then it was well worth the risk.

"Very well, then." I said. "I'll go."

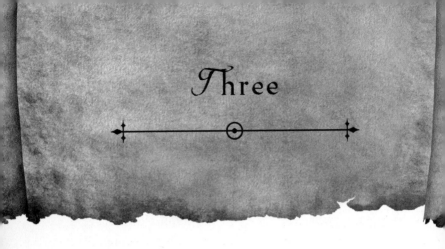

Three

The next morning, we loaded five casks of wine into the rear of the cart. It took all of us to manage it. Only Brother John, built even slighter than I, was exempt. And he had the equally difficult task of holding the harness of the skittish mule. He stroked its nose without ceasing, crooning to it until we had the casks safely stowed away for the journey.

"Are we ready?" he asked, still patting the mule's twitching nose.

Fernando nodded, wiping his dusty hands on his habit. "We must consult with Francis first. Then we are gone."

I followed Fernando inside, down the corridor past the dormitory and up the steps to the abbot's chambers. We found him hunched over a huge desk strewn with papers, bits of parchment, and several obviously well-chewed quill pens. He was nibbling on the end of a quill, which he held poised above a ledger, as we walked in.

"Well?" He laid the pen down beside a stained inkwell and glanced up at us. "How many casks are we sending to Journet?"

"Five," Fernando replied. "That leaves two for us."

"When can we expect the next harvest?"

"In a few weeks. That should net us at least six more casks. We might have one more small harvest after that, but that will be all until next August."

"Then it will have to suffice." The abbot picked up his pen and nibbled on the end again while examining the ledger. "Fortunately, we are well stocked with flour and salt for the winter. But we are low on cheese. See if you can pick up one or two from that cheesemonger, whatever his name is. He always has a goodly supply."

Fernando snorted. "That is because he overcharges so much."

"Then haggle him down a few deniers." The abbot made a few notes in the ledger. "Pretend you are at a street market in Florence. Be ruthless. We will have one more mouth to feed this winter and we must be prepared."

I bristled. Why was he so sure that I would still be here when winter came? Once more, I reminded myself that my stay in this monastery was only temporary. I would be leaving before the first snowflake fell, to go to wherever fate would lead me.

"Is there anything else we need?" Fernando peeked over the abbot's shoulder at the ledger.

The abbot scanned the page for a moment. "We could use a few more candles for the sacristy."

"Perhaps you had better write that down so we don't forget," Fernando said. "It's likely to be a busy morning."

The abbot pulled a scrap of parchment from a stack on the table and dipped his pen in the inkwell. "Make sure you get beeswax," he muttered over the scratching of the pen nib, "and not those dreadful tallow things. They always reek like overdone mutton. There." He handed me the scrap.

"We should return well before supper," I dimly heard Fernando say. "Unless we run into difficulties, which I don't anticipate. Are you ready to go, Michael?"

I studied the florid handwriting on the scrawled note in my hand for a moment. Frowning in puzzlement, I looked up from the note and watched the man who had penned it as he continued to scribble in the ledger. Then I lowered my gaze to the parchment again.

I had seen that handwriting before. Last night, in the monastery library.

"Michael?" Fernando's voice abruptly brought me back to the present. "Is there something wrong?"

I glanced up at him and forced a smile. "No, no. I am merely trying to make this out."

Fernando merely chuckled. "You will get used to his scribble eventually. We all do. Now, come. It grows late."

I glanced at the parchment one final time before tucking it into the pocket of my doublet. There was no time now to allay my suspicions. I would have to wait. With a sigh, I followed Fernando out the door.

The cart clattered down the hill towards the village. I bounced so hard on the seat that I was sure the wheels had found every bump and rut in the dirt road. It was difficult to carry on any sort of conversation with our teeth rattling so, and Fernando had his hands full attempting to keep the mule from wandering all over the road. We narrowly missed a cartload of hay coming the other way.

I breathed a sigh of gratitude when we finally pulled off the main road into the gravel and dust of the village square. Sainte Felice was tiny and compact, with several small rough stone huts topped by grayish thatch that clustered around a stone fountain. Women hoisting baskets of laundry gathered at the rim, dipping their clothes in the water and slapping them against the side.

One or two of them waved as we clattered by, and Fernando waved back with a cheerful smile. My gaze fell upon a maiden washing her clothes beside an older woman, possibly her mother. She looked no older than I, but her figure, tucked into the lacing of her bodice, was as full and ripe as a rosy apple. Rich chestnut hair fell across her arms, and she looked up at me with beautiful amber eyes. She smiled briefly, then returned to her washing.

A sudden desire to kiss her sweet mouth and to stroke her soft white skin thrilled through every nerve in my body. I swallowed hard and forced myself to look away from her, but I could still feel an ache of longing that arose within me. Even several deep breaths failed to quell the heat that flushed my loins.

Her beauty served as a stern reminder that if I stayed at the monastery, I would have to forgo such pleasures. Was I willing to do that?

Fernando finally reined in the mule in front of a tavern north of the central square. I noticed that the sign seemed freshly painted. The whitewash on the stone walls looked as though it too was new.

"My heavens." Fernando stroked his chin. "This place is done up like a Roman courtesan." He jumped down from the wagon seat as an old man appeared at the doorway and waved. The man was, I noticed, the same one who had greeted Father Francis when we first journeyed to the monastery. Had it only been a few short days ago?

Fernando greeted the old man warmly. I clambered down from the cart as well, silently blessing the solid earth beneath my feet.

"You are not one day too soon." The old man wagged his finger as Fernando tied the mule to a post behind the tavern. "I was beginning to draw the dregs of the last cask. You only sent me three, you know."

"That was all we had from the first harvest." Fernando waited until the mule was munching happily on a pile of hay before making his way to the back of the cart. "The late spring, you know."

"Bother the spring." The old man eyed the casks in the back of the cart. "How many do you have here?"

"Five. And possibly three more before the summer is over. Will that do?"

The old man grunted. "I could sell five times that much."

"I'm sure you could." Fernando lifted an eyebrow. "Well, we will see what we can do after the next harvest. Come, Michael," he called to me. "Let us get these casks into the back of the tavern."

Reluctantly, I went around to the back of the cart. The old man eyed me with interest. "This must be the young man that rat constable was looking for yesterday."

I caught my breath as cold fingers of dread clutched at my heart. But Fernando only chuckled. "It is, indeed." He clapped me on the shoulder and brought me forward. "Michael, this is Emil Journet, tavern keeper and connoisseur of fine vintages."

Unable to find my voice to speak, I could only bow my head politely.

But Journet hardly seemed to notice my distress. His expression had darkened at the idea of the constable. "Thought as much," he snorted in obvious distaste. "Sent that ruffian on his way, I did. Didn't like him sniffing about. And all that talk about sorcerers and all."

"He...he said that?" I squeaked. "About me?"

"Rubbish. That's what it is. I told him we had no sorcerers in Sante Felice. Only the holy monks from the monastery with their blessed wine."

"But, what if a sorcerer did come here?"

"Then the abbot will surely see to his redemption,"

Journet replied with a grunt as he helped Fernando unload the casks from the cart. "I have no doubt of that. A truly saintly man, the abbot."

His remark startled me. Abbot Francis? Saintly? But there was no time to ask questions. I grabbed one end of the nearest cask while Fernando took hold of the other. Journet held up the middle and, after several minutes, we finally managed to get all five casks stacked in the rear of the tavern. Journet, panting and breathless, leaned back against the wall, mopping his brow.

Fernando watched him for a moment, a look of concern furrowing his brow. "You look weary, Emil. Are you well?"

"Well enough." Journet dug a small bag of coins from a pouch at his belt and pressed it into Fernando's hand. "My age creeps up on me sometimes, and I miss my son. But life goes on, doesn't it? Here is the twenty crowns as we agreed."

Fernando kept his gaze on Journet's flushed face while tucking the bag of coins into his girdle. "Still, there must be something we can do for you."

"Have your sainted abbot say a novena for me." Journet gave him a wan smile. "That should do me just fine."

"You need more than a novena," Fernando said sternly. "You need someone to help you."

"Oh, I should be able to manage for a few years yet."

"And then?"

Journet mopped his face in silence for a moment.

"God will provide." He turned away abruptly and shuffled back towards the bar.

"He's a stubborn old man," Fernando said, turning to me with a sigh. "And a proud one."

Something about Journet both touched my heart and irritated me at the same time. "What happened to his son?"

"He was taken ill with fever in his fourteenth year." Fernando watched as Journet mopped the bar with a rag. "His death affected Journet greatly. The boy was his only son."

"That is truly sad," I murmured, as painful memories intruded into my mind. I was no stranger to tragedy. My own father had been struck down when I had but thirteen years—literally falling from the scaffolding where he had been repairing the roof of the Cathedral of St. Etienne. But what had kept my mother and three sisters from starvation was my father's stonemason guild, not God. "Do you really think God will provide for him?"

Fernando's reply was cut short by the sudden clatter of hooves on the hard-packed earth, punctuated by the creak of carriage wheels. He turned around. "It sounds as though Journet has customers."

Journet was heading towards the door of the tavern, and we followed in his wake. I peered past Fernando's shoulder out into the courtyard.

I had been right. It *was* a carriage. But such a carriage! It was painted white with gilded trimming, drawn by a team of four horses. A groom climbed down from the running board and held the heads of the lead horses. The door opened and a man emerged, the golden thread on his scarlet velvet doublet and cloak winking in the sunlight.

To my amazement, Journet grinned and rushed forward as two ladies also climbed out of the carriage. One was an older woman, thickly set, her graying hair swept back into her jeweled hood. Her gray eyes looked as though they never missed a thing. The other woman was younger, and looked frail and sickly. But her gown was no less sumptuous, and she was wearing the tall, cone-shaped hennin that had been so much the rage in Paris.

"I do not wish to be rude," I whispered into Fernando's ear, "but they seem a bit out of place in this humble village."

"So they do." Fernando lifted an eyebrow. "Come. Let us see what is going on."

"Good day, Your Grace." Journet ushered the three into the tavern.

"Your Grace?" I echoed softly.

Fernando put his finger to his lips as we slipped through the door after them.

Journet waved his customers to seats and drew three cups from one of the new casks. "You are just in time, Your Grace," he said over his shoulder. "A new shipment has come in just this morning and each one is better than the last."

We made our way along the wall to the counter and waited for Journet to finish serving his resplendent customers. I noticed that they sipped at their earthenware cups as though they were golden chalices. Journet edged towards us, keeping a watchful eye on them.

"You see?" He gave Fernando a conspiratorial wink. "I told you. Word has spread far and wide of the magical virtues of your wine. They say that it will cure anything from toothache to ague. It will relieve fevers, get rid of bad humors without leeches, and hasten the healing of sword wounds. Some folks are even giving it to babies for colic. That," he gestured discreetly, "is His Grace the Duke of Orleans. They have been coming every week for the past month. His wife, the Duchess, insists on using your wine in her communion chalice. And his mother, that older lady over there, will take no other cure for her gout."

The older woman was taking in the entire room with a sweep of her keen gaze. "Monsieur Journet?" she called.

"Yes, madam?"

"Is that by chance one of the monks from the monastery?"

"Yes, madam."

All three nobles turned to us at once. I edged back towards the wall, but I need not have bothered. Their attention was fixed on Fernando, who gestured frantically to Journet in silent protest.

"Tell me, good brother," the Duke asked Fernando with a pointed look. "Just what do you do to this extraordinary wine of yours? Pray over it?"

"Ah, Your Grace, how clever of you to have guessed our little secret," Fernando replied, forcing a grin. "Yes, that is precisely what we do. We pray over it. And God is pleased to bestow His blessing on our humble vintage. But now, we must be on our way. May God grant you good day."

Grasping me firmly by the arm, Fernando turned and headed resolutely for the door, pulling me behind him.

"Let us hurry, Michael," he muttered under his breath. "Before His Grace's curiosity becomes more insistent." Vaulting up onto the seat of the cart, he grasped the reins firmly, pulling the mule's nose out of the hay. It brayed in protest as he yanked it round, away from the tavern. I jumped up onto the back of the cart as it clattered down the road.

"So that is the reason for the new paint on the tavern," I said as we were safely on the other side of the square. "The keeper is catering to the nobility now. No wonder he's becoming so prosperous."

"Yes," Fernando said ruefully. "Let us hope that wine is all they are interested in. Now we must visit the cheese-monger before we leave."

"And the chandler." I fingered the parchment in my pocket.

"Yes, yes, the chandler. We shall have to do penance for a month if we forget Francis' candles."

Finally, our errands were accomplished. Fernando flicked the reins across the mule's hindquarters to get it moving. Further conversation proved nearly impossible amid the bone-rattling trek up the hill. I fingered the parchment in my sleeve and felt more confused than ever.

Over supper, Abbot Francis listened with keen interest as Fernando related our adventures. "So," he mused, rubbing his chin, "that is the secret of Journet's sudden prosperity."

"I don't like that bastard Duke nosing around this close to our front door," Marcel said, with his characteristic frown.

"So long as he stays in the village, I can see no harm in it." Antonin laid aside his star charts. "Besides, if he is that devoted to our wine, he will see to it that we continue to make it, unmolested by Montaigne and his minions, will he not?"

Even Marcel had to agree to that. Abbot Francis chuckled and rose to his feet, clapping Fernando on the shoulder. "It seems that you have your work laid out before you, my brother. Are you certain that you can squeeze another half a dozen casks out of this harvest?"

"If you can manage to keep the rain at bay for at least a few more weeks, until we have gathered in the last of the grapes."

Startled by Fernando's almost careless remark, I waited for the abbot's reply. But all he did was smile enigmatically and make his way back to his chambers. The other monks cleared the table with a nonchalance that puzzled me. They had seen what Abbot Francis had done at their front gate during the visit from the constable. Surely they also knew what he had done in the town square of Orleans. Did he do such things often?

I retreated to my cell and sat down on the bed, pulling the scrap of parchment from my pocket. I squinted at it in the fading light. The florid hand was indeed the abbot's—I had watched him pen the words with my own eyes. I let my breath out in a long sigh as I remembered the abbot's thundering invocations to the angels of the elements. Causing rain. Causing earthquakes. Stopping rain.

Could it be true? Was Abbot Francis really who I suspected he was? I had to be sure, or I would go mad.

Finally, the last glow of sunlight faded from the sky. Grabbing my candle, I tiptoed down the stairs into the library. My eager hand made straight for the manuscript and I propped it open at a particular page—the invocation to Gabriel, the Archangel of Water. *Let the blessed tears of Heaven pour forth from thine eyes.*

With my pulse pounding in my ears, I unfolded the parchment scrap and compared the writing, noting the ascending *d*'s and descending *f*'s. I took a deep breath and let it out slowly. There was no doubt in my mind. The hand that wrote the invocation that had saved my life was the selfsame hand which had so recently penned the humble request for candles.

I needed no further proof. The abbot of this strange and wonderful monastery was none other than Seratois, the Wizard of Alceste.

I gazed down at the manuscript in my hands one final time and then carefully slid it back into its niche in the shelf. God, what I would not do to be able to study under the famous Seratois. What a feather in my cap that would be. I, who was nothing but the son of a stonemason from a nondescript town in Lorraine, would finally come into my own.

An image flashed into my mind of the Count de Sainte Jacques on the last day I had seen him. He had been a small and frail man, whose satin and velvet robes draped over his skinny shoulders like bedding over a laundry rack. His eyes had been small and beady, and they would peer at me with raptor-like intensity as he expounded on the books he had read.

But in the year I spent in his service, I had never actually performed any magical rituals with him. I had begged many times to be able to practice what he had been describing to me. "You aren't ready yet," he would tell me. "You must prove yourself worthy." But I never had proven myself worthy to do much except dip his candles, sweep his floor, and blow up the embers of his fire.

I let out my breath in a shudder, as a sorrow I had not had time to feel welled up inside me. I had always thought the fault was mine—I was just not worthy to practice the sacred art. And yet it now occurred to me that I had never witnessed him doing any magical work, either. The monks in this strange monastery had demonstrated more magical knowledge in three days than I had seen from the count in an entire year.

The thought brought me up short, nearly taking my breath away. Could it be that the count might not have actually had the knowledge and the power that he claimed to have had? And if he was nothing but a fraud, what might I learn if I was apprenticed to a real magician?

Like the great Seratois.

Shutting my eyes, I relished a vision of myself striding

into the hall of the Fratres Illuminati in Rome, announcing to the astonishment of the assembled company that the great Seratois did not die in the Tiber. He lived, and I was his apprentice and—dare I even think it—heir to his title. But would he even be willing to take me on as his apprentice? I had to know at once or I would go mad.

Taking the candle with me, I left the library and made my way down the corridor to the steps leading to the abbot's chambers. The soft glow of candlelight that showed around the edges of the door told me that he was still up. I eased the door open and tiptoed in.

I found him sitting at his desk, cradling his chin in one hand and absently tapping the tip of his quill on the edge of the ledger book. He seemed to be lost in thought, making no sign that he knew I was even there. I stood motionless for several seconds before I summoned enough nerve to speak.

"Father Francis?"

My voice, although soft, rang out in the silent room. He started, dropped his pen, and looked up. "Ah, Michael. I did not hear you come in."

"I should have knocked, I suppose," I babbled, my heart racing. "Please, forgive me for disturbing you at this unholy hour but I had to speak with you. I … I have a confession to make."

"Oh?" He lifted an eyebrow and regarded me with a faint smile. "Rather out of character for you, is it not? Superstitious peasant nonsense and all of that."

I lowered my gaze and bit my lip hard. "It is not that kind of confession. It is more of an apology."

Something in my face must have betrayed my agitation, for he dropped the teasing tone and lowered his voice to a gentle hush. "For what, my son?"

"I have discovered who you really are." My voice dropped to a whisper.

He paused for a brief moment. "And who might that be?"

"You are Seratois," I replied. "The Wizard of Alceste."

"Oh, I am, am I?" His voice seemed deceptively calm. "And what has brought you to that conclusion?"

I reached into my pocket and pulled out the scribbled parchment. "I compared this to the Grimoire of Light in your library. That manuscript is written in your hand."

"It is, indeed," he returned. "Still, how do you know that I did not merely copy it from another?"

"You crossed out some passages and wrote others ... passages that I recognized as being from the copy that the count possessed. Had you merely copied it, you would not have done that. But you would have done so if you were revising your own work."

"I see."

I paused, considerably taken aback by his apparent lack of concern. "I wish you to know that there is no torture the Holy Office can devise that will cause me to betray you. I swear that I will keep your secret until I no longer have breath to speak. I ask you ... no, I beg you to believe that."

"If I didn't believe that, I assure you that you would

not be here." He waved towards an earthenware pitcher on the table. "Now, pour yourself a little wine and calm down so we can talk this over sensibly."

It took several swallows to quiet my trembling. The abbot waited patiently for me to take a deep breath and sit on a bench in the corner.

"Now," he continued. "You were saying?"

"I find it difficult to believe that you are not angry with me."

"Angry? Should I be?"

"You would have every right to be," I said. "I should have asked you outright, I suppose, rather than sneak about."

"How do you know that I would have told you?" he countered. "I might have refused to confirm your suspicions … or denied them altogether."

Somehow, I could not imagine him doing so. "I suppose I would have done just that, were I in such a position. All things considered, I understand that the pyre would burn hotter for you than for the rest of us."

"It matters little how hot the pyre burns," the abbot returned. "The end result is the same."

"I suppose so." I lowered my gaze to my clasped hands.

"Still, you seem to have taken a great deal of trouble to ferret out my secret. May I inquire why it meant so much to you to do so?"

I glanced up and found myself looking straight into his blue eyes. His voice never lost its gentle softness, but his gaze nearly pinned me to the wall. I looked down at my clasped hands. "I wanted to be able to study under you."

"Study what?"

"Magic."

"And I did not qualify for this honor as Father Francis?"

"No, no, I didn't mean that," I protested, becoming more and more flustered by the moment. "But to be able to sit at the feet of the great Seratois, no matter what name he goes by, was ... too much like a dream come true."

"And just what did you expect to learn from me?"

His voice had taken on an edge. I felt panic rise in my throat.

"I ... I hardly know."

"Would it perhaps be the parlor tricks that so impressed the Roman dilettantes of the Fratres Illuminati?"

I did not answer. I could not, because it was true. And to make matters worse, he knew it.

He sat back in his chair and heaved a weary sigh. "The threat from the Holy Office is not the only reason why I am reluctant to reveal my rather colorful past to newcomers. I must admit that your curiosity on that subject does concern me, but not because I fear the pyre." He pressed the tips of his fingers together and studied me for a long moment. "I will tell you this. If you decide to stay, I will teach you what I can. But if you expect me to suddenly become the notorious Seratois once again just to give you the satisfaction of calling yourself my apprentice, then I fear I must disappoint you."

"I never expected you to doff your priestly disguise,"

I retorted a little sharply. "Especially since it seems to be working so well."

"Michael," he said sternly. "I am not merely disguised as a priest. I am a priest. In a way, the man I was did indeed die in the Tiber on the way to the pyre. When I left Rome, I also left Seratois behind, to live in the past." He paused for emphasis. "And that is now the only place where he must live—in the past."

I made no reply. His words had caught me off guard, and I had no idea what to say. Was he trying to tell me that he had recanted his heresy and renounced his sorcery? Was that why he was no longer Seratois?

He gave me another of his piercing looks. "Do you understand?"

I nodded, the bitter taste of chagrin stinging my mouth. I didn't want to learn mere priestcraft. I wanted to learn magic, the kind of magic that Seratois had been so famous for. But it apparently was not to be.

"Very well. Now, allow me to suggest that you go to bed and get some sleep. Morning comes early and we have much to do tomorrow." His tone suggested that he had no intention of discussing the matter further.

Numbly, I rose to my feet and stumbled out the door, shaking with utter humiliation. I had been a fool to just barge into the abbot's private chambers and blither like an idiot about such a forbidden and dangerous thing as magic. No wonder he had brushed me aside like a pesky child. But had he truly renounced magic, or did he simply not think I had the wit to learn the kind of magic that the great Seratois had practiced?

I finally reached my cell and sat down on my bed as the ache of disappointment grew within my breast. I shook my head in disbelief. No, no ... it wasn't possible that he had recanted. How could a man, invested with magical power that awed the most illustrious men in Rome, now just be content to live in a ruined monastery catering to a lot of ignorant townsfolk? Could he not return to Rome, reclaim his title, and avenge himself on the rogue that had betrayed him? If he were to do so, I would willingly be at his side, Holy Office or no.

I lay back on the straw with a sigh and shut my eyes. What in heaven's name was I going to do now? I had nowhere else to go, and I was sure that Montaigne and his soldiers lurked outside the monastery walls like prowling wolves. I had no choice but to remain in this drafty ruin.

But I wasn't going to give up my quest. I wanted to study magic, real magic. And I would do so or die trying. Before sleep finally engulfed me, I determined to find some way to make the abbot change his mind and teach me the magic of Seratois.

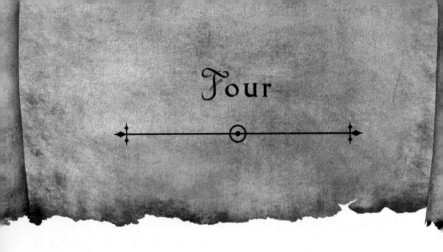

Four

The next morning, the peal of a bell jolted me awake from a deep pre-dawn slumber. I listened to it for a moment as I watched the first struggling rays of sun filter in my window. I frowned, musing on the fact that this was the first morning since my arrival that my sleep had been thus disturbed.

Still, the bell continued is raucous tolling. I climbed out of bed, pulled on my doublet, and trotted down the stairs—and almost collided with Brother John, who was running at full tilt down the corridor towards the front gate. He had a white surplice tossed on over his black habit. It made him look like an altar boy.

I realized with some shock that that was precisely what he was.

Framed in the parlor doorway, the morning sun shining behind him, stood Abbot Francis, bedecked in stole, mantle, and cope. "Come, John," he called with frantic gestures. "The people are assembled."

The sight of the abbot in his priestly garb startled me for a moment. Then I chided myself for being surprised. It must be Sunday and, of course, Abbot Francis would say Mass for the villagers. Not to do so would certainly have invited suspicion. And yet, knowing what I now knew of the abbot's identity, it seemed decidedly incongruous for the notorious Seratois to be performing an act of such pious superstition.

I found the other brothers milling about outside the south transept. At a gesture from the abbot, they filed into the church and I fell into line behind them. I had not been to Mass since I had left Lorraine, and there was no reason why I had to attend one now. And yet my curiosity was piqued by the idea of the notorious Seratois celebrating Mass. It would hardly be an ordinary service. Would I see the Wizard of Alceste in action?

I dropped out of the procession and tucked myself into a pew at the rear of the nave. The rest of the brothers followed Abbot Francis down the center aisle behind Brother John, who was hoisting a golden cross up over his head. They, too, fell out of the procession at the entrance to the choir, leaving the abbot and Brother John to approach the altar.

I settled back in the hard wooden seat as the service began. It was the first time I had been inside the monastery church, so I took a moment to look around with the eyes of the son of a stonemason. Notre Dame Cathedral it was not. The arches that lined both sides of the nave were small and rounded rather than tall and high, and fashioned of the same gray stone as the rest of the monastery. They remained unadorned save for six stone gargoyles, similar to those that had confronted me in the monastery library, which squatted atop the columns and regarded the people below them with baleful gazes.

All the other ornamentation, if indeed it had ever existed, had long since broken or crumbled. Even the rood screen consisted of plain ironwork, with only tiny finials at the ends. The statuary consisted solely of a large statue of the Virgin on the left side of the high altar and an equally large figure of Christ Crucified on the right. Above them both, in surprisingly good repair, the rose window glowed in red, blue, green, and purple as it captured the morning sun and splashed it onto the floor below.

The nave was extremely narrow and looked like it would hold only fifty or so people comfortably. And yet there were nearly twice that many crammed into the wooden pews, clustered under the archways, and even kneeling on the worn stones of the floor.

Most of the people wore the simple homespun clothes of the village. But I also noticed clusters of men and women in velvets and furs taking up many of the front pews; the stylish trains of the women's skirts swept the floors as they passed down the aisle. I even saw the Duchess of Orleans and her mother-in-law kneeling in the pew across from me, their heads bowed over pearl rosary beads.

I frowned in puzzlement. These people, obviously

wealthy, could have heard Mass in the fine cathedral in Orleans. Why on earth were they coming here?

"*Dominus Vobiscum.*" The voices of the monks echoed between the stone arches in such a way that their four voices sounded like many. "The Lord be with you."

I found myself chanting with them under my breath as the words of the liturgy echoed once more in my mind. I had served at the altar myself as a young boy, in the Cathedral of St. Etienne in Metz, and had learned to read passable Latin in the Cathedral school. This had so pleased my father that he bid his guild master to arrange for me to learn the rudiments of the secret science of Geometry, with the intention that I might follow his trade.

I had been excited about the prospect at first, until I discovered that being a stonemason was less about divining the mysterious secrets of sacred numbers and more about pounding on stone blocks with a chisel and mallet. I sensed that my father's trade was less about superior intellect and more about bulging muscles, an idea that appealed to me less and less as the years passed.

"*Sanctus, sanctus, sanctus,*" the monks chanted. "Holy, holy, holy. Lord God of Hosts." I could pick out Brother Juan-José's melodious baritone from the chorus of echoing voices. And Antonin's thin tenor. And Fernando's slightly nasal one. And Marcel's tuneless rumble. Still, I found the sound oddly comforting. It took me back to my childhood, before my life had become so turbulent and complicated.

With a sigh, I sat back in the pew and stared up at the ceiling. The arches had never been elaborate, and the

65

ribbing was crumbling a bit around the edges. But for all that, the vault had a rough austerity and a purity of line and curve that I found strangely graceful and elegant.

My father's guild master once told me that the secret of God's creation lay in numbers, proportions, and the Golden Mean. Masons were cocreators with God, and the cathedral was a microcosm of the Divine realm, a portal to heaven where the angels dwelt. Through that portal, mortals could commune with the angelic host and listen in rapture to the Music of the Spheres.

His words had echoed in my memory for years after that. Sunday after Sunday, I would gaze up at the vaulted ceiling of the cathedral while my mother told her beads and my older sisters ogled the boys in the adjacent pews. I studied the triangles, trapezoids, and pentagons, half-hoping to see angels and wondering if I could talk to them and get them to talk to me.

One Sunday at Christmas, they did. Or at least it seemed so to me.

As I gazed up at the vaulted ceiling of the cathedral on that bitter cold morning, I fancied that I could almost hear the divine music. To my amazement, the ceiling had suddenly turned into the vault of heaven. Angels came and went therein just as people came and went in the street below.

A voice I couldn't identify proclaimed that there existed a sacred wisdom that the buffoon bishop and his clerical toadies either didn't know or didn't see fit to impart to the ignorant faithful. The angels of heaven could be called upon with secret rites and rituals. This was known to the profane as magic, but in reality was the sacred art of invocation. The blessed angels could, when asked properly, impart sacred and hidden knowledge that could be used to help the less fortunate, rather than further ensuring their enslavement by a greedy and authoritarian church.

But that knowledge carried with it a risk and a price. If I wanted to learn to use that knowledge, I would have to devote my life to study and endure great sacrifices.

I would have to become a Sacred Magician.

Later, when I inquired of my father if he knew of such things, he crossed himself, glowered at me, and declared that we were a pious family and I was not to speak of such things to him again. It was impossible for me to tell if he even knew what I was talking about, or, if so, if he was simply constrained by fear of reprisal (from the Church and his guild) from divulging it to me. I determined to discover the secret lore for myself and redoubled my efforts in my studies at the Cathedral school.

Then my father fell from the scaffolding and broke his head open. And my studies abruptly ended—or so I thought at the time. I was convinced that the angels had found me unworthy to practice the sacred art and had abandoned me.

Now, sitting in a worn wooden pew staring up at a far more humble ceiling, I couldn't help but wonder at the events that had brought me here to the feet of the most powerful magician in all of France. Maybe, just maybe, the angels hadn't abandoned me after all. Did I dare believe that?

Something I couldn't name brought me out of my reverie and made the back of my neck prickle. I looked around at the people in the seat beside me and noticed something odd. Instead of leaning back in the pews and tucking themselves in for a sleep, as they had done in my childhood, they leaned forward in anticipation, watching the altar expectantly. Children were squelched if they so much as uttered a peep, and indeed the entire church seemed to be couched in a hushed silence. What was it that they expected to happen?

"*Hoc est enim corpus meum*," the abbot chanted. "This is my body." His sonorous baritone voice reached even the back rows. He genuflected, then took the wafer off the silver platen and raised it high above his head, moving it in a circular motion. I noticed that he discreetly waved his hand.

A gasp rose up from the small congregation and I could barely make out a faint sobbing noise from somewhere in the nave. The sobbing grew louder until it filled the entire church. The statue of the Virgin in one corner began to glow, as if lit by candles. My eyes wide with astonishment, I watched large tears roll down the plaster cheeks and drip onto the cracked stone floor. Several people crossed themselves, but most bowed their heads in prayerful awe.

The abbot genuflected again, as if nothing out of the ordinary had happened, and lifted the chalice next. "*Hic est enim calix sanguinis mei*. This is the cup of my blood."

Everyone's gaze turned to the rood screen, and mine with them. The crucifix glowed with the same eerie light.

Blood welled out of the painted wounds on the hands, feet and side of the wooden Christ and ran down the carved cross.

Old women wept and crossed themselves continuously, and children gazed up at the abbot in awe and wonder. I heard frequent prayers, Pater Nosters, Ave Marias, and Amens whispered up and down the aisles as the other monks ushered the villagers up to the communion rail.

Finally, the abbot stood before the altar, the sunlight from the rose window forming a yellow and crimson halo around his head and shoulders. I caught my breath in spite of myself. He gave the crowd a final benediction, reminding them they were blessed and that God loved them.

"The Mass is ended, go in peace." He made a final sign of the cross in the air in front of him and led the way out of the church.

He was soon engulfed in a veritable swarm of people, all seeking to touch his hands or his robes. Mothers thrust their babies into his arms and a tiny old woman knelt to kiss the hem of his habit. He didn't appear to be annoyed and greeted them with genuine warmth, stooping to kiss a small child or lay a comforting hand on the white hair of an old man, calling them all by name.

My attention was caught by the young Duchess, who was hovering on the steps and tangling her rosary in her trembling fingers. Her huge eyes were wide with adoration as she watched Abbot Francis move through the crowd. Her mother-in-law motioned Journet over to her side and whispered something to him. He nodded and stepped forward.

"Father Francis, I would like to present the Duchess and Dowager Duchess of Orleans."

As the abbot turned around, the young Duchess sank to her knees and took his hand in both of hers, kissing it ardently. "Oh, Blessed Father." She gazed, enraptured, into the abbot's blue eyes. "I am so pleased to finally be able to meet you."

Abbot Francis, looking oddly discomfited, gently but firmly pulled his fingers out of her grip. "Simply address me as Father Francis, I beg of you. I am no more blessed than any of my brothers."

"Of course," she murmured, clearly unconvinced but obviously even more impressed with his modesty.

"I must say that I have never been quite so uplifted at Mass before." The Dowager Duchess pressed her wrinkled hands together. "Truly extraordinary."

"Your Grace is most kind," the abbot replied, doing his best to be gracious. The young Duchess continued to gaze at him as though he were some kind of saint. Finally, Brother Fernando, looking as though he had done this many times before, wedged himself firmly between the duchess and the abbot. He thanked the women for their attendance and kind words and allowed the abbot to escape into the cloister.

We all quickly convened in the refectory as Brother John served yeasty bread and ripe apples for breakfast. While the others ate, I sat silently in my chair, picking at the food on my trencher. The entire performance had irritated me—not because it wasn't impressive, but because it was. Flawless. Moving, even. That is, if I had been of a pious mien.

But I wasn't. I wanted to learn serious magical rituals. And I found myself acutely disappointed that the one man in the world I wished to have as a mentor would waste his considerable talent and knowledge on impressing superstitious townsfolk.

His vestments doffed, Abbot Francis leaned back in his chair and nursed his goblet with a satisfied look. "It went well, did it not?"

"Father Francis," I protested, "you tricked them."

"Into what, pray tell?"

"Into … well, into believing in …"

"Miracles?" His voice took on an edge. "In their own worth and blessedness? In the fact that they have the grace of God to pull themselves out of their own wretchedness and poverty? If so, then I plead guilty."

I was not convinced. "Still, it's as bad as the so-called miracles that I saw as an altar boy in St. Etienne's. The parish priest used to make the statues bleed and cry using levers, pulleys, and colored water."

"Show me what levers, pulleys, and colored water I have used."

"That is not the point." I frowned, remembering how my superstitious mother had cried like a babe at such spectacles and put an extra denier into the collection plate—a denier we could ill afford to spare. "You give them false hope."

"False hope?" he echoed. "My young friend, it is not

my modest illusions which make Sainte Felice prosperous, I assure you. The people feel blessed by God, which gives them the courage to make their world a better place. If my harmless little tricks serve to renew their faith for another week, why do you fault me?"

"Because I had expected that the infamous Seratois would have better use for his magic than to resort to performing religious tricks for peasants," I replied sullenly.

Everyone's gaze turned to me. "What was that?" Juan-José leaned forward, fixing me with a fiery scowl.

"It's all right, my brothers," Abbot Francis put in with a sigh. "He knows."

"How?" Marcel demanded. "Did you tell him?"

"I had no need to. He figured it out on his own." The abbot smiled ruefully. "We have a young man of unusual perception among us. We would do well to mind ourselves."

"So I see." Juan-José studied me for a moment from beneath his furrowed brow. "Yes, my young friend," he said finally, "our abbot is, indeed, the Wizard of Alceste. When did you discover this?"

I felt my face flush fiery scarlet. "I suspected as much the first night I came," I replied. "And yet, I was not sure until... until I compared his handwriting with the Grimoire of Light in your library."

"Well!" Antonin exclaimed, rubbing his chin. "Fine bit of deduction, I must say."

"So, what are you going to do with your newfound knowledge, eh?" Juan-José scowled.

"What do you mean?" I demanded.

"Whenever he rescues one more of us, the risk of the Holy Office discovering his presence here grows greater…as does the risk of betrayal."

I finally turned to face him, hot with indignation. After all I had been through, how dare he accuse me of being a snitch? "Do you think me a traitor?"

"How do I know that you are not?" he returned, fixing me with a smoldering stare.

"I owe Abbot Francis my life, even as you do," I snapped. "And I fully intend to keep his secret as you have done. Now, I have trusted you by remaining here. Either trust me as well or run me through with your sword."

The abbot leapt to his feet in an instant and positioned himself between us as though we were snarling dogs. "Now, my young friend," he said, placing his hand on my shoulder, "do calm down. I fear our brother has been in the army longer than he has been in the cloister and is used to dealing with soldiers not with monks. Please do not take his lack of tact for insult."

I need not have worried. A hint of a smile showed itself from beneath Juan-José's dark mustache. "I have to admit that I entertained doubts about the truth of your story until now."

My eyes widened. "And what has changed your mind, pray tell?"

"A man who has stared death in the face, no matter what age he is, behaves very differently from a man who has not. He knows the difference between that which is important to the body and that which is important to the soul." He shrugged. "Besides, who am I to question Francis' trust in you? He had every reason to doubt me, as well."

"Indeed I did." The abbot sat back down again and reached for his goblet. "Although, my good brother, it was never your loyalty which I doubted. Nor your swordsmanship ... having had the unnerving experience of crossing blades with you."

"I did not know who you were," Juan-José retorted.

"There was no time to introduce myself, if you recall."

"You actually attacked Father Francis?" I stared at him, aghast. "With your sword?"

"The soldiers of the King of Castile had me surrounded," Juan-José protested. "They had several priests in their company—priests from the Spanish Inquisition. For all I knew, Francis was one of them. How was I to know that he was attempting to rescue me?"

"And you dueled?" I gazed in amazement from one man to the other.

"If you can call it that," the abbot replied with an amused smile. "When he lunged at me with that sword of his, I could only snatch up another and defend myself as best I could, until ..."

"Until what?" I demanded anxiously.

"Until he turned my saber into an eel," Juan-José muttered. "At least, that's what it seemed like to me."

The abbot laughed at the swarthy Spaniard's sheepish expression. "I had no choice. You are a far better swordsman than I. You would have skewered me like a roasting fowl."

"Was that how he discovered your identity?" I asked the abbot.

"That was rather a dramatic introduction, I will grant you," the abbot replied. "The rest were a bit more discreet."

"Francis, you must admit that having such a celebrity as yourself in our midst is a difficult secret to keep," Fernando commented with a mischievous smile. "I doubt whether there is any student of the arcane arts in the whole of Europe by now who has not heard of your exploits."

"My master spoke of you often," I said eagerly. "He was quite impressed by you the few times you had met."

The abbot suddenly looked uncomfortable. "I can imagine," he commented sourly, frowning into his goblet.

I mistook his obvious embarrassment for modesty. "His favorite story had to be how you, at a banquet with the Papal nuncio, brought the roasted pheasant back to life from beneath the nuncio's very knife. Ah, I would have given anything to have seen the look on his face as his supper began to squawk and flap its wings."

I left off my tale as the abbot fixed me with a gaze that would freeze water.

Fernando, oblivious of my plight, fairly shrieked with laughter. "Did he really?" he demanded. "I, too, would have loved to have been there. Why, I remember a time when he..."

"That will be all, Fernando," Abbot Francis ordered

sharply. "Such things are in the past. Kindly allow them to remain there, if you please."

Fernando and I glanced at one another for a moment like chastened boys.

"Forgive me, Father Francis," I finally said. "My remarks were uncalled for. I had no wish to offend."

"No, of course you did not," he replied, keeping voice even with an obvious effort. "But I must insist that you refrain from regaling us with further... anecdotes."

"But are they not true?" I asked.

"It doesn't matter," he returned. "Wagging tongues must be curbed lest they unwittingly wag before the wrong audience. You are new to this, but Fernando knows better. I'll thank you both to use a bit more discretion in the future."

With that, he rose abruptly and stalked out of the refectory.

"Now you've done it," Marcel grumbled. "He'll be bad tempered for the rest of the morning."

"Does he do this every time his real identity is brought up?" I asked.

"God, yes." Antonin rolled his eyes heavenward.

"I cannot understand why he would be so reticent about it," I persisted, as Juan-José cleared the breakfast dishes. "I would have found it something of which to be proud."

"Not when you have the Holy Office after you because of it," Juan-José said.

"I suppose," I conceded, feeling very sheepish. "Still, I am sorry that I aroused his wrath."

Fernando only laughed. "My boy, you have yet to see his wrath." He clapped me on the shoulder. "He has merely had his feathers ruffled. He'll get over it by dinnertime. Now, we must attend to the vines or we shall both be in even deeper trouble."

I followed him obediently through the cloister to a small gate. Fernando opened it with a creak. A small path led up the green hillside towards the rows of grapevines, heavily laden with large green leaves and purple grapes. The scene was most idyllic. I half expected a buxom shepherdess to appear at any moment.

Cradling a bunch of grapes in his palm, Fernando cut the stem with a small scythe and dumped the bunch into the basket at his feet. I reached for another bunch and did the same, almost slicing my palm. The process took more dexterity than I had expected. For a moment I watched Fernando snapping grape stems with a practiced hand. He easily cut three bunches to my one.

I cupped my hand around a bunch of grapes and examined it closely. A few of the grapes at the tip still held a greenish tinge. "How about this one?"

He examined it carefully, then shook his head. "Save it for the next harvest. Better to have them too ripe than not ripe enough."

I nodded and left it on the vine. After cutting a few more bunches, I began to get better at the technique—at least enough so I didn't cut off my finger in the process.

I wanted to hear more stories about the abbot's nefarious past, since the more I heard, the more they seemed incongruous with the image of a humble priest in a backwater monastery. I sensed there was a side to Abbot Francis that I had yet to discover, one that would fit the stories only too well. Maybe I could get Fernando to tell me, now that the abbot wasn't around to hear us.

"You knew Abbot Francis in Rome, didn't you?" I asked, as we filled basket after basket with purple grapes.

Fernando nodded. "I, too, was a member of the Fratres Illuminati, God help me." He smiled ruefully. "And a more unholy bunch of ruffians never were, believe me, even though a good half of them were churchmen of various sorts."

I frowned. "Churchmen?"

"Oh, indeed. Bishops, cardinals, even the Pope himself at one time, or so I was told. I came into the order just about the time that Francis, or Jean-Phillipe as he was called then, became Grand Master."

"Were they all magicians?"

"Hardly." Fernando snorted in derision. "Most of them were just dilettantes who had read a book or two and then fancied themselves Great Magi. They dressed in robes and played a role as though they were on the stage. Only Jean-Phillipe had real power. I sensed it the first time I met him."

I leaned forward eagerly. "What was he like back then?

"I didn't know him all that well. But I can tell you that he certainly cut an impressive figure. I remember that he wore his hair in blue-black waves down to his shoulders and had a penchant for emerald velvet and gold brocade. Everything he did had a dramatic flair to it. And his temper was the stuff of legend." Fernando rolled his eyes expressively. "Francis doesn't take kindly to being reminded of those times, as you have noticed."

"How did you know to come here?" I persisted, my curiosity still unsated. "Did you know that he did not drown in the Tiber?"

Fernando laughed aloud. "I honestly thought he had, along with everyone else in Rome. Then I received a mysterious letter inviting me to the University of Paris. It was signed by a Father Francis Duchienne, a name I had never heard of. Still, going to Paris was certainly safer than remaining in Florence. So I took a ship to Marseilles and hired a carriage to go to Paris. I stopped for the night in Sainte Felice. Francis met me in Journet's tavern and, well, as you can guess, I never went on to Paris."

"Did you recognize him?"

"Yes indeed. He had only cut his hair and donned a black habit. Everything else about him was the same."

"But didn't you think it odd that he would have become a priest?"

"I did at first." Fernando replied. "I wondered, as did you, if he was just hiding behind a false identity. Then I watched him say Mass for the first time. He performed the ritual with such genuine sincerity that it nearly moved me to tears. There are many things a man can counterfeit, little brother, but sanctity is not one of them."

79

I pondered this, a bunch of ripe grapes staining my palm with purple juice. I remembered Abbot Francis playing with the children and comforting the old people after Mass. It did not match the image of the flamboyant sorcerer in velvet and brocade bringing dead fowl back to life. "What happened to him?"

Fernando shrugged. "I have no idea. Who knows what changes take place in a man's soul when he is given a second chance at life?"

Fernando's remark brought me up short. It reminded me that I, too, had been given a second chance at life—by the man who had once been known as the notorious Wizard of Alceste. The life I had once known had ended, just as his had. His words of the other evening echoed in my mind. Was that what he had meant? Had "Seratois" really died in the Tiber on the way to the pyre?

"Brother Fernando," I asked finally, "is he still Seratois?"

"Ah, yes. He is still Seratois." Fernando smiled to himself. "Brilliant, theatrical . . . and, at times, damned temperamental."

"So, how is he different from the man he was in Rome?"

"He has fallen in love with the people of Sainte Felice." Fernando snapped the last of the grape stems and tucked the curved knife into a leather scabbard at his belt. "His magic now serves them, not himself. That's the difference."

I helped Fernando stack the baskets beside the press and then followed him into the refectory for supper. As I sat at the table, watching the monks pass the bowls and platters of bread and fruit, I pondered how all of these men, skilled in the hidden arts, had abandoned positions of power and influence to live in a half-ruined monastery with simple food, drafty accommodations, and austere black habits. I remembered Fernando's description of the Fratres Illuminati: men like my former master, playing magician like it was a child's game. But men with real knowledge, like the ones seated beside me at the huge refectory table, seemed to have no need to impress anyone. It was the magical work that mattered, not what other people thought of it.

I realized that they were the real Illumined Brothers.

I glanced down at my stained linen shirt and tattered doublet, the clothes I had innocently put on the morning before the life I had known had been turned upside down. That morning, I had been a student at the University apprenticed to a magician. Now, I was neither. As kind as the monks had been to me, the stark contrast between their dress and mine reminded me yet again that I was an outsider—maybe even an intruder that threatened their very existence.

Supper finally being over, Antonin began to clear the table while John disappeared into the kitchen to bake the bread for tomorrow's breakfast. As the others rose to leave the table, I reached over and caught Abbot Francis' sleeve.

"Father Francis, how does one go about joining a monastery?" I almost said "your" monastery but then decided to keep my request impersonal, as if it were merely a matter of curiosity. I wasn't quite ready to admit my interest to Abbot Francis—or to myself.

"Normally, one would enter the order as a postulant." He leaned back in his chair and pressed the tips of his fingers together. "After that, if the candidate were found suitable, he would become a novice. Then, in a year or so, he would take provisional vows of obedience, stability, and conversion of life for a period of three years. At least, that is how it is according to the Rule of St. Benedict. However, what works for a large Benedictine house does not work for a small and select company such as we are. So, I have combined the novitiate period with the provisional vows. Vows are quite important in the practice of magic, as you no doubt have noticed." He paused for emphasis. "Especially the vow of obedience."

I bristled. Obedience had never been one of my virtues—particularly when I had to obey seemingly senseless and arbitrary rules. My father had once beaten me severely, one of only a few times he had done so, for disregarding his order forbidding me from climbing on the scaffolding while he fitted the dressed stones into the wall of the cathedral. I had watched the workmen scurry up and down the wooden planks like so many squirrels. Why couldn't I do the same? It was perfectly safe. And the view of the valley from the roof was truly breathtaking. My father was just being a tyrant, seeking to control my actions simply because I was his son.

It was only after he died that I realized he had been right.

"Then what?" I asked, annoyed at the lump that had risen in my throat.

"After the three years have passed, he would take his final vows, which bind him to the order for the rest of his life. That is, unless the abbot chooses to release one from those vows, which occurs only under extraordinary circumstances."

"Does one have to become a priest?" I asked with some trepidation.

The abbot shook his head. "No, indeed. I happen to be the only one actually ordained. The others are monks, not priests, but they have taken the same vows."

"I see." I pondered this for a moment, not finding it quite to my liking. I never did fancy being told when to rise, when to eat, when to sleep and so on, as my mother had complained on more than one occasion. But I particularly didn't like the prospect of being told what not to do, to say, or to read. Would Abbot Francis impose such restrictions upon me if I came under his authority?

"Why do you ask?" he inquired with a faint smile, looking as though he knew full well what the answer was. It was a quirk of his that I was beginning to find extremely disconcerting.

"I had just thought that, well, it might be safer for me to wear a black habit too. I would be less obvious as an outsider that way."

He leaned forward and studied me for a moment. "Michael, do you wish to join our order?" he asked, as though he had not heard a word I had said.

"I don't know." It was the most honest answer I could give. "But I feel very uncomfortable sticking out like a goose in a chicken coop. If I'm going to be staying for any length of time at all, I want to at least look like I fit in."

"To whom?" he countered. "To Montaigne and his soldiers, or to yourself?"

"To myself, then, since you are so insistent about it," I snapped. "What, pray, is wrong with that?"

"These black habits are not costumes," he replied firmly. "We are legitimate members of the order of St. Benedict. Now, I will grant you that our observance of the Rule is not strict, but we are not pretending, any of us. Were you to don the habit and cowl, you, too, would have to join the order of St. Benedict as a lay brother, just as the rest have done … and take the same vows as they have." He gave me one of his impaling looks. "Are you ready to do that?"

"No," I muttered, feeling both chastened and extremely annoyed about it. Once more, he had caught me out. "Does that mean I have to leave?"

The abbot shook his head gently. "We offered you sanctuary for as long as you required it. But if you actually wish to join us, you must make the decision yourself and inform us of that fact. Then, and only then, will you truly be a member of this monastery." He regarded me with a maddening smile. "And privy to the remainder of its secrets."

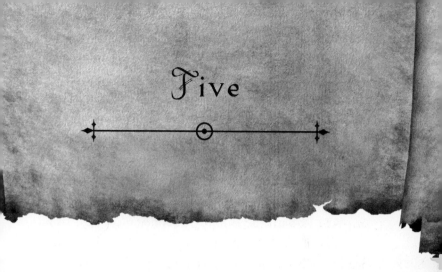

Five

For the next several weeks there was little time to think about anything, much less monastery secrets. I was too busy cutting vine stems and piling bunches of sweet, purple grapes into a basket almost as tall as I was, which I then had to lug down the hill through the gate into the cloister. I stacked the basket next to the wine press, grabbed another, and hurried back up the hill to fill it.

Each of us had a row. Even Abbot Francis rolled up his sleeves, hiked up the hem of his habit, and grabbed a basket. It took nearly an entire day to gather all the ripe grapes from that row. On the next day, all the grapes that weren't ripe the previous day were now ripe, so we had to work the row again. And again—until nearly all the grapes were harvested.

God, what a job it was. And even then, it turned out that we were only half finished.

"I think we are finally ready to press the grapes," Fernando said cheerfully after supper as the rest of us nursed our wine and our sore muscles. His face and hands were purple with grape juice, and his eyes shone with enthusiasm. "I would like to begin tomorrow, so that we can bung up the casks before the full of the moon."

The rest of the monks groaned in chorus.

"As you wish, Fernando," Abbot Francis said, rising slowly to his feet. "Now, I suggest that all of you retire to your cells. We will begin at dawn."

The other monks filed out of the refectory. I followed them into the corridor, then managed to catch up with Fernando on the way to my cell. "What is it that we have to do?" I asked, not sure I wanted to know.

"We have to load the grapes into the press and turn the crank," Fernando explained, gesturing with his hands. "It is quite a task. It takes all of us to do it. We could surely use your help for just a bit longer, if you are willing."

"I suppose so," I said with a resigned sigh. The whole business had begun to irritate me. It wasn't the labor that bothered me so much—I certainly wasn't working any harder or longer than any the others. But I still felt like a hireling. Maybe if I was actually a member of this strange company, I would feel differently about the work. I might even enjoy it. The thought surprised me, which irritated me even more.

"Good." Fernando rubbed his hands together, ignoring my lack of enthusiasm. We stopped at the base of the stairs and Fernando pointed off to the left, towards the base of the bell tower. "Go up and ask Antonin when the planetary aspects are favorable to bless the wine. He'll know what that means."

I nodded eagerly, remembering the abbot saying that Antonin had his own observatory up in the tower. I had never seen such a thing before. Forgetting my sore muscles, I hurried up the serpentine staircase and found myself in the bell tower. Frowning, I turned around and made my way back down the steps, wondering if I had made a wrong turn somewhere.

A door suddenly opened at a turn in the staircase and Antonin peeked out.

"So, it's you scurrying about up here." He raised an eyebrow. "What is the matter? Are you lost?"

"Yes," I replied petulantly. "I was looking for you, but all I found was the bell tower."

"My cell is just below it." He drew me into the tiny room. "It is a bit difficult to find, I will admit. But I have a window which faces east. It affords a wonderful vantage point for determining which planets and stars are rising over the horizon on any given day."

"But doesn't the ringing of the bell awaken you?"

"Not when my task is to ring it," he replied. "A bargain I struck with Francis for the privilege of a cell with such a view."

"I see," I murmured, gazing out of the window. From the monastery's vantage point on the hill, one could see the entire countryside spread out below, for surely a hundred miles.

"Now, what can I do for you, hmm?" he asked.

"Brother Fernando wanted to know when to bless the wine," I said, still transfixed by the view from the window.

"Oh, of course." He grabbed a large leather-bound volume from a stack by the window and opened it onto a bookstand. "Let's see now. The Sun is almost in Libra. He's a bit behind schedule this year, isn't he?"

I finally gazed around the tiny cell. Aside from a cot and a washstand, the rest of the tiny circular cell was crammed with books. "You must have more books here in this room than there are in the entire library." Stacks of leather-bound volumes served the dual purpose of chairs and tables. One pile in the corner had a goblet on top of it. Another pile held a strange brass instrument. "What do you do with all of them?"

"These are all the ephemerides, Tables of Houses, and other references that I use to chart the course of the planets." Antonin motioned me to his side. "Here is one for this year—1480."

I stared at the page for a moment until my vision swam with all the numbers and strange symbols which filled the ruled columns. I glanced up and found him watching me with curiosity. "Do you know how to read an ephemeris?" he asked.

I shook my head sheepishly. "I know the symbols for the planets and the signs of the zodiac. But as to more than that, I'm afraid I'm still woefully ignorant."

He regarded me for a moment with his head cocked to

one side. "How long did you study under your esteemed count?"

"A year. I had just begun my studies when I was arrested." I heaved a sigh. "There is so much I have to learn."

Antonin chuckled softly in reply. "Francis would say that is the first wise thing a man ever says. Come."

He led me back to the window. Dusk had fallen, leaving the sky indigo. "It should be dark enough to see the stars in a few minutes. Then we shall see what is rising tonight."

My fingers, resting on the windowsill, caught on something. I looked down and found that a curved strip of wood had been carefully affixed to the sill and carved with numbers: 0, 30, 60, 90, and so on. Glancing up, I also noticed that a notch had been cut out of the stone arch which framed the window, a notch which lined up with the 0 on the wooden strip on the sill.

"That notch marks due east," Antonin explained. "Each constellation will rise directly under that notch at certain times of the year. One can track the course of the planets throughout the year in that fashion."

"Is that how you determine when the time is right for Brother Fernando to perform his alchemical operation and bless the wine?"

"No, for that I consult the ephemeris and the Mansions of the Moon." He selected another volume from the stack and leafed through it. I watched him for a brief moment as the candlelight played off his flaxen hair and finely chiseled features. It was difficult to tell how old he was. When I first saw him, I had thought he was only a few years older than I. Now, noting the fine lines around his eyes and mouth, I figured he had to be well past thirty. "Here," he finally said, pointing with his finger. "The times when the Sun conjuncts the lunar mansion are the times to perform the operation."

"Won't it work any other time?"

"Oh, it will work," he replied. "But the results may not be what we wish. I don't know whether Fernando has mentioned this, but if the wrong celestial alignments are present during the alchemical process of distillation, then inharmonious influences will be reflected in the finished wine and the elixir which heals will be the elixir which poisons."

"I see," I said, more than a little awed by the sudden solemnity of his tone.

"So, Fernando must distill by…" He paused and studied the scribbles on the page for a moment. "…the end of October, it appears, or else not at all. Certainly before the Sun enters Scorpio and is squared by Saturn, the Greater Malefic."

The candle flickered, sputtered, and finally went out as blackness descended on the room. But instead of relighting it, Antonin rose to his feet and gestured for me to follow him to the window. The stars gleamed in the night sky like diamonds sewn to a black velvet doublet. Antonin grabbed the brass instrument from the top of the book pile. I had never seen one like it before. It looked like a triangle nestled into a crescent. He held it up to his eye and adjusted a small lever.

"Ah. Fifteen degrees and thirty six minutes of Sagittarius rising due east." He grabbed a flint and steel from the top of the bookcase and relit the candle. "Now, let us see what the ephemeris has to say."

He grabbed the volume again and propped it up on the window sill. "There." He pointed to a place in one of the endless columns. I noted the glyph for Sagittarius, along with the numbers 15 and 30. "Six minutes off. Not bad for an old sextant."

"I don't understand," I said. "Why do you bother to measure what is on the horizon when you have it here in the book? Didn't someone else measure it for you?"

"Not 'measure,' my dear boy," he replied sagely. "Calculate." He tapped a slender finger on the parchment page. "These planetary positions were calculated many years in advance, using ancient mathematical formulae for the motions of the constellations across the heavens. It does well to check the accuracy of these calculations with actual observation from time to time. It shows that the calculations are dependable...dependable enough to employ in predicting events."

But I was still gazing out the window at the gorgeous stellar display. "And so the stars march in orderly formation across the sky," I said, remembering a comment that my master had made. "Like a legion off to some celestial war."

"So it seems," Antonin said with an enigmatic smile. "But often Nature is not what she appears."

"How do you mean?" I asked.

"What if it is not the stars which move above us? What if it is we who move below them?"

I frowned. "We? Moving? I fear that I do not understand."

The enigmatic smile broadened. "What if the Earth not only turns on her axis but rotates in an orbit around the Sun? The other planets revolve about the Sun as well, some faster than the Earth, some slower. That explains why some of them appear to move backwards through the constellations, while the Sun never does."

"But that's absurd," I protested. "Why, the ancients knew that the Sun revolved around the Earth."

"Not all of them." He looked around the room for a moment, then swooped down to grab a volume off a stack by the cot. "The Greek philosopher Aristarchus suspected that it was the Earth that moved and not the Sun. But he lacked the instruments and mathematical formulae to prove it."

"Then it can be proven?"

"Oh, indeed. I have the calculations here somewhere." Antonin gestured helplessly at the piles and stacks around him. "They actually match the observed planetary positions much more accurately."

Then a thought struck me. "But that directly contradicts the Scriptural account of creation."

"That was precisely what the Emperor thought," Antonin agreed ruefully, "after I published a modest little treatise upon the subject … which is why I am here."

"How exactly did you get here?" I leaned forward eagerly.

"Not altogether willingly, I must admit. I escaped from

Bruges, with everything I owned in two sacks slung across the withers of my horse. I thought to head for Italy, but such was not to be. It was dusk, as I recall. I was racing down the road through Sainte Felice and I'll be damned if my horse did not run headlong into Fernando's blasted mule cart. They tell me that I lay senseless for nearly a day. In the meantime, Fernando had examined the contents of my bags and knew who I was. We had corresponded briefly while he lived in Italy, but I had never met him. I have to admit that I was as skittish as you were about being in a monastery until I discovered that he was here as well."

"And Abbot Francis? Had you heard of him before?"

"As if anyone had not heard of the Wizard of Alceste." Antonin laughed brightly. "And I must admit that I was as eager to meet him as you were, just to discover if the stories were true."

"And are they?"

"If they are not, then they should be. He is a truly extraordinary man."

"Then are you glad you stayed here and took your vows?"

"Not a moment's regret." Antonin studied me for a moment. "Are you thinking of remaining as well?"

"I don't know," I replied. "It is not a decision one takes lightly, I am told."

"Then think on it." He rose and replaced the book on the stack. "While there is still time."

"Still time?" I echoed. "Before what?"

"Before this monastery meets its fate."

My eyes widened. "What fate is that?"

"Never mind." Antonin brushed my inquiry aside briskly. "We can speak of it later." He turned and regarded me with a raised eyebrow. "That is, if you are still here."

Baffled and a bit annoyed, I bid Antonin good night and made my way back to my cell, resolving to meditate upon my decision further.

Meditation on anything had to wait for the next several days while we pressed the grapes into juice. We worked in shifts. It took four men, two on either arm, to turn the huge wooden beam of the press. While they toiled, the others gathered the remainder of the grapes in the baskets and hauled them across the hills to the monastery gate. After awhile, two of the men at the press retired to rest while another two took their places. Thus rotating, we labored until dusk and had just enough energy left to nibble on some bread and cheese before staggering to our cells.

Finally, we had all the grapes pressed and the juice bunged up in the casks to ferment—and not a day too soon. My arms ached so badly I thought they would fall off. The others, even those who were two decades older than I, did not seem to fare as badly. The years of physical labor and simple diet seemed to have made them somehow hardier. And I, who had spent so much of my youth lifting nothing more heavy than a book, was exhausted. At supper, I could do little more than listen to their conversation while allowing the wine to ease my pains.

"The vines have produced remarkably well this year," Fernando said with some pride, as though he were personally responsible for the fertility of the vines. "We can have seven more casks for Journet before the feast of All Saints."

"Perhaps if we planted more vines, we will increase our yield," the abbot suggested.

But Fernando shook his head. "We would have to grow them from seed, and that would take years."

"Besides," Antonin put in, "if we increase our yield, Journet will have to sell the wine he has for less. If his supply is limited, he can charge more—especially to his increasingly wealthy clientele."

"A pity that the wine goes to the proud nobility," John mused, "rather than to the good folk of Sainte Felice."

"The good folk of Sainte Felice have more need for the money," Marcel said. "One cannot feed and clothe children with wine."

"You have a point, Marcel," the abbot said. "Still, it would be nice to increase our yield, if only to provide even more of an income for the villagers."

"Perhaps if I can get cuttings, we could have more vines sooner." Fernando sighed. "I'll see what I can do."

I glanced up as a sudden rumble of thunder echoed off the stone walls, as if some monstrous giant was stomping through the monastery corridors. Another crack—then came the furious patter of rain on the wooden roof.

"Francis?" Fernando glanced over at the abbot, who sat at the head of the table with his fingers pressed together, beaming a beatific smile.

"All for the glory of God, Fernando," he said.

As the storm raged outside the walls, Fernando lit the

fire in the great hearth. We all clustered about it, nursing our wine and letting both the outer and inner sources of life and warmth ease our soreness.

Dusk fell, and soon the fire served as the only light in the room. Finally, Abbot Francis stifled a yawn.

"Surely it must soon be Compline," he said. "I fear that I am getting too old for this kind of work."

"Pah!" Fernando retorted. "You only have five years on me, and I am not sore."

"Wait until tomorrow morning," Juan-José replied sourly. "We will hear your groans."

The abbot sat back in his chair. "I am senior to all of you by several years," he announced. "I'll thank you all to show the proper respect."

Antonin laughed lightly. "Francis, you old reprobate, you'll outlive us all."

"Will all of us live? Or will we all die?"

I turned abruptly to John, who sat directly in front of the fire, staring unblinking into its dancing flames. He had said nothing during the entire conversation and I had thought that he had been dozing. But his eyes were open wide, showing the white rims. His remark made no sense. And yet, something about the tone of his voice sent a sudden chill up my spine.

"Eh?" Juan-José looked askance at John's entranced expression. "Are we to be lectured by his pesky angels again?"

Abbot Francis threw him a withering look and held his

finger to his lips for silence. "What is it, John?" he asked gently. "What are they showing you?"

"They show me a great evil stalking this monastery. It is like unto a wolf on the prowl, hungry for blood." John broke off, his eyes wide as though he alone saw a horror to which the rest of us were mercifully blind.

Antonin leaned forward. "What is the nature of this evil, John?"

John, lost in his vision, pressed his knuckles into his closed eyes. "Oh, God," he cried. "The wolf! He has caught one of us. I see a man being dragged away from the monastery…to the flames."

"Which of us is it?" Marcel demanded. "Tell us, damn it!"

Juan-José shook his head in disgust. But Abbot Francis ignored them and laid a gentle hand on John's shoulder.

"John?" he coaxed.

"No more." John buried his face in his cupped hands. "They show me no more." He fell silent, leaving only the moaning of the wind, the rumble of thunder, and the occasional crackle of the dying fire.

Just then, we heard a furious pounding on the front door. John jumped up with a shriek. The rest of us turned as one man and faced the door, motionless in our nameless dread. The pounding continued.

The abbot slowly rose to his feet and opened the door. I could see the tow head of a small boy peeking out at us from around the abbot's robes. He handed the abbot a letter and bolted back down the stone walkway.

"What is it, Francis?" Juan-José eyed the letter suspiciously.

Abbot Francis broke the ornate red wax seal and examined the parchment for a moment. "It seems we are to expect a visit from the bishop tomorrow morning."

"I knew it," Marcel muttered.

Brother John silently crossed himself.

"Oh, come now," Abbot Francis chided. "What are you all worried about? The bishop has been here before."

"And always with some complaint from Montaigne," Juan Jose shot back. "I will wager that this visit is hardly a social call either."

"Probably to do with young Michael, here," Antonin said.

"No doubt," said Fernando.

"Mother of God," John intoned solemnly.

"Now, now, my brothers," the abbot said in a soothing tone. "I assure you we have nothing to fear from Sorel. He is probably inquiring merely as a matter of form. He will ask a few questions just so he can assure Montaigne that he has done so. We'll send him off with another jug of wine and that will be the end to it."

"Or so it has been in the past," Marcel retorted. "How long until someone gets wind of what is really going on here?"

"As long as we can keep our wits about us," the abbot replied sternly. "And not give ourselves over to fearful imaginings. Come, my brothers." He draped his arm around

John's shivering shoulders. "Let us leave the night to the elements and hope for better in the morning."

He led the way out the parlor with John leaning heavily on his arm. There was nothing to do but follow. I made my way back to my cell, my gaze constantly searching the shadows, jumping at every creak and rumble from the storm outside.

For what seemed like hours I remained awake, staring wide-eyed at the darkness of my cell and listening to the rage of the storm outside. I could not get John's vision out of my mind, and I continued to tremble at the words that had tumbled from his mouth. Montaigne would somehow invade the sanctuary of the monastery and get one of the monks—maybe all. Again, I shuddered.

In order to still my near panic, I asked myself whether it was possible that Brother John could really be on intimate terms with angels, as Enoch was, or was he just hopelessly mad? If he was merely mad, then his ravings constituted nothing but meaningless noise. And yet, if he was truly conversant with angels, then it meant that one of these monks would be dragged out to meet the same horrid death that had awaited me, had not the abbot intervened.

I shut my eyes against the surge of remorse that threatened to flood my eyes. Abbot Francis had risked his monastery to save me from the flames, and now all were in danger because of it. Ambition, and ambition alone, had prompted me to stay here, hoping to become a powerful magician like the count. But in doing so, I was posing a threat to these strange monks who had taken me in as a kindred soul. I suddenly could not bear the thought of any of them going to the stake along with me.

The next morning at breakfast, Brother John was conspicuous by his absence. I had not been able to shake the feeling of dread which had soaked the previous night along with the rain. Still it persisted, even though the sun shone clear and bright through the refectory window.

"Maybe he is ill," Fernando suggested. "His constitution really is not strong enough for such intense visions."

"Go to him, Antonin." The abbot gestured towards the dormitory. "If he is ill, he must be tended whether he wants it or not."

With a nod, Antonin rose to his feet. Just then, John, looking pale and spectral, padded noiselessly into the refectory.

"Here you are, my brother," Juan-José greeted him. "We were just now sending a ministering angel to you. Or have you had enough of angels for one night?"

John, his thin lips pressed together, pointedly ignored the remark and took a seat. "The wolf is on the prowl even as you scoff."

I pricked up my ears at the rumbling of distant cartwheels on rutted ground. It grew louder and louder.

"He comes." John turned to Juan-José with a stern look. "Just as the angels foretold."

"Then let us make ready, for heaven's sake." The abbot pointed to the remains of breakfast that littered the refectory table. "We've no time to argue. Hurry!"

All the monks jumped to their feet and scurried about collecting platters and sweeping up crumbs. I followed Fernando into the kitchen and hung back while he drew a pitcher full of wine out of the barrel by the back door. "What shall I do?"

"Stay out of sight." He gave me a sidelong glance on the way out the door, pitcher in hand. "I hope Francis can persuade the bishop not to linger."

I crouched behind a pillar near the entrance to the cloister, watching as the bishop's carriage lurched up the path and pulled up to the door. The Bishop of Orleans exemplified everything that I had come to dislike about the Church. Fat and dissipated looking, he had packed his bulk into robes of white silk stitched with gold thread. It mattered little that the golden threads depicted the Chi-Rho and a cross.

"God grant you a good day, Your Grace," Abbot Francis greeted him as John took the reins of the carriage horses.

"Spare me the cheerfulness until I get down from this accursed thing." With a grunt, the bishop eased his massive form down from the carriage steps. He landed on the ground with a thud, his cassock hiked up around his fat ankles.

"Ah, there is the good Brother Fernando with wine." Abbot Francis glanced over his shoulder as Fernando, pitcher and goblet in hand, scurried down the corridor towards the parlor. "That is," he turned back to the bishop with a wink, "if Your Grace wishes some."

"It's the only thing that helps my lumbago these days." The bishop smoothed his sumptuous robes to preserve his modesty, if not his dignity, and took the abbot's arm. "I've already gone through that jug you sent me."

"Then we shall just have to send you back with another." The abbot escorted the bishop through the gate and vanished through the front door.

Brother Fernando emerged from the parlor. Silently, he gestured to the rest of us and we followed him up a small set of stone steps to a small corridor that led behind one of the archways on the way to the bell tower. I began to ask why we were going there, but Fernando just put his finger to his lips and motioned for me to follow. I received the distinctive impression that they had done this many times before.

Indeed, off the corridor, there opened a small chink in the wall through which the entire parlor spread out below us. We gathered at the tiny but convenient opening and watched the bishop ease himself into a chair almost directly below us. Abbot Francis, playing the role of affable host to the extreme, took the pitcher and goblet from the sideboard and poured the bishop's wine himself. The bishop took a long draught and settled back with a contented sigh as the abbot took a seat opposite him.

After another swallow from his goblet, Bishop Sorel looked up and glowered over the rim at the abbot. "One might even say you were trying to bribe me, eh?"

Abbot Francis merely smiled beatifically. "We must be generous with the gifts that God has given us."

The bishop seemed in no mood for banter. "Don't be coy, Abbot Duchienne. I am not here on very pleasant business. There is the little matter of the condemned heretic that you pulled from the flames in Orleans. Montaigne has complained loudly to the Archbishop of Paris."

"I saved a young man from a hideous...and needless...death," Abbot Francis replied, unruffled. "My conscience would not have allowed me to stand by and permit it."

The bishop leaned forward with a scowl. "That young man was duly convicted by the Holy Office before he was turned over to Montaigne."

"To die unrepentant in the flames?" The abbot's voice suddenly took on an edge. "Is that the purpose of the Holy Office these days, to provide such grisly entertainment for the good people of Orleans? God forbid that I should persuade the heretic to repent and spoil their show."

Alarmed, I wondered if the abbot was about to let his righteous indignation, commendable as it was, get the better of his judgment. Surely the bishop would not allow himself to be spoken to in that fashion. I held my breath as Abbot Francis' clear-eyed gaze met the bishop's rheumy one for a long moment.

The bishop heaved a weary sigh. "My good abbot, do be reasonable. Whatever your sterling motives might be, you cannot just elbow the king's authority aside like this."

"And why not?" the abbot returned. "The secular arm, in the person of Giles de Montaigne, would not have had him in the first place if the Holy Office had done its job which, I am told, is to save souls, not incinerate bodies. If I have succeeded in saving a soul that the Holy Office could not, then that is their problem, not mine."

"I will not even begin to debate that issue with you." The bishop's heavily jowled countenance took on a pained expression and he rubbed his face with his fat hand. "I suggest that you save your eloquence for Cardinal de Joinville—who will be here this day next week—to determine whether or not this is a matter for an Inquisitor to investigate."

His eyes widening, Abbot Francis froze for a brief moment. "Whatever for? He does not doubt our orthodoxy, surely."

"Your orthodoxy is only one of the things he is interested in." If the bishop noticed the abbot's momentary loss of composure, he did not reveal it. "He also wishes to examine your handiwork of reforming a convicted sorcerer for himself. I trust you will make him as welcome as you have me."

Abbot Francis only frowned. "I had hoped to merit better at your hands, Your Grace."

The bishop rose to his feet with a grunt. "Abbot Duchienne, please do not think me totally unsympathetic. I have defended your methods, as highly irregular as they are, to both Montaigne and De Joinville for the simple reason that they seem to work. You and your motley little band have taken this miserable collection of daub and wattle and turned it into a prosperous village. The people of Sainte Felice are happy with you. Therefore, I can ill afford to be unhappy with you. But you have made a bitter enemy in

Montaigne—an enemy more powerful than you seem to be willing to admit."

The abbot snorted in derision. "That little weasel?"

"That little weasel speaks with the voice of the king," the bishop returned sourly. "And we of the Church must learn to heed that voice, as much as we may disagree with what it says. Still, the Church sees to her own affairs. So, have a care with De Joinville. I do not wish the Holy Office to get involved in this any more than you do."

"I can assure you that he will be most impressed."

"For your sake, I certainly hope so. And now, God grant you good day." The bishop, no doubt wishing to return to his sumptuous palace in Orleans, lumbered out the door with the abbot at his side and we could see no more.

"Come," Fernando whispered. "We will meet him in the refectory."

We heard the creak and clatter of the bishop's carriage wheels fading off into the distance as Abbot Francis, immersed in deep thought, entered the refectory. It was time for supper, but I was hardly hungry. It seemed that none of the others were either.

"Well, here's a fine mess!" Marcel growled. "What are we going to do now, oh exalted abbot?"

Abbot Francis ignored the sarcasm. "We prepare for the Cardinal's visit," he replied with deceptive calm.

"We prepare?" Marcel's voice rose to a shriek. "Just like that?" He waved his hand to encompass the entire monastery. "We just hide all of our books, our star charts, our glass flasks, and all will be well?"

"Have you another suggestion, Brother Marcel?"

Again, I shuddered at the abbot's penetrating gaze, only grateful that I was not the target this time.

"We run!" Marcel leapt to his feet, his eyes wide with terror. "Anything is better than just sitting here and waiting for them to come and haul us away."

"And where will you run?" the abbot asked pointedly. "Back to Anjou? Will you be safer there?"

Marcel, casting his gaze about him like a cornered animal, stumbled into a chair. He sat down, clutching at the chair leg to keep from tumbling over. Abbot Francis grabbed another chair and straddled it, facing Marcel squarely.

"My dear Marcel," the abbot began. "I understand that you are uneasy. As are we all—I no less than you. We all face a horrible death at the hands of the secular arm if our secret is discovered. That is why we all must remain. To flee would surely show the Inquisitor that Montaigne is indeed right and that we have something to hide. If he were to think that, then none of us should be safe. And we would have nowhere to go."

"Why can't we just give Michael back to Montaigne?" Marcel retorted. "Then they would all leave us alone."

His words cut through me like a dagger blade. I glanced over at the others in panic, searching their expressions for any sign of assent. Juan-José, glowering fiercely, opened his mouth to protest, but Fernando put his finger to his lips and shook his head.

"No, Marcel," the abbot replied, laying a gentle hand

on Marcel's shoulder. "We must see this through together … with faith, patience, and fortitude. We are all wanted by someone or other. Were I to hand Michael over to Montaigne, might I not have to eventually hand John over to the English, Antonin to the Emperor, Juan-José to the Spanish, Fernando to the Pope … and you, Marcel, to the townspeople of Veronnes?" He paused for a moment, his gaze searching Marcel's face. "The sacrifice of one brother is not worth the risk."

"But Michael isn't our brother," Marcel persisted. "He has not taken the vows. We are risking ourselves for one who is not one of us."

"We risked ourselves for you before you had taken any vows." The abbot's voice remained hushed, like the swish of a rapier. "Do you not remember?"

Marcel, his mouth working at a protest he dared not make, stared down at his sandled feet.

The abbot rose and turned to us. "What say you, my brothers?" he asked the company at large. "Shall we now begin abandoning future brothers to the stake because of the likes of Montaigne?"

None of the brothers could meet his eyes. I, too, lowered my gaze to my clasped hands. Silence hung in the small refectory like a pall.

Finally, Juan-José heaved a deep and audible sigh. "Very well, Francis," he said. "We have trusted you up until now. We will continue to trust you. All will be made ready for the Cardinal and whoever he drags along behind him."

"God help us," John murmured.

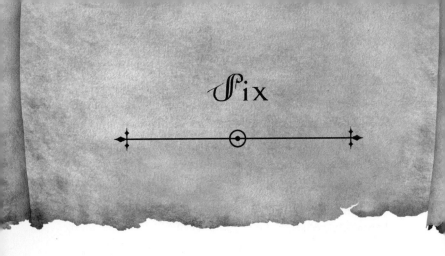

Six

I spent the next day busying myself with small tasks, too engrossed in my own thoughts to converse much. The brothers seemed to have accepted the inevitable. With amazing vehemence, they argued like so many housemaids about repairing this, scrubbing that, and sweeping out the other thing.

Even John, his visions fading before the hard reality of stocking the larder for the Cardinal's visit, sat at the refectory table scribbling a list of supplies to be purchased in the village upon the morrow. I tried to ask him if he foresaw disaster, but he merely waved my question away.

"Have faith, my young friend," was all that he would say.

Heaving a resigned sigh, I nodded and made my way up the stairs to my cell. By the time dusk fell, I knew what it was that I had to do. I waited for the others to retire to their cells before I made my way along the corridor and entered the cloister.

The night was crisp and clear, the chill breath of autumn in the air. The moon had risen and her silvery light bathed the garden, gleaming off the ancient stones and bestowing upon the humble granite the whiteness of the finest alabaster. But the beauty only deepened my gloom, reminding me of how difficult my decision was to be.

I had been at the monastery long enough to feel comfortable there—the peace and serenity, the companionship of kindred souls, the proffered tutelage of brilliant minds; not the least of which was, despite his protests, one of the most celebrated magicians in all of Europe. I bit my lip against the surge of grief that washed over me. I suddenly did not want to have to leave.

I had thought that at this late hour, all of the monks would have retired to their cells. I was not expecting to stumble over a dark form crouching on the pathway, half hidden in the shadows of the trees. I found it even more disconcerted to discover that it was Marcel, on his hands and knees, grubbing in the dirt of the garden.

"Forgive me," I stammered, backing away. "I was trying to find my way back to the kitchen. I did not mean to disturb you." My voice hoarsened. "I don't want to be a nuisance."

He glowered up at me. Then I saw his expression soften in the moonlight. "Oh, sit down." He waved me to a nearby stone. "None of this is any fault of yours." He heaved a sigh and absently toyed with the soil around the base of one of his plants. "Francis is right. He always is."

Reassured somewhat, I perched on a stone and watched as he examined each leaf of a row of plants. "What are you are doing?"

"Tonight the moon is full," he explained. "The flowers of the hyssop must be gathered on this night for it to have the maximum potency."

"What is it used for?" I asked, fascinated in spite of myself.

"For contusions. Difficult to treat except with hyssop."

"Does one eat it?"

Marcel glanced up at me and I felt suddenly ashamed for having asked what I feared was a stupid question. But he merely shook his head. "It is steeped in hot water. Like a tea." He studied me for a moment with an expression that was almost indulgent amusement. "What do you know of herbs?"

"Very little," I replied, falling back on the humble truth. "I know very little about many things. I had hoped to stay and learn . . . from all of you."

"Then learn quickly," he muttered. "Before the vultures descend."

I leaned over, suddenly emboldened. "Do you not feel that Abbot Francis can keep those vultures away?"

Marcel picked the plump flowerlets in silence for a moment. "Francis is a brave man," he finally said. "But he relies too much on books, clever talk, and his position in the Church. There are some things he chooses not to see."

"Such as?"

"He trusts that fat bishop." Marcel spat on the ground in contempt. "He won't see that we could be sold out just as well by some greedy prelate as by a lackey of the king."

An image of the bishop's heavily jowled face flashed into my mind. I shuddered.

"But, really, Brother Marcel, I don't see where the abbot has much choice. It seems to me that Montaigne is worse."

"Montaigne is like a jackal," Marcel said. "He is what he is and does not try to pretend to be anything else. You can tell just what he will do. Those pompous bishops, archbishops, cardinals, and all the rest of them … they tell you they are so terribly holy, they pray, they preach, then they knife you in the back and rob you blind."

It was my turn to be silent for a moment. "Do you think that the monastery is in danger?" I asked softly.

"I don't know." Marcel heaved another sigh. "I know nothing of the laws of Church or king like the rest of them. I know only herbs and charms. But I do know that if Francis keeps his gaze too firmly fixed on the heavens, he may not see the viper coiled at his feet … until it is too late."

He brushed the dirt from his hands and piled the flowers into an earthenware crock. "Have a care, boy." He rose to his feet and tucked the crock underneath his arm. "Maybe it is you who are in danger by staying here with us, not the other way around." With that, he scuffled back towards the kitchen.

I stood alone in the dark shadows of the garden, tears blurring my eyes. I was even more sure now that I had to leave the monastery. Marcel was wrong. All of the monks were in peril because of my presence. The cardinal would come, see me here, and order Montaigne to arrest them. I couldn't let that happen, no matter what happened to me. I resolved to leave at once rather than waiting until the dawn, lest I gaze once more into the abbot's blue eyes and allow him to change my mind.

Quietly, I made my way across the dark garden towards the iron gate, wondering if I dare take anything with me in the way of provisions or a blanket. I decided against it. I had come to the monastery with nothing but the tattered clothes on my back, and I should leave the same way.

The full moon flooded the countryside as I walked along the road towards the village. The pearly light threw shadows from the major ruts in my path, enabling me to avoid them. But I made very little progress, and the moon was setting by the time I reached the first of the shops on the edge of Sainte Felice.

A chill wind blew up out of the darkness and I fervently wished that I had dared to take away the warm blanket that enveloped my cot. I suddenly bit my lip against the surge of longing to turn around and make my way back up the road. I could return in time for breakfast and none would notice my absence.

I marched into the silent village square, deserted except for a stray cat or two that lurked in the shadows and watched me with eyes that glittered like jewels. I sat on the edge of the fountain for a moment. What had kept me walking thus far was fear—not for myself, since I knew that very likely I was headed back into the jaws of the Jackal of Orleans.

No, my fears were for the monastery. I had put them into danger and I knew that I must try to lure that danger away again. Maybe I could return to Orleans and somehow make it known that I was leaving for England. Montaigne would then chase after me and leave the monastery alone. I had no idea how I would actually get to England, nor what I would do once I got there, but that wasn't important. I would figure that out once the monastery was safe.

However, in the meantime, I knew that I needed rest. When I could barely keep my eyes open, I picked out Journet's tavern out of the many shops that lined the square. Perhaps if I curled up under the eaves, I could close my eyes for an hour or two, sheltered from the wind. I would, of course, be gone before Journet opened the tavern in the morning.

However, the warm straw in the rear of the tavern proved more comfortable than I had imagined it would. I awoke in the full morning sun with Emil Journet peering down at me, twirling his mustache.

"Michael, isn't it?" he said good-naturedly. "What on earth are you doing sleeping in my donkey pen?"

I rose with such shreds of dignity as I had left. "Forgive me, Monsieur Journet," I said respectfully. "I meant no harm."

He waved it away and reached out his hand to pull me

out of the straw. "I should have gladly given you shelter if you had only asked me."

"I did not wish to disturb you," I said, brushing bits of straw from my doublet. "It was only for a moment's rest."

His fists planted upon his hips, he scowled at me as he would an errant child. "Does your abbot know you are here?"

"No," I retorted. "And there is no need for him to know. Besides, he is not my abbot. I am taking my leave of the monastery and returning to Orleans."

Journet looked at me quizzically. "Oh?" he inquired. "Back to that rogue Montaigne?"

I grimaced, not wanting to answer.

But Journet only chuckled and clapped me on the shoulder. "Well, you might as well continue your journey fed as well as rested. Come."

He drew me into the tavern and settled me down with warm bread, cheese, roasted mutton and, of course, wine. I ate with near desperation, not sure when I would have such a meal again. He watched me for a moment, then drew a goblet himself and sat beside me.

"You know, you really should have told the abbot that you were leaving. He will surely be concerned, and will no doubt come looking for you."

"I realize that." I stared down at my empty plate. My stomach was pleasantly full, but my heart ached. "And believe me, I had no desire to cause him worry. But I felt that it was better to leave without saying goodbye. He might have … made me change my mind."

Journet smiled. "He is very persuasive, isn't he?"

I could only nod.

Journet swirled the wine in his cup for a moment. "He has always been so, from the day he first came here."

I mused into my trencher for a long moment. Brother Fernando's words still rang in my ears: *He has fallen in love with the people of Sainte Felice. His magic serves them, now.* What had this tiny village done to the notorious Wizard of Alceste?

"When did he come to Sainte Felice?" I asked.

"Nearly ten years ago." Journet smiled. "I remember it was around Eastertide, and it was raining so hard that I thought we should all wash away like Noah and the Ark. He came to my tavern soaking wet, having ridden all the way from Orleans in the downpour. I feared he should catch his death of cold right there and then. Ah, but he proved to be far tougher than that."

I leaned forward, interested in spite of myself. "Did he tell you who he was?"

Journet looked surprised at my question. "He told me that he was Father Francis Duchienne and that his order had sent him to try to revive the monastery up on the hill. I'm afraid I wasn't too enthusiastic about it. The monastery had been abandoned for over thirty years. It was nearly in ruins. But it didn't seem to discourage him at all. After the rain let up, he made his way up there." Journet smiled at the memory. "That night, he lit candles in the church. We stood in the town square and watched. The clouds had parted, and the light from the window shone through the darkness like a beacon from heaven. We crossed ourselves. It was truly a sign from God that He had not forgotten us. The next morning, we couldn't contain our curiosity any longer. We gathered up food and linens and made our way up there. He had cut a small path through the undergrowth leading to the church door. It was open, and we peeked in. The church had been swept, the furniture cleaned and put back in place, the altar pieces polished, and new candles put in the sconces. We found him fast asleep, draped over one of the pews. He had worked all night and had no doubt fallen asleep at his devotions. Well, we left him where he was, and the women went to work in the cloister. They swept the floor, dusted the furniture, put up fresh linens, and made the beds. By the time he emerged from the church, rubbing his eyes, we had supper laid out in the refectory." Journet chuckled softly. "I shall never forget the look on his face."

"And that is why *he* stayed," I murmured, more to myself than to anyone else.

"The next day was Easter," Journet continued. "He said Mass for us. There were heavenly voices, as of angels, singing the Kyrie and the Sanctus from the choir. We all heard it, every last one of us, although we could see no one there. We knew then that he was a saint."

I frowned. "But did he not tell you who he had been before he became a priest?"

"Some kind of scholar from a great University," Journet replied with a shrug. "He had nearly died in a fall from a wagon, or something, and decided to become a priest."

Journet fingered his mustache thoughtfully. "Like St. Paul on the road to Damascus."

"And the others?"

"Brother Fernando came about a year later. Had been a winemaker, he said, before taking the vow. And the Spaniard followed upon his heels. He had been a soldier and I am not surprised, from the look of him. And the fair-haired one, Brother Antonin, the physician, cured all the children of a mysterious disease not long ago. They had come down with it nearly every year in the summer. We had thought that it was the pox. But he claimed it was some kind of stomach ailment caused by the water in the well. He was right, bless him."

"And Brother Marcel," I prompted. "What do you know of him?"

"We do not see much of him," Journet said. "He keeps to himself, I'm told. But it was his medicines that helped to cure the children. Brother Antonin said so."

"Is that all you know about them?" I asked, trying to phrase my question carefully as to avoid suspicion.

"What else should we know?"

"Oh, like how they all happened to come to the monastery."

"I suspect that they were in trouble with the king's men, just as you were." Journet seemed totally unconcerned.

"That does not bother you?" I asked in astonishment.

"Those who do good are always persecuted by those in power. Our Lord teaches us that."

"But what if they were in trouble with the Church?" I

probed. "What if the abbot had disagreed with the churchmen in Rome and was guilty of heresy? Or worse." I broke off, feeling as though I were treading on thin ice.

Journet drained his cup with one long swallow. "I am only a tavern keeper. I know nothing of theology like the scholars in the university. But I know the monks of Sainte Felice and their saintly Abbot have been a blessing to this village. And if the churchmen in Rome don't agree with the abbot, maybe they should shed their palaces, their fine clothes, and their mistresses and listen to him. They might learn something."

With that, he rose, as other customers noisily entered the tavern. But before seeing to them, he gazed down at me with an abruptly serious expression. "Go back to the monastery, lad. Join the holy brothers. Peace and blessedness has come to all those whom the abbot has taken in."

But I shook my head. His story had made me all the more resolved that I should not risk the safety of the monastery with my accursed presence. "I thank you for your concern, Monsieur Journet, but I cannot. I must return to Orleans. And now, as much as I appreciate your hospitality, I must be on my way." I felt his gaze follow me out the door.

I mingled with the crowd in the square, dodging chickens, pigs, and goats that squawked, grunted, and bleated their way past me. Not a soul paid any attention to me, even when I had to push past a market woman with a basket of turnips on her head or jump out of the way of a pack of ragged children chasing a wayward goose.

The sun shone overhead as I wandered around the village, trying to find the road to Orleans. It eluded me for some reason. All the shops and houses looked the same, even down to the thatch on the roofs. I went down one pathway, then another, only to find myself back at the fountain in the center of town. After the third time, the women doing their washing began to regard me with grins on their faces. They elbowed each other, pointed to me, and giggled.

I finally sat down on the stone steps and rubbed my stinging eyes, trying to sort through my confused and distracted thoughts. It shouldn't have been so hard to find the blasted road. It was true that I hadn't been paying too much attention to landmarks the last time I was here. Still, the village wasn't large, and there couldn't have been too many roads that led away from it.

Except that I didn't really want to leave. I wanted to go back to the monastery, just as Monsieur Journet had counseled me to do.

I couldn't help thinking about Journet's tale of how Abbot Francis first came to Sainte Felice. I could easily picture the look upon his expressive features that morning when he discovered what the townspeople had done. From what my old master had told me, the membership of the magical order had been rather a cutthroat bunch. The abbot, as Seratois, would have had to constantly strive to outdo his rivals, trusting no one, befriending no one, in order to not only maintain his position but to avoid being cut to pieces . . . as he eventually was. How different the unconditional trust and acceptance of the townspeople must have seemed after such company. No wonder he was so deeply touched by them that he would make their cause his own.

I, too, had been touched by how the monks had accepted me. They had treated me as one of them, even though I wasn't and never could be.

I sighed and rose again to my feet. The women were packing up their laundry, and I asked one of the older ones the way to the road to Orleans. She pointed back the way I had just come. I thanked her with a wan smile and set off again.

I found a path out of the village and followed it until I finally reached the main road. I should have been relieved. But I wasn't. Off in the distance, I could see the monastery roosting on the top of its hill, just as I had first seen it from the seat of the mule cart beside the man who had saved my life.

Tears stung my eyes. As much as I wanted to return to that ramshackle ruin, I just couldn't bear the thought that my presence would bring any harm to five men that had become my friends and, for the short time I was there, my mentors. I gazed at it for a long moment, fixing the image in my memory for the rest of my life—however long or short that proved to be. Then I turned on my heel and headed down the road.

A rumble behind me stopped me in my tracks, turning my blood to ice water. Horses, several of them, thundered down the road after me. What if they were soldiers, with Montaigne in their midst?

Turning, I headed towards a cluster of trees off the side of the road. I crashed through the undergrowth in my panic, heedless of the bushes and brambles that tore my hose into shreds. The rumbling grew louder, and I ran as fast as I could. I finally threw myself onto the ground beneath one of the oaks. Squeezing my eyes shut, I waited for the thundering hoofbeats to pass by.

After a long moment, they faded into the distance and my heartbeat slowed back to normal. I pushed myself to my feet and brushed the leaves and twigs from my tunic, then turned around to go back to the road. It was then that I realized that I had another problem.

I was lost.

I swallowed my sudden surge of panic and wandered around in the forest for a time. Eventually I found the barest trace of a footpath and followed it for a time, expecting it to take me back to the road. But it did not. Instead, it narrowed further until it was nearly swallowed up in the vines and brush that choked the ground beneath the trees of the forest. Then, it vanished altogether.

Thoroughly alarmed, I made an effort to calm myself and turned around, hoping to at least make my way back to the village. Perhaps I could discover where I had made a wrong turn and try again. However, the sun was already dipping below the horizon, throwing deceptive shadows across my path. Just when I thought I had found the way back through the undergrowth, the path, as though it had a mind of its own and was toying with me, would vanish once more.

Turning around, I tried another direction, and then another until I found nothing but trees around me at every point. The light was rapidly dying and the clicks, chatter, and hoots of the forest creatures commenced their nightly choir practice. Most I did not recognize, having grown up as I had in a rather large town rather than in the country. And while I was able to reassure myself during the day that the creatures were more frightened of me than I was of them, night found me terrified that I could possibly be supper for a wolf or a bear.

Finally, it was pitch dark and there was no reason to even try to walk any more. My legs finally grew too weak to support me upright and I sank down beneath a tree, to live or die as my fate would have it. I sat with my back up against the trunk as tears came unbidden to my eyes. I lacked any strength to fight them off, so they rolled unchecked down my dirty nose.

Journet was right. I should never have left the monastery. Destiny had heard my plea after the death of the count and had led me there to learn everything about the arcane arts that I had ever wanted to know. And I, ungrateful dolt that I was, had left it all behind. I deserved whatever fate lay in store for me.

What ever made me think that just because I left the monastery, Montaigne would not still hound the others? After all, every one of them, including Abbot Francis himself, had run afoul of some authority, any of which could press for an arrest.

My noble sacrifice, then, was nothing of the sort. It was only the rationalization of a coward. And now my punishment was to die in this dreadful forest, serving the only purpose of providing food for carrion birds.

Why, oh, why had I ever thought myself worthy to study magic under the great Seratois, miserable wretch that I was? Why had I ever thought myself worthy to study magic at all?

So lost was I in my self-pity that I did not hear the approach of gentle footsteps. I lifted my head with a start as a black-robed figure knelt beside me.

"What are you doing out here?" John asked in his soft voice. "The night promises to be cold. And Francis is beside himself with worry. We've been searching for you all day."

"Brother John!" I had to stifle the sudden urge to grasp his hand and kiss it. "How did you find me? *I* don't even know where I am."

"*They* showed me where you were." By "they," I knew that he meant the angels he talked to. Somehow, the idea did not seem quite so mad as it did before. "Now, we must return to the monastery before it grows late."

"Oh, Brother John, I cannot. I must not. I am the cause of all of this trouble. I could not bear it if anything ill happened to the monastery because of me. I'd sooner burn."

"Michael," he said, as he lay his hand on my hair. "We have all brought disgruntled authorities to the door of Sainte Felice, only to have them turned away. In my case, it was the Archbishop of Canterbury who braved the stomach-churning waves of the channel to come and fetch me. Francis convinced him that I was hopelessly mad, but that the monks of Sainte Felice, in the name of Christian charity, would care for me and that I should not trouble the archbishop again. After all, what use is there in hanging a madman?"

I paused, gazing into his pale eyes for a long moment. I knew that those eyes saw things which no one else could see. Did I dare to trust what they were seeing now? "Brother John," I asked softly, "do you really think that he will fool the Holy Office?"

"Francis has his ways, to be sure. But he is only one man. We must all do our part. We must keep our faith, and our vows."

"But I have taken no vows."

"You will." He gave me a mysterious smile. "Before the archbishop comes."

I frowned in annoyance. "How do you know that?"

"Because you wish it."

A feeling of chagrin washed over me. As if I could have tried to fool John, or his angelic confidants. My secret desires must have been obvious to him despite all the lies that I had told myself of where I wanted to go and what I wanted to do with my life. The inescapable truth was that I had finally found my magical teacher, and I wanted nothing more than to remain at the monastery and learn whatever he was willing to teach me. And if that meant donning a black habit and taking monastic vows, then so be it.

"Will Abbot Francis have me?"

"You only have to ask him." John rose to his feet and held his hand out to me. "He will be waiting for you in Journet's tavern. Come. We mustn't keep him waiting."

I took his hand. With a strength I never would have given him credit for, he pulled me to my feet. He picked his way, with the surety of a man guided by divine intelligence, through the enveloping shadows of the forest. I followed behind him and held onto the fold of his habit to keep from losing him amid the trees and undergrowth. We were soon at the road, flooded by the light of the moon now unobscured by branches. I felt as though I had truly been led out of the darkness of my own folly, into the light of illumination.

Wordlessly, I followed John back to the cozy safety of the village. The lights blazed in the windows of Journet's tavern. John stepped over the threshold, but I still hesitated. Standing near the blazing fire, Abbot Francis looked around and saw me.

"Michael!" He stepped forward, holding out his hands. "Thank God you are safe."

Abruptly, I lost whatever composure I still possessed and hurled myself into his arms, sobbing like a lost child. He draped an arm across my shaking shoulders and led me to a chair. I pulled myself together with an effort as another black robed figure slid into a chair beside me.

"Damn fool thing to do," Marcel muttered. "Running off like that."

I dried my eyes on my sleeve. "I didn't want to be a threat to your safety."

"No more than we are a threat to yours, my boy." Juan-José was hovering at Marcel's elbow. "If you had any sense, you would have left us the day after you arrived. But you didn't. Any more than the rest of us did."

I raised my head as Fernando knelt beside my chair. "Join us, Michael." A smile played at the corners of his mouth. "I have never had a more capable assistant."

"I want to, Brother Fernando. More than anything in this world." My voice hoarsened to a whisper. "But I am not worthy."

"As if any of us are." I glanced up and found Antonin standing beside Fernando. "Still, someone must have found you worthy or you would not have been led here, would you?"

I looked about the small tavern. Were they all here? Had they all been looking for me? I bit my lip as the tears threatened again.

"Will you accept me as your brother?" I asked softly, gazing at each one in turn.

"If you will accept us. It goes both ways, you know. But we aren't the ones you should ask." Fernando took my arm and firmly drew me to my feet. Taking me by the shoulders, he turned me to face the abbot, who stood quietly by the hearth.

I slowly knelt before him, took his hand and kissed it. "Will you take me into your monastery?"

"Is that truly your wish, my son?"

"Yes, it is." I felt the tears threaten again, but managed to blink them away. Instead, I gave him a sheepish smile. "I suppose it took me a while to admit it."

He chuckled softly. "Fair enough."

He laid his left hand on my head and made the sign of the cross over me with his right. It was a simple gesture, one that I had seen a thousand times before. But this time, it felt like an exorcism. A black cloud of doubt, anger, and disillusionment lifted from me. Feeling euphoric and light-headed, I rose to my feet again.

"This calls for wine." Journet grinned like a fox who had found his way into the hen house.

I whirled around to face him. "You told on me."

But he only laughed. "I knew where you needed to go. Just like the Prodigal Son."

"We are facing considerable trouble with Montaigne over this, Emil." Seating himself at one of the tables, Abbot Francis motioned for Journet to join him. "He has managed to convince the Archbishop of Paris, Cardinal De Joinville, that we are worthy of investigation, possibly by the Inquisition. He will be here in Sainte Felice next week."

"The Archbishop of Paris?" Journet's eyes widened.

"Why would he bother you? He should just excommunicate Montaigne. That would solve the problem, eh?"

"I fear that it is not that simple," the abbot explained in a patient tone. "The archbishop does not wish to offend the king by disciplining one of his ministers."

"Pah! Are they so gutless that they have sold themselves to the king like ... like the Whore of Babylon?" He gestured with his wine cup, threatening to slop the wine onto the floor.

The abbot reached out and lowered Journet's waving hand. "I wish I had a rational answer for you, Emil. But I do not. All I can say is that Montaigne would dearly love to chase me, and all these good monks, out of Sainte Felice."

"Well, he won't succeed," Journet said, squaring his shoulders. "God will see to it, and so will I."

"Your faith is commendable, Emil." The abbot rose to his feet. "It will soon be sorely tested. In the meantime, tell the good people of Sainte Felice that young Michael will enter the Order of St. Benedict at Mass this Sunday. And then, we must all brace ourselves for whatever happens."

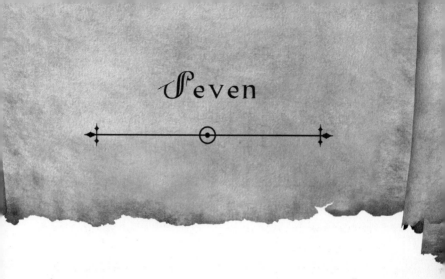

Seven

Sunday morning arrived in hushed silence. I knelt, cold and numb, in the pew, watching the flicker of the lamp that burned on the altar before the Blessed Sacrament. Dawn had just started to soften the darkness inside the monastery church. Soon, someone would come for me and prepare me to enter the monastery as a novice.

All during my dark vigil the previous night, I had examined my soul to its depths. What on earth was I about to do? The last place I had expected to find genuine instruction in the magical arts was in the very church that I so despised, and from which I had tried so hard to escape. And yet here I was, in a ruined chapel gazing at an altar with a cross upon it, about to dedicate my life to a part of that selfsame church.

Had I gone mad?

Doubts continued to haunt my mind like unquiet spirits demanding rational answers that I didn't have. I knew only one thing for certain. Celestial powers must have heard my Christmas prayer after all and, despite my protests, had led me here.

There was much that I still did not understand about Abbot Francis and his monastery. But it didn't matter. Here was the magical education that I wanted ... and wanted badly, desperately, achingly so ... enough to take monastic vows for it. I had decided, long before the first rays of the sun filtered in through the stained glass, that I would do whatever was required of me if I could obtain the knowledge that I craved.

I found myself ready—possibly even eager, if I were not so nervous—when Antonin and Fernando came for me. Neither of them spoke a word, but stoically stripped me of my tattered shirt, doublet, and hose, bathed me in water so cold my teeth chattered, and enfolded me in the black habit and scapular of the order of St. Benedict. Fernando finally produced a pair of shears and snipped off my brown curls, leaving my hair clipped close to the nape of my neck. They wound a flaxen cord about my waist and led me into the church.

Murmurs of approval rose from the pews as I knelt once again in the place prepared for me in the front. The abbot entered and began the Mass, with the other monks chanting the responses from the choir. I waited, my heart pounding with trepidation, all through the Introit, through the Credo, and through the Communion.

Finally, the abbot turned to me and held out his hand. I froze in my seat for a moment. Panic rose in my throat and I suddenly wanted to run out of that church, far away from the monastery. All this was nothing but a ruse and a sham. Was it worth trading my youth for?

And Abbot Francis, who stood before me shrouded in white vestments, colored light from the rose window playing about his head and shoulders ... just who was he? Did he have everyone in Sainte Felice in thrall to his singular personality? Had I, too, fallen under his spell? And was I merely to play the role of pawn in his ruthless and elaborate power struggles with Church and State?

Finally, I found my feet. Biting my lip, I crossed myself and approached the altar. I gazed up into the abbot's eyes, losing myself in their azure depths. What I saw there made me tremble, not but with fear. Something awe inspiring and wonderful shone from those eyes, something that moved me to the depths of my soul. In that instant, I saw him for the first time as he really was—someone that I had begun to doubt really existed.

A Sacred Magician.

All doubts fled in a wisp of incense smoke. Whether he was truly a saint or merely a very clever sorcerer, or perhaps a bit of both, it didn't matter. He had saved my life. I would go to the wall for him, to the pyre if need be.

I knelt before him and placed my hands in his. My heart pounding within my breast, I swore my vows. I felt my old self wither away and die, leaving me newly reborn. There was no terror at that moment, no regret. Just relief, as though I had finally come home after a long journey. Abbot Francis laid one hand on my head and made the sign of the cross over me with the other. I rose to my feet, a novice monk.

Without fanfare, I took my place in the choir with the others and the abbot finished the Mass. However, warm and enthusiastic congratulations from the townspeople greeted me on the church steps. Monsieur Journet thumped me on the back, grinning from ear to ear. The Duchess even took my hand and kissed my cheek. I felt my face flush pink with embarrassment, but I had to admit to being pleased with the sincere attention.

In the cloister, I discovered that John had prepared a special breakfast in my honor—honey cake with raisins and hazelnuts, baked apples with sweet cream, aged cheese, and a pitcher of the new wine. Tears in my eyes, I exchanged warm embraces with my new brothers as the abbot, beaming like a father who has just added one more son to his growing brood, looked on.

The tasty fare was soon reduced to crumbs. I glanced up and noticed the abbot missing from the table. He reappeared after a moment with a weighty volume tucked under his arm.

"Brothers," he announced, waiting for their attention. "I do hate to cut our celebration short, but there remains the small matter of the visit from the archbishop. There is much to do, and we must begin our preparations at once."

"Very well, Francis." Juan-José put down his goblet with a resigned sigh. "What have you in mind?"

"Several things," the abbot replied. "First, we will take those things of our art that the Holy Office might object to and store them in the passageway to the Tabernacle. That includes all books and manuscripts of a possibly heretical or even questionable nature. Your astrolabe, sextant, and ephemerides, Antonin…"

Antonin nodded in agreement.

"Your herbal preparations and other, shall we say, paraphernalia, Marcel?"

Marcel grunted.

"I fear that you will have to dismantle most of your laboratory, Fernando."

Fernando sighed and threw up his hands in a gesture of resignation.

I tugged at Juan-José's sleeve. "What is the Tabernacle?"

He gave me a maddenly secretive smile. "You will see soon enough."

"Surely that is not all you have in mind," Antonin said pointedly. "I doubt whether just expurgating our cells and libraries will be sufficient to convince the cardinal of our piety."

"No, my dear Antonin, it surely will not. What we will have to do is rigorously follow this." The abbot tossed the book down onto the table with an ominous thump. "The Rule of St. Benedict. We will follow it to the letter as long as our visitors are here."

"But Francis," Fernando protested, "you know as well as I that few Benedictine houses these days actually follow the Rule."

"True enough. However, few Benedictine houses are full of wizards, heretics, and magicians, either. It behooves us to appear as traditional as possible. Besides, the less time he actually has to examine us, the better."

"So, what do you suggest we tell him?" Juan-José demanded. "He is sure to ask us awkward questions about who and what we were before we came here. Do you want us to lie?"

The abbot shook his head. "That should not be necessary, and could prove to be dangerous if you are caught contradicting yourselves. I suggest that each of you come up with a story that is as close to the truth as possible without revealing too much. Speak only when spoken to and tell no more than you are specifically asked. After all, we are Benedictine monks and our Rule forbids us being too chatty. The cardinal will be apprised of this and will be expected to comply."

"But surely that will make him angry," I said.

"Good," Juan-José said. "Maybe he won't stay so long."

"Still," I persisted. "If he is uncomfortable, will he not try all the harder to find fault with us?"

"Michael has a point, Francis," Antonin said. "Making him testy may not prove to be in our best interests."

"My goal is not merely to make him feel discomfort," the abbot said, "but to make him feel guilty about his discomfort. It will make him far more amenable to the other more subtle influences that I have in mind."

He obviously was working up to revealing the high point of his plan and I, for one, was content to allow him to unfold it before us in his own time. My new brothers, who had no doubt seen this performance many times before, were not so patient.

"What subtle influences, Francis?" Juan-José demanded. "Come out with it. What are you going to do?"

The abbot looked pained. "I will tell you if you will allow me to." He waited until Juan-José sat back in his chair and waved him to continue. "Now, once we have the cardinal primed with lack of sleep and the drone of chanting…" His voice trailed off and he began to fiddle with the gold cross that hung on his breast.

I had always assumed it was merely a harmless habitual gesture, like Journet pulling at his mustache. But the others clearly thought otherwise. Fernando frowned and shook his head. "Francis, I am not so sure that is wise."

"And why not," the abbot asked coolly, still twiddling the cross in his fingers. "It would certainly be effective."

"Under the very nose of the most powerful churchman in France?" Marcel jumped to his feet, his eyes widening in alarm. "Francis, are you out of your mind?"

Antonin reached up and yanked the folds of Marcel's habit, pulling him back into his seat.

"No, Marcel." The abbot remained unruffled, his mouth set in lines of grim determination. "Far from it. And I assure you I will not be as obvious about it as I was when I rescued our new brother."

"Still," Antonin said. "What if the cardinal proves to be unmoved by such a—shall we say—demonstration of sanctity?"

"Then he will send for the Inquisitor," Marcel said

with characteristic bluntness. "Who will find Francis guilty of sorcery. That's what."

"Therefore he must be moved," the abbot insisted. "Therein lies our only hope. This is France, and only De Joinville has the authority to turn us over to the secular arm, not an Italian Inquisitor. If we can manage to convince De Joinville of our blessedness, then there is a good chance that the Holy Office will not even be consulted. Now do you understand?"

I was certainly beginning to, and growing increasingly more uneasy with the prospect. I thought back to that awful moment on the pyre when I beheld Abbot Francis for the first time, reaching to heaven and commanding the elements. I remembered that he clutched the cross all during his invocation. Was he now planning to do likewise for the archbishop?

"I still don't like it, Francis," Juan-José was saying. "Is there no other way?"

"Can you think of one?" the abbot asked.

Juan-José thought for a moment, then shook his head with a rueful grin. "Not any that would work nearly as well."

"Then, have I your consent, my brothers?" The abbot encompassed the room with a wave of his hand. "John, we have yet to hear from you."

John gazed at him for a moment with a look that was almost sad. "The angelic host will serve you as they have pledged to do so long ago. But beware, my dear Francis. Your power grows, in ways even you do not realize."

"I shall be sure to rein myself in, my good brother," the abbot said. "And you shall be my tether. Now, are we agreed?"

We were, some of us more reluctant than others. But all of us immediately trotted off, each to his own cell, to gather up whatever we would deem unsuitable for the archbishop's perusal.

Soon I noticed that wooden crates and cloth bags began to accumulate in, of all places, the kitchen. Antonin carried in a leather folio stuffed with his horoscopes and charts, plus all of his ephemerides and other instruments. Neither John nor Juan-José had much to contribute except a book or two each, and I, of course, had nothing.

Marcel, however, hauled in several large crates of bottles filled with strangely colored liquids and powders; boxes of stones; and piles of leaves, feathers, bones, and other oddly shaped objects that I did not really want to investigate too closely.

After dinner, Francis made a thorough inspection of the entire abbey. Putting himself in the place of an Inquisitor, he examined all of our cells, the library, the refectory, the kitchen, and, lastly, Fernando's workshop.

I noticed that the furnace had been dismantled enough to look like part of the hearth, and the aludel was nowhere in sight. Still, everything else appeared to be in place and three casks of wine lay on the rack against the wall.

Fernando looked decidedly unhappy as he packed up several crates of swan-necked flasks and copper tubing.

"There will not be time to bless the remainder of this wine before the cardinal arrives."

Abbot Francis, wearing a mysterious smile, sat down on the bench and motioned Fernando to sit beside him. "That, my dear Fernando"—he laid a conspiratorial hand on Fernando's arm—"is part of my plan."

Fernando shook his head slightly, his brow furrowed in confusion. "I don't see your point."

"The wine stored in your workshop will not be blessed," the abbot continued. "It will be ordinary wine. Tasty perhaps, sweet and of a fine bouquet, but only wine."

"But why?"

"Cardinal de Joinville is a man of wide culture. He is particularly enamored of fine vintages. If we offer him your blessed variety, he will surely notice the fact and will demand your secret. You will be hard pressed to come up with a convincing answer. However, if what we serve our guests is just wine, then they can only wonder at the stories of a miracle liquor. Do I make myself more clear?"

A slow smile crept from beneath Fernando's beaked profile. "Francis, your ingenuity still amazes me after all these years."

"Good. Now, let us go in to supper, and then we must retire to our beds. Tomorrow we will begin chanting the offices so we will at least be able to present a decent performance while De Joinville is here."

Fernando gave him a pleading look. "Even Matins?"

"Especially Matins." A chorus of groans encircled the table, accompanied by pained expressions. But the abbot remained firm. "Oh, come now. It's only for a week. Then you can all return to your dissolute and heathen ways."

"I will tell you one thing," Marcel muttered. "If I have to get up before dawn and go sing in a frigid church, so does he."

"And he will, I assure you." The abbot leaned back in his chair and pressed his fingertips together, his mouth set in hard, determined lines. "If it is orthodoxy he seeks, by God, we will show him orthodoxy. We will be so orthodox, we will be positively annoying."

I had no doubt of that. But whether it would do any good or not remained to be seen.

—⚊—

On the evening before the cardinal's expected arrival, we gathered by the hearth in the parlor, nursing goblets of the blessed wine. I savored every sip, knowing that I should have to do without it for the next week. It wasn't the only thing that I wasn't relishing about the cardinal's impending visit.

"Have we thought of everything, Francis?" Antonin asked.

"I believe so," the abbot mused, over the rim of his wine cup. "Can we chant the offices convincingly?"

Marcel grunted.

"All magical paraphernalia is ready to go into the Tabernacle?"

"It will take a week to reassemble the apparatus for blessing the wine," Fernando grumbled.

"We will assist you in that task as soon as all of this is over." The abbot glanced at each of us in turn. "You all have your stories?"

I bit my lip, remembering the nights I had lain sleepless between Matins and Prime, going over mine. I realized why the abbot had insisted that it at least be partly true. A bald-faced lie would not be convincing. But deciding which details of my past to include and which to exclude still had to be the most painful thing I had ever done.

The abbot fell silent for a moment, a distant look in his eyes. He finally sighed heavily. "There remains one final thing."

My new brothers exchanged meaningful looks, as though this pronouncement was something they had been expecting and they were wondering why the abbot had taken so long to mention it.

"The ritual, I take it," Juan-José finally said.

The abbot nodded in reply.

Ritual? My eyes widened and my breath caught in my throat. *What* ritual?

"Do we perform it as before?" Fernando asked as the monks got to their feet.

"I don't see why not." Abbot Francis turned to Antonin. "Where is the Moon tonight, Brother Astrologer?"

"In Pisces," Antonin replied. "Squaring Jupiter, in Gemini. A difficult aspect, Francis. It presents a great possibility for overconfidence."

"I shall take that into account. You all remember your parts, I trust?"

All the monks nodded. My gaze fell upon each in turn. I wanted to speak up and say that I had no idea what my part would be in whatever they were about to do, but I held my peace. It would be enough to be permitted to watch whatever it was that transpired.

"Then let us be about it." The abbot pushed himself out of his chair. "To the Tabernacle, my brothers."

Abbot Francis led the way into the kitchen from the refectory. Taking a ring of keys from a hook in the wall, he selected one and inserted it into the lock of a small cupboard that lay tucked in behind two larger ones bolted into the stone wall. The cupboard, to my surprise, contained nothing but a lever. But my surprise turned to astonishment when he pulled the lever and one entire block of the stone floor slid aside, revealing a staircase leading down into almost infernal blackness.

"Is that the Tabernacle?" I asked in wonder.

"It is." Abbot Francis lit a torch from the hearth fire and led the way down the steps, motioning for me to follow at his heels. The rest of the monks fell into line behind me. "Many years ago, the abbot of this monastery used it for a wine cellar. This abbot, however, uses the cellar for a rather different purpose."

A different purpose indeed!

At the bottom of the staircase, we made our way, single file, down a narrow passageway cut into the heart of the mountain. After several yards, the passageway opened into a circular chamber easily ten or twelve feet in diameter. Waiting for the flame, torches sat in holders at each of the four cardinal points. To the east stood a small altar covered by a white cloth. Two silver candelabra on it flanked a brazier, which sat on a tripod of brazen lions' paws. Painted on the rough stone floor was a triple circle containing the names of the four archangels, the signs of the zodiac, and the symbols of the planets.

I gazed all around me in awe, at what I realized was the heart of this magical monastery. For a moment, I looked down at the front of my habit and gently stroked the rough black wool. I knew now that if I hadn't taken vows, particularly that of obedience, I would not be standing in this place.

The books, the instruments, the manuscripts, the horoscopes were certainly dangerous enough if the cardinal discovered them. But this! This temple was what made the Monastery of Sainte Felice what it was—and would surely send its abbot to the flames if it were to be discovered.

I caught at Abbot Francis' sleeve, my heart pounding in my throat. He could only be about to do a ritual of angelic conjuration. And I was going to be there to aid him. I could scarcely contain my enthusiasm. "What would you have me do, Father Francis?"

He glanced over at me, stroking his chin, and thought for a moment. "You may serve the incense. Fernando did it last time, but since you are here, you may do so."

I turned to Fernando, just to make sure he approved of this change of procedure.

"Just as well." Fernando wrinkled his substantial nose. "Frankincense makes me sneeze."

"Very well," I said eagerly, turning back to the abbot. "How is it to be done?"

"Stand by the altar and scoop the incense into the brazier." He took a small bronze box filled with a light brown powder from the altar and handed it to me. "Not too much, lest it smoke us out of here, but enough so that a steady column rises to the ceiling. Do you think you can do that?"

"Oh, yes." The job pleased me enormously, since it involved standing by the altar so as to get the best look at the proceedings.

"Good. Now let us begin."

We stood in silence, cowls thrown over our faces and hands tucked into our sleeves, as we began the ritual. I trembled with excitement at the commencement of my first real magical operation. This was precisely what I had taken my vows to God for, and God was honoring His side of the bargain.

Still, it was a solemn moment. I remembered reading in my old master's books that a rite of conjuration required a mindset of reverence and devotion. It was never to be done with frivolity or jest. After all, we were summoning holy angels, not demons. And it was a ritual as sacred as the Mass in its way, even if Church authorities disapproved of it. I took several deep breaths to quiet my pounding pulse.

"*Gloria Domine*," we chanted in a hushed monotone as we circled the cavern, keeping always within the confines of the magic circle. We circumambulated thrice, then halted with Antonin in the east, Juan-José in the south, Fernando in the west, and Marcel in the north. John sat in the center, on a three-legged stool in front of the altar.

Juan-José pulled his sword from the scabbard upon his belt, saluted the altar with it, and handed it to Antonin.

"I summon, stir, and call ye forth, O Spirits of Air." Antonin pointed the sword in the direction of east and slowly traced a pentagram in the air before him. "Guard ye the portal of the east and allow no evil to trespass therein. In the name of Almighty God." He lit the torch on the eastern wall and passed the sword back to Juan-José.

"I summon, stir, and call ye forth, O Spirits of Fire," Juan-José traced another pentagram in the air and lit the torch on the southern wall. He in turn passed the sword to Fernando, who performed the same invocation in the west.

Then the sword was passed to Marcel, who was clearly unused to this kind of magic and did not find it entirely to his taste. All the same, he invoked the spirits of earth in the north, lit the torch, and gingerly handed the sword back to Juan-José.

When all the torches were lit, Juan-José slipped the sword into its sheath once again and turned to face the altar. The others did the same. Abbot Francis lit the candles on the altar and then pulled his golden cross, chain and all, over his head. He cradled it in his hand. Turning it over, he pushed a tiny latch on the side.

To my astonishment, the entire back of the cross sprang open, revealing a tiny brass talisman. It was no bigger than a coin, but exquisitely engraved with a pentagram in the center that was encircled by the holy names of God and the blessed archangels. I recognized it from one of my former master's books. King Solomon was said to have had such a talisman, which he wore on his finger as a ring—it enabled him to command the spirits of air, of water, of fire, and of air.

The abbot pressed the cross and the talisman to his lips, then placed it upon the altar and sank to his knees. He began to pray. "I beseech thee, O Almighty and everlasting God, thou who didst create all things visible and invisible, have mercy upon me, thy most humble and unworthy servant, and look kindly upon my most heartfelt petition. Forsake me not, O my Lord, but grant me grace and forgiveness of my sins. Put forth thy hand and touch my body and my soul and make them clean as a newly scoured sword."

His prayer grew more impassioned with every phrase. He crossed himself repeatedly until his voice, almost breaking, trailed off and he bowed his head over his folded hands. I thought for a moment that he would break down and weep. But he did not.

Rising to his feet abruptly, he raised his hands in invocation and cried out, in a commanding voice that rang off the rough stone walls of the cavern, "I call upon thee, thou great and powerful Archangel Raphael. Come! I call thee hither by the name of He who spake and it was done, by the glorious name Elohim Sabaoth by which the elements are overturned, the earth trembleth, the air is shaken, the sea turns back, the fire is generated, and all the hosts of things celestial, things terrestrial, and things infernal do tremble and are confounded together."

A slight nod from Fernando served as my cue to begin

scooping the incense from the box into the brazier. The amber buds of frankincense sizzled on the glowing coal for a second, then released their wisps of pungent but fragrant smoke into the air. It curled up from the dish of the brazier in swirls and strands, like the flaxen locks of a maiden's hair blowing in the breeze. Fernando, pinching his nose firmly between his thumb and forefinger, stifled a sneeze.

"We do humbly beseech and entreat you, O benevolent and magnificent archangel, descend from your celestial mansion and appear to the sight of our eyes," the abbot continued, his tone lowering into a sing-song drone. "And your voice unto our ears that we may visibly see you and audibly hear you speak unto us, and give therefore unto us a sign of your merciful presence."

I suddenly began to grow very uneasy. I felt as though I could sense someone—or something—approaching unseen behind me in the dark. I swallowed hard and forced myself to remain calm.

"Descend, I say!" The abbot's voice rose abruptly, making me jump. "O, glorious archangel, appear before us as servants of the Most High God, whose works shall be a song of honor and praise before all Creation. Come!"

I suddenly gasped, as the hairs on the back of my neck stood up and a tingling sensation coursed up and down my spine. The wisps of smoke gradually took a roughly human form, still swirling and gyrating. The form raised its arms and seemed to reach out for the abbot.

John suddenly let out a soft moan. His eyes rolled back, showing only the ghastly whites. He opened his mouth and a voice issued forth—a voice which was not John's usual lilting tones, but was deeper and stronger. And not quite human.

"Thy petition has been granted," the voice said, in tones which made me shiver to the depths of my being. "The dual-edged sword shall protect and guard that which thou dost hold dear. But beware of the price that will be asked of thee."

"The price will be paid willingly." Abbot Francis turned to face Juan-José. "Your sword, my brother." He held out his hand and waited.

Hesitantly, Juan-José pulled it once more from its sheath and handed it to the abbot, hilt first. With a nod, Abbot Francis took it in his hand and saluted the altar with it. Then, to my utter horror, he bared his left forearm and drew the blade across it. As the trail of blood welled up from the cut, he strode to the altar and knelt before it, resting his clasped hands upon its surface. The blood slowly dripped onto the altar, and onto the cross and talisman that lay upon it, as he shut his eyes and bowed his head once again in silence.

We waited breathlessly until the moment when, heaving a weary and resigned sigh, Abbot Francis unclasped his hands, kissed the altar, and rose to his feet.

"I give thee thanks, holy Archangel Raphael for thus heeding the sacred rites of magic. I bid thee now to depart, and may the peace of God remain forever between me and thee."

The energy in the room fell almost at once, as the

smoke from the brazier faded and vanished. John moaned softly and crumpled to the floor. Marcel strode forward and pulled him to his feet, shoring him up with an arm around his waist. The abbot extinguished the candles and handed the sword to Antonin.

Antonin nodded, then turned and saluted the east. "I dismiss you, Spirits of Air, to your own realms. In the name of Almighty God, I bid you hail and farewell." One after the other, fire, water, and earth were dismissed and the torches snuffed, leaving one taper to light the way out of the Tabernacle.

We filed up the steps and back into the familiar, earthy realm of the kitchen. Then we grabbed all the boxes, bags, and piles and stacked them in the passageway, successfully blocking any entrance to the magic circle. It now looked, to a casual observer, like any other storage room.

Abbot Francis threw the lever and guided the stone slab back into its niche in the floor. "*Per omnia saecula saeculorum.*" Raising his hand with forefinger and middle finger extended, he made the sign of the cross over the slab. "World without end. Amen."

Finally, he locked the cupboard and hung the keys onto his girdle. Then, bidding us all a good night, he vanished up the stairs to his chambers.

Full of questions that demanded immediate answers, I pulled at Fernando's habit. But he put his finger to his lips and shook his head. "Discussing a rite of magic afterwards lessens its power." I began to protest, but he only smiled and cuffed me gently on the shoulder. "Later, little brother," he said, and sent me off to bed.

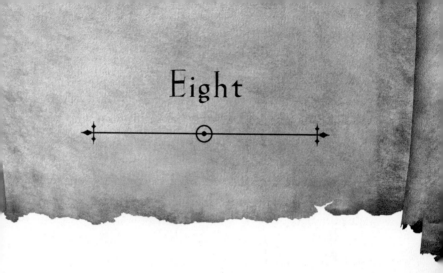

Eight

Late the next morning, my brothers and I gathered in Antonin's cell and watched the ornate carriage lumber up the road, straining at the grade until it reached our front gate. It opened and disgorged the cardinal, along with one other priest, several men in secular clothes, and two young boys. I gazed at the cardinal in dismay. If I had thought Bishop Sorel the epitome of what I did not like about the Church, I had been much too generous.

Cardinal de Joinville was also a mountain of a man, but well built and hearty looking, as if he had long ago mastered the art of fine living. His scarlet robes and wide-brimmed cardinal's hat shone like a fresh wound against the dull gray of the stone wall.

Antonin leaned over the window sill and watched the arriving company with interest. "His Excellency does not like to travel alone, I see."

"God in heaven, how are we going to feed them all?" John wailed. "The larder will be bare in no time."

Juan-José rubbed his chin. "None of them look like they would be satisfied by bread and water."

"Well, they will have to be," Fernando grumbled with a frown. "This is a monastery, not a tavern."

"But who are all those people?" Marcel demanded. "And why does he have to bring them all here?"

"That other priest is probably a clerk." Antonin pointed. "The boys are pages, and the rest are servants. After all, a man of the cardinal's position would not dream of writing his own notes or cutting his own meat."

"Or wiping his own backside," Marcel muttered.

"Just be thankful that he didn't bring a mistress," Juan-José commented sourly. "Francis says that he has at least two. One is rumored to be quite beautiful."

Antonin cocked an eyebrow. "No doubt he has a plain one for fast days."

The others laughed heartily, but about all I could manage was a weak smile. Bishops with mistresses didn't surprise me. The Bishop of Metz, where I grew up, had a mistress. She even went to Mass at the Cathedral every Sunday all painted up like a carnival statue. My parents would never discuss it, but the local boys made crude comments every time she passed by in the street.

Still, I shuddered. This was the man who was to determine whether or not we should be examined by the Inquisition. The prospect did not bode well.

"Well, my brothers," Fernando finally said. "Let us go

and play our parts in this little masquerade. Hopefully it will be over soon."

We trotted down the stairs to the parlor just as the bell to the front gate began ringing furiously. Fernando went out to answer as the rest of us took our prearranged places. John trotted out to the kitchen to work on preparing supper, Marcel went out to his garden and Juan Jose retired to the church. Only Antonin remained upstairs, preparing to ring the bell for vespers.

Although my task was simple—seeing that the cardinal's goblet never became empty—my role was the most difficult of any. I was to play the penitent heretic. And how well I could play that role would determine whether or not the Inquisitor would be called. I shuddered again, then firmly put the thought from my mind. I decided that I would be so thoroughly repentant that the saints themselves could not help but rejoice at my salvation.

Fernando ushered the cardinal and his entourage into the parlor, where the abbot awaited them. My heart sank as I watched Abbot Francis humbly kneel before that scarlet monstrosity and kiss his ring. Would I have to do the same?

"Welcome, Your Excellency," the abbot said. "I trust you had a pleasant journey."

His polite greeting, I noticed, was lost on the cardinal, who couldn't help looking around at the grimy stone walls and splintering beams in the ceiling. "Bishop Sorel hardly did your austerity justice, Abbot Duchienne. I had understood this monastery to be in ruins. It appears that it still is."

"We are protected from the wind and rain, Excellency." The abbot smiled beatifically. "That is all we require."

"Yes, of course," De Joinville replied, gazing dubiously at the water stains around the windows and doors.

"But come, you must be weary." Abbot Francis gestured to Fernando. "Brother Fernando will show you to your quarters. Afterwards, I would be honored if you would join me in the parlor for some refreshment before holy office."

Fernando led the way up the stairs. De Joinville's entourage followed hesitantly, picking their way carefully up the crumbling stone steps. I had never seen anyone go up those particular steps before.

"Where is he taking them?" I whispered to the abbot.

"There is an old section of dormitory above the library. It hasn't been used since I came here." He paused, his eyes narrowing. "We'll show him austerity, by God."

De Joinville and the other priest reappeared after a few moments, looking decidedly displeased with the accommodations. I took up my pitcher and goblet and joined the abbot in the parlor. I took my place at a discreet distance behind De Joinville, hoping that I wouldn't have to run to the kitchen to refill the pitcher too often.

"I trust the rooms are satisfactory," the abbot said innocently.

De Joinville grunted. "They will do." He eased himself down into a chair. I noticed that the cushions had been removed. "And now, my Lord Abbot, on to business."

"Oh, but surely you will have some wine." The abbot

motioned me forward. "We make it ourselves, with some success." I poured a goblet full and handed it to the abbot, who presented it to De Joinville with a flourish.

De Joinville's broad face suddenly came to life. "Ah, yes." He swirled the wine around in the cup and sniffed it. "The famous vintage I've heard so much about." He took a long swallow, frowned, and gazed down into the cup once again.

"Is something wrong?" the abbot inquired.

"No," De Joinville replied in a puzzled tone. "Indeed, it is quite tasty, rich, full bodied. And yet..."

"Brother Fernando, our cellarer, was a vintner in his youth. There are herbs he uses, I am told, that gives the wine a distinctive flavor."

"Still," De Joinville persisted. "I had heard such stories about this wine."

"Stories, Excellency?"

"Oh, you must have heard them. It's supposed to cure all manner of diseases and distempers that mortal man is heir to. But this..." He paused, gazing into the cup as if he had expected to see demons crawling up out of it. "This is only wine."

The abbot laughed brightly. "Of course it is only wine. What else would it be? Some kind of magical elixir?"

I caught my breath and stared at the abbot in alarm.

But De Joinville only shrugged his massive shoulders. "Damned peasant nonsense." He drained the cup and held it out for more wine. I obliged, filling it to the brim. But he had barely raised the cup to his lips when the peal of the bell shattered the silence. Startled, De Joinville jumped, spilling the wine down his scarlet cassock. "God in Heaven! What was that?"

"The bell for Vespers," the abbot replied calmly. "Will you join us?"

"Join you?"

"Yes," the abbot replied firmly. "In church."

"Oh." De Joinville rubbed his hand over his red face. "Yes, yes of course."

Obediently, we all lined up outside the door to the south transept, our cowls over our faces and our hands tucked inside our sleeves. We filed into the choir and began to chant the office—with Antonin prompting us from a hymnal on a lectern beside the pews.

We had only had a week of practice, and were stumbling badly on the chanting. But De Joinville rumbled along with us, missing nearly every other word and chanting a tune that had only a passing acquaintance with what the rest of us were singing. His clerk, if that indeed was who the other priest was, remained silent throughout the entire service. The servants and the boys were not present. I could not help wondering if it had been wise to leave them alone in the cloister while we were all in church.

I need not have worried. We had barely emerged from the transept when the two young boys came towards us, barreling down the corridor and throwing themselves against De Joinville with cries and shrieks.

"Whatever is the matter?" he demanded.

"The gargoyles," one of them whimpered. "They growled at us."

"One of them snapped at me," the other boy claimed staunchly. "Like this." He snapped his teeth together several times, grimacing horribly.

"Where are these gargoyles?" De Joinville demanded.

Both boys pointed down the corridor.

"Ah, those would be the gargoyles in the library," the abbot said in a curiously offhand manner. "Would you like to see them? They are exquisitely carved."

The boys hung back, clutching De Joinville's robes as the abbot led the way to the library.

"These are the gargoyles?" De Joinville leaned closer to inspect them.

"Very striking, are they not? I commissioned these, and the ones in the church as well, from a local mason in the village. His work is truly excellent. And such carving is nearly a vanished art, you know. I wished to preserve it at its finest." The abbot paused meaningfully. "I also wished to provide another source of income for the villagers. It is a great boost to the local economy."

But De Joinville heard little of the abbot's conversation. Instead, he scowled down at the boys, who had never taken their eyes off the fierce stone faces.

"But they did too snarl," one insisted. "I swear to God."

The abbot beamed an indulgent and amused smile. "Boys that age have such wonderful imaginations."

"Too wonderful, sometimes." De Joinville dismissed

them with a wave of his hand. "Now go back to the parlor, you two, and cease your snooping about. It is nearly time for supper." The two miscreants slunk away, eyeing the abbot with awe.

"And now, Abbot Duchienne…" De Joinville strolled beside the abbot across the cloister and into the parlor with me at his heels, carrying the pitcher I had grabbed as I left the church. "As you know, the magistrate of Orleans has complained loudly and long to His Majesty about your continual flaunting of royal authority."

"It is truly a pity that His Majesty must endure such annoyance from one supposedly capable of administrating such a great city as Orleans." The abbot shook his head. "I shall pray for him."

De Joinville scowled briefly, then cleared his throat and continued. "Since this is a Church matter, His Majesty has sent me to look into Montaigne's complaints to see if they have any validity."

"Eminence," Abbot Francis said, heaving a long-suffering sigh, "please be assured that I am more than willing to allow the king's ministers to do their duty—even when they place onerous taxes upon the poor people of this district, taxes that they can not always pay without being reduced to further poverty. Still, I am not here to advocate disobedience to the king's law…"

"Except for snatching condemned criminals from the stake."

"Except where it compromises the spiritual welfare of the people," the abbot finished archly. "That is God's law."

"Allow me to remind you," De Joinville said, "that the magistrate was merely carrying out the king's justice against a condemned criminal."

"Not a criminal." The abbot held up his hand in protest. "A heretic, whose crimes were against the Church, not the State. Since I, by the grace of God, was able to persuade him to repent and be taken back into the embrace of Holy Mother Church, then he was a criminal no longer, was he?"

"He was when he was condemned by the Holy Office," De Joinville returned. "Before he was even turned over to the secular arm. Surely you do not question the judgment of the Holy Office?"

"God Forbid!" The abbot crossed himself and raised his eyes briefly to heaven. "Still, the Church, like a loving mother, forgives the prodigal son, even at the eleventh hour, as Our Lord taught us. I would have thought that the Holy Office would rejoice at the fact that the lost sheep had finally been found and brought back into the fold. It shouldn't matter which shepherd it was that actually fetched it back again, should it?"

"That depends upon whether the shepherd in question brings the lost sheep back to the proper fold."

Abbot Francis blinked. "I fear I do not understand."

"I think you do," De Joinville said sharply. "However, I shall put it more plainly. Montaigne has accused you ... and the rest of your monks as well ... of the practice of sorcery."

"Oh, good heavens!" the abbot said indignantly. "Is

that the kind of rubbish that he is filling the king's ears with? God save us!"

"They are serious charges, my Lord Abbot."

"This world has come to a sad state when the good works and spiritual devotion of the monastic life is considered so strange that it is confused with sorcery," the abbot said with a frown. "Surely His Majesty does not take such ravings seriously."

"Seriously enough to bid me to investigate them."

"Then why did you not just bring the Inquisitor here with you to examine me and my monastery for himself?"

I gasped, terrified at the very thought. For a moment, I wondered if the abbot had let his temper get the better of him.

But no. The remark had been calculated to have an effect, and it did. De Joinville backed down from his position and leaned back in his chair to have another sip of wine. I discreetly glanced at his goblet and noticed it was nearly empty. I discreetly filled it to the brim.

"It was not my wish to involve the Holy Office unless I first determined if the charges were true," De Joinville said. "This is a French matter, and neither His Majesty nor I wish to involve the Italian clergy in any way. So, in light of that, I will examine your monastery myself and decide if the Holy Office is to be summoned."

"Then the doors are open to you. I am very sure that you will find everything in order. If I can be of any assistance …"

"I wish to see everything," De Joinville stated flatly.

"Every book, every manuscript, every nook and every cranny. And I wish to question all of your monks until I am satisfied as to their orthodoxy."

"Of course." The abbot rose as the bell began to ring again. "But I see that it is time for supper. Please feel free to take a seat in the refectory. I shall join you in a moment."

"Very well." De Joinville, obviously eager to eat, lumbered out of the parlor. As soon as he was out of sight, the abbot grabbed a book from the bookcase and motioned me to his side.

I glanced behind me with a frown, hoping De Joinville was out of earshot. "I don't like him," I whispered.

"God knows I don't either. But hopefully we will not have to endure him for long." He opened the book, leafed through it briefly, marked one of the pages, and closed it again. "Here." He handed the book to me. "Tell Antonin to read this during supper. Now hurry."

I helped John serve a simple meal of bread, fruit, and wine, which I could sense did not satisfy the raging hunger De Joinville's journey had induced in him. Antonin stood at the lectern, his soft and soothing tenor voice contrasting sharply with the harshness of the Rule from which he read.

We were to eat in silence, according to the Rule, signaling each other with gestures if we required anything. Idle conversation, jests, and laughter were discouraged. A meal, it appeared, was considered a holy office like Matins or Compline, nestled between grace said beforehand and afterward. Likewise, silence was prescribed after Compline, the last office of the day. We were not to linger, speaking together, but were to retire to our beds after the abbot's blessing.

The chapter was long, and several times Antonin glanced up at the abbot to see if he should read further. But the abbot waved him on. Page after page he read, his voice taking on an edge of hoarseness, until the chapter was concluded. Easing himself into a chair with a grateful sigh, he drained his wine cup as the abbot rose to say the final grace.

"And now," De Joinville said, "I want to speak with that monk who ..."

But Abbot Francis put his finger to his lips and shook his head. "I am afraid that it will have to wait until tomorrow."

De Joinville frowned darkly. "My Lord Abbot, you have just assured me that you would cooperate fully with my investigation."

"And so I shall," Abbot Francis said in a soothing tone. "But surely you recall that the Rule prescribes that all the brothers must now retire to their beds. Allow me to suggest that you do the same. Matins comes very early. Now, may God grant you a good rest."

Grunting in reply, De Joinville made his way down the corridor towards his quarters. Heaving a relieved sigh, I also made my way up to my cell, grateful for the short reprieve. I suspected my rest would be over all too soon.

It was.

It seemed I had barely fallen asleep before the peal of the bell cut through the night announcing Matins. I had no idea what time it was; all I knew was that it was pitch dark outside my window. Telling myself that this was only for a few days, I pulled myself out of bed and assembled with the others in the cloister. De Joinville joined us, rubbing his eyes and looking decidedly displeased.

I realized with a start that the unused rooms in the dormitory were the ones right next to the bell tower. De Joinville would have been awakened by the bong of the bell right next to his pillow. I turned to Abbot Francis with a questioning look. However, he only smiled and led the way into the church.

It was bad enough attempting to follow the prayers while half asleep, but we could barely hear ourselves over the snoring that emitted from De Joinville, who sat with his head lolled against the back of the choir stall. The abbot motioned Marcel to prod him awake, which Marcel did with more force than was perhaps required. De Joinville awoke with a snort, mumbled a few more phrases, then fell asleep again. Finally, his point made, the abbot decided to abandon the remainder of the prayers and allow us to return to bed.

Three hours later, Antonin rang the bell again, this time for Prime. We all had to rise again and file into the church. John and I were able to hide in the kitchen, preparing breakfast, while the abbot dealt with the sleepy cardinal.

Right after breakfast, we assembled in the parlor for Chapter meeting. We sat silently in our chairs, our hands tucked into our sleeves, while Abbot Francis took his place in his chair near the hearth. De Joinville and his clerk took seats on the abbot's left.

"My brothers," Abbot Francis began, in a solemn tone. "It is my humble pleasure to welcome Cardinal de Joinville, the Archbishop of Paris, to our monastery. As you all know, he is here to investigate several complaints regarding us made to the king by the Magistrate of Orleans. I know that you will all cooperate with His Eminence in every way possible, and I am sure that God will bear witness to our innocence."

De Joinville scrutinized all of us for a moment, one by one. "Good brothers, I deeply regret that I must disrupt the discipline and serenity of your lives in this manner. However, I assure you that it is only for a few days. I will question each of you in turn about the various activities that this monastery engages in, and I will trust that you will keep your vow of obedience and answer with the truth."

We all nodded our heads in silent assent, as if there was anything else we could have done. Clasping his hands together, the abbot shut his eyes and began to pray. "We beseech thee, O Lord, to aid these thy servants in their search. Guide them with thy divine counsel, lead them not into error, but show them thy divine truth which shines like a lantern in the darkness. Thou who judges the quick and the dead, mete out justice to those who would transgress the laws of God, and shelter the sheep from the wolves. *In nomine Patris et Filii et Spiritus Sancti...*" He crossed himself and we piously followed suit. After a long, scowling moment, De Joinville did the same.

Abbot Francis and I hung back while the other monks quickly scattered out of De Joinville's reach, off to attend to their various duties. When it looked as though De Joinville would storm out of the parlor after them, I grabbed my pitcher and refilled his goblet to the brim. Without so much as a glance at me, he took a deep swallow. For a long moment, he peered into the goblet, sloshing the wine inside it to and fro. Then he raised his head sharply and gave Abbot Francis a piercing look.

"And now, my Lord Abbot, the first thing I wish to see is where this legendary wine of yours is made."

Abbot Francis nodded calmly, as though he were expecting that very request. "As you wish, Your Eminence."

Motioning for me to follow, he led the cardinal and his entourage out past the church and through the cloister to Fernando's workshop. We found Fernando there, nonchalantly sweeping the floor. He looked up, holding his broom, as the abbot waved everyone inside.

De Joinville gazed around the tiny cottage, his expression indicating that he wasn't altogether impressed. "The wine is made in here?"

"Yes, Your Eminence." The abbot moved to Fernando's side. "This is Brother Fernando, our wine maker."

De Joinville waited impatiently as Fernando knelt and kissed his ring. "And how did you come to make this wine, Brother Fernando?"

"My father was a vintner," Fernando replied easily. "In Tuscany. I turned a wine press as soon as I could walk."

"I have no doubt of that. How do you make this wine of yours?"

"It is very simple, Your Eminence," Fernando replied. "If you will be so good as to follow me, I will show you." He led the group out the door again to the shed where the press was kept. The cardinal's clerk began scribbling notes onto a slate with a stub of a pencil, but writing became difficult for him as he struggled to keep up.

"The vines are over there on the hillside." Fernando pointed over the wall at the hill that rose behind it, studded with vines now bare and skeletal. "We gather the grapes and press them in this press. Then, we bung the juice up in these casks, add the yeast, and wait."

The clerk scribbled furiously for a moment, then Fernando led the way back into the workshop. "We store them in here until the wine is fermented. Then it is strained and returned to the casks."

But De Joinville was not paying attention to the wine. "Brother Fernando, you have been here the longest, I understand."

"Yes, Eminence," Fernando replied.

"Have you ever seen any evidence of the black arts being practiced in this monastery?"

"God forbid!" Fernando gave the cardinal a horrified look and crossed himself. "Why in the world would anyone even think such a thing? This is a holy place. We pray, work, and serve the people of the village. What would we wish to practice any black art for?"

"Your wine, Brother Fernando," De Joinville said pointedly, "is rumored to have magical properties. Is this true?"

"Your Eminence," Fernando replied, his tone firm. "God has granted me the knowledge of wine making, and He is pleased to allow me to turn out an excellent product. But the excellence of my wine is entirely due to the excellence of the grapes and the healthfulness of the herbs that God has provided us with. Nothing more."

De Joinville's gaze lit upon something over by the hearth. He pushed Fernando aside abruptly and reached down, grasping in his hand one of Fernando's alchemical vessels, one of the tear-shaped flasks used to collect the Elixir as it flowed from the aludel.

"And I suppose this..." He held the flask up triumphantly. "...is also used in the making of wine, and for some more arcane purpose?"

I held my breath. Had Fernando forgotten to hide the flask? In spite of all of our careful preparations, were we going to be condemned for some silly oversight?

Fernando appeared totally unruffled. He gently took the flask from the cardinal's fingers. "This is a special flask that is used to prepare the tincture of the herb that flavors our wine."

"And it isn't used in the practice of alchemy?"

"No indeed, Eminence. There is a superficial resemblance, to be sure. But, you see, the leaves are placed in the flask, so..." He indicated the neck. "...and then covered with cold water. Then it is boiled for several minutes, until the mixture turns a deep green. Then the liquid is added to the wine in the proper proportion and mixed with..."

De Joinville waved his hand for silence. "Very well, Brother Fernando," he said impatiently. "We have seen enough. Come, let us move on."

He turned and led the way back out the door. The abbot stood aside to let them pass, looking decidedly displeased with De Joinville's behavior. I hung back from the party in order to refill the pitcher that I carried. Heaven forbid that it should be empty if De Joinville required a refill of his goblet.

Fernando poured the wine from a special barrel by the door. "Rude old windbag," he whispered in my ear. "Isn't he?"

I only had time to nod in agreement before trotting to catch up with the cardinal's party. Abbot Francis was leading the way to the kitchen, where a column of white smoke curled up from the chimney. The yeasty smell that wafted across the garden announced the baking of bread.

"Brother John prepares most of our meals," Abbot Francis was explaining as I came up behind him. "Even though he is decidedly of a mystical bent, he bakes a truly wonderful loaf."

We entered the kitchen to find John enshrouded in a white halo of flour. He tenderly patted a mound of dough, as though he were trying to comfort it before consigning it to the hot oven. He turned as De Joinville approached him and knelt to kiss his ring.

"And are you a baker, Brother John?" De Joinville asked.

"I am now, Your Eminence," John replied with an innocent smile.

De Joinville glowered at him suspiciously for a moment. "You are English."

"Yes, Eminence."

"Then what, pray tell, are you doing in a French abbey?"

"The English did not want me," John replied with his disarming smile. "So they sent me here."

"And why was that?"

"I was mad."

"Mad?"

"Oh, yes, Eminence. I had been possessed by a demon. An English demon, I am told. The English priest that I was taken to could do nothing with me. But Abbot Francis offered to take me in and the demon left me."

The cardinal glanced up at the abbot with a frown, then turned back to John. "He did not...exorcise this demon, did he?"

"He had no need to. As soon as I entered this holy place and put on the habit of the Benedictines, the demon fled in a puff of sulfurous smoke and quite dreadful shrieks." Brother John crossed himself and gazed towards Heaven in rapture.

De Joinville glared at the abbot, who smiled indulgently. "Brother John's visions are quite inspirational."

But De Joinville merely grunted, then fell to coughing as the flour rose in the air. Desperately waving at us to follow, he stumbled out of the kitchen as John, his smile now reflecting more smug satisfaction than ecstatic rapture, returned to his mound of dough.

The bell rang for Sext at noon, then it was time for our dinner. Although the cardinal was eager to eat, he looked singularly annoyed that he was required to cease his investigations in order to do so. But the abbot remained adamant that the Rule be observed, and the cardinal ate in silence while Antonin read still another chapter from the book.

I noticed that the abbot again deliberately dragged the meal out much longer than it took to actually eat in order to allow Antonin to finish the chapter. The cardinal fidgeted like a horse too long in harness. Finally, when I was positive that he would voice his complaint, the abbot rose, said a final grace, and dismissed us from the refectory.

I braced myself for another round of questioning, but Abbot Francis had other plans. Dinner had taken so long that by the time the table was cleared, it was past time for None. No sooner had we sung the office then it was time for Vespers. We sang another office, and then it was time for supper, and then Compline. By this time the sun had set and it was bedtime. With a sigh of relief, I plodded up the stairs to my cell.

The next morning, De Joinville grimly continued his investigation despite the fact that he was getting little, if any, sleep. Right after breakfast, he insisted on heading out to the cloister and examining the herb beds that lined the pathway. I followed at his heels, stifling a yawn with the back of my sleeve.

Would this horrible man never leave?

We found Marcel kneeling in the black dirt, pulling tiny weeds from between the rosemary and the verbena. I harbored great doubts about whether or not Marcel would be able to mask his contempt for De Joinville with the façade of piety that the situation required, and I approached him with some trepidation. He glared up at the cardinal with obvious distaste, then slowly rose to his feet and brushed the dirt from his habit. He hesitated, then, at a stern look from the abbot, he knelt and kissed the cardinal's ring.

"This is Brother Marcel, our resident apothecary," Abbot Francis explained cheerfully as De Joinville pulled the hem of his scarlet robes out of the mud. "His herbs contribute much to our good health as well as to our table."

"What manner of herbs do you grow, Brother Marcel?" De Joinville eyed the orderly rows of plants with some suspicion.

"I have fennel," Marcel replied, pointing to a tall, graceful plant with a lacy yellow flower. "It aids in the digestion. And there is parsley for the colic." He indicated another lacy green plant. "And coltsfoot, for cough."

The cardinal stroked his chin for a moment. "You wouldn't, of course, have such things as mandrake?

Marcel shook his head emphatically. "A bad root, mandrake. No good comes from it. Kills everything else in the bed."

"And henbane?" De Joinville persisted. "Or nightshade? Or aconite?"

"What use would I have for those?" Marcel gave the cardinal a disgusted look. "My job is to make medicines to help sick people, not ride through the night on a broomstick."

"Ah, then you know of such things."

Marcel snorted. "You can't know the herbs without knowing what some folk use them for."

"But you do not fly to the Sabbat yourself."

"No." Marcel's look was defiant. "I don't."

"Never?" De Joinville pressed.

"Never. My herbs serve the glory of God and the health of the people in this village," Marcel returned staunchly. "I don't have the book learning that the others have, but I keep my vows."

De Joinville regarded Marcel with a stern and imperious look. But Marcel, undaunted, returned his gaze, scowl for scowl. Finally, it was De Joinville who turned away, obviously displeased with Marcel but having no more questions to ask. Like it or not, there was nothing to fault Marcel for. Merely possessing forbidden knowledge constituted no crime, and De Joinville knew it. It was proof he needed, and there was none.

"Thank you, Brother Marcel. We shall leave you to your work." Abbot Francis stepped back onto the stone walkway and waited firmly for De Joinville to do the same as the bell rang for Sext. After the office, it was time for dinner and another endless chapter of the Rule. So, it was after None before De Joinville could continue his investigation. But he did, with a dogged determination not to let the afternoon slip through his fingers as it had the previous day. With a resigned sigh, I took up my pitcher and followed at his heels.

It appeared that Juan-José featured next on De Joinville's list. But in order to find him, De Joinville had to follow Abbot Francis back to the church. Juan-José, his cowl thrown over his head, knelt in one of the pews near the statue of the Virgin, head bowed piously over clasped hands.

"Good brother." De Joinville's voice intruded loudly onto the silence of the sanctuary. "We would like a word with you."

Juan-José slowly pulled back his cowl and glared up at De Joinville. He shook his head, threw the cowl back up, and bowed his head once again. De Joinville scowled in anger.

But Abbot Francis stepped forward and put his hand up for attention. "Your Eminence, this is Brother Juan-José. I fear that he cannot speak with you."

"And why not?" De Joinville demanded archly.

"He has taken a vow of silence in gratitude to the Virgin for saving his life. We must not disturb him."

"Well, he will have to resign himself to being disturbed," De Joinville retorted ungraciously. "I wish to ask him a few questions."

"But Eminence..."

"I insist."

The abbot heaved a sigh. "Oh, very well." He knelt by Juan-José's side and laid a gentle hand on his shoulder.

"Dear brother, I hereby release you from your vow for a little while. It is vital that Cardinal de Joinville speak with you on a matter of great urgency. Please answer him."

Juan-José sat back in the pew and, after a moment's reflection, nodded. "What does the cardinal wish to know?"

"How came you to take such a vow?" De Joinville asked.

"I was a soldier," Juan-José replied slowly. "In the service of the King of Spain. We were fighting the Moors and I was thrown from my horse in the battle. As I fell, I knew that I would be cut to pieces before I hit the ground. In despair, I beseeched the Virgin that if She were to save my life, I would enter a monastery and devote my life to prayer and contemplation."

"But why a vow of silence?" De Joinville prompted, interested in spite of himself.

"Because I, who had been such a braggart in my youth, could conceive of no greater sacrifice than silence."

"I see." De Joinville rubbed his chin for a moment, obviously impressed. "Then how did you find your way to this monastery?"

"Our Lady appeared to me in a dream and guided me here. Another abbey, perhaps one in which the monks were worldly and licentious rather than pious and austere, would not do for me." Juan-José paused for emphasis and studied the cardinal pointedly for a moment. "Is there more that you wish to know? I would return to my prayers."

De Joinville, annoyed at being brushed off but unwilling to deny such obvious piety, rose to his feet. "Yes, of course." He waved for his clerk to follow him.

Abbot Francis made the sign of the cross over the motionless Juan-José kneeling once again in the pew, and accompanied De Joinville out of the church. I followed with a sidelong glance at Juan-José, who pulled back the cowl from his face and winked at me.

The bell rang for Vespers, which effectively put an end to the cardinal's investigations for the evening. Supper followed on the heels of Vespers, which, in turn, dragged out to Compline and then to the peace and quiet of bed.

I made my way back to the dormitory and noticed a faint glow coming from behind me. Making a quick detour, I followed the light to the kitchen. I discovered that Juan-José had climbed up onto the table and had his head thrust deeply into one of the cupboards. Curious, but not wishing to startle him by calling to him, I waited impatiently until he had pulled his head out of the cupboard. With a triumphant expression, he reached in and pulled out an earthenware jug, well covered with dust.

I cleared my throat softly and he grinned at me. "Ah, Michael, you've caught me in the larder like a mouse." He held up the jug. "Care to join me?"

"What have you found?" I craned my neck to get a better look.

"Some of the real wine." He pried the cork out with the tip of his dagger. "I thought we had a bit of it left after that last cask. I saw Fernando put it into this jug with my own eyes."

He pulled out the cork as I fetched two goblets from the hearth. He sat on the table as if it were a bench, the jug in his lap, and motioned for me to join him. Eagerly, I jumped up onto the table beside him and he poured me a generous portion.

"Father Francis will be terribly angry if he finds us here," I said, feeling five years old again. "He was adamant that we go directly to bed after Compline."

"That is to keep us out of the clutches of that blasted cardinal," Juan-José replied, taking a long swallow. He brushed his mustache off with his sleeve and heaved a contented sigh. "God, but I've missed this blessed brew."

"I don't see how we can avoid him," I retorted, also taking time out for a healthy drink. "He seems to have taken over this monastery."

"No, he hasn't. The Rule of St. Benedict has taken over this monastery. I must say it's a brilliant plan Francis has concocted, even though I don't much like it."

"De Joinville certainly doesn't like it much either," I commented.

"Did you for a moment think that he would?" Juan-José raised an eyebrow. "But not even he dares to violate the Rule. That would reduce whatever credibility he has, if he has any at all, with the Holy Office. It is a battle, Michael, a battle of wills rather than swords, but a battle all the same."

"But Father Francis will win," I said. "Surely."

"He is defending his homeland, and that always gives a soldier an added advantage," Juan-José said. "But De Joinville is no fool. You mark my words, he will put up some kind of fight. Francis has the upper hand now, but there are chinks in the best of armor. It won't take De Joinville long to figure out where to aim."

"I guess I have difficulty imagining that Father Francis would have any chinks in his armor," I said. "He seems so . . . well, it doesn't seem possible that an ordinary man like De Joinville would have much of a chance against him."

Juan-José smiled to himself. "Ah, my young friend. Even a man with *baraka* has his weaknesses."

"*Baraka*?" I echoed. "What on earth is that?

"It's a Saracen word. I suppose you could call it 'magical power,' or you could call it 'sanctity.' The Moors use it for both. Francis did not have to transform my sword to prove to me that he possessed it. I had only to look into those eyes of his and I knew." Juan-José thrust the cork back into the jug and put it back into the cupboard.

"Is there still some left?" I asked hopefully.

"Yes," he replied. "But let us save it for Antonin. He will need some to soothe his throat after doing all that reading. Now, let us toddle off to bed as the Rule prescribes before the De Joinville catches us and asks embarrassing questions."

"Like, what you're doing talking to me?" I asked with a grin.

He laughed and gave me a shove that nearly knocked me over. "Be off, boy," he ordered. "And not another word until morning."

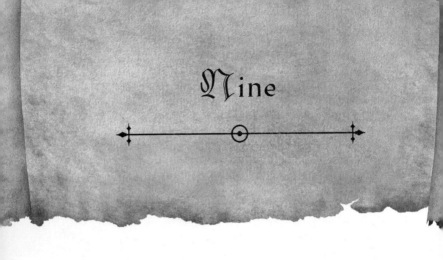

Nine

"I fear that we will have to postpone the remainder of our tour until tomorrow," Abbot Francis mentioned at Prime the next morning. "Since this is Sunday, and I seem to be the only priest between here and Orleans, I must offer services for the villagers."

"Do you do this every Sunday?" De Joinville asked.

"And feast days as well," the abbot replied. "Now, if you will excuse me, I must prepare."

De Joinville moved his huge bulk between the abbot and the door. "I will say the Mass this morning."

The abbot froze for several heartbeats, a startled look on his face. "Eminence?"

"You heard me." De Joinville peered at him from beneath low-hanging brows. "There isn't a problem, my Lord Abbot, is there?"

Abbot Francis recovered his composure. "No, indeed.

It would be an honor, Eminence." The shadow which had crossed his features clearly indicated that it would be nothing of the sort. "The sacristy door is behind the altar."

"Good."

De Joinville lumbered towards the church while the two boys brought his vestments from the carriage. Instead of the abbot's simple white cope and mantle, he allowed the boys to array him in heavy velvet that was lined with silk and embroidered in gilded thread and gold bullion. He reached for his equally gilded miter and placed it on his head. "The entire village attends, does it not?"

"As a rule," the abbot replied, his nonchalance betrayed by a tightness around his mouth.

"Then we will show them how a proper Mass is performed." De Joinville picked up his crosier. "Even in such rude surroundings."

I watched the abbot's blue eyes flash in sudden anger at the insult, but he could do nothing but stand back while De Joinville, followed by his clerk, took their places at the head of the procession. The two pages, dressed in their own copes and surplices, came next, one holding the crosier, the other waving a thurible that put out a cloud of incense smoke.

We silently lined up behind them and followed them through the south transept into the sanctuary. "*Introibo ad altare Dei*," we chanted. "I go to the altar of God."

Everyone glanced up as we entered. I heard several gasps and whispered comments as a ripple of confusion worked its way through the crowd in the pews. Nobody recited the opening prayers. They were too busy watching De Joinville and his entourage with suspicion.

He ascended to the altar, followed by his boys, as we peeled off into the choir. The whispering grew perceptibly louder, and did not abate even when De Joinville chanted the first psalm.

"*Sancti, Sancti, Sancti*..." he intoned solemnly.

Abbot Francis sat fuming in the choir stall. "That should be '*Sanctus*,' you imbecile," he hissed under his breath. Fernando shot him a reproving look and leaned back in the pew with a sigh, shutting his eyes with a pained expression.

I watched the abbot with growing concern. I could well understand that it must be difficult for him to sit back and watch while De Joinville mangled the Mass at his altar in his church. The abbot was a proud man and De Joinville had insulted him at every turn. I was certain it was deliberate.

How long would the abbot manage to keep his legendary temper in check?

There came a brief respite from the torment when De Joinville served communion. Several of the villagers paused before approaching the altar rail, and many did not venture forth at all.

Juan-José, his voice masked by the scuffling of feet, leaned over and whispered to me, "If resisting temptation is a sign of sanctity, then Francis is a saint indeed."

I frowned in puzzlement. "What temptation?"

"The temptation to bludgeon that bastard with a wall sconce, that's what."

I could barely stifle my shriek of laughter. Fernando glanced sharply at me, then put his finger to his lips. I looked over at Juan-José reproachfully, but he merely winked and bowed his head with mock piety.

Finally, the Mass ended and we processed back to the cloister. I glanced behind me and noticed the people of the village still clustering about the abbot as though it was he who had said Mass and not De Joinville. Many of the care-worn faces bore worried looks. Apparently the presence of the cardinal, with all of his pomp, had aroused suspicion and concern. The abbot spent many minutes stroking withered features with reassuring gestures and quieting crying children. Several knelt and kissed the hem of his habit, as they seemed always to do.

Their devotion was definitely not lost on De Joinville, who watched the scene for several minutes before vanishing behind the altar to divest himself. In his careless haste, he knocked over an old woman who was kneeling at the corner of the communion rail, wooden rosary beads dangling in her shriveled fingers. He heedlessly strode past her, his pace unchecked. She tumbled to the floor, frantically clutching the railing.

Abbot Francis came up behind her and knelt to help her to her feet. As he did so, he glowered up at the cardinal's retreating form with a look of barely concealed fury, the likes of which I had never before seen. His gaze darkened as with gathering storm clouds, and I sensed that lightning would soon flash. I carefully backed out of the sanctuary and followed the other brothers out into the cloister.

John dutifully headed for the kitchen to see what he could make for dinner. But he soon came into the parlor with a worried look, anxiously motioning for Abbot Francis. The rest of us exchanged concerned glances and decided to follow.

"Francis," John whispered, drawing the abbot into the kitchen. "We are nearly out of food. I have only enough flour to last one more day. That cask of unblessed wine is down to the dregs. The cheese is gone, as is the butter, and we must have the last of the eggs for dinner. Thank God that tomorrow is a fast day, at least according to the Rule..."

"Then put him and his entire mob on water and day-old bread," the abbot declared, his eyes narrowing. "Until he decides to leave."

I watched with a heavy heart as he turned on his heel and stalked out of the parlor. I turned to find John watching him as well. A worried frown creased his brow, showing me that he, too, was concerned that the abbot might finally lose his legendary temper—a revelation that didn't comfort me in the slightest.

"What is he going to do?" I asked softly.

"I don't know." John crossed himself. "But if he gives in to his anger, we are doomed."

—✺—

As soon as Antonin rang the bell for dinner, De Joinville led his entourage into the refectory as though it were he who was abbot. At the moment the cardinal began to say grace,

Abbot Francis appeared and wordlessly took his accustomed place at the head of the table. He said nothing, but I could see him smoldering like the coals in Fernando's athanor.

Everyone sat in silence as John and I served the meager fare. Antonin read yet another endless chapter of the Rule. De Joinville eyed the sparse platters set before him with obvious displeasure, but Abbot Francis pointedly ignored the cardinal's inquiring looks.

The abbot ate virtually nothing, I noticed with some concern, and he waited pointedly until after the chapter was read before dismissing us from the refectory. He informed De Joinville tersely that he had to attend to some urgent monastery business the rest of the day and could not possibly conduct any further tours until after Prime the next morning.

De Joinville watched impassively as the abbot stalked out of the refectory. Then he turned to his clerk and they conferred in hushed whispers for a moment.

"I doubt very much whether His Eminence will be content to pass the afternoon in prayer and contemplation," John observed as I helped him carry the platters back into the kitchen.

I glanced at him in alarm. "Do you think that he will investigate on his own?"

John looked over at me with a sad look. "Do you not think that he has been waiting for such an opportunity ever since he arrived?"

"But why is Father Francis allowing it?"

"We will soon see."

His chair squeaking in protest, De Joinville rose to his feet and motioned his clerk to do the same. "Brother Fernando," he called.

Fernando approached the head of the table, wiping his hands on a towel. "Yes, Eminence?"

"Since you have been here the longest, you might be able to answer a question for me. I understand that there was once a tunnel beneath this monastery. Is this true?"

I clutched John's hand in terror.

"It is," Fernando replied with a shrug. "But Abbot Francis had it bricked up and sealed years ago." He leaned forward and lowered his voice delicately. "Rats."

"Still, I wish to see it. Will you show it to me?"

Fernando faltered for a moment. "Of course, Eminence. But perhaps I should go and fetch the abbot. He knows far more about it than I."

De Joinville dismissed the suggestion with a brusque wave of his hand. "There is no need to disturb your hardworking abbot. He must be very busy. You may show me, Brother Fernando."

Fernando swallowed hard. "Very well, Eminence. Come this way."

John and I tried to appear busy with the baking as De Joinville trooped into the kitchen. I fumbled the bread dough, nearly dropping it onto the floor. John took my shaking hands in his for a moment in silent reassurance.

"Trust," he mouthed. "Trust Francis."

De Joinville looked around with a scowl. "The entrance was here? In the kitchen?"

"I am told it served as a wine cellar, Eminence," Fernando replied.

"But surely you would have need of such a cellar," De Joinville said pointedly.

Fernando shook his head. "Actually, no, Eminence. Most of our wine goes to the village. We keep very little of it here." He patted the oak barrel on a stand near the back door. "One cask is all we require."

"I see." De Joinville still looked unconvinced. "Still, show me where it was."

Heaving a resigned sigh, Fernando indicated the outline of the slab on the floor. "This stone section slid aside to reveal a passageway under the floor. It led to a chamber carved out of the rock of the mountain. It was vented by another small opening by the river. That was how the rats got in."

De Joinville clearly was not concerned about the rats. "How was it opened?"

"By a lever," Fernando replied. "In one of the cabinets."

I began to shake again. Although Fernando was doing the best he could, he had not rehearsed this possibility. I could see beads of sweat popping out upon his high forehead.

I refused to think about what would happen if De Joinville discovered the Tabernacle.

De Joinville looked about at the cupboards, examining each one in turn, until he found the one which was locked. "This is where the lever is, is it not?"

"Yes, Eminence."

"Pray, open it for me."

"I cannot, Eminence." Fernando spread his hands in a helpless gesture. "I have no key."

"Then we will have to break the lock." Picking up a knife from the table, De Joinville slipped the blade between the two edges of the tiny doors. The ancient wood squeaked in agony and split apart. With a grunt of satisfaction, De Joinville yanked the door open and grasped the lever. I felt as though I would faint as he pulled the lever up.

Nothing happened.

Frowning, he pulled again. Still nothing. Whatever it was that the abbot had done to it, the slab held fast and no amount of pulling by De Joinville could release it.

Fernando, a look of intense relief washing briefly across his features, moved forward in an elaborate gesture of helpfulness. Grasping the lever himself, he jiggled it a little from side to side. "The mechanism was disengaged after the entrance was sealed. I suppose that was so it could not be opened by mistake."

"Give me that." De Joinville shoved Fernando out the way and grabbed the lever with both hands. He pulled it back, grimacing with the effort. With a loud crack, the lever broke in his hands, sending him flying backwards. He landed on his backside on the floor.

I turned my head away, trying to stifle my laughter. Fernando tut-tutted in concern and offered De Joinville his hand. De Joinville scowled and opened his mouth to say something, but his voice was abruptly drowned out by the bell for Vespers.

"Ah, Your Eminence, I thought I might find you in

the kitchen." Abbot Francis appeared in the doorway and looked around for a moment, clearly assessing the situation. "I trust that supper is being prepared to your satisfaction?"

"Yes, quite." De Joinville heaved himself up off the flagstone floor and glared at the abbot for a long moment. Abbot Francis met his gaze calmly. Eventually De Joinville turned away, knowing that he had lost this round.

"Then perhaps you would join me in church and allow our good brothers to finish their work." Standing aside with a flourish, the abbot allowed De Joinville to pass before him out the door. He and Fernando exchanged a brief look. "It held, I take it."

Fernando nodded.

"Good. I trust he will keep his prying fingers to himself in the future." Abbot Francis dug into the pocket of his habit and pulled out the long iron pin that had fastened the lever to the mechanism. "Here." He handed it to Fernando. "We can fix it later." He turned on his heel and followed De Joinville out the door.

Fernando ran a shaking hand across his sweaty brow. "Francis," he murmured, "you will be the death of me."

After Compline, we all gratefully made our way back to our cells. It had been a trying day, and I should have slept like a corpse. But I found that I could not. Restless, I took my taper and made my way back down the hall. My instincts were telling me that something was afoot, but I had no idea what. A faint glow shone down the hallway. I followed it.

It came from the abbot's chambers. I crept closer and heard his voice muttering from behind the door. At first I thought he was talking with someone, but then I caught phrases here and there, enough to realize that these were much the same prayers I had heard in the Tabernacle.

Unable to suppress my curiosity, I pressed my eye to the crack in the door. I couldn't help gasping in awe. There, splayed out against the rough stone wall, was the abbot's shadow, huge and black, holding the cross before him as though it were the consecrated host.

What in God's name was he doing?

I gasped as the realization hit me. He was doing a summoning, of the kind that I had watched him do in the tabernacle. But why? What did he want the angels to do? Was he asking them to smite De Joinville with a thunderbolt and reduce him to a pile of smoking ash? Had the abbot's anger and pride gotten the better of him?

If they had, then we were doomed.

Before I even realized what I was doing, I crossed myself. Whispering a small prayer of my own to the blessed angels, I turned my back on his door and made my way up the stairs to my own cell.

De Joinville's absence at Matins the next morning was duly noted, but ignored. We sang the office anyway, at least most of it, much to my disappointment. It wasn't that I had been sleeping that well and missed my bed. There were so many questions that I wished to ask, mostly to ally my fears, which grew by the hour. But Abbot Francis was unusually taciturn and dismissed us from office with little more than a wave of his hand. I had heard tales of his legendary temper, but the possibility of seeing it finally unleashed was not something I relished. So, for the first time since I arrived at Sainte Felice, I feared to approach him.

Dawn came, and with it the bell for Prime. De Joinville and his company appeared in the refectory for barely more than dry bread and a couple of withered apples. But De Joinville touched nothing, not even the wine. His face was drawn and haggard, with deep bags beneath the eyes. Whatever else he had been doing in the dead of the night that caused him to miss Matins, it obviously wasn't sleeping.

I felt a shiver course down my spine. What had Abbot Francis done to him?

The abbot, however, was most solicitous. "You look unwell, Eminence."

De Joinville shook his head. "I had a miserable night," he grumbled, rubbing his eyes. "I slept little, and when I did, I dreamed ... most disturbing dreams."

The abbot smiled faintly. "Allow me to call upon Brother Antonin. You have not yet spoken with him, I believe. He is our physician. I'm sure that he could be of great assistance."

Antonin, having emerged from the tower, came into the refectory and looked up at a gesture from the abbot. De Joinville moaned softly and rested his head in his hands as Antonin glanced from him back to the abbot with a genuinely puzzled look.

"Brother Antonin, His Eminence is feeling rather poorly. Perhaps there is something you might do." He gave Antonin a mischievous wink.

Antonin suddenly flashed the abbot a knowing smile. "To be sure. Allow me to fetch my bag."

De Joinville watched Antonin exit the refectory. "I had no idea that you had a doctor of medicine among your brothers."

"Oh, yes, Eminence," Abbot Francis replied with a touch of obvious pride. "Brother Antonin not only sees to our health, but to that of the villagers as well."

"I see."

Antonin returned, carrying a large bag of black leather. He set it on the floor and knelt beside De Joinville, examining his swollen and bloodshot eyes.

"You are a true doctor of physik?" De Joinville asked pointedly. "Where did you take your degree?"

"University of Cologne, Eminence," Antonin replied, busying himself with the delicate task of taking De Joinville's pulse. Frowning slightly, he concentrated upon it for a long moment, then shook his head gravely.

"What is it?" De Joinville asked with obvious trepidation.

Antonin gave him a solemn look. "We will know in a moment." Reaching into his sack, he brought out a glass flask. It bore a vague resemblance to Fernando's aludel. But I discovered the resemblance was, at best, superficial. "Now, Eminence, if you will be so good as to piss into this flask, I shall be able to examine your water and tell you for certain what ails you."

De Joinville started. "You want me to do what?"

Antonin regarded him with a look that one might give

to a balky child. "I must have a sample of your urine to make a proper diagnosis, Eminence."

"Why?" De Joinville scowled in suspicion.

Antonin heaved a long-suffering sigh. "In order to determine whether your humors are properly balanced. The Greek physician Galen teaches that when the humors of a man are out of balance, then disease results."

"How so?"

Rubbing his chin, Antonin regarded him sagely for a moment. "I would say that you were a man of bilious humor, and an overbalance of phlegm could be the cause of your trouble. Of course, I cannot be sure without a sample of your urine."

"Is it … serious?"

"It well could be. However, fear not. We can always do a bloodletting."

"A bloodletting?" De Joinville jumped to his feet in alarm.

"We shouldn't need much. A few leeches ought to do the job nicely." Reaching into his bag once again, Antonin pulled out another tiny flask, this one with a cork plugging the top. It was about half full of murky water, in which several slug-like creatures floated.

De Joinville grew visibly pale. "I hardly think that will be necessary, Brother Physician. I am feeling much better at the moment." Rising to his feet, he turned to the abbot. "I think we have enough time to see the library."

Since it was before Sext, Abbot Francis had no choice but to agree. De Joinville eyed the gargoyles with increased suspicion as the abbot led the way past them into the library. I followed with a full pitcher and a heavy heart. If Juan-José was right, De Joinville would let loose one final volley before all of this was done.

"I hope I can be forgiven for saying that we have a fine library for an abbey of our size," the abbot said. "As you have noticed, our brothers come from several countries, and each has brought to the library at least one or two rare volumes."

"Rare volumes, indeed." De Joinville took one from the shelf, which, I noted, was placed prominently to command his attention. "*The Pimander of Hermes Trismegistus*," he muttered, reading the frontispiece. "You have some heretical works here, Abbot Duchienne. The Pimander is considered to be a book of sorcery."

"Only a less well educated man than yourself, Eminence, would consider such a work to be sorcery," the abbot said smoothly. "The ignorant always consider as magical those things that they do not understand."

"Even when they speak of the planets as though they are gods?" De Joinville demanded. "And describe ways of gaining their aid?"

"Such books glorify God by acquainting the scholar with the intricacies of His divine work," the abbot replied. "The thrice great Hermes, living as he did before the Incarnation, would of course, make significant errors in his interpretation of such intricacies—say, ascribing to the planets, in his pagan ignorance, glory that belongs to God alone. However, such errors are to be understood in light of that and are no more heretical than, say, Aristotle. We Christians do not have to worship the planets nor do we have to invoke them to do our bidding in order to appreciate the wonder of God's universe."

"There are those who would say that knowing how such things might be done leads to the temptation to do them, whereas if one is in ignorance, one is not so tempted."

"To know sin is to avoid sin," the abbot returned. "And many are those who stumble into forbidden practices through ignorance. Still, one can, I'm sure you would agree, gaze up into the heavens and contemplate the movements of the stars and planets without ever entertaining a thought of casting a horoscope. However, there are those who are so greedy that the idea of admiring God's handiwork without attempting to make a profit by it would be so incomprehensible as to appear to be sorcery itself."

De Joinville could not argue with that, but continued the tour with suspicious looks at the shelves. "Still, you do seem to have an inordinate number of pagan works."

"I also have Aquinas, Augustine, and Duns Scotus." The abbot pointed to another shelf. "Although our collection is not large, we try our best to ensure that there is more truth than error. Besides, the works we read and study the most, such as the Rule of St. Benedict and other works of Christian devotion, are normally circulated amongst the brothers, while the pagan works stay here for only occasional consultation."

"I see," De Joinville said with a frown. I could not be sure if he believed the story or not, but there seemed to be no evidence to the contrary. He spent the next several minutes scrutinizing the shelves, occasionally taking a book or manuscript out, leafing through it, then putting it back.

Abbot Francis, who never took his gaze from De Joinville throughout the entire examination, looked visibly relieved when De Joinville turned towards the door. "I trust everything is in order, Eminence?"

De Joinville turned to the abbot with a stern frown. "You seem an extremely well-educated man, Abbot Duchienne, and your austerity is to be commended. However, you are aware that the Devil tempts the intellect as well as the flesh."

"I pray daily for the Divine guidance to avoid falling into such a trap," Abbot Francis said. "However, if you find that I have, indeed, been guilty of such unorthodoxy, do be good enough to tell me so that I can duly repent of my errors."

De Joinville ruminated for a moment, wondering, no doubt, if he should take the abbot up on his challenge. However, something must have caused him to decide against it, for he only frowned and headed for the parlor.

The abbot, unable to help a smug smile, quickly caught up with him. "I trust you are satisfied with the piety of our little company.

But De Joinville suddenly turned on him like an enraged bear. "No, Abbot Duchienne, I am not satisfied. I wish to see that sorcerer that you fished from the flames. We've been dancing like damsels around this issue for four days now. There is no use hiding him from me any longer. I demand that you produce him at once."

"But Your Eminence, he has never left your side." Abbot Francis turned to me. "Brother Michael, His Eminence would like to ask you a few questions."

Finally, it had arrived—my moment of truth. I put the pitcher on the ground, genuflected, and kissed De Joinville's ring. I glanced up and found him gazing at me in astonishment.

"My God, he's only a boy." A pointed look from the abbot kept me from protesting. "What was that wretched Montaigne trying to do, for heaven's sake—burn a child for sorcery?"

"Now you see why I interfered as I did," the abbot said quietly.

"I still do not believe it." De Joinville shook his head. "To hear him tell it, he had bagged a powerful sorcerer."

"No doubt he meant my master." I began my carefully rehearsed story at a slight nod from the abbot. "The count."

De Joinville frowned. "Your master?"

"Yes, Your Eminence. He was the one arrested for sorcery. I was only his... his servant."

"His servant?"

"Yes, Your Eminence."

"And you never actually practiced sorcery with this ... this count?"

"No, Your Eminence." Tears welled in my eyes at what was, after all, the bitter, bitter truth. Fernando had been right. The count had been nothing but a fraud and a poseur. I had gone to the stake and nearly died ... for nothing.

"Then why did you not tell this to the magistrate?" De Joinville demanded.

"I did," I protested with a sniffle. "But he refused to believe me."

"And you did not share the count's heretical ideas?"

"I did not understand them. But if I did not agree with what he said, he would beat me." I clutched at De Joinville's robes. "Oh, Your Eminence, I was lost, body and soul, before Abbot Francis rescued me from the pyre. Whatever wickedness I have done, I have confessed and have gladly taken my vows as a Benedictine novice. I thank God every day for God's grace in bringing me here."

"But what happened to this count?" De Joinville asked.

"He died in prison, Eminence," I replied. "In Paris. I escaped to Orleans where Montaigne arrested me."

"Thinking, of course, that young Michael here was the count in question." The abbot waved his hand in my direction. "An understandable assumption, perhaps. But a mistaken one, which nearly cost an innocent youth his life."

I caught my breath and stared at the abbot, my eyes wide with astonishment. Could this have been true? Had Montaigne actually thought I was the count? Or was this a clever ploy on the abbot's part, to convince De Joinville, once and for all, that there were no sorcerers at the monastery?

Most importantly, would De Joinville believe it?

"Well!" The archbishop rubbed his chin. "It seems that we might have had a ... a slight misunderstanding here."

Abbot Francis smiled like a cat with a bird in its mouth. "I was sure that Your Eminence would appreciate our position once you were acquainted with the actual facts in the case. It is obvious that the magistrate, in his zeal to uphold the law, simply tried to punish the wrong man."

De Joinville heaved a sigh and rubbed his eyes. "He always was nothing but a damn fool."

"I deeply regret that you had to undertake such an exhausting journey to discover such an obvious mistake."

De Joinville waved the abbot's solicitation away with an impatient wave of his hand. "It was hardly a wasted journey, Abbot Duchienne. I must admit that I was extremely curious about you and this monastery of yours, after hearing all of the stories."

The abbot allowed himself a soft chuckle. "I do hope that we have not disappointed you."

De Joinville gave the abbot a sidelong glance and shook his head. "No, indeed. It has been a most constructive visit. However, I must take my leave in the morning. My servants will see to my carriage."

Abbot Francis nodded in assent as the bell rang for Sext. At a beseeching look from Antonin, he requested that Fernando read from the Book of Hours during dinner. The remainder of the day was once again filled with offices, and after a meager supper, the abbot asked Antonin to ring the bell for Compline early. For once, De Joinville did not seem to mind.

I lingered in the church after the office, watching the others return to the dormitory. Abbot Francis glanced over at me and smiled.

"Well done, Michael. You were most convincing. We

will soon have the cardinal packed off back to Paris with his tassel between his legs." He studied my long face for a moment. "Why, what is the matter?"

"It was all true," I muttered. "That is the matter. Everything you suggested I say to him, it was all true. The count was nothing but a charlatan and all I ever was to him was a servant ... a servant whose job it was to sweep the floor, dust the books and listen to his claims of knowledge and tales of magical prowess."

Abbot Francis smiled gently. "Ah, Michael, why do you think I suggested that you say as much to the cardinal? You would not have been nearly as convincing if you were merely telling a story."

I opened my mouth in astonishment for a moment. "You knew all along that the count was a pompous old fool."

The abbot chuckled. "He certainly was when I met him. There was no reason to think that he would have changed over the years. But, my dear Michael, you certainly would not have allowed me to tell you that when you first came here, would you? Now, go on to bed. We are going to send the cardinal off right after Prime."

"Very well," I said. "Good night."

"Sleep well, my son."

I reached the door, then turned and watched him putter at the altar for a moment.

"Father Francis?" I called softly.

He turned to me, the light from the candles glinting off the silver in his hair. "Yes, Michael?"

"The stories I had heard about you do not do you justice at all." I smiled at his puzzled expression and headed for the dormitory.

—⁓—

De Joinville piled his entourage into the carriage immediately after Prime. He had turned down the offer of breakfast—as if we had anything to feed him even if he had accepted.

"No, thank you. I must be on my way. It has been a most instructive visit." He paused at the doorway and chuckled to himself. "In the future, I will pay more attention to my dreams."

"Dreams, Your Eminence?" the abbot asked innocently.

"Yes," De Joinville replied ruefully. "For the last two nights I have had an angel appear to me, waving a flaming sword in my face. 'Beware!' he shouted, in a voice that seemed to shake the shutters. 'Beware the desecrators and the despoilers. Preserve this holy place.' Such a vivid dream! I would have sworn it was real until I woke up alone in the darkness, with that blasted bell of yours ringing in my ears." He regarded the abbot in silence for a moment with a look that I finally decided was grudging respect. "You know, Abbot Duchienne, Bishop Sorel frequently refers to you as a burr in his backside, a needle in his miter, and a splinter in his crosier."

For a moment, I wanted to laugh. But the abbot clearly did not think the appellation at all amusing. "It was never my intention, Your Eminence, to cause the bishop trouble. But the will of God is not often comfortable or convenient. Is it?"

"No, it's not." De Joinville paused. "Did you also know there are those as far away as Paris who call you a saint?"

"I was ordained to serve God's people," the abbot replied simply. "And that is what I attempt to do. Nothing more."

"Perhaps," De Joinville mused, stroking one of his many chins. "Then again, perhaps not. In any case, I see no reason why we have to bother the Holy Office with this matter. A gadfly, you certainly are. But you do not seem to be either a heretic or a sorcerer. I will advise His Majesty of my conclusions."

"And Giles de Montaigne?"

The cardinal snorted in contempt. "I shall speak to His Majesty regarding him. If we let royal lackeys like that roast every priest that disagrees with them, then we should have none left, should we? God grant you good day, Abbot Duchienne."

The abbot knelt and kissed De Joinville's ring with the most warmth I had seen from him during the entire week. With enthusiastic wishes for a good journey, John and Fernando bustled De Joinville into his carriage.

"There," Fernando said, returning to the doorway where we stood. "He's gone."

Abbot Francis leaned against the wall and closed his eyes. "*Deo gratias.*"

"Amen," I breathed in response.

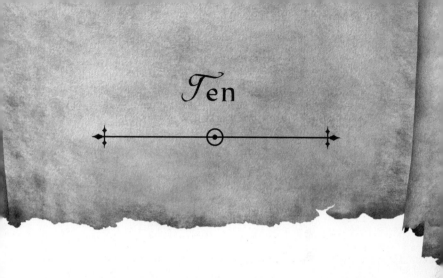

Ten

De Joinville's huge shadow passed like a dark cloud, leaving the days that followed sunny and warm by comparison, even as it neared the end of October. We all returned to our normal round of activity as though the storm had not occurred. I helped Fernando reassemble his alchemical laboratory and we blessed the last of the wine. It was only three casks, and would be the last we would have until next summer.

"That will only make it more precious," Fernando said as we stacked the barrels against the wall. "We will deliver this batch in time for Christmas. Journet will be so grateful he may pay more for it."

"He'll just pass the cost on to the duke," I said, wiping my hands on my habit.

Fernando laughed. "As if he hasn't been doing so already. A man like the duke doesn't value anything he does not have to pay dearly for. Journet is turning into quite the well-to-do merchant. He wanted to open a wine shop a year or two back, but Francis persuaded him to abandon the idea."

"Why?" I asked. "Journet would do very well."

"Too well," Fernando replied. "That would be the problem. By selling the wine by the barrel rather than the goblet, as he does now, he would eventually increase the market for it, possibly as far away as Paris. We cannot supply that much."

"Then he could charge all the more."

"Possibly. However, some enterprising Parisian merchant might decide to cut Journet out of the process entirely and try to buy the wine directly from us."

"Is that even possible?" Somehow, I could not imagine Journet putting up with such a state of affairs.

"Oh, indeed. Francis owns the wine as well as the vineyard which produces it. It is his by right, as abbot of this monastery. From what I understand, the abbots of Sainte Felice used to be liege lords over this entire area, with the villagers as their serfs. When the monastery was abandoned, the villagers learned to fend for themselves. But Francis could, if he chose, exercise his feudal right at any time and sell the wine to whomever he wished."

"Father Francis would never do that," I retorted. "Would he?"

"Francis may not have a choice," Fernando replied. "Especially if the merchant in question was rich enough. Kings require money to rule, and if they cannot squeeze enough of it out of the peasants or townspeople, they borrow it from merchants. Therefore, merchants have far more influence with kings than nearly anyone else … including the Holy Office."

"Are you telling me that the king could offer Father Francis immunity from the Inquisition, if he agrees to sell our wine to some wealthy Parisian merchant and leave Journet and all of Sainte Felice in ruin?" I demanded. "He would never do it. He would go to the stake first."

"Yes," Fernando agreed ruefully. "So, you see what a dreadful tangle this could turn out to be. Prosperity has its price, little brother, doesn't it?"

I nodded solemnly. As Fernando and I tidied up the workshop and made our way across the cloister to the refectory, I made up my mind that I would not have the abbot's job for anything.

I noticed that Abbot Francis was seeing several villagers out the front gate. I thought I recognized the cheesemonger and a woman I gathered was his wife. There was another older man, another older woman, and a younger man. It seemed to be a joyful gathering, with the parties embracing each other and shaking each other's hands. They all knelt in turn to kiss the abbot's hand and then went on their way, their loud voices echoing off the nearby hills.

"I see we've had company," Fernando observed to Juan-José, who was making his way to the kitchen.

"They came to see Francis." Juan-José shrugged. "Something about a marriage arrangement. They want him to perform the nuptial Mass this Sunday."

"They seemed like a jolly group," I said.

"You should have seen them when they arrived," Juan-José said with a snort. "I have attended councils of war that were more civil."

"What seemed to be the problem?" Fernando asked with a smile. "Or did you not see fit to listen in?"

"Of course I listened in. The dispute was about the dowry. The groom is the son of your miserly cheesemonger. He desperately wishes to marry a local peasant girl who, it appears, has only her charms as her portion. The cheesemonger, as you might expect, was hardly satisfied with that and wanted cash. And so it went."

"What happened?" I asked, suddenly interested. Unlike the disputes of kings and cardinals, this one seemed comfortably resolvable.

"Well, the bride's father has a cow that will drop her calf soon. If it is a heifer, it will go to the cheesemonger as part of the dowry. I believe they agreed upon three heifers in all, and part of the milk. Or something to that effect. It was difficult to follow the discussion, with everyone talking on top of each other."

"So, we are to have a wedding," Fernando said. "I hope we aren't expected to provide the feast."

"The cheesemonger will see to that," Juan-José said as we entered the refectory. "Good for business, you know."

We sat down at the table in the refectory and waited for Abbot Francis to say grace. Fortunately, he kept it short, and John and Antonin served the steaming platters.

"So, did you sort the dowry business all out?" Juan-José asked between bites.

"I wish all of the world's problems were resolved so easily." The abbot chuckled. "We are all invited to the wedding feast, by the way, if any of you wish to go. Journet is holding it in his tavern. Should be quite an event."

"It might be useful, to see if we can glean some interesting bits of information," Antonin put in. "There is nothing like a wedding feast to loosen everyone's tongue."

Fernando laughed. "Not everything said at a wedding feast is the truth, my brother."

"Then we will go to the feast," Juan-José said. "If only to satisfy Antonin's insatiable curiosity."

"And your insatiable thirst, Juan-José?" Fernando asked with a mischievous wink.

"Bah! I will wager you a month's kitchen duty, Fernando, that he waters down the wine."

"Done." Fernando reached over and shook Juan-José's hand. "Francis, you are witness to this."

"Never have I seen a more elaborate excuse to attend a feast," the abbot commented with an indulgent smile. "And how about you, John? Will you go as well?"

"I don't see why not," John replied, with a slight shrug.

"And you, Marcel?"

Marcel only scowled in reply.

"Oh, do come, Marcel," Fernando cajoled. "Just this once."

"Francis?" Marcel turned to the abbot with a beseeching look. "Must I?"

"Of course not," the abbot replied. "If you don't wish to. But you might enjoy it."

"Not while I'm constantly guarding my back," Marcel growled.

"Really, Marcel," Antonin said. "We understand your past unpleasant experiences, but don't you think that you are taking this a bit far?"

"No," Marcel shot back. "I don't. This whole nasty business is not over yet. We have only had a lull in the storm. Go to your feast, my brothers, if you want to. But I warn you, don't get too comfortable. The wolves are still on the prowl."

The abbot watched sadly as Marcel stalked out of the refectory and headed back out to the garden.

Heaving a sigh, Fernando rose to his feet. "Well," he said, "no one can say that we didn't try. Come, my brothers, let us clear the table."

Juan-José and John rose also, gathering up plates and platters to take to the kitchen while the abbot returned to his chambers.

I reached over and grabbed Antonin's sleeve. "You have cast the horoscope for the monastery, have you not?"

"To be sure," he replied. "Why do you ask?"

I bit my lip. "I'm worried."

"About what?" He lifted an eyebrow. "Surely you haven't let Marcel frighten you."

"It isn't just Marcel. I have been talking to Fernando

about how the popularity of the wine might also compromise our safety. We might escape the Inquisition, but suffer a far worse fate. Besides," I continued boldly, "you hinted at something that was about to happen to the monastery, remember? You wouldn't tell me because I had not yet taken my vows. Well, now I have, and your fate is now mine."

Antonin drew back in surprise for a moment, then smiled. "I had nearly forgotten how astute you are, Michael. Very well. Come and I will show you."

I followed him up the coiling steps to his tower cell. He reached into one of the piles by the window and extracted a parchment scroll, of which he seemed to have several. Motioning me to sit beside on the bed, he unrolled the scroll onto the floor. It revealed a large square, with a smaller square in the center. The intervening space was marked out into triangles arranged around the smaller square. But inside this geometric figure I recognized the signs of the zodiac, the symbols of the planets, and, in the center of the center square, the date *12 April, Anno Domini 1473*.

"I cast this for the day Francis arrived here in Sainte Felice. You will notice Jupiter in the tenth house sextile Mars in the eighth and trine Mercury in the sixth. Such a well-aspected Jupiter placed in the house of prosperity can keep both king"—he pointed to the Sun in the first house—"and Church"—he pointed to the Moon in the seventh house—"at bay."

"Then, are we in any danger at all?" I asked, "Or is everyone, including me, just skittish?"

"Oh, there is danger," Antonin replied. "But not from

either Church or king. Look." He pointed to Saturn in the twelfth house in direct opposition to Mercury. "This is the house of things kept hidden. Our greatest danger comes from within these walls, rather than from without. In short …" He looked up with a sudden serious expression. "One of us will betray Francis to the Holy Office."

My mouth dropped open. "For God's sake, who?"

"There is no way of knowing that." He looked at me sadly for a moment. "And thank God there is not."

"Have you told this to Father Francis?"

"Indeed, I have."

"And what did he say?"

Antonin's mouth tightened. "He merely waved it away."

"He waved it away?" I echoed. "Why?"

"He reminded me that the stars impel but do not compel. We still have our God-given free will and the ability to change our fate." Antonin sighed. "Which is true enough, I suppose. And if there exists a man who is the master of his fate, then our abbot is that man. Still, that quality which makes Francis what he is might be the very quality which will lead to his downfall. I have warned him. I can do no more. Sometimes, knowing what fate has in store for someone is not a blessing but a curse." He rose to his feet and rolled the parchment back up. "So, there you have it. What will you do now?"

"Do as you have done," I said, lifting my chin in what I hoped was a gesture of bravery. "Keep silent and hope for the best."

He smiled and clapped me on the shoulder. "Good. Now, go and think no more on it, lest it drive you to distraction."

I nodded and turned to leave. As I reached the door, though, I turned around and watched Antonin put the parchment scroll back in its place.

"Antonin?" I asked softly. "How do you do it?"

He turned to me. "Do what, Michael?"

"Keep silent, when you know something terrible is about to happen to someone for whom you care deeply."

"Faith." A look of deep sadness shadowed his dove-gray eyes. "In God's Divine Plan. It is all that I, or anyone else, can do."

Sunday, the day of the wedding, dawned clear and warm. Cowls thrown over our heads, we processed into the church in the now familiar manner and took our place in the choir. The air fairly sparkled with anticipation and festive enjoyment. Everyone in the packed church wore their brightest, gayest attire. Jewels sparkled in the light that poured in through the window. And the people in the front pews, probably family and friends of the bride and groom, whispered and giggled, no doubt about the feast and merrymaking to come, once the necessary but exceedingly dull business of the Mass was over.

"*Kyrie eleison*," we chanted. "Lord have mercy."

Not that it mattered much to the couple who knelt at the railing. The groom was obviously worshipping at a far different altar. The bride, veiled and demure, kept her head down, whether out of maidenly modesty or acute embarrassment I could not tell. Did she love him too? I wondered.

It wasn't until the elevation of the host that she finally looked up and, as she did, my heart sank down to my feet. It was my nymph at the well, who I couldn't help but remember every time I went to the village square. I left off chanting and bit my lip so hard that it bled. It was insane. I had not even met her. She probably didn't even know who I was. She would soon have a prosperous husband who obviously adored her. She would have a good life.

I tried to console myself with that thought. But it helped little. I watched, heartsick, as the abbot blessed the pair. Even though it was near November, the distinct aroma of roses and orange blossoms filled the church. I heaved a sigh. The abbot would probably have cherubs singing in the aisles next.

Finally, the Mass was over and we all trooped out to the steps to congratulate the happy pair. I hung back, in my monk's habit, sadly watching her, in her bridal dress, greet her friends and relations and kiss her new husband. What possibly might have been, I mused, now would never, ever be.

Fernando had harnessed the mule to the cart and driven it down to the front of the church. Antonin, John, and Juan-José climbed into the back and clattered on down the road as the rest of the wedding party walked or rode back to the village. Finally, the bride and groom climbed into another cart amid a flurry of other maidens and youths, and I could see them no longer. Feeling tragic, I turned to return to the cloister.

"Are you not going to the feast, Michael?"

I looked up and found Abbot Francis watching me, his eyebrow raised in that infuriating gesture of his. I had no idea how long he had been observing me, reading my conflicting thoughts in the expression on my face. But I had no doubt that he knew exactly what I had been thinking. He had been too much a man of the world not to, or so I had heard.

"No," I said bluntly. There was no point in giving a reason, and I was far too miserable to invent an excuse. My face flushing, I pushed past him and headed for the gate.

He ambled behind me, easily catching up to me with his long strides. "By the way," he commented nonchalantly, "now that you have joined us, have you given any further thought to becoming my apprentice?"

I halted in my tracks and turned to him. All thoughts of unhappiness and melancholy miraculously vanished. "I ... you mean it?"

"You had requested it, as I recall." He lifted his eyebrow once again, an amused smile playing about his mouth. "Surely you haven't changed your mind."

"No!" I fairly shouted the word, then brought my voice under control with an effort. "That is, no, I haven't changed my mind. I thought ... I mean, I didn't know that you had even considered my request."

"When you first asked me, you had not yet taken your vows. I decided to wait to give you an answer. Now that you have taken those vows, I will give you that answer. Come with me."

"Now?" I asked incredulously.

"Would you rather wait?"

"No! By all means, let us begin at once."

Trembling with excitement, I followed him once again into the abbey library. He went to the shelf in the rear where I had originally found the Grimoire of Light, but he reached not for that manuscript but for another that rested beside it.

"Here." He pulled it from its place on the shelf and handed it to me. "This is your first lesson."

I leafed through the volume for a moment. The florid handwriting was the same. "Is this your work also?"

"Dear me, no," he replied. "Although it is my copy. This, my young apprentice, is the Sworn Book of Pope Honorius the Great, from which all later grimoires, mine included, sprang. It contains the rituals for the conjuration of angels."

"But, my master—that is, the count—claimed that the Sworn Book was only a legend," I protested. "It never really existed."

"Oh, but it does, and there it lies in your hands," Abbot Francis said with a wink. "There are few enough copies, I will grant you, and there are those who will say that it does not exist rather than admit that they are not privileged to have a copy."

I held the book to my breast with great reverence. "And I may read it?"

"You will do more than that." The abbot motioned me to a small alcove, cunningly placed so that the sun shone in through a window, illuminating the alcove without shadows. "You will copy it, as I did when I was not much older than you. Here."

He opened a cabinet by the wall and brought out several sheets of vellum. "I found these amid a pile of rubbish in the workshop when I first arrived here. Most had gone to the rats, but I managed to salvage enough for a book. You will find ink and pens in the cabinet. If you run out, I have a supply."

I swallowed hard, considering the gargantuan task before me. "Could I not just read it?"

The abbot shook his head firmly. "You must copy it in your own hand. That is the only way that you will adequately commit it to memory. Once you can recite the invocations in your sleep, then you will be able to perform them in a magical rite. Not before."

No doubt I still looked dubious, for he smiled and sat himself down on the ledge in the alcove, motioning me to sit beside him. "A grimoire, Michael, is not just a book. It is a companion. By copying it in your own hand, putting your own effort into it, feeling the cramp in your fingers and the ache in your back, you form a sacred pact with the work that you will never forget. Never will anything be more precious to you. Nothing will you prize more highly nor guard more closely. It will become a part of you and will go to the grave with you."

I considered this for a moment. "When I am finished with this one, may I copy the Grimoire of Light?"

"If you wish. But perhaps one day you will write your own invocations and not rely upon mine. Now, to your task." He gave my knee an encouraging pat and rose to his feet. "Keep me informed of your progress, and when you are finished, we will proceed further."

He left me sitting alone in the alcove, still cradling the book in my lap. I had to admit that, despite his explanations, I felt a little irked. I had had enough of books. I wanted to do magical operations, like the one I had observed him do. But there seemed no help for it.

Heaving a sigh, I pulled the tiny table into the alcove—there seemed to be no copy desk—and sat down before it, my back to the window. It was an annoyingly awkward arrangement, since there was no room on the table for both the book and the vellum. But I soon discovered that if I opened the book on the seat beside me, I could glance down from time to time while holding the vellum on the table.

When I was as comfortable as was possible, I opened the bottle of ink, took the pen in hand, and began to write. At first I tried to keep my penmanship graceful and even. Soon, however, I found myself less concerned with how the script looked and more intent on getting the words down upon the vellum as quickly as possible.

Within the pages of the Sworn Book, I found everything I had ever wanted to know about angels—who they were, what they would do, and how they were called.

Angels ruled every day of the week, every month of the year, every cardinal direction, every element, and every planet.

The Sun's angels, I noted, would give love, favor, riches, and good health. Painstakingly, I drew the sigils upon my vellum. I found Mercury's angels even more interesting. They knew the past, present, and future, and would tell you all the secrets of the spirits and of men. Anything that I might desire in this world or the next I could ask of some angel or other. I found myself writing faster and faster.

I lifted my head as I heard the sounds of the mule cart clattering up the road. So engrossed had I been in my work that I had not noticed that the light had faded from the window. The other brothers must be returning from the wedding feast.

With an effort, I tried to remember the events of the morning—the nuptial Mass, the bride, my chagrin. There was no trace of grief remaining within my heart. Indeed, it was difficult to remember what it had felt like. It was as though the whole thing had occurred years ago rather than just that morning. Had it really only been a few short hours since I had begun my task? It seemed that I had been writing for an eternity.

I tried to set the pen down and suddenly whimpered. I could barely move the fingers of the hand which had been curled around the pen. Using my other hand, I pried the pen loose and massaged my aching joints. I ran from the library to the parlor just as Fernando, John, Antonin, and Juan-José jumped down from the mule cart.

Abbot Francis met them at the door and crossed his arms in mock disapproval. "The revelers have finally decided to return, have they? So, tell me. Who won the wager? Who do I pester to get supper together?"

"Neither of us won," Fernando replied with a grin.

"Neither of you?" the abbot echoed. "Why ever not?"

"He served ale, the wretch," Juan-José replied.

Abbot Francis laughed in delight. "That will teach you to try to outsmart a tavern keeper. A man like that has more savvy than all the scholars in Paris."

Fernando and John quickly served bread and cheese while Juan-José poured the wine.

"Well, he certainly had that cardinal pegged," Antonin said as he reached for the cheese platter.

"How so?" the abbot asked.

"After De Joinville left our door, I wondered what would happen if he stopped in at Journet's tavern for a goblet of wine to smooth the road and actually tasted Fernando's blessed brew," Antonin explained.

"I wondered that too," I said. "He really would have been suspicious then."

"We need not have worried," Fernando put in with a chuckle. "Apparently, the villagers were so outraged at his arrogance at Mass that the children pelted his carriage with rotten fruit as soon as he pulled into the village. He did not even dare to open the door, much less go into the tavern. Instead, he ordered his driver to continue on to Paris."

Even Marcel, dour as he was, grinned at that.

"You must admit that there is an element of Divine

Justice in that," Antonin continued. "The Archbishop of Paris, a man presumably with an army at his command, run out of a tiny village by a brigade of street urchins armed with overripe tomatoes."

"Let's hope that he doesn't take his vengeance on some other hapless village along the way," Marcel said.

"Oh, I doubt it," Antonin said. "Most likely he'll take himself back to his palace and his mistresses and have done with tiny villages for a while."

It was my turn to clear the table, and I did so with some effort. Just grasping the stack of plates was excruciatingly painful. I dropped them onto the table in the kitchen as soon as I could and held my throbbing fingers in my left hand with my teeth clenched.

Antonin came into the kitchen behind me. "What is the matter with your hand, Michael?"

"My fingers ache," I replied with a grimace. "I've been copying a manuscript all afternoon."

"Have you, now?" Antonin reached over and took my right hand in both of his. "What manuscript might that be?" I gasped as he began to massage my fingers, expertly working out the stiffness in my knuckles with every stroke. After the first sharp pain, I felt such great relief that I never wanted him to stop.

"The grimoire," I replied. "That is, the one Father Francis uses for his conjurations. I am supposed to memorize it, if I am ever to try to do one myself."

"Wise advice." Antonin continued to work on my fingers, pulling each one until the joint cracked. I thought it would hurt, but it did not. "You must have the reference memorized before you try an operation. It would be like trying to trephine someone's skull and consult Galen at the same time."

"I suppose," I said petulantly. "However, I have not yet copied even as far as the prayers, and my fingers feel as though they are locked in place."

"You can massage them yourself with your other hand. Start at the base of the finger and work towards the tip." He showed me as he talked. "Do that several times. Also, bathe your hand in warm salt water. That will help, too. And for heaven's sake, don't try to copy the entire book in one sitting."

"Thank you," I said as he released my hand. "I'll try to be careful. But I am in a hurry to finish it. He won't let me try my first invocation until I do."

"So he has taken you on as an apprentice, has he?"

"Yes," I replied, unable to mask the pride in my voice.

"I thought he might," Antonin said. "Sooner or later. Just don't learn any of his bad habits, now." He winked at me as I turned to go back to the library.

It took a week of nearly constant work to copy the book. I tried to follow Antonin's advice and massage my fingers, but after a few days even that did not help. They felt fine while I was massaging, but after I took up the pen, the ache returned. And my back! I could not believe how terribly my back would hurt after being hunched motionless over a desk for hours at a time. But it did, much to my dismay. I would wake in the morning nearly unable to move and wanting nothing more than to be able to remain in bed.

That is, until I remembered what work I was doing. The book drove me onward—every prayer, every list of angels and their attributes, every conjuration I copied made me all the more anxious to begin to do the actual rituals. I heard the words of each invocation ringing in my head even as I scrawled them.

Finally, a day came when I could bear it no more. It was a Thursday, and the weather was dismal. It had rained on and off for much of that afternoon, but the sky was so gloomy that I had no light to copy by even in my usually sunny alcove. I took a candelabra from the church and lit every candle of it, but it still remained too dark to see properly. It was not long before my eyes began to ache as well as my back. Finally, I took the unfinished manuscript in my arms and trotted up the stairs to the abbot's chambers.

I found him standing by the small hearth, consulting a volume that he had taken from a shelf on the wall.

"Father Francis?" I called softly. "I'm sorry to disturb you, but…"

"But what?" he inquired, with an indulgent smile.

"I have a magical working that I wish to do."

"Have you finished copying your grimoire?"

"Nearly," I said, rubbing my aching hands. "But, Father Francis, must I finish copying it completely before I can do a magical operation?"

He considered this for a moment, rubbing his chin. "That depends. What operation did you have in mind?"

"I wish to do an elemental invocation."

"Very well," he said. "Which element?"

"Air."

"For what purpose?"

"Knowledge," I stated.

The abbot chuckled softly. "You would do better to summon earth for patience. However, as you wish. Air it is. Which is the angel that rules the element of air?"

"Cerub."

"And the day of the week?"

"Wednesday."

"And the suffugations?"

"Balsam, camphor, and olium olmarum."

"Very good, Michael." Abbot Francis nodded in approval. "You have indeed been studying diligently. Now, can you recite the prayer?"

Taking a deep breath, I pictured the page of the volume in my mind, remembering the words that I had so painstakingly written. I recited it up to, and including, the sign of the cross.

"Excellent! And the conjuration?"

I searched my memory and began. But halfway through it I faltered on the many holy names of God, which had seemed so incomprehensible to me when I wrote them that now I could not remember. I grew nervous, fearing that Abbot Francis would not permit me to do the operation.

But he only smiled. "The Hebrew names do take a bit

of effort to memorize, I will grant you," he said. "So, for your first attempt, I shall stand by with the grimoire in case your memory fails you. However, do your best to do it without aid, and try not to depend upon my prompting. Agreed?"

I nodded, nearly beside myself with excitement.

"Now," he continued, "you will do as I instruct. Take no food after dinner and spend the evening alone in church, contemplating the magnitude of what you are about to do. Beseech God to bless you. At midnight, you will meet me in the kitchen and we will descend into the Tabernacle. And there will be no words between us until we begin. Understood?"

Again, I nodded.

He rose and indicated that I, too, should do the same. "Until then," he said, "kindly stay out of trouble." He shooed me out of his chambers.

Finally, the hours passed and I followed the abbot down the stone steps to the Tabernacle, clutching my grimoire in my trembling hands. It was a moment that I had been waiting for ever since I could remember—the moment of my first magical operation. Not merely hearing it described, not merely reading about it, and not even assisting someone else. This operation was mine. I had every reason to be exhilarated. But I was terrified instead.

It was true that Abbot Francis stood beside me to coach me. And yet I could not help but think that his presence served to make me all the more nervous. There was no man in this world whose approval I desired more, and there was not a demon that dwelt in the infernal regions that frightened me as much as the possibility of failing this, my first operation as his apprentice.

I took several deep breaths and put such thoughts from me. I laid my book upon the altar and lit the candles. The first thing to do was invoke the aid of the holy archangels. Since I had no sword, I pulled my dagger from my belt and approached the east.

"I summon, stir, and call thee forth, O Mighty Archangel Raphael, guardian of the eastern quadrant of the magic circle ..."

I lit the torch and heaved a sigh. This was easy. Flushed with confidence, I approached the south.

"I summon, stir, and call thee form, O Mighty Archangel Michael, guardian of the southern quadrant of the magic circle ..." Finally feeling like a real magus, I lit the torch in the south with a flourish and went on to the west.

"I summon, stir, and call thee forth, O Mighty Archangel Uriel ..."

"Gabriel," the abbot said softly.

I turned to him with a frown, annoyed at the interruption. "What?" I demanded.

"Gabriel," he repeated, "The guardian of the west is Gabriel, not Uriel."

"Oh," I said sheepishly, my confidence draining away. "Of course."

I hesitated for a moment. Had I blundered the ritual already? Was there any hope of recovering it?

"Continue," he prompted.

Taking another deep breath, I began again. "I summon, stir, and call thee forth, O Mighty Archangel Gabriel …"

Feeling considerably less like a mighty magus, I lit the torch in the west and moved to the north. I swore that I would get it right this time.

"I summon, stir, and call thee forth, O Mighty Archangel Uriel …" I lit the final torch.

Finally, I laid my dagger upon the altar. I bent down to kiss it as I had seen the abbot do, then knelt in the center of the magic circle to pray.

Never could I remember ever uttering a more fervent prayer. The words that I had painstakingly committed to memory flowed forth easily. I beseeched Almighty God, Christ, and the Blessed Virgin to aid me in my operation, vowing piety, chastity, and reverence for all my days to come.

Suddenly, I knew why a magician begs the Almighty to aid in his operation. So many things can go wrong, and human memory fails at the most inopportune time. I breathed a silent prayer to the holy archangels. I hoped with all my heart that they would be patient with me.

I got to my feet and glanced over at the abbot. He nodded briefly. Heartened, I turned back to the altar and scooped a mound of incense on the glowing coals—too much incense, I discovered too late. The cloud of acrid smoke that billowed up from the thurible filled my throat and set me to coughing. I stood back for a moment, then cleared my throat, took up my dagger, pressed it briefly to my lips, and began.

"Powerful angel, Cerub, come. You are summoned by the sacred rites of magic..."

I hardly knew what to expect, but in my heart of hearts I had hoped for something—anything—to let me know that my summons had been answered. But all I saw was the column of smoke from the thurible shrivel and disappear, leaving only silence.

I glanced over at the abbot once again, but all he would do was raise an inquiring eyebrow at me. Frowning slightly, I turned and put another scoop of incense into the thurible. My second conjuration was worded far more strongly, and I pronounced it with as much of a commanding voice as I could.

"I call, beseech, and require of you, powerful angel, Cerub, to be obedient unto the seal of God."

The incense died away again.

Setting my jaw with grim determination, I tried a third and final time. "Quit your obstinacy, Cerub. I urge you not to impede this work, nay, I urge and request you rather to come peacefully before this circle..."

Silence and the sputtering of the candles was all that greeted my thundering conjuration.

Finally, I could stand the humiliation no longer. "It's hopeless!" I cried, hurling my dagger back onto the altar. "Nothing has answered me and nothing will answer me."

"Now, Michael." The abbot reached out to pat me on the shoulder. "You must have patience. Calm yourself and try once more."

But I was beyond placating. "I could stand here and

invoke all night and nothing will ever answer me. I should have known better than to even imagine that I could ever be a magus." I turned towards the door.

"Michael!" Abbot Francis called after me. "Do not break the circle. You must banish what you have summoned."

I ignored him as the hot tears of disappointment and frustration threatened to roll down my cheeks. Pushing past him, I stormed out of the circle, up the stairs, and through the kitchen. The cold night air slapped me in the face as I ran down the corridor towards my cell.

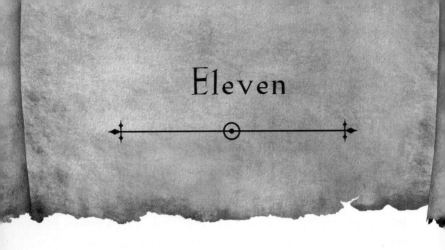

Eleven

The next morning, I made my way down the corridor to the refectory with considerable trepidation. Throughout most of the night I had fretted, wondering if I would merit the abbot's anger or disappointment at my failure. I was not sure which would be worse, but I braced myself for whichever it would be.

To my astonishment, Abbot Francis said nothing whatever about it. He greeted me warmly, then sat down at the table while John served up bread and wine.

"Fernando, have we the casks ready for Journet?" he asked, as though absolutely nothing unusual had happened. "It seems to me that he was inquiring about them after the wedding last week."

"I have three for him," Fernando replied, talking around the piece of bread in his hand. "I was hoping to wait until after Christmas to deliver them. It will be a long time until summer."

"Yes," the abbot agreed with a sigh. "Still, you had probably best deliver them, or else he will continue to pester me about it."

"As you wish. We can deliver them either today or tomorrow." Fernando rose from the table and headed towards the kitchen. I rose as well, since it was my duty to clear the table that week. I was secretly grateful that I had something to busy myself with; I didn't want the rest of the brothers to suspect that something was amiss.

As I leaned over the refractory table, I noticed to my astonishment a little whirlwind of dust swirling around and around. I had seen such a thing many times in a courtyard, when a breeze would blow the leaves about. But this was happening in the center of the refectory floor.

Antonin suddenly shivered and rubbed his arms. "Odd," he mused with a frown. "I don't remember this room being quite this drafty before."

We all glanced up at the distinct sound of hoofbeats and carriage wheels coming up the road towards the monastery.

Juan-José frowned. "We aren't expecting visitors, are we, Francis?"

"Not that I am aware of," he replied, looking as puzzled as the rest of us.

"Maybe it is Journet coming for his wine," I suggested.

Antonin went to the door and craned his neck to see

past the gate. "Not unless the tavern business has become far more profitable than it was a week ago. What we have here is a handsome carriage with a team of matching roans."

Fernando joined him in the doorway and whistled. "My God, it is the duke. I'd know that carriage anywhere. He visits Journet at least once a week." He turned to the abbot. "He probably wants a cask of wine."

"I'll wager he wants more than that," Juan-José put in.

Marcel frowned. "What if he wants to look around?"

"He will not be permitted to," Abbot Francis replied sternly, rising from his chair. "I will receive His Grace in the parlor while the rest of you lay low. John, go and draw one of those earthenware jugs full of wine and keep it in the kitchen until I call for it."

We scattered like chickens as the carriage pulled up at the gate.

"Michael," the abbot called to me, "would you be so good as to conduct our guests to the parlor? See to their refreshment, but don't be too liberal."

I nodded briefly and reached the gate just as the carriage door opened.

"Good day, Your Grace, mesdames." I greeted them with my best manners. "Welcome to the Monastery of Sainte Felice. Abbot Francis awaits you in the parlor, if you would be pleased to follow me."

The duke descended from the carriage and stood aside as the groom helped the duchess and the dowager duchess down from the step. Both were cloaked against the mist which lingered from the previous night.

"How did you know we were coming?" the duke inquired brusquely.

"We saw your carriage coming up the road."

"I told you that we would not take them unawares," the dowager duchess scolded, gripping the duke's arm. "That tavern keeper warned us that the blessed angels themselves guard the abbey. You will not get away with this, I warn you."

"Mother!" The duke frowned and pulled his arm out of her grasp.

"This way, if you please." I led the way through the gate, skirted the cloister garth, and directed them into the parlor. I noticed the duke hanging back a bit, straining to catch a glimpse of whatever lay beyond the gate. But he could see little of the cloister past the wall of the church, and soon he left off and pushed past me into the parlor.

Abbot Francis stood waiting for them. As they entered, the young duchess knelt and kissed his hand, not once but several times. Her mother-in-law did the same. The duke himself hesitated, with a slight frown. But under the accusing glare of both women, he too knelt and brushed his lips against the abbot's fingers.

Abbot Francis, smiling beatifically, blessed them with the sign of the cross and motioned them to chairs. "To what do we owe the honor of this rather sudden visit?"

"Do forgive us, Blessed Father," the young duchess

replied in a breathless voice. "Our visit is but a mere whim. We were in the tavern in the village and we…"

"We come there every week," the dowager duchess finished, her strong features and robust figure contrasting sharply with the frailty of her daughter-in-law. She did not appear to be a woman I would care to cross. "I must have a goblet of that blessed wine of yours every evening or else my knees ache so terribly I can barely move. It is the only remedy that works, you see. Those miserable doctors in Paris could do nothing for me." She scowled darkly. "With their leeches and their…"

The duke leaned forward in a pointed gesture. "My Lord Abbot, as you see, both my wife and my mother are devoted to your extraordinary wine. They wished to see your abbey so that they might satisfy themselves that it was, indeed, made here on earth and not in heaven."

"To be sure, it is," Abbot Francis said with an indulgent chuckle. "You can see the vines on the hillside behind the cloister wall. The wine is made by a very ordinary process, I assure you."

I quickly ducked into the kitchen and grabbed the pitcher and four goblets that John had ready. I noticed that the goblets were small ones.

"You must be weary after your journey," the abbot was saying as I brought the wine into the parlor. "Please accept our humble hospitality and slake your thirst."

I poured the wine and handed it round. The women took their goblets in both hands, as though they were communion chalices, and slowly sipped the contents, smiling with utter bliss.

The duke, obviously not as enraptured as his womenfolk, took a long swallow. "I will come to the point, my Lord Abbot." He studied the abbot over the goblet's rim. "I wish to buy a cask of this wine."

The abbot's smile grew chilly. "I fear that would be quite impossible."

"And why is that?"

"We sell all of our wine in the village," the abbot replied. "Our vines are not so extensive that we can produce more than a few casks in a season. There is enough to provide an adequate supply to Monsieur Journet, but, save for that which we use ourselves, there is really none to spare. I'm sure that Monsieur Journet would sell you a cask if you inquired."

"I do not wish to buy it from him," the duke returned sullenly.

"I certainly hope you were not expecting me to sell it to you for less?" The abbot, his voice still silky soft, fixed the duke with a gaze so stern it made the duke fidget. "Our wine is the main source of income for the village of Sainte Felice. It keeps the people prosperous, and encourages them to give back of their abundance to both Church and king in the form of tithes and taxes. Were I to sell the wine to you, even at his cost, I would be depriving him of his profit—profit that, in turn, he spends to support the other merchants in the village."

"Abbot Duchienne." The duke leaned forward intently.

"I am prepared to offer you twice as much as Journet pays you for a cask of your wine, provided that it comes directly from this abbey and not from some tavern. There are merchants in Orleans who will pay three times as much. I need only inform them that the wine is available, and they will vie with each other for the privilege of being the sole vendor for your blessed vintage. "

"Your Grace." The abbot's tone hardened. "This monastery is in the business of saving souls, not selling wine."

"But think of the income for the abbey," the duke persisted. "You could build a great cathedral."

"A house of worship is more than a building," the abbot declared. "It is built of Christian faith, hope, and charity."

"You cannot eat faith," the duke retorted. "And charity will not keep the rain out."

"That is certainly true, and the modest income from our wine does serve to keep the wolf from the door. However, we require nothing more than that. Our purpose here is to serve God and minister to the needs of His people. Were we to allow wine-making to become our first priority, rather than our works of charity, then the wine that you consider blessed would be blessed no more. We should become nothing more than a winery with stained glass windows." He rose to his feet, clearly indicating that the discussion was at an end.

"I urge you to reconsider," the duke persisted.

"I'm sorry, but the answer is still no." Abbot Francis merely smiled. "Still, you have come far, and I do not wish to send you away empty-handed." He turned to me. "Brother Michael, be so good as to put some of our wine in one of those jugs for His Grace."

I nodded and went back into the kitchen. John had the jug already filled and was standing on tiptoe ramming the cork into the top.

"There," he said softly. "Give the Devil his due."

I couldn't help smiling. "Aren't you being a bit hard on His Grace?"

"Am I?" he replied with a disapproving frown. "Consider what he just tried to persuade Francis to do. 'Thou shalt not tempt the Lord thy God.'" Handing me the jug, he waved me out the door.

The duke glanced up in surprise when I entered the parlor with the crock in my arms. "I thought that you refused to sell me any wine."

"And I have," the abbot replied. "This is my gift to your good mother. May her pains be eased by the love of Christ. Madame, there will always be wine in this monastery for you."

I handed the crock to the older woman who clutched it to her breast and gave the abbot a look of utmost gratitude. The younger woman crossed herself as the duke regarded the abbot with an odd mixture of distrust and awe.

"And now, if you will accompany me to the church, we shall pray for your safe return to Orleans."

"We should like to see where the wine is actually made," the duke said again. "I have wanted to inspect your process for quite some time."

The abbot looked at him with a pained expression. "I am afraid that would be quite impossible."

"And why is that?" the duke asked sharply, clearly annoyed at being refused yet another demand.

"Entrance to the cloister is forbidden to anyone not of our order," the abbot explained in a reasonable tone. "And since our workshop is located in the cloister, I cannot take you there. Please try to understand. And now, Brother Michael, please assemble the other brothers for Holy Office."

I nodded silently and ran down the corridor to the kitchen.

"What does he want us all in church for?" Marcel demanded as I returned with the abbot's latest request.

"So that we look pious and devout," Fernando replied.

"Well, someone is going to have to keep an eye on that blasted duke," Juan-José commented.

"It might take all of us to do that," Antonin said with a worried look. "His Grace seems determined to investigate."

"And what will we do if he does?" Marcel persisted. "Say 'very sorry, Your Grace, but you aren't supposed to go in there?'"

"That is precisely what we will do," Fernando stated flatly. "And if he doesn't like it, he can take the matter up with the bishop."

Marcel snorted. "Well, I'm comforted."

"Come, my brothers," John insisted, trying to herd us

out the door into the cloister. "We can argue about it later. Now, we must do what Francis bids. Hurry!"

Cowls thrown over our heads, we processed into the church through the south transept. Juan-José, in his strong baritone, led us in one of the chanted prayers that we had lately performed for De Joinville. It was, I noticed, a prayer for the office of Compline and not for Sext, but I doubted that the duke would know the difference.

We filed into the choir stalls as Abbot Francis led the duke and the two women in through the front door. The duke followed his mother into the pew and edged down towards the end so that, or so it seemed to me, he could slip out during the office.

Instead of following her husband into the pew, the duchess caught at the abbot's sleeve and gazed into his face with a beseeching look. "Please, Blessed Father," she whispered. "Would you hear my confession? It would give me such great comfort."

"Of course, my daughter," Abbot Francis replied, not looking at all sure that he relished being closeted with a woman who so obviously worshipped him. "Come with me."

"So much for getting them out of here by dinnertime," Marcel muttered as we watched the duchess follow the abbot into the confessional like a devoted spaniel.

"Let us hope that she has not sinned too much," Fernando said. "Or too often."

"She might even make up a few sins," Antonin said

with a shrug. "Just to keep him in the confessional with her a bit longer."

I turned to him, aghast. "But surely she doesn't expect him to return her affection, does she?"

"Of course not. That would quite ruin the appeal. Forbidden fruit and all of that. But it doesn't prevent her from adoring him from afar. No wonder it takes the woman so long to be shriven. With every sin she confesses, she commits two more." Antonin leaned back in the pew with a sigh. "We could be here until Vespers."

I jumped as Juan-José suddenly dug his elbow into my ribs. "Watch the duke," he whispered.

Sure enough, the duke had risen to his feet and was inching his way along the side aisle towards the door leading into the cloister garth.

"Shall I follow him?" I whispered.

"Yes," he replied. "And I shall follow you."

I slipped out of the choir stall with Juan-José behind me and left the south transept just as the duke found his way into the cloister. Juan-José and I crouched behind one of the columns as we watched him look around for a moment, as if trying to decide in which direction to investigate. I heard an audible grunt of satisfaction as he caught sight of the wine press next to Fernando's workshop and took off at a trot across the cloister garth.

"Damn it!" Juan-José hissed. "He's heading for the workshop."

I gasped, knowing full well what sight would meet his gaze as soon as he peeked in through the open door.

Not knowing what else to do, I shut my eyes and crossed myself. "Oh, blessed angels," I breathed, in a silent but heartfelt prayer. "Stop him. Please."

My eyes flew open at a sharp exclamation from Juan-José. A sudden wind had blown up, shrieking through the trees, echoing off the far hills, and stirring up a cloud of dust and leaves that grew larger by the second. A wispy but definite angelic form appeared within the cloud, its wings undulating as leaves do in a brisk breeze. The angel held before him a wand that looked for all the world like a quarter staff, with which he blocked the duke's path.

I stared. "Cerub?"

The duke let out a yell and fell back, blown off his feet by the cross breeze, and landed heavily on the ground. He tried to scramble back up but was knocked down again, as the breeze strengthened into a gale that whipped the cloud of leaves and dust into a whirlwind. The duke yelled again, and kept yelling as he desperately clutched at the trunk of a tree to keep from becoming sucked into the swirling air.

"For the love of God, what is going on?" the abbot's voice bellowed behind me. I turned and found the rest of the brothers, along with the duchess and her mother-in-law, gathered beneath the arches of the corridor.

The duke suddenly lost his grip and rose into the air with a howl. He whirled around and around several times, often rising to the level of the workshop roof. The duchess shrieked and clutched at the abbot's arm for support. But the abbot shoved her unceremoniously into her mother-in-law's arms and ran out into the cloister.

Shouting something above the whine of the gale, he reached up and grabbed ahold of the duke's hand. The wind died down almost immediately and the duke tumbled down into the abbot's arms, sprawling in an extremely undignified posture on the grass. The two women rushed to his side, but he rose to his feet abruptly and pushed them aside.

"You were forbidden from entering the cloister," Abbot Francis scolded, pushing his rumpled hair out of his eyes. "Why did you disobey?"

"I wanted to see how that marvelous wine of yours is made." Summoning what was left of his dignity, the duke scrambled to his feet and brushed himself off. "I had no idea that the wind would be this strong."

His disgruntled gaze met the abbot's implacable one. Then, like a small boy who has just been rescued from a tree that he was forbidden to climb, he lowered his gaze to the ground and knelt at the abbot's feet. "Forgive me."

The dowager duchess strode forward. "What did I tell you?" She grabbed her son's arm and shook it as though he were a small child. "This monastery is guarded by angels."

The duke pulled his arm out of her grasp. "Be that as it may." He straightened the hem of his velvet doublet. "I think that it is high time that we leave these good brothers in peace."

The women gathered up their cloaks and the valued crock of blessed wine. I followed the abbot as he escorted them to the gate and watched in relief as all three piled into the carriage. The duke sat back in the plush seat with a sigh. But the young duchess reached out of the window, grasping the abbot's hand and seeming most unwilling to let it loose. "Might we come again, Blessed Father?"

"Any time you wish, madam." Abbot Francis reached out and gently pried her fingers loose. "May God grant you a safe journey."

We stood at the gate, watching the carriage recede down the hill until it was out of sight. Then we joined the others in the refectory for dinner. I glanced over at the abbot several times during the course of the meal, wondering if he would bring up the strange events of the morning. But he seemed to have no intention even mentioning them.

Why not?

I busied myself with helping John in the kitchen until supper, but it was difficult to keep my mind from thrashing itself to pieces in confusion. I had no doubt that I had succeeded in summoning Cerub; he had manifested his presence in an undeniable way. And I had totally underestimated his angelic power.

I glanced up from the vegetables I was peeling and found John watching something in the corner. I didn't see anything, but it was obvious that John did, and his frown told me that he wasn't too pleased with whatever it was. He finally turned away to stoke the fire in the chamber under the clay oven, then glanced over his shoulder at the corner again and shook his head in annoyance.

I felt the hairs on the back of my neck prickle in alarm. Cerub was still there. I didn't have to see him to sense his strong presence. He was waiting for me, shadowing my every move. I had to do something. But what?

When the sun set, Fernando blew up the fire in the hearth while John went about the room lighting the candles with a long taper. It was late in the year, and the nights were growing long.

"It looks as though that wind has blown up again," Juan Jose observed. We listened for a moment. It rattled the shutters, crying and mewing like so many stray kittens.

We all started. With a horrific crash, every window and door in the monastery slammed open and a rush of wind blew through the parlor, snuffing out every candle in the room and spreading the sparks from the fire like tiny fireflies all about the room. Finally, it blew out, leaving the room in blackness.

"Francis!" I heard Juan-José bellow. "What in God's name is going on?"

John emerged from the kitchen with a small lantern. The breeze still blew about the room, and the tiny flame of the lantern quivered behind the glass panes as John held the light aloft. Quickly we all set to closing the shutters and doors and relighting the candles. But a gust of wind would playfully blow some of them out, while leaving others burning.

I glanced over at the abbot and found him fixing me with a stern gaze, his arms folded across his chest. I gulped as the realization of what was happening began to dawn upon me. But there was no time to ponder what to do about it.

A thick book rose off the table and sailed across the room, narrowly missing Marcel. With a yell, Marcel dove under the table as the book hit the far wall and fell with a thump on the floor, its pages turning as if by some invisible hand. An earthenware pitcher flung itself off the mantle and landed at Fernando's feet, exploding in shards of crockery. The rest of the brothers scattered and ran for cover as the air was filled with flying objects.

Fernando, crouching in the doorway, glared up at the abbot in fury. "Francis," he said though clenched teeth, "I don't know what you and Michael are up to, but you must *do* something. Now!

"Well, Michael," Abbot Francis said, oddly calm amidst the chaos. "Are you ready to dismiss that which you have summoned?"

I stared down at my feet, my face burning with humiliation. I didn't know how I was going to dismiss the angel, and wasn't sure I even could. "I would rather you dismiss it."

But the abbot shook his head. "No, my son. You called it, you dismiss it. Learn to rectify your own mistakes. One day there will be no one there to do it for you. Now, come." Taking me firmly by the arm, he propelled me into the kitchen and threw the lever to open the trap door.

Meekly, I followed him down the steps into the Tabernacle. He quickly lit the torches and the altar candles, then ushered me into the center of the circle. "Now, finish your ritual as though there had been no interruption."

I swallowed hard and nodded. Stirring up the coals in the brazier, I scooped a little of the incense into the bowl, managing to coax a small wisp of smoke out of it. It wasn't much, but I desperately hoped it would be enough.

"Blessed angel Cerub," I asked, "in the name of Almighty God, give to me a sign, that I may know of your presence."

Suddenly, the candles on the altar flickered. I rubbed my eyes and stared. They flickered again, then burned steady. I felt the hairs rise on the back of my neck, as though my spine were a hazel wand quivering over the site of an underground stream. My pulse began to pound and I fought panic with every measure of will power that I possessed.

"Michael?"

The abbot's voice, although barely audible, served to shore me up enough to take my dagger from the altar and raise it in salute.

"Because thou hast diligently answered my request, I do hereby license thee to depart. And may the peace of Almighty God ever remain between me and thee. Depart, depart, depart, I say, and begone!"

I picked up the candle snuffer and put out the candles while the abbot laid a brass plate over the bowl of the brazier.

"Is that it?" I asked hopefully.

But he shook his head. "Not quite." He waved his hand at the torches on the wall.

"Oh," I said sheepishly. "Of course."

Positioning myself at the east, I raised my dagger again. "I dismiss you, spirits of air, to your own realms. In the name of Almighty God, I bid you hail and farewell." I went to the south and repeated my dismissal, then to the west and finally to the north.

Then, and only then, did the abbot nod for me to quit the chamber and make my way back up the steps. I watched him slide the slab back into place and seal it. I stood in the kitchen for a moment, wanting desperately to say something but hardly knowing what.

"Father Francis," I finally said. "I'm sorry."

"I should hope so." He turned to me with a half smile that made me wonder if he was more amused than angry at my bungled ritual. "Still, have you learned a lesson from all this?"

"God, yes!"

"Then tell me what you have learned."

"Well," I said, "I have learned that the elemental forces are real indeed."

"And?"

"That they are not to be toyed with."

"Splendid. Anything else?"

I heaved a sigh. "And that I need to learn to be more patient."

"And will you finish copying your grimoire?" He lifted an eyebrow.

I nodded.

"Now, I do not want to hear anything more about doing magic until you have finished your work. Agreed?"

I nodded again, but my reply was cut off by John bustling into the kitchen with another bowl of flour. He regarded us with an exasperated look. "If you two are quite done with your conjuring, I have supper to prepare."

"Come, Michael," the abbot said with a smile. "We mustn't anger the cook."

—⁂—

Although it was nearly a week before Marcel stopped eyeing the crockery with suspicion, all seemed to be quiet and peaceful with no sign of the angel's unexpected return. The November air brought a chill with it, and the vines dropped their leaves and stood bare and skeletal against the hillside. Fernando and I delivered the last of the wine to Journet, much to the tavern keeper's delight. I held my breath while he chatted with Fernando about the duke and duchess' continued interest in the wine, but to my intense relief, Fernando made no mention of the duke's adventures in the cloister.

Still, I decided that I wasn't going to bungle any more rituals ever again. I had taken vows in order to learn magic, and I had better do it right.

It was early December before I finally finished copying the grimoire. That evening after supper, while the others were busy with their respective studies, I clutched the precious stack of parchment to my breast and ran up to my cell. I was determined that the next time I tried a conjuration, I would know the prayers by heart and wouldn't need prompting.

I arranged the pages on my nightstand, lit a candle to

illuminate them, and stood in the center of my cell. Raising my arms in front of me, I solemnly intoned, "O Lord God, from whom nothing is hidden, to whom nothing is impossible, thou knowest that I perform these ceremonies not to tempt thy power, but that I may penetrate into the knowledge of hidden things. I pray thee by thy mercy to cause and permit, that I may arrive at this understanding of secret things ..."

I broke off, as the distinct sound of hoofbeats echoed off the hills and into my open window. The prayer fled from my mind as I ran to the window and stared out in horror.

Soldiers, twelve of them at least, thundered up the road towards the monastery.

I ran down the stairs and joined the other monks in the parlor. Juan-José had his head out the door, watching the front gate. The hoofbeats grew louder, then stopped.

"God in heaven," Fernando grumbled. "Now what?"

"I thought I heard horses." Abbot Francis finally strode into the parlor. "Who is it this time, Juan-José?

"Soldiers," Juan-José said over his shoulder. "Swarming at our front gate."

"What do they want?" I asked in trepidation, hoping it wasn't me.

"I have no idea," Juan-José replied. "But it looks like they are heading towards the church."

The abbot frowned in puzzlement. "The church?"

Over the noise of the horses, we heard a thin wail echo off the mountains. I could not make out the words, but

Antonin turned to the abbot in alarm. "Someone is crying out for you, Francis."

The abbot ran for the door and raced down the corridor to the church, with us at his heels. He ducked in through the transept door and found a small boy, no more than seven, huddled in the pew crying and shaking. The child caught sight of the abbot and flung himself in the abbot's arms just as the door burst open.

A dozen soldiers, their swords flashing in the candlelight, stormed inside the nave of the church. With them, his thin face drawn and pitiless, strode Giles de Montaigne.

"How dare you enter the house of God with naked steel," the abbot said sternly. "Sheath your swords at once!" Clearly nervous, the soldiers glanced at each other. The abbot glared at them until they put their swords away. "Now, what is this all about?"

"We caught him stealing, Father," one of the soldiers said.

The abbot knelt beside the sobbing boy and wiped the tears from the boy's face with his sleeve. "What is your name, son?"

"Pierre," the boy replied between hiccups.

"Where do you live?"

"Down by the river."

"Did you steal from someone?"

The boy swallowed hard, then nodded. "A man in the tavern dropped some coins out of his purse onto the ground. I grabbed them and ran away."

"Why did you take the man's coins?"

The boy's voice dropped to a whisper. "I was hungry."

"Then you will have supper with us." Abbot Francis held out his hand and gave the boy a stern look. "Now give the coins to me."

Slowly, the child pulled three gold crowns out of his pocket and laid them in the abbot's palm. Abbot Francis rose to his feet as the child hid behind the folds of his habit.

"There is your stolen property." He tossed the coins on the floor. One of the soldiers bent down to gather them up. "Now leave us in peace."

"Not good enough, Abbot Duchienne." Montaigne stepped forward as the child began to whimper. "A thief must still be punished. It is the law."

"Don't let him hang me," the child whimpered. "Please, Abbot Francis, don't let him hang me."

"God's law is forgiveness," the abbot said.

Montaigne clenched his fists in fury. "Again, you have defied the king's law by harboring a common thief."

"Have you no other criminals to hang that you must chase down hungry children?" The abbot's eyes narrowed dangerously.

"Enough!" Montaigne reached suddenly for the boy. The child shrieked and gripped the abbot around the waist.

Abbot Francis, his arm around the child's shoulders, backed up against the communion rail. "I warn you," he hissed.

"Take him!" Montaigne ordered. The soldiers pulled out their swords.

From high atop the columns there arose a throaty roar which echoed off the vaulted ceiling and bounced from arch to arch. I stared in astonishment as the six gargoyles seemed to turn their red-eyed gaze onto the soldiers. The roar deepened, growing louder and more menacing.

The soldiers hurled their swords away, turning and running from the church as though the Devil and all his legions were at their heels. Only Montaigne remained, standing alone and unarmed. With a courage that I could not help but admire, he faced the abbot squarely across the nave of the church as the gargoyles, still growling within their granite throats, watched him with their wary gaze.

"I warn you, Abbot Duchienne. You have hoodwinked everyone else, but I know what you are. I demand that you give me the thief before I call the Inquisition."

"Get out of my church!" the abbot bellowed, pointing a shaking finger at Montaigne. Of its own volition, a candle sconce detached from the wall and flew at Montaigne, all its candles blazing. It hit the wall two feet from Montaigne's head, falling to the floor in a shower of sparks.

Montaigne backed out the door, his features twisted in rage and terror. "You'll burn for this, Abbot Duchienne," he snarled. "If it is the last thing I do, I will see that you burn."

Abbot Francis, his gaze as cold as the midwinter snows, continued to embrace the terrified child until the sound of the hoofbeats faded into the distance.

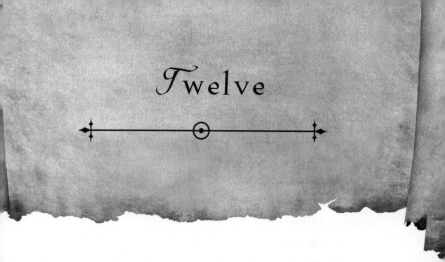

Twelve

The morning of Christmas Eve, I rose from my bed and gasped as my bare feet touched the frigid floor. And yet, despite the fact that my breath came from my mouth in wisps, something drew me to the window. I opened the shutters and stared, ignoring the cold air that made my ears numb. The morning sun gleamed on a white blanket of snow, pure as the Virgin Herself, which covered the hillside surrounding the monastery.

I closed the shutters, pulled on my leggings and leather shoes, and trotted down to breakfast. Fresh bread and warm spiced ale greeted me. But Abbot Francis was not at the table.

"He's been in the church since before dawn," Fernando replied when I inquired. "Polishing the candlesticks, trimming the wicks, sweeping the floor, such things as that."

"He is certainly putting young Pierre to work," Antonin

said. "He can get into places that none of us could fit. I found him wedged between the altar and the rood screen cleaning the wax off the floor. Michael, I don't think that even you could have fit back there."

"Still, we need to figure out what we're going to do with him," Marcel said. "He's been here for weeks. He's too young to enter a monastery. We can't keep him here too much longer. "

"Why can't we just take him home?" I suggested.

"He doesn't appear to have a home to go to," Antonin replied. "His mother and father are both dead of that fever that has been plaguing the village. And any other relatives might not be able to feed an extra mouth."

"Well, I suppose we could keep him here until he is a bit older," Juan-José put in. "But even if he decides to be a novice, he certainly cannot be one here, you know. Maybe there is another abbey we can ship him off to."

Fernando chuckled and shook his head. "I doubt whether that will work. He sticks to Francis like a burr. He would not even stay in a cell by himself—I had to fix him a pallet at the foot of Francis' bed. I wonder if Francis can even visit the latrine without a shadow."

"That will get tiresome soon," Juan-José commented.

The abbot finally appeared, blowing on his hands to warm them. Little Pierre followed, gave Fernando a shy smile, and sat down at the table, falling on his food like a ravenous animal. His bread vanished in no time, but the portion which satisfies a grown man is not enough to fill a growing boy. Pierre still looked hungry. Marcel watched him for a moment, then, with a wordless gesture, took his own bread and dropped it in the child's bowl. The boy looked up and met Marcel's gaze for a moment, then grinned and munched the proffered food.

"Well, Francis," Fernando inquired. "Are we ready for the onslaught?"

"If you are referring to Mass tomorrow," the abbot replied, "I believe we are."

"That church will be packed," Juan-José observed. "I'll wager we will have people from as far away as Paris."

Juan-José was right. The next morning, even before the sky turned from black to gray, carriages began to gather despite the continuing snowfall. Antonin rang the bell and kept ringing it as the sun eased its way up over the mountains.

I ran to the church even before the bell, stamping my feet to keep my toes from becoming numb. It was my first time assisting the abbot at Mass, and I felt myself growing excited as well as nervous. I hadn't been overjoyed at the prospect of being an altar boy again, but I had a feeling that this particular Mass would be far different than anything I had experienced at the Cathedral of St. Etienne.

"Are you sure that this will teach me to be a magus?" I asked, as I helped Abbot Francis into his chasuble and grabbed the stole from the altar.

"The Mass is a magical ritual." He took the stole from my hands and draped it around his shoulders. "As much so as anything we might do in the Tabernacle. The form of the ritual is slightly different, but that is all."

"I guess I never thought about it that way before." I bit my lip and gathered up the heavy cope from the chair. "It never seemed like a ritual when the Bishop of Metz performed it."

"Well, it is when it is properly performed," the abbot said, winking at me. "Perhaps one day you will be ordained. Then you will discover this for yourself."

I draped the heavy cope about his shoulders and found myself fumbling with the clasp for some moments before managing to fasten it. The notion of becoming a priest myself bothered me, but I didn't quite know why.

"Michael?" Abbot Francis asked softly. "Your hands are trembling. Are you nervous?"

"Yes."

"Whatever for?"

I bit my lip for a moment. "I want you to be proud of me."

"Well, I already am proud of you, so don't waste any time worrying about it. Now go." He gave me a little shove. "We've a church full of people out there."

Taking the censer, I preceded the abbot out into the church just as the rising sun began to gleam through the stained glass windows, flooding the altar with colored light. The other monks chanted the Introit as we slowly processed down the aisle. I swung the censer back and forth, sending wisps of incense smoke over both sides of the aisle.

I realized with a start what the incense was. It was

frankincense—the same incense I had scooped into the censer while Abbot Francis invoked Raphael.

I stepped aside and let the abbot approach the altar. He stood motionless while Antonin ascended to the lectern and read the Christmas story from the gospel of Matthew. The words echoed, the same story that I had heard that cold Christmas morning when I first heard the voice of the angel challenging me to become a Sacred Magician.

A magician just like the three magi who offered frankincense to the newborn Christ child. It all made sense to me now.

Antonin finished reading and resumed his seat in the choir. Shaking myself out of my reverie, I turned to the altar. It was time for Abbot Francis was to begin the consecration, and I had a part to play in the ritual. But instead, he turned to the crowd kneeling at his feet and began to speak to them.

I had never heard him give a sermon before. I had suspected that he did so only on major feasts, such as this was, as part and parcel of his priestly role. And yet I found that, instead of preaching to them of sin and punishment, as seemed to be the usual Christmas fare, his words conveyed compassion and encouragement.

"For you are blessed." He lowered his voice to a sing-song tone that I found irresistibly entrancing. I realized he was weaving an enchantment over the entire congregation. "Every one of you is blessed, from the poorest among you to the richest. Always remember that—no matter what prince may say otherwise, whether it be a prince of this world or a prince of the Church. You are all blessed by God, and you all walk in the light of Christ, even as the light dawns upon this Christmas morn. Bear that light within you all your days, and you will know the true meaning of peace."

He finally ceased speaking, the ringing echo of his voice gradually fading into hushed silence. I heard muffled sniffles and whispered responses as people shuffled, wiped their eyes, and crossed themselves. As I looked around, I caught sight of an old woman off to the side in the front pew gazing at the abbot in utter rapture, a smile lighting up the harsh creases of her face like a candle in a window.

I realized then why they revered him so. It was not just the bleeding statues or the visions of angels. He lifted their spirits and offered them hope for a better life in this world, not just salvation in the next. He had cast a magical spell on them, but it was a spell of comfort and love that enveloped all the bodies packed like herring into the tiny stone church, a spell like a blazing fire warming the hearts and souls of all those who had ventured forth on this bitterly cold midwinter's morning. I found that I too was moved.

It took a sharp nudge from Abbot Francis to draw my attention back to the task at hand. Flustered, I quickly took up the platen with the host as he began the chanting the words of the consecration. A hush descended on the crowd as the abbot elevated the host. From somewhere near the vaulted ceiling, I distinctly heard the sound of a baby's cry. It faded just as mysteriously as it arose.

Again, at the elevation of the chalice, I heard another

sound near the ceiling. This time, it was the voice of a woman softly singing a lullaby. It, too, faded after a moment and was replaced by the whispers and murmurings rising up from the pews. Although I should have been accustomed to the abbot's apparitions by now, I still felt a chill run suddenly up my spine.

Finally, the people lined up at the rail for communion and the Mass drew to a close. Pierre, who had been kept at bay all during the Mass, fastened himself once again to the abbot's robes, all the more determined not to let go. The sky had cleared, letting the warming rays of the sun gleam upon the snow that dusted the steps of the church. I followed the abbot outside and, with the rest of the brothers, tried to keep order as he performed his usual greetings and blessings on the ever-expanding crowd.

After a while, Fernando took the abbot by the arm and drew him to one side. "Francis, I have been thinking. We have here a son without a father. Over there"—he pointed to Journet—"we have a father without a son. Perhaps..."

Abbot Francis gazed over at Journet for a moment as a smile spread over his features. "Fernando," he said finally, "that is a brilliant idea. Wait here."

Taking the boy gently but firmly by the arm, the abbot propelled him through the crowd. At first the boy clung desperately to Abbot Francis' robes as he reached out and drew Journet out of a knot of people.

After a moment, however, the boy who seemed very much taken by the tavernkeeper's twitching mustache and kindly smile, gradually loosed his hold on the abbot's surplice. Then, after much coaxing and reassurance by the abbot, the boy put his small hand in Journet's gnarled one and they headed down the church steps. Smiling broadly, Abbot Francis waved to them as they climbed into Journet's donkey cart.

"Observe, little brother," Fernando said to me with an air of satisfaction, "what a noble virtue charity is. By one small act, we have succeeded in solving two rather large problems."

"*Gloria in excelsis Deo.*" John pressed his palms together and cast his eyes heavenward. "Glory to God in the highest."

"And on earth," Antonin finished, "peace to men of goodwill."

That Christmastide held perhaps the most contentment I believe I had ever known. Wrapped in serenity and enveloped in a soft blanket of snow, the earth rested from her labors and so did we. I spent the short hours of light in the library, musing over one book or another, often staring at the same rubricated folio for long moments before the bell for supper would jostle me from my reverie.

The evenings we spent before a roaring fire, nursing mulled wine or spiced ale. Often we spent hours in silent companionship where even the slightest word was shunned lest it shatter the fragile web that often links kindred spirits, one to the other. I felt almost as if we could, at any moment, answer an unspoken thought with a spoken reply, and a verbal observation with silent agreement.

It was on such a night, near Twelfth Night, that the

winter began to grow restless. A storm blew up, hurling snow and hail in angry flurries as it howled and shrieked against the ancient stone walls. We all huddled especially close to the fire, carefully tending it lest it die and leave us to the mercy of the storm's icy breath, which found its way under the doors and between the shutters.

At first, we paid no heed to the hammering at the door, taking it for the wind. But the hammering continued.

John raised his head from his arms and listened. "There is someone at the door."

"Mother of God!" Juan-José exclaimed. "On a night like this?"

Fernando rose and opened the door a crack, drawing into the parlor a snow-covered figure. At first I thought it was one of the villagers, but I had never seen this tiny man before. Snowflakes dusted his dirty hair and beard, and his woolen clothes were torn and shredded. He stood shivering, whether with fear or the cold I could not be sure.

Catching sight of Abbot Francis, he knelt and clutched him around the knees, much to the abbot's astonishment. "Please, blessed Father," he sobbed. "Please, come. Before she dies."

Raising the little man to his feet, Abbot Francis brushed him off and gazed intently into his reddened face, shaking him slightly. "Now, my good man, kindly calm down and tell me what it is that you wish of me."

The little man crossed himself. "My daughter, my little rose … she is dying and needs God's blessing," he replied, his speech halting and difficult to understand, as though he had never learned to speak properly. "If she does not have the final prayers, she will go to Hell. Please, Blessed Father, come to her, I beg of you."

"Where do you live?" Fernando asked.

The little man dropped his gaze. "Germaine-de-Bris."

I gazed at him in morbid fascination. I had heard the villagers speak of Germaine-de-Bris. Not even a village, it was little more than a knot of peasant hovels clustered by the tiny stream that trickled at the foot of the hill. When it was spoken of, it was with horror, as it was a veritable morass of pestilence and desperate poverty.

Abbot Francis, however, gave it not a second thought. "Then let us be off," he said, reaching for his cloak and cowl.

"Francis," Antonin protested. "You can't be serious."

"Absolutely." He swung the woolen cloak over his shoulders.

"But it is nearly five miles from here. And with a storm such as this?"

"I must," the abbot stated, in a voice that permitted no disagreement.

"Then you will not go alone." Before the abbot could forbid me, I jumped to my feet and grabbed my own cloak. "Keep the coals burning for us, John."

"Michael, you are as mad as he is," Marcel told me. "Look after him now."

I met his gaze with a smile. "I shall."

"Well, if you are coming with me, you had best get

moving," the abbot called to me over his shoulder. "Or else I will leave you behind."

Wrapping my cloak tightly around me, I ran to the door and we followed the little man out into the angry night. The wind screamed at us, hurling snow and sleet in torrents as we trudged down the road. The man, guided by experience alone, finally led us off the road onto a track that I could barely see in the swirling flakes. Catching hold of a fold of the abbot's cloak, I lowered my head to avoid being slapped in the face by the wind-driven snowflakes.

Slowly, putting one foot before the other in a seemingly endless succession, I brought up the rear of the tiny procession that made its way, single file, along the path. It was like a journey into a world where every single feature of the landscape—every tree, every rock, every hill or valley—had vanished, engulfed in an ever-shifting but unchanging shroud of white. For a moment, I thought that I had passed into the colorless limbo of unbaptized souls who waited, suspended, neither in Heaven or Hell, for the Second Coming. Only the chattering of my teeth reminded me that I was still a living man.

I could no longer feel my feet, and the hand that clutched the abbot's robes was so numb that it did not seem like a part of me. Then we halted abruptly, and I nearly plowed into the abbot before I realized that we had come to a small hut. Our guide opened a small slat that served as a door and we entered a room lit only by a ruby glow from the hearth.

A woman, also tiny, her lined face aging her beyond

her years, rose from a pallet of straw and rags and kissed the abbot's hands. To my extreme discomfort, she did the same to me, wiping her tears on my sleeves.

"You have come," she whispered. "God be praised."

Taking the abbot by the hand, she pulled him over to the pallet. There lay a little girl of about four years or five. Her hair, bright and shimmering like the gold thread that trimmed the bishop's mantle, fanned out behind her head like a halo against the filthy rags of her pallet. She could easily have served as a model for any of the painted cherubim on a cathedral ceiling. And yet to see such innocent beauty lying cold and still in a place of such squalor, her angelic face pale and bloodless, filled me with pity.

The child's mother, for the tiny woman could be nothing else, buried her head against her husband's shoulder and sobbed as Abbot Francis knelt beside the pallet. He stroked the child's fair hair for a moment, shaking his head sadly, then he reached into the pouch at his girdle and brought out a vial of holy water.

Softly muttering the prayers for the dead, he made the sign of the cross above her still form. Then he dipped his fingers in the holy water and anointed her eyelids, her ears, her nostrils and finally her lips. He blessed her with the sign of the cross once again, then fell silent, leaving only the mother's muffled sobs and the wail of the wind outside.

Long after he finished the last prayer, he continued to stroke the child's brow, gazing wordlessly into her angel's face. What thoughts passed through his mind or what feelings moved his heart during those long moments, I could not begin to fathom. But finally, I noticed the lines of his mouth tighten in determination, as though he had made up his mind about something.

Pulling his golden cross over his head, he laid it on the child's breast. He covered her brow with his hand and tilted her head back slightly. Then he leaned over the pallet. Gently placing his lips on top of hers, he abruptly blew his own breath into her mouth—not once, not twice, but thrice. I gazed in utter amazement as the child drew a hesitant breath of her own, coughed a few times, then drew another and another. Then she opened her eyes and began to cry.

Her astonished and overjoyed parents rushed to her bedside as Abbot Francis picked up his cross from the rumpled blankets and rose to his feet. Taking me roughly by the arm, he backed away towards the door.

"We must leave at once," he said in a hoarse whisper. I began to protest, but his look cut me off cold. "Now!"

I meekly followed him out of the hut.

We spoke not a word on the journey back to the monastery, in the iron gray of the dawn. The storm had eased, leaving only a few furtive flurries, but the snow now came up to our knees and each stride took some effort. The abbot had thrown his cowl over his face and tucked his hands into the sleeves of his habit. He strode beside me, lost in his own thoughts, keeping a pace that was difficult for me to follow. I contented myself with staying behind him, treading in the furrows that his feet made in the snow until we reached our front gate.

We entered the parlor just as the others were gathering in the refectory. But the abbot stomped past them without a word or a glance and mounted the steps to his chambers. I, too, ignored their inquiring looks and stumbled up the stairs to my cell. My habit and leggings were soaked from the waist down and I was shivering. I undressed and wrapped myself tightly in my blanket. The sun cleared the horizon as I fell into a troubled sleep.

I awoke to the sound of cart wheels and the ill-tempered braying of the mule. Looking out my window, I watched Fernando and John lurch their way up the hill, back to the front gate. They had gone into the village as though it were an ordinary day.

I ran down the stairs as they entered the parlor and shed their damp cowls by the fire.

"It never ceases to amaze me," Fernando was saying, "what stories people will tell."

"Interesting tidings from town, eh?" Juan-José strode in from the kitchen, wiping his hands on a towel. "What have you heard this time?"

"Now they have Francis raising the dead." Fernando sank into a seat by the fire and rubbed his hands to warm them. "I have no idea how the story started, but we heard nothing else the entire morning. I felt rather dimwitted for not knowing anything about it. But I suppose we can hardly keep track of every mad tale that is told."

"The story is true," I said dully. Immediately, I felt every gaze upon me.

"What?" Fernando frowned in puzzlement.

"He did raise the dead. Last night."

"I thought he was performing last rites for someone's child," Antonin said.

"He did," I said, as all the brothers took seats around me. "But he did not stop with that."

As if relating a dream to a trusted friend, I told them all what had happened the previous night. Even though I sat near a warm fire, the awful wonder of what I had witnessed set me to shivering yet again. Stunned, the others remained silent for a long moment.

Finally, John crossed himself. "He has finally crossed the threshold from Sorcerer to Saint."

"God Almighty," Juan-José muttered. "They'll burn him for sure."

Silence again fell, save for the crackle of the fire. Finally we heard footsteps on the stairs.

"Francis is awake," Fernando whispered. "Now, not a word about this, any of you, until he tells us about it himself."

We all nodded in agreement as Abbot Francis appeared in the refectory doorway. "Here it is Terce already," he chided good-naturedly. "Why did not someone fetch me?"

His smile was a pale ghost of its normal self. I felt a stab of alarm.

"You were so late returning last night, we thought we would let you rest." Fernando rose to his feet but his smile, too, seemed a mere shadow. "Don't worry, we planned on waking you for supper."

"I should hope so." The abbot's voice suddenly dissolved into a fit of coughing so severe that he was forced to clutch at the table to keep his balance. Rasping and hoarse, he coughed for several seconds before he finally could catch his breath.

I glanced over at Antonin and found him as alarmed as I was. "I don't like the sound of that," he muttered, shaking his head. He reached out and took the abbot's arm, but Abbot Francis waved him away.

"It's nothing. Just the wretched damp."

Antonin, clearly unconvinced, stood aside and let the abbot ease into a chair at the table. We all sat down as well, save for Fernando, who bustled back and forth from the kitchen. Antonin and Marcel exchanged worried looks across the table as the abbot fell to coughing again, his complexion growing more pale by the moment.

"Francis," Antonin said sternly. "I really must insist that you return to bed. You are far more weary than you will admit. You are but mortal flesh, remember?"

The coughing fit finally subsided, leaving the abbot gasping for breath. "Perhaps … for a few more hours."

He rose slowly, then collapsed onto the floor in a dead faint, knocking over his chair. I leapt to my feet in horror, but Antonin had already raced to the abbot's side with Marcel close at his heels.

Antonin felt the abbot's brow. "He is burning with fever," he muttered. "I knew it. By God, I should have never allowed him to run out last night in that storm."

"As if you could have stopped him," Marcel put in. "Now we must get him to his chambers."

It took all five of us to raise the abbot to his feet and carry him up the stairs. Undressing him down to his tunic, we laid him on his bed.

Antonin took charge of the sickroom protocol with a firm and practiced hand. "We will need a basin of water. Cool, but not too cold. And some clean cloths." Fernando nodded and trotted off down the stairs. "Marcel, you have some excellent poultices for fever, do you not?"

"Willow bark," Marcel replied. "And coltsfoot in a tea."

"Excellent. If you would be good enough to fetch them."

Marcel was out the door before Antonin could finish his request.

"What about us, Antonin?" Juan-José asked. "What would you have us do?"

Antonin did not answer. Taking the abbot's hand in his, he felt for the abbot's pulse with his long fingers. Then he ran his hand over the abbot's brow and frowned. Beads of sweat had begun to form on Abbot Francis' face, dampening his silvery black hair, and an unhealthy flush had crept into his pale cheeks.

Fernando returned with the basin and the cloths and set them down on the night table.

"We must get this fever down." Antonin dipped a cloth into the water and laying it upon the abbot's brow. "We should bathe him, but since we have no balinary, this will have to do. Change the cloth frequently to keep it cool, and continue to swab him."

All night we worked, in shifts of four hours or more, bathing the abbot's face in cool water, changing the poultices, and watching his breathing become more and more hoarse and labored. Often he would thrash about, moaning and muttering. At those times, Antonin would take him by the shoulders and press him back into the mattress, speaking to him in a quiet, soothing voice. Then he would lie quiet in deathly stillness for a time, until the delirium seized him once more.

Morning dawned and Fernando saw to breakfast, although wine and a bit of bread were all we cared for. Juan-José had taken the early morning watch, relieving Marcel for a few hours of rest.

I glanced up at the sound of voices outside the gates. Fernando went to the window and looked outside. "The townspeople are coming up the road." He frowned. "What are they doing?"

"Coming to Mass," John replied. "It is the feast of Epiphany."

"Oh God, that's right." Fernando rubbed his brow wearily.

"What will we tell them?" I asked. "They expect Father Francis to say Mass."

Fernando heaved a sigh. "They will have to be told something, I suppose." Grimly, he made his way towards the church. I decided to follow.

The entire populace of the town sat expectantly in the pews as the weak sunlight leaked in through the colored windows. Fernando and I slipped into the side transept. He hesitated for a moment. I reached out and laid a hand on his arm. He looked over at me, smiled weakly, and patted my hand. "Let us hope that divine inspiration will descend at the last moment and I will know what to say."

We approached the rows of pews as the crowd hushed and turned to us. Fernando cleared his throat. "Good friends," he began, his tenor voice bouncing eerily from stone column to stone column, "I truly regret to have to tell you that there will be no Mass today. Abbot Francis has fallen gravely ill. He burns with a fever and lies senseless upon his bed. We fear for his life."

His voice trailed off and he glanced over at me, unable to mask his worry and deep concern. I fear that I could do no better. We exchanged solemn looks as the crowd began to murmur.

Journet rose from the front pew and turned to the rest of the congregation. "Then let us pray for his swift recovery."

All heads bowed in silence. Many crossed themselves and pressed rosary beads to moving lips. Fernando listened for a moment, too deeply moved to reply. He wiped his eyes abruptly with his sleeve, then turned to me.

"Go and see if Antonin needs assistance," he whispered into my ear. "I will stay here until they are gone."

I nodded silently and made my way back to the cloister.

"Are they still here?" Marcel asked as I entered the

abbot's chambers. "I thought that they would go away once they learned that Francis wouldn't say Mass."

"They wanted to remain in the church," I said. "To pray for him."

"By themselves?" Marcel frowned.

I shook my head. "Fernando is with them."

"Well, all right," he conceded. "For all the good that it will do."

Juan-José grunted in agreement.

John turned on all of us with a rare flash of anger in his pale eyes. "Have our hearts become so hardened and so cynical that we so totally discount the power of prayer?" he demanded. "If so, then we are no better than the pompous and hypocritical Church from which we have fled. Which one of us, in his darkest hour, did not raised his voice to heaven and have it answered by the hand of the Almighty, leading us to this door? And now we dare to look down our monkish noses at the sincere prayers of the townspeople who want not their own succor but that of our abbot? We ought to be ashamed."

I stared hard at the floor. Even if the others were not shamed by John's words, I certainly was. I turned and moved over to the abbot's bedside, gazing for a moment at his flushed face and heaving chest. I could not help but think that he now burned with the selfsame fever that had taken the little girl. In giving her life, had he willingly sacrificed his own? God forbid that it should be so. Slowly, I sank to my knees by the bed, bowing my head over my clasped hands.

One by one, the others joined me—first John, then

Antonin and Juan-José, and finally Marcel. We knelt in a silence broken only by the roar of the fire and the abbot's gasping breath. Finally, I heard Juan-José's voice, hoarse with emotion, begin to pray.

"All wise and loving God," he murmured, crossing himself, "what an unholy mess we have made of thy church. Surely the stink of it must rise to Heaven itself. Still, we beseech thee, have mercy upon one who does his best to bring thy love into world in the midst of greed and corruption. Please, God. Grant Francis his life."

"Amen," we chorused.

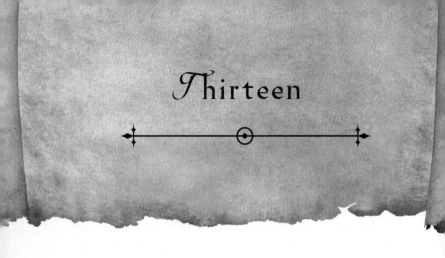

Thirteen

We spoke little the next day, each of us taking our turn rotating between the abbot's bedside and the kitchen, stoking the fire and preparing the meals. None of us were willing to acknowledge that, despite all of our ministrations, the abbot's fever had grown worse rather than better.

That evening, Antonin failed to come down to supper for the second day in a row, preferring, or so he told us, to keep his vigil by the abbot's bedside. Shaking his head in disapproval, Fernando filled a wooden tray with bread, cheese and mulled wine.

"Take this upstairs." He thrust the tray into my hands. "Tell Antonin to eat or else he will fall ill and we shall have to care for him as well."

I carried the tray up the stairs to the abbot's chambers, pushing my way in with my foot. I paused by the door as

Antonin, his face drawn and pale, sat at the abbot's table before an untidy pile of books and parchments, gazing up with resigned weariness at Marcel pacing the floor beside the abbot's bed.

"All I am saying, Marcel, is that we tried the infusion of lungwort." Antonin seemed to be trying his best to keep his tone reasonable. "It has not been effective."

"Then you find a remedy," Marcel retorted furiously. "You are the one with the fancy degree, not me. Look in those books of yours."

"I have," Antonin snapped. "Repeatedly. Backwards and forwards, upside down and sideways. I can find nothing more. That is why I asked you, with your knowledge of the herbs…"

"I have done all I know." Marcel threw up his hands in a gesture of utter despair. "I can do no more." Turning on his heel, he stormed past me out of the door into the hallway. I heard his footsteps thundering down the stairs as Antonin closed his eyes and heaved a sigh.

"Antonin?" I said softly. "Fernando sent this up." I set the tray on the desk. "He was concerned when you failed to come down for supper."

Antonin gave me a wan smile and picked up the goblet of warm wine, swirling it about in the cup before taking a sip. "That was most kind of him."

"You are supposed to eat," I continued. "Fernando insisted. He said that doesn't want to have to take care of you too."

But Antonin only heaved a weary sigh. "I fear I have not had much appetite of late."

I glanced over his shoulder. He had before him yet another horoscope drawn on a parchment scroll. Scrawled in the center square was the date *14 December, Anno Domini 1434*. I realized that I was gazing at a natal chart, and it did not take the wisdom of Solomon to figure out whose it was.

"That is Father Francis' chart," I said, "is it not?"

Antonin nodded. "He once told me the date of his birth. Although he failed to tell me the time, I cast the chart anyway."

"Can a horoscope be accurate?" I asked. "Even if you do not have the exact time?"

"I can rectify the hour from certain events in a person's life," Antonin continued. "Nearly always I am right. In his case, however…" He broke off for a moment, rubbing his bloodshot eyes. "I hope to God that I am wrong."

I shivered. "Is it possible to predict a man's death from his chart?"

Antonin glanced up at me sharply, then slowly shook his head. "I certainly would not dare to do so. Still, there are times in a person's life when the gates of death swing open and the soul is free to go if it wills. These times are clearly indicated by the placement of the planets."

I looked over at the abbot lying on his bed, his face pale against the black wool of his habit, gaunt shadows outlining the planes of his features. I felt tears sting in my eyes. An astrology lesson was not what I sought.

"Will he die?" I whispered.

"Saturn, the Greater Malefic, is transiting the sign of Aries, the sign that rules fevers," Antonin replied softly, tracing the dour planet's path across the parchment chart with his finger. "It now squares his natal Sun from his eighth house, the house of death. If Francis leaves this world, it will be tonight."

"Is there nothing we can do?"

"No." Antonin shook his head again. "What happens now is up to him. He has claimed numerous times that a man's will is stronger than his stars. We can only wait... and hope that he is right."

I numbly refilled the lamp, preparing for the night's vigil. Antonin took his a seat on a low stool while I perched on the abbot's bedside.

"He is much calmer tonight," I observed, resting my hand on the abbot's brow for a moment. "The delirium seems to have passed."

But Antonin made no reply. I looked around. The strain of the last three days had finally taken their toll, and he had fallen asleep draped across the foot of the abbot's bed. I reached over to shake him, then decided to let him be. I would remain awake and watchful, and call him only if I needed to.

The long, cold winter night dragged on, timeless, eternal. No wind rattled the windows, no bird or insect chirped to remind me that there was a world of life beyond the stone walls. I imagined myself entombed in an endless blackness, kept at bay only by the tiny flame of the small lamp and the abbot's labored breathing.

Antonin's words echoed in my mind. At certain times in a man's life, the gates of death swing open and the soul is bidden to pass through … if it wills to do so. What if the soul is unwilling? Is there something that passes through the gates from the world of the dead to the world of the living to seize the soul by the scruff of the neck, dragging it kicking and screaming through the cavernous portals into the darkness?

I looked up, my gazed fixed upon the shutters of the window in the abbot's room. In the flickering lamplight, the window seemed to me to grow larger and larger until it encompassed the entire wall. I heard a moan, then a wail, as of a woman weeping and lamenting. Then the shutters flew open, snuffing the feeble light of the lamp and revealing not the starry sky but blackness—nothingness—the void of nonbeing. The blackness began to undulate, like water in a dark well, writhing like a dying thing.

Then it took form … but such a form! Terror clutched at my throat and I fought for breath. Larger than a man it was, with outstretched arms shrouded in filmy black sleeves that undulated as if an unholy wind blew through them. The black cowl about its head fell back, revealing nothing but a skull for a face, which grinned and leered at me from its empty eye sockets. It reached out towards the abbot with long, skeletal fingers that snatched and picked at his bedclothes, trying to catch hold of his hand.

"No!" I cried. "You shall not have him this night, not

if I have anything to say about it. Back, you fiend! Begone, I say! Go back to the realms of the dead. The living are not for you."

How it happened, I know not. But I discovered the abbot's pectoral cross in my hand, larger than I remembered it, the gold shining with a light of its own. I held it up before my face, placing my body between the abbot's still form and the hideous thing that approached. With a shriek, it folded in upon itself and faded back into the night. The shutters closed with a snap and shrank to their normal size.

I sat up with my heart pounding, gazing about the room. Antonin had not stirred, and the tiny light of the lamp still glowed. I watched the abbot's chest rise and fall with long, labored breaths, and heaved my own sigh of relief. It was only a dream, a phantom of the night born of my weariness and worry.

Then I noticed something gleaming in the lamplight. The abbot's cross, which we had removed while undressing him for bed, lay on the night table. I reached over and picked it up, turning it in my hands for a moment. It occurred to me that taking it off him was a mistake. We should have left it hanging upon his breast.

How superstitious, I thought. And yet I still did not fully understand the depth and breadth of the power it contained. All I really knew was that Abbot Francis was dying and I was unable to just sit and wait for the Angel of Death's next attempt to fetch him away. Holding the cross between my clasped hands, I closed my eyes.

"Holy archangels," I prayed, my lips moving silently.

"Bright messengers of Almighty God, here lies, for all his power, a mortal man at the gates of death before his time. Dash not the hopes and dreams of those who have placed their trust in him. Please do not let him die, I beseech you." I felt the tears fill my eyes once again, but sternly held them back. "Not for my sake, but for these monks and the good and simple folk they serve. In the name of our Lord and Savior."

I could not go on. Swallowing my tears yet again, I crossed myself and raised the gold cross to my lips. Then, leaning over the abbot's still form, I slipped the gold chain over his head and arranged the cross on his breast. Now, truly, there was nothing to do but wait.

For another eternity, I watched as the tiny flame of the lamp flickered and danced, throwing shadows against the walls. Then it seemed as though the light grew in brightness. It came not from the tiny lamp, but from somewhere behind me.

I turned, and my eyes widened in awe and wonder. Another portal was opening in the eastern wall, but this time light, brilliant and glowing with life and love, poured through, filling the room with its healing rays. A being emerged, his face radiant and haloes of light shining off his fire-colored hair. His white robes swirled around him as he floated across the room, borne up by radiant wings that fanned out behind him.

I crossed myself once more. "Raphael..." I breathed, as memories returned of the icons pictured in my old master's books.

The archangel approached the abbot's bedside, float-ing above his body, enveloping him in light. With a tender-ness that made me want to weep yet again, Raphael reached out and touched the abbot's brow, stroking it once, twice, thrice.

My eyelids flew open at the sunlight that blazed through the shutters. I rubbed my eyes in confusion for a moment, then, without thinking, glanced over at Abbot Francis. He lay still and quiet. Cold fingers of dread clutched at my heart. If I had let him pass from this life while I slept, I would never, ever, forgive myself.

"Antonin!" I cried aloud. "For God's sake, wake up."

Antonin was at my side in a moment. Leaning over, he listened for the abbot's breath while feeling at the point of the abbot's jaw for a pulse. I held my breath.

Finally, Antonin felt the abbot's brow with one hand and laid the other on the abbot's chest. I felt my heart leap as his hand rose and fell with the abbot's regular breathing. Antonin turned to me with an incredulous expression on his weary features.

"He is sound asleep," he announced, barely able to contain his own relief. "The fever must have broken some-time during the night. I have no idea how, but his brow is cool and dry and he is breathing easily."

"Then he will live?" I asked eagerly.

"Yes, yes, he will live. Go and fetch the others. Quickly."

Jumping to my feet, I ran down the stairs, nearly tripping

over my own enthusiasm. I raced down the hallway towards the kitchen as fast as I could go.

Fernando looked up in astonishment, carving knife poised above the loaf of bread as I clutched at the door frame, gasping for breath. "Michael!" he exclaimed. "Whatever is the matter? Oh, my God, Francis…"

"He lives," I said breathlessly. "Antonin said that the fever broke during the night."

Fernando tossed the knife back onto the table and made for the door, wiping his hands on his habit. "I must go to him," he called over his shoulder. "The others are in the parlor."

The rest of the monks, having heard the commotion in the kitchen, were already on their feet. At my tidings, John crossed himself as Juan-José exclaimed something in his own language. But Marcel proved to be the first one out the door, heading for the stairs.

"Hush." Antonin held a finger to his lips as we congregated at the abbot's bedside. "He's coming around."

Abbot Francis heaved a sigh and stirred. His eyelids fluttered briefly, then opened, blinking several times at the bright sunshine.

"Good morning," Antonin greeted him cheerfully. "How do you feel?"

The abbot moaned softly and passed his hand over his eyes. "Like I've been hurled out of the bell tower. God, I ache in every joint." He paused, as he gazed in puzzlement at all of us. "What is the matter? Has something happened? Fernando, why are you weeping?"

"You have been wracked with fever for the last three days," Antonin told him. "We feared for your life. Don't you remember?"

The abbot heaved a sigh. "I fear it is all so muddled." His eyelids drifted closed and his breathing deepened into slumber once more.

"He must rest." Antonin shooed us out of the room like so many geese. "I will tell you when he awakens. Now be gone!"

"My Lord Physician has spoken." Juan-José waved us towards the stairs. "Come, before he turns his leeches loose upon us."

—◊—

Several days went by and the weather, as well as our spirits, brightened considerably. The crisis having passed, Abbot Francis improved daily, spending more and more time awake and talkative. Even so, I had not wanted to distress him by asking the question that had burdened my heart ever since our journey to Germaine-de-Bris.

Finally, I got my chance. "How is he this morning?" I asked as Fernando bustled about preparing the abbot's breakfast tray.

Juan-José chuckled. "Well enough to try to argue with Antonin," he replied as I gathered up the tray and headed towards the stairs. "Have a care, lest you find yourself caught in the fray."

I had to smile as I heard the voices coming from the open door of the abbot's chambers.

"Now, Antonin," Abbot Francis was saying, "do be reasonable. I feel fine."

"And so you claimed just before you collapsed," Antonin said sternly. "No, Francis, absolutely not. You cannot get up yet. I forbid it!"

"Antonin, you are a tyrant," the abbot replied with a note of petulance.

"And I advise you not to forget it. Now, you will remain in that bed if I have to chain you there myself. Do you understand?"

I heard a resigned sigh in reply as Antonin emerged from the doorway.

"Ah, Michael," he said. "You are here. Good. Maybe you can distract him with food."

I had to chuckle at his exasperated expression. "I take it that he is being a difficult patient."

Antonin rolled his eyes heavenward. "I swear that he will drive me mad. Now, watch him. If he so much as steps over this threshold, I want to know about it immediately."

He trotted down the stairs past me as I carried the tray in through the open door. Abbot Francis lay back on the bed with his eyes closed as I set the tray on the table.

"Are you feeling better?" I asked.

He opened his eyes and gazed at me reproachfully. "As a matter of fact, I am," he replied. "However, I am under strict orders not to act like it."

I could not help smiling. "Antonin is merely being cautious. You had us all very worried."

"I am seldom ill." Abbot Francis heaved a sigh. "Therefore, I fear that I am not very good at it."

"Well, the first thing you do is to obey your physician. If he tells you to stay in bed, that is where you must stay."

He chuckled softly. "I see that he has allies." The abbot's voice, although still weak, had regained a measure of its richness. I felt relieved to hear it. "Very well, then. I will stay here until I am told otherwise. But I cannot promise to do so with any good grace. There is no doubt much to be done."

"Nearly all of which can wait until you recover," I returned. "Now, do you need help with your breakfast?"

He pushed himself up into a sitting position and regarded me with a raised eyebrow. "I think I can manage," he replied. "Thank you."

I hesitated for a moment, wondering if I should bring up the subject that had haunted me for these past days. "Father Francis?" I began. "I want to ask you something."

"And that would be?"

"Why did you do it?" I whispered.

"Do what?"

I frowned. "Surely you must remember. You healed that little girl."

He shut his eyes, a pained expression crossing his face. I hoped that I had not troubled him.

"Ah, yes," he finally replied. "I have asked myself that selfsame question many times over these last few days.

279

Would you believe me if I told you that I don't quite know? Suddenly a power I had never experienced before surrounded me like a corona, and I became merely an instrument of some higher will." He turned to me. "Do the others know?"

I nodded. "I told them. I had to. The news was all over the village."

I broke off in alarm as a coughing fit seized him. It eased after a long moment, leaving him gasping for breath. I rose to my feet in alarm. "Shall I fetch Antonin?"

Unable to speak, he shook his head emphatically and motioned for me to resume my seat. "No," he finally replied, his voice hoarse. "It will pass ..." I waited until he cleared his throat and turned again to me. "Speak no more of this," he said in a tone that permitted no argument. "Let it remain just another story, like singing angels and magical wine."

He fell to coughing again until his eyes glistened with tears. I waited, my hand resting on his arm, until the spasm passed.

"Very well, Father Francis," I replied gently. "If that is your wish."

"It is," he whispered, clearing his throat again. "Now, go down to your breakfast and do not worry about me. I promise to follow Antonin's advice to the letter."

By the end of the week, however, the abbot's requests to rise from his bed became even more insistent and persuasive. Finally, even Antonin could refuse him no longer. We wrapped a blanket about him, helped him down the stairs to the parlor, and sat him in his chair by the blazing hearth fire.

Nursing a steaming cup of wine, he leaned back with the smug look of a man who has finally gotten his own way.

"There," Antonin said as he tucked a cushion behind the abbot's head. "Now will you at last be content?"

"I shall," the abbot replied with a mischievous smile. "At least for now. Perhaps I might stroll in the cloister later."

"In a foot of snow?" Antonin retorted. "I think not. And you had best resign yourself, my dear Francis, to returning to bed after dinner. I will not tolerate any argument."

"I wouldn't think of it," the abbot said with an innocent look.

"See that you don't." Antonin scowled down at him. "You are being a dreadful pain in the rump, you know."

Abbot Francis took a sip from his cup. "I'm told that I do it rather well."

Antonin gave an indelicate snort and whirled out of the room.

Our attention was suddenly riveted by the muffled clop of horses making their way through the snow. The noise grew louder, then ceased. Fernando and I ran out the door and watched the bishop's carriage plow through the snowdrift and dock, like some unwieldy ship, at our front gate.

"What in God's name is *he* doing here?" Fernando muttered in annoyance as the carriage door creaked open. He turned to me. "Fetch the others and go to the tower, quickly."

I hurried back inside and motioned frantically to John, Marcel, and Juan-José. We climbed the steps to the tower and took our places at the chink in the wall as the bishop lumbered in the door like some gigantic bear, swaddled in furs against the bitter cold.

"I don't like the look of this," muttered Juan-José.

Marcel scowled. "Neither do I."

"Ah, Abbot Duchienne," Bishop Sorel said as Fernando ushered him into the parlor and relieved him of his mantle. "I see that God has been merciful and I find you still in the land of the living."

"Your Grace!" Abbot Francis glanced up in surprise and attempted to rise to his feet. "Forgive me, I had not been expecting you."

"There was no time to send word." The bishop waved him back into his chair. "Please, sit and rest yourself. This will take but a moment."

The abbot glanced pointedly over at Antonin, who was returning from the kitchen with a steaming pitcher. "Thank you, my brother. I should be fine for the moment."

But Antonin, busy pouring hot tea into an earthenware cup, failed to notice the abbot's look. "Now, Francis," he said, "You must ..."

"Antonin," the abbot said firmly. "Please." His tone, although soft, clearly indicated that he was not making a request.

Startled, Antonin glanced up, saw the bishop looming over him, and colored deeply with embarrassment. "I shall be in the kitchen if you need me." Turning quickly, he trotted out of the parlor.

The bishop watched as Antonin disappeared through the door. "You are being well cared for, I see."

The abbot leaned back in his chair with a sigh. "I fear I've been unwell."

"Unwell!" The bishop lowered himself down onto a stool, which creaked beneath his bulk. "The word all over Orleans was that you were on your deathbed. I came here half expecting to find a funeral in progress."

The abbot smiled faintly. "A bit premature, I think."

"Well, God be praised for that. Still, that was what we had heard." Bishop Sorel leaned forward and studied the abbot from under heavy brows. "And we thought it true... true enough for His Grace the Duke of Orleans to petition the Pope to begin the proceedings."

"The proceedings?" The abbot frowned in puzzlement. "For what?"

"For your canonization."

The abbot's blue eyes widened in astonishment. "My canonization?" The word died on his lips. He stared at the bishop, aghast for a moment. "I don't understand. There need to be miracles."

"Oh, we have miracles aplenty." The bishop rolled his eyes. "More miracles than we know what to do with. This whole county has been beset with miracles ever since you arrived here."

The abbot grew visibly pale, but he quickly composed himself. "Harmless tricks." He waved his hand in a gesture of dismissal. "Engineered to bolster the faith of the unlettered masses. You and I have spoken of this before, if you recall."

"And so we have. However, the fact remains that there have been occurrences of late that are not explained away by tricks." The bishop scooted his stool closer to the fire and lowered his voice so that I could barely make out the words. "My good abbot, I ask you to tell me, in this holy place in the presence of God, are you Seratois, the Wizard of Alceste?"

My breath caught in my throat, and I heard gasps of surprise from the others. Had our worst fears finally come to pass? I whimpered softly and felt my knees turn to water.

I felt a gentle hand on my shoulder. "Steady, Michael," John whispered in my ear. "We must keep our heads for Francis' sake."

The abbot was silent for a long moment, only the tension around his mouth betraying his agitation. I knew he wouldn't lie outright, but how else could he answer such a question?

Finally, he nodded. "Yes." His voice was so soft I could barely hear it. "I am."

"Ah." The bishop leaned back and stroked his chin. "I thought as much."

"But, after all these years," the abbot mused incredulously. "How did you find out?"

"After the duke's petition for canonization reached Rome, I received a letter from the Grand Inquisitor wondering just who this Father Francis Duchienne is." Bishop Sorel glanced searchingly around the room. "It seems the Inquisitor has heard some amazing tales about you, and he wondered whether you were perhaps the sorcerer called Seratois, who was supposed to have drowned in the Tiber River some ten years ago. Just in case you proved to be the notorious Seratois, I sent a letter of my own to His Holiness to block your canonization. I hope that will end the matter. The last thing I need is for the Holy Office to come prowling all over this diocese chasing after one of their sorcerers." He scowled. "But I must warn you, my efforts might not prevail over the voices clamoring for a Saint Francis Duchienne."

The abbot lowered his gaze, his mouth tightening. "I am no saint."

"That is not what the people of Sainte Felice say. Or the Duke and Duchess of Orleans. But I see that I am tiring you. We need not speak of this now. Whether you are a saint or not remains a moot point while you yet live, does it not?" The bishop rose to his feet with a grunt. "Now I must be on my way."

I followed the other monks down the stairs to the parlor and tried to pretend we had heard nothing. Fernando escorted the bishop to his carriage while the rest of us hurried to the abbot's side. He sat motionless in his chair, his face the color of chalk. I feared that he would fall to the floor in a dead faint.

"Francis?" Antonin laid his hand gently on the abbot's shoulder. "Are you all right?"

The abbot did not seem to hear. With a soft cry, he buried his face in his hands. "God help me," he whispered. "I am lost."

"As are we all," Marcel muttered under his breath.

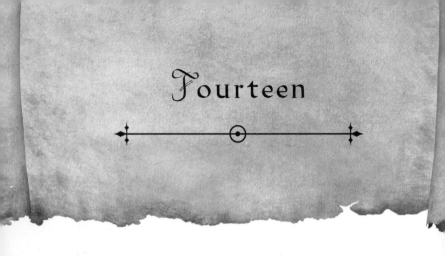

Fourteen

Dusk finally descended as we supported the shaken abbot up the stairs to his chambers. Fernando blew up the fire in the hearth as the rest of us settled him back into bed. I could not help but worry if the shock of this latest revelation would cause him to have a relapse of his illness. Antonin, taking no chances, felt for the abbot's pulse.

Abbot Francis sighed heavily and slowly shook his head. "What a fool I was to think that he would never find out."

"The only thing I don't understand," Fernando said, "is why it took him so long."

"He could have suspected for some time," John commented. "And not said anything before this."

"It is truly incredible that he had the wit to figure it out at all," Juan-José said. "It seems that we might have under-estimated him."

"Even if he has known from the beginning, it seems that he has just as much of a vested interest in keeping it quiet as we have," Antonin put in. "After all, he obviously does not want the Holy Office coming to France and depriving the county of a source of income."

Marcel laughed harshly. "For once the greed of both Church and king is on our side."

A week of bitter cold passed as January drew to a close. We spent our days between the hearth and the kitchen in a desperate attempt to stay warm. Despite his recent shock, Abbot Francis continued to recover his health. After he pointed out, with irrefutable logic, that it was considerably warmer in the parlor than it was in his chambers, we had no choice but to allow him to preside from his chair by the fire.

However, cold or no cold, the larder began to grow bare. We decided there was nothing to do but to chance a trip into town and bring back some sorely needed supplies. I went with Fernando, leaving the others behind to take care of the abbot. I had wanted to remain behind as well, but someone had to accompany Fernando. And perhaps it was better for me to have something to occupy my time other than fretting.

We rattled down the road between the furrows of melting snow. It was slow going, and Fernando had to guide the mule carefully between patches of sticky black mud. It afforded us no time to talk and I, for one, was grateful.

Maybe I could convince myself that the bishop's revelation had been nothing but a terrifying dream.

Journet greeted us at the door with a broad smile and ushered us into the tavern. A fire roared in the hearth and I rubbed my hands before its welcome warmth. Young Pierre, who seemed to be taking well to tavern life, appeared with two goblets and a pitcher of warm ale. He set them down in front of us as we sat down at a table in the corner.

"Thank you, good Pierre." Fernando gave him an encouraging smile. "By God, you must have grown at least two inches since Christmas. You will soon be as tall as Journet."

Pierre beamed at the compliment and scurried off to tend to the mule.

"And your sainted abbot?" Journet inquired as he sat down beside us. "I hope he is doing better."

"His health improves daily," Fernando replied, sipping at his cup. "As does his disposition. Brother Antonin has finally given up on the task of keeping him in bed and we've been forced to let him return to his work before he drives us all mad. He is not a man accustomed to inactivity."

Journet chuckled in reply. "To be sure. Still, may God be praised for his recovery. Will he say Mass this Sunday?"

"I am sure that we will be unable to prevent him," I said.

Fernando politely but pointedly refused a second cup and we rose to leave. I untied the mule while Fernando shook Journet's hand, reassuring him yet again about the cuttings and how there would be more wine next year.

I glanced behind me and noticed a small procession come down the road and pull off at the tavern. Several armored soldiers rode along, flanking a man on horseback dressed in a habit of white shrouded in a black mantle.

Nudging Fernando with my elbow, I pointed. "That is the habit of the Dominicans, is it not?"

I had hardly expected Fernando's reaction to my innocent question. He whirled around and froze, his eyes wide an alarm. "God Almighty!"

"Fernando?" I asked with a concerned frown.

"Michael, do you not know? ... no, how could you?" He took a deep breath and calmed down with an effort. "There, little brother, walks the worst of all our fears."

"Is he not a Dominican?"

"Michael, he is not only a Dominican, but an Inquisitor," Fernando replied grimly. "A man named Fra Pagnelli, the most thorough inspector who ever wore the insignia of the Holy Office."

"You know him?" I asked, aghast.

"He is the Inquisitor that condemned Francis to the stake in Rome."

I could only watch in sick horror as the Dominican friar dismounted and vanished into the tavern, followed by the soldiers. Gripping my arm, Fernando pulled me around the outside of the tavern, towards the back door.

"Come," he whispered. "Let us find out what is going on."

Inside the tavern, we found the Inquisitor asking Journet in broken French how far it was to Orleans. He was rather short of stature, and thin, with a bony frame and deeply sunken eyes, as if years of austerity had left their mark.

Here, I thought with a sinking feeling, was the opposite extreme of the self-indulgent corpulence of a Bishop Sorel or a Cardinal de Joinville. And yet, at that moment, I would have preferred either one of them, or even both, to the man who now stood before me.

Fra Pagnelli turned and conversed with the soldiers for a moment in what sounded like Italian. Motioning me to stay back, Fernando inched his way around behind the casks of wine and ale so that he could hear them more clearly.

Pagnelli spoke to the soldiers for several minutes. Then, without stopping for either wine or ale, he motioned the soldiers out of the tavern. They remounted their horses and took off down the road.

"Marcel was right," I said as we emerged again into the street. "The bishop must have betrayed Father Francis to the Inquisition despite his denials."

But Fernando shook his head. "Fra Pagnelli was summoned by Montaigne, not Bishop Sorel. I overheard one of the soldiers ask where Montaigne was."

"Montaigne?" I echoed incredulously. "Is that possible? Can he summon the Holy Office without telling the bishop?"

"It appears that he has done just that," Fernando replied grimly. "Sorel will awaken tomorrow morning and find the Inquisition on his doorstep, and he will have no choice but to cooperate." Fernando shook his head slowly. "This is not good, little brother. Not good at all."

I swallowed hard. "What do we do now?"

"We must warn Francis." Fernando climbed up into the cart beside me and whipped the mule into a trot back up the road.

John met us at the gate and took the reins as we climbed out of the cart. He searched Fernando's face with a worried look. "The wolf is at the door."

It was a statement, not a question. Fernando only nodded.

John crossed himself, then unharnessed the mule and led it back to the stable.

"What's going on?" Juan-José appeared in the doorway. "Has Journet been watering the wine again?"

Frowning, Fernando shook his head and pushed past Juan-José into the parlor. "Where is Francis?"

"Antonin sent him upstairs to rest." Juan-José scrutinized Fernando, then me, then Fernando again. "Why?"

"We need to talk to him at once."

"About what?" Abbot Francis appeared in the kitchen door. He looked pale and leaned heavily against the door frame—almost as though he already knew what had happened.

"Fra Pagnelli is on his way to Orleans," Fernando said gently. "We saw him in Journet's tavern. It appears that Montaigne summoned him."

"That bastard," Juan-José hissed.

The abbot sank into his chair with a heavy sigh. "I must admit that I have been expecting it."

"Well, we pulled the wool over the eyes of that bastard archbishop. We can do the same for the Inquisitor," Juan-José said, jumping to his feet. "Come, my brothers. Let us be about it."

I glanced over at a sudden movement by the hearth. Marcel, who had been sitting in silence in the corner, rose to his feet. He gazed at me with an expression that was difficult to name. "What did I tell you?" he said under his breath, then turned and left the room.

I found myself shuddering.

—⁓—

I spent the remainder of the afternoon helping Fernando dismantle his laboratory yet again. Since he had packed it away only a few short months before, the task took only a few hours. He wasn't happy about doing it yet again, but had complied with Juan-Jose's request anyway. And I was relieved at having something to do other than worry.

We worked in silence save for the clatter of glassware. Fernando's face was drawn and haggard, and he said little beyond necessary instructions. I had hoped to get some information about Pagnelli out of him, but he was too lost in his own thoughts to chat.

"You're worried about Father Francis," I finally ventured, hoping to get him talking again. "Are you not?"

He nodded with a sigh. "He is still weak. I hope that he can withstand this latest onslaught."

"Is there anything more we can do?" I asked.

Fernando shook his head.

I watched him in silence for a long moment.

"Is it over?" I finally whispered. "Will they finally take him away?"

He turned to me in fury, his eyes flashing. "Do not say that, Michael!" he hissed. "Do not ever say that. We must not give up on him. Do you hear?"

I could only nod dumbly.

Running a trembling hand through his black hair, Fernando shut his eyes as a look of anguish crossed his features. "Forgive me, little brother. I had not meant to vent my rage upon you."

I reached over and laid my hand upon his shoulder, feeling the tension in every muscle.

"Fernando," I began, "does Fra Pagnelli have the authority to arrest Father Francis?"

Fernando swallowed hard and nodded.

"Even here in France?"

"Yes," he replied. "Once Pagnelli has condemned Francis for sorcery, he will be turned over to the secular authorities for execution, which Montaigne, damn him, will be only too happy to carry out."

"But Pagnelli still requires proof, doesn't he?" I asked, a knot of fear settling in my stomach. "Isn't that why we are hiding your alchemical apparatus? So Pagnelli won't find any evidence of sorcery?"

"It does not matter what we do," Fernando muttered through clenched teeth. "Pagnelli has methods of persuading people to tell him what he wants to know. He will find the proof he requires."

"And then, what?"

"Then, little brother." Fernando turned to me, his eyes brimming with tears. "It will be only the grace of God that will keep Francis from going to the stake."

We finished packing as it grew dark, then we picked our way along the icy flagstone path to the refectory for supper. Even without observing the Rule, we ate in silence. Fernando, maintaining his composure with an effort, busied himself serving the bread and wine. Marcel was decidedly conspicuous by his absence and Juan-José frowned as he passed the empty place at the table.

"He is most likely brooding again," Antonin commented. "You know how he is."

"Well, he won't have the luxury of brooding for long," Juan-José grumbled. "He needs to collect his rubbish and put it in the Tabernacle again. We don't have much time."

"Oh, I am sure he will come through," Antonin said staunchly. "As he did last time."

I glanced over at John, who silently met my gaze and shook his head slightly. I thought of Antonin's chilling prediction that one of us would betray Sainte Felice. I found that I could not finish the rest of my supper.

The next morning dawned sunny and a bit warmer. Heartened, I helped John prepare breakfast and noticed that even Abbot Francis looked a good deal better.

Fernando turned in his seat at the sound of footsteps coming in from the garden. "That must be Marcel," he said brightly. "Perhaps he has decided to join us after all. Marcel, have you…" His voice trailed off and his brown eyes grew wide in astonishment.

We all turned as Marcel strode into the refectory, dressed in tattered shirt, tunic, and leggings, with a patched mantle thrown over his shoulders. He carried a small sack in one hand and his black habit bundled up in the other.

Abbot Francis slowly rose to his feet. "Marcel?"

"Francis," Marcel began, his voice hoarse with emotion. "Please release me from my vows. I wish to leave the monastery and return to Anjou." He tossed the habit onto the table in a rumpled heap.

The abbot flinched, as though he had been struck in the face. "May I ask why?"

"The reason should be obvious," Marcel replied, looking around like a trapped animal as we all stared at him in disbelief. "We are in great danger here. That bishop now knows who you are, and it won't be long before the soldiers of the Inquisition come to arrest you. I, for one, don't want to be here when they do."

Juan-José vaulted to his feet. "You coward!"

The abbot waved him quiet. "Very well, Marcel," he said quietly, maintaining his dignity. "If you truly wish to go, I will not keep you." He paused for a moment, only his eyes betraying his grief. "Is there anything we can provide for your journey?"

"One thing only." Laying his bundle on the floor,

Marcel knelt at the abbot's feet. "Please, Francis, give me your blessing."

His hand visibly shaking, Abbot Francis made the sign of the cross over Marcel, as though he were blessing one newly dead. Marcel then stood and met the abbot's eyes for a long moment. Abbot Francis reached out his hands, but then abruptly drew back. Marcel scowled ferociously and whirled around, snatching up his bundle. We stood as though turned into stone as he stalked out of the refectory, and remained that way until we heard the clang of the iron gate as it slammed shut.

"I suppose I should have expected this," the abbot finally said, with a heavy sigh. "Marcel has never felt entirely safe within these walls."

"Still, that is no excuse," Juan-José fumed. "He took vows."

"To God," the abbot replied sharply. "I have released him from his vow of obedience to me as abbot." He gazed sadly about the room. "And I shall do the same for any of the rest of you, should you decide to follow Marcel."

"Not bloody likely," Juan-José muttered.

"How could you even think we would?" Fernando demanded.

"You would do well to consider it," the abbot persisted, his expression stern. "And let me know what you decide." Moving as though he had aged twenty years in the last twenty minutes, he turned towards the door. "Until then, we must carry on as best we might under the circumstances."

A pall of sorrow hung over the entire monastery, almost

as though one of us had died. It pervaded every room like a bone-penetrating chill. We spoke only when necessary and except for exchanging an occasional meaningful glance, avoided each other's gaze. I busied myself hauling wood from the shed to the hearth and helping John keep the fire stoked in the oven as he baked our bread for the day.

The hot soup and fresh bread that John served for dinner lifted our spirits only a little. We kept our conversation to trivialities such as the possibility of planting carrots and parsnips in the spring, how the repairs on the roof should be made, and whether we should consider keeping a few chickens in the cloister in order to have our own eggs. Too often, we fell suddenly silent as our chatter failed to keep the gloom at bay. We would glance at each other in near desperation, and another brother would try a different subject.

Abbot Francis tried his best to remain genial, but his thoughts were clearly elsewhere and his comments were uttered in one or two words. Often he would drift off into his own reverie and not hear us at all. After dinner, he thanked John for his culinary efforts and retreated to his chambers.

Antonin watched him until he was out of sight and then sadly shook his head. "I wish there was something we could do."

"Damned if I know what," Juan-José put in.

"Someone must go into the village this afternoon," John said softly. "We need supplies."

Fernando shook his head. "I don't wish to leave him."

"Nor I," Antonin said.

"Then, I shall go," I said. "I can handle the mule."

"And I shall go as well," Juan-José spoke up. "In case Michael needs assistance."

"Very well," John replied. "We will require butter and eggs and cheese, if you can pry some out of the cheesemonger."

"I will do my best," I assured him.

Fernando harnessed the mule while I climbed into the cart. Juan-José vaulted up beside me and something made of metal clanked against the wooden beams of the cart. I glanced over and saw to my astonishment that he had his sword strapped to his belt. Tendrils of fear prickled down the back of my neck. "Do you really think that is necessary?"

He did not reply, but his look told me clearly that he felt it was. With many misgivings about the entire trip, I grabbed the reins and urged the mule down the path to the main road.

As we clattered along, I could not shake the feeling that something was decidedly wrong. It took me a moment before I could put my finger upon exactly what it was. I finally realized that it was past midday and we were the only ones on the road for as far as I could see. No hay wagons, no travelers on horseback or in fine carriages. This was the main road from Paris to Orleans, and it was deserted.

I turned to Juan-José to comment, but I discovered him gazing intently off into the distance like a stag sniffing the air for the scent of the wolf.

"Pull off the road." He pointed towards my left. "Quickly."

I steered the mule into the grass. The cart had not yet come to a halt before Juan-José jumped down and ran around the back. Reaching up, he dragged me out of my seat.

"What are you doing?" I demanded.

He silenced me with a scowl and pulled me down behind the cart. I heard the hoofbeats of a multitude of horses coming down the road from the north. "Soldiers," he muttered in my ear. "I saw them over the hill."

"What are they doing here?" I asked.

"I don't know. But I'll wager that they are not out gathering daffodils." He laid his hand on the hilt of his sword as the hoofbeats grew louder.

Finally, the soldiers rode by us. There had to be at least a dozen of them. They escorted a man on a horse who rode as best he might with shackles on his hands and feet. He glanced around as the procession passed the cart. I saw his face only for a moment, but that moment was enough.

"Oh my God," I whispered. "It's Marcel."

"Yes," Juan-José said dourly. "They probably captured him on the road to Paris."

"But how would they know who he was?"

"No doubt they stopped to question every traveler on the road. Marcel, in his panic, must have tried to run away. That was probably when they figured out who he was and arrested him."

"But where are they taking him?"

"To Orleans, from the look of it," Juan-José replied. "That Inquisitor will pump him like a well. We shall have no secrets at all when they are through with him. Come. Butter or no, we must return and warn Francis."

I nodded in agreement. But when I peeked around the cart, I stared straight into the face of a soldier. With a shout, he reached out and grabbed me while three more soldiers raced around the other side of the cart.

Juan-José already had his sword drawn. With lightening speed, he skewered one immediately, but the other two came at him from either side. He backed off and lunged at one assailant, then, when that one was recovering, struck at the other. One soldier howled as blood flowed from a cut in his arm. The other backed Juan-José up against the hill.

I gasped as Juan-José stumbled and fell. But, as though he had planned it all along, he rolled out of the way just as the soldier made what he must have thought was a killing thrust and scrambled to his feet once again. The soldier looked up to face a flashing blade, and blocked the blow just in time.

The abbot had been right. Juan-José was a brilliant swordsman. But he was one man against two. I glanced over at my captor, who was watching the battle with a glee-ful grin. I quickly decided that I was not about to stand there wringing my hands like a maiden in distress. With a sudden movement, I yanked my arm free, pulled away from the soldier holding me, and made a dive for the fallen one, grabbing a dagger from his belt.

With a yell, my captor came at me. But I rose to my knees and buried the dagger up to its hilt in the stomach that swelled beneath his breastplate, feeling the soft flesh give way before the sharp blade. He grunted and fell, knocking me over. He kicked several times, but I kept ahold of the dagger, feeling the warm wetness bathing my hand. Finally, he rolled over on top of me, belched up blood which splattered on my habit, and lay still.

The ruckus caused enough of a distraction to allow Juan-José to dispatch one of the other two soldiers, leaving him facing only one. Feeling a strange rush of fury, I kicked free of the body pinning me to the ground, grasped the sword from the dead fingers and swung at the remaining soldier. He easily blocked my clumsy blow, but received another in the chest from Juan-José. He fell, and the battle was over.

I found myself shaking and dropped the sword on the ground, feeling for a moment as though I would be sick. Juan-José glanced over at me in some surprise.

"Well!" he exclaimed, brushing his hair from his eyes. "Fine work, my boy. I thought you had never fought before."

"I haven't," I replied dully.

"Well, now you have." Nonchalantly wiping his blade on his habit, he slipped his sword into its sheath. Then, he took up the blade lying on the grass and wiped it clean also. He rolled the body of my dead captor over with his foot and pulled the scabbard off the belt. "Here," he said, handing both blade and scabbard to me. "It is yours, now. Consider it the spoils of war."

Draping his arm around my trembling shoulders, he led me to the cart and pushed me up into the seat. Vaulting up beside me, he took the reins himself and turned the mule's head around, toward the path to the monastery.

It was nearly sunset by the time we pulled up to the gate. Fernando ran out and held the reins as we climbed down. He glanced at the empty wagon with a slight frown.

"Where are the supplies?" he asked. "You remember, the butter and cheese from the village?"

"We never got to the village," Juan-José muttered.

Fernando's eyes grew wide at the sight of my blood-stained habit. He quickly tied the reins to the iron spikes and followed us into the parlor as John emerged from the kitchen.

"Sorry about the butter, John." Juan-José unbuckled his sword belt and tossed it on the table. "But we ran into a little trouble."

"Holy God!" Abbot Francis stood in the doorway, staring at us in utter horror.

"The village is swarming with soldiers, Francis," Juan-José said grimly. "There must have been an entire garrison out patrolling the road. They had Marcel in chains and were taking him back to Orleans when we came upon them. They tried to take us as well." He glowered darkly. "But they did not succeed."

John crossed himself. "God only knows what they will do to him."

Clutching the arm of his chair, Abbot Francis sank into it with the soft cry of a man stricken to the heart. "Oh, Marcel, Marcel," he murmured, his voice torn with anguish, "You warned me so often and I paid no heed. Now, you must suffer for my accursed pride. Forgive me, my brother. Forgive me."

"Please, Francis." Antonin knelt and laid his hand on the abbot's arm. "You must not blame yourself. Remember that Marcel chose to leave."

"As all of you must," the abbot declared, fixing us with an intense gaze. "At once! There is no time to lose. It may be today or tomorrow, but the Inquisition will now surely come for me. I beg you, begone! Lest they take you as well."

We all held our breaths, glancing around at each other. Finally, Fernando spoke, voicing that which lay in all of our hearts. His eyes were bright with emotion, but his voice remained calm and assured.

"Francis," he began, laying his hand on top of the abbot's own. "There is no power on earth that can force me to leave you. I will remain here, and if it is God's will that I share your fate, then so be it."

Antonin reached up and laid his own hand on top of Fernando's. "I can say it no better than that."

"Nor I." Juan-José did the same.

I hurried to place my hand on top of Juan-José's as John placed his atop mine. "It looks as though you cannot chase us away, Father Francis," I said. "Any more than you could the rats in the Tabernacle."

Fernando could not suppress a snort of laughter. But the abbot gazed up at us for a moment, his eyes growing moist.

"My brothers," he whispered hoarsely, "I have no words…"

"None are needed." Juan-José rose briskly to his feet. "We've had too many words around here as it is. What we need now is action."

"The Inquisitor will come tomorrow morning," John said softly.

"Then we will give him a proper welcome," Juan-José declared. "And if it is a fight that they want, a fight they will have."

That night, my tormented heart forbade me the comfort of sleep. Frightened and distraught, I lit my taper and made my way to the church, hoping against hope that I might find some little solace there.

The glow of candlelight told me that someone was there before me. I tiptoed in and halted at the sacristy door. A figure knelt in the pool of light from the flickering lamp that glowed before the Sacred Host. Muffled sobs echoed off the walls.

I stood still as one of the statues while Abbot Francis wept at the foot of the altar that he had vowed to serve. I wanted to go to him, to think of something reassuring to say to comfort him. But I could not bring myself to approach him. If the thought of his rage had frightened me so, his despair filled me with such dreadful awe that I could do nothing but turn and flee from the church, fighting back my own tears until I could vent my grief in the silent safety of my cell.

At dawn, we assembled in the parlor. We said nothing,

only listened to the roar of the fire in the hearth. John made no move to prepare breakfast, but sat near the door, staring at it as if he expected it to open any moment. The rest of us looked at each other in growing concern as the moments dragged by. Only Abbot Francis seemed resigned to his fate, sitting in his chair by the hearth, pressing his interlaced fingers to his lips in what looked like a gesture of prayer.

We had not long to wait. Someone pounded on the door and we all jumped to our feet. Fernando glanced around, stricken, then slowly made his way to the door and opened it.

Abbot Francis rose gracefully to his feet as a triumphant Giles de Montaigne, flanked by several heavily armed soldiers, pushed Fernando aside and strode into the parlor. Looming behind Montaigne was Fra Pagnelli. I swallowed hard as I recognized the insignia of the Holy Office.

Montaigne turned to Pagnelli and pointed to the abbot. "Is this the man you found guilty of sorcery in Rome?" he demanded. "Is this the Wizard of Alceste?"

Pagnelli nodded. "It is." He looked the abbot up and down, stroking his long chin. "Good day to you, Signore Seratois. We meet again."

"So we do, Fra Pagnelli." The abbot strode forward with deceptive calm. "Welcome to my monastery. What brings you to Sainte Felice?"

"You."

"I?" The abbot raised an eyebrow. "Why would the Holy Office be interested in the humble abbot of a tiny monastery so far from Rome?"

"Don't toy with me." Pagnelli scowled in sudden anger. "Do you think that we have not heard tales of the miracle worker of Sainte Felice, who has angels at his beck and call? I suspected that it was you. The letter from the Magistrate of Orleans accusing you of sorcery only confirmed my suspicions. It is no use, Signore. You escaped the pyre in Rome. I am here to see that you do not outrun justice again."

"Fra Pagnelli," the abbot said slowly. "If I recall correctly, you are nothing if not thorough. By now, you must have learned from Bishop Sorel that I have recanted my heresy, been absolved, taken holy orders, and become a Benedictine abbot. And I credit you and the Holy Office for guiding me into seeing the error of my sinful ways." He nodded briefly. "I am indeed in your debt."

Pagnelli did not appear impressed. "Clever, Signore. Very clever. However, I don't believe you. If anything, you are an even more dangerous heretic now than you were in Rome. While it is true that you have joined the Benedictine order, it is not true that you have abandoned your accursed art. Even within these hallowed walls, you still practice your sorceries."

"Monsieur de Montaigne has repeatedly accused me of that," the abbot returned. "Even though Cardinal de Joinville could find no proof."

"Oh, we have proof." The Inquisitor gestured to one of the soldiers. My heart sickened as the soldier dragged Marcel into the center of the room and tossed him, ragged and bleeding, onto the floor at the abbot's feet. "One of your brothers has made a full confession. It is all the proof we need. And now—Abbot Duchienne, I believe it is—you are under arrest as a sorcerer and relapsed heretic. You will come with us."

I could not help gasping as the soldiers drew their swords and reached for the abbot.

His blue eyes flashing fire, Abbot Francis stepped back, grasped his pectoral cross, and reached up towards the ceiling. Immediately we heard a low rumble, a sharp crack, and the throaty sounds of unearthly growls coming from the direction of the church.

The soldiers drew back and dropped their swords, eyes wide. Six stone gargoyles, their red eyes glinting in the gray dawn, appeared in the doorway, waiting only for one gesture from the abbot to tear the soldiers apart with their granite jaws.

"Fools!" the Inquisitor shouted over the din. "Do not be put off by his phantoms. Seize him!"

But the soldiers, to a man, refused to come anywhere near the abbot despite Pagnelli's exhortations. It appeared to be a standoff. Then, as Marcel got to his knees and began to crawl towards the safety of the abbot's feet, Montaigne pounced upon him like a cat after a mouse. Catching Marcel around the neck, Montaigne drew his dagger and held the tip to Marcel's throat.

"Call off your devils, Abbot Duchienne," he snarled. "Or your monk dies."

"Don't do it, Francis," Marcel gurgled hoarsely. "Please! Don't listen to them. Let me die and save the others."

Slowly, Abbot Francis heaved a sigh and released his

grip on the cross. The gargoyles vanished and the roaring subsided, leaving only the crackle of the flames in the hearth. He pressed his fingertips together and bowed his head in a gesture of defeat.

"Very well," he finally said. "Release him."

"Francis!" Marcel cried out in protest.

The abbot gazed down at Marcel and shook his head. "No, my brother. I will not endanger your life. I accept my fate." Pulling the cross and chain from around his neck, he placed it on the table and held out his wrists to the astonished soldiers. "Take me."

Juan-José could bear it no longer. Pulling his own sword from its scabbard, he lunged forward. "Touch him and die!"

Two of the soldiers drew their swords in response and it looked as though there would be a battle.

Abbot Francis turned to Juan-José and shook his head. "Put your sword away, my brother."

"But, Francis..."

"Do it!" the abbot snapped.

Clearly torn, Juan-José met the abbot's gaze for a long moment, then scowled and slipped the sword back into its scabbard. "As you wish, Francis."

Montaigne glared around the room, peering at each of us in turn. "What about the rest of them?" He turned to Pagnelli. "Shall I arrest them all?"

"Leave them be." Pagnelli waved his hand in a gesture of dismissal. "They are of no consequence. I have the man I came for."

Montaigne hesitated, then released his hold on Marcel.

As Marcel crumpled to the floor, Montaigne motioned for one of the soldiers to come forward. Nervously, the soldier fastened iron manacles around the abbot's wrists. We watched, rooted to the floor in unbelieving horror, as the soldiers led Abbot Francis out the door, shutting it behind him with a resounding thud.

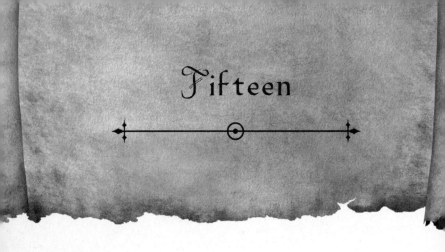

Fifteen

"No!" Fernando flung himself at the door, pounded it with his fists, then sank to his knees with a anguished sob. John knelt at his side as Juan-José turned in fury on Marcel, who lay weeping silently in a crumpled heap on the floor.

"Betrayer!" he bellowed, drawing his sword. "Judas himself was no worse a scoundrel than you!"

"Go ahead," Marcel murmured. "Kill me. I would rather die than live with what I've done."

Antonin knelt beside him, glaring defiantly up at Juan-José. "If you kill him, then you must kill me, and perhaps the rest of us as well. We might well, any one of us, do that which Marcel has done. I don't know about you, my brother, but I could not long endure the tortures of the Holy Office without confessing everything."

Juan-José scowled darkly for a long moment as the

bloodthirsty sword trembled in his hand. Antonin point-edly turned away and began examining the oozing lacera-tions on Marcel's hands, wrists, and ankles. I shuddered as I thought of what wounds might lie beneath his tattered clothes.

Finally I could stand it no longer. "Please, my broth-ers. Let us not fight among ourselves this way. It does not matter who did what. Father Francis has been arrested and God only knows what instruments of pain and torment they have reserved for him."

I broke off, my voice threatening to break. But John rose to his feet, gazing intently at something, or someone, behind me.

"Listen to Michael, my brothers." His soft voice echoed in the strained silence. "He speaks with the voice of angels, and his words are wise."

Everyone turned to face me. Even Fernando had left off sobbing and raised his head.

"We can rescue him," I went on, my voice strangely strengthened by I knew not what. "By whatever power and knowledge that we each possess, we can save him from the pyre. But we can only do so if we lay aside our jealousies and rivalries and work together. Please, let us do so at once. We don't have much time. I beg of you, let us not argue while our beloved abbot burns at the stake."

Slowly, Juan-José eased his blade back into its scabbard and unbuckled his sword belt. He reached down and offered Marcel his hand. Marcel stared at him in utter disbelief for a moment, then took the proffered hand. Juan-José pulled

Marcel to his feet as Antonin took his other arm. Together they carried Marcel up the stairs to his cell.

I let my breath out in a shuddering sigh and tried to ease the trembling which had taken hold of my limbs. I turned to find John watching me with a smile. "You are doing well, my young magus."

"I'm not a magus," I said.

"Not yet, perhaps. But you soon will be." He held out his hand to me. "Come. Let's see what we can find to eat."

After dinner, we assembled by the hearth fire, nursed the last of the wine, and held a council of war. Juan-José presided from the abbot's chair and surveyed the lot of us from beneath his furrowed brow. "What we need, my brothers, is a plan of attack. Every trick, every scheme, and every ally must be called upon if we are going to not only save Francis but ourselves as well. Now, let us begin with allies. Who do we have in our camp?"

"Emil Journet and the people of Sainte Felice," Fernando said, lifting his chin in determination. "With Journet's help, we can rally the entire village into revolt if necessary."

"A good place to begin," Juan-José replied with a nod. "Now, who else?"

"The Duke and Duchess of Orleans," Antonin said. "Particularly the dowager duchess. They surely would have some influence with the king, who might be persuaded to grant Francis a royal pardon. I will ride out to their castle as soon as it is dark."

"But what if you're stopped like Marcel was?" I protested. "There are soldiers swarming all over the road."

"I will travel by night," Antonin replied with his usual calm. "And stay clear of the road."

Juan-José considered this. "Very well, but have a care, and go armed." He turned to the rest of us. "Now, have we left out anyone?"

"Bishop Sorel," I put in. "In spite of everything, he might be persuaded to help."

"How do you propose to do that, Michael?" Juan-José asked pointedly.

"By playing upon his pride," I suggested. "Surely he cannot be overly pleased about having Montaigne call in the Inquisition without his consent."

"Good point," Juan-José conceded. "But you will have to take the cart to Orleans alone, and that will be dangerous."

I couldn't help a knowing smile. "I, too, am armed."

"That covers our earthly allies," John said. "We have celestial allies as well, you know. I advise you not to forget them." His pale-eyed gaze met Juan-José's dark one without wavering or flinching.

Finally, Juan-José heaved a sigh of defeat. "Very well, John. What do you suggest?"

"They will warn us of danger and advise us as to further action if we will trust in their wisdom, even if what they advise goes against our reason or lies beyond our control."

Juan-José clearly did not find this to his taste. His

frown deepened. "I do not fancy relying on unarmed apparitions."

"Unarmed only to you, my brother." John glared pointedly at Juan-José for a moment. "Do you doubt their power?"

Juan-José slowly shook his head.

"Then, we must call upon them and implore their aid." John turned his gaze upon me. I rose from my chair, slowly moving to the table by the door. The abbot's golden cross lay where he had dropped it. I took it in my hand and turned it over in my fingers.

"I will invoke them tonight," I said.

"But who will you invoke, Michael?"

John's voice faded for a moment into echoes. Michael … Michael … Michael … Of course. I remembered that Abbot Francis had always called upon Raphael. I would need my own patron, and who better than the angel whose name I bore?

"Michael?"

"Yes," I replied, rather distracted. "Indeed. I will invoke the Archangel Michael."

John smiled broadly. "Ah, my brother, you are indeed learning to heed the angelic voices." He turned to Juan-José with a satisfied look. "Have we all of our legions in place?"

"Celestial and terrestrial, at any rate," Antonin said. "Shall we try for infernal?"

Fernando sniffed with contempt. "I think we have quite enough infernal legions to deal with, thank you."

"Then let us begin." Juan-José rose to his feet and we all followed suit, each preparing for his own task. I felt both strangely heartened and nervous at the same time. I wandered for a moment into the library and laid my hand on the abbot's Grimoire of Light. Although I gained some comfort from it, I knew in my soul that this was to be my ultimate test as a magician and that I would have to rely on my own knowledge, not the abbot's.

Still, there was someone whose assistance I had not yet sought. I left the grimoire on the shelf and made my way to the kitchen, following the fragments of a melody that emerged from the doorway. Singing softly, John stood at the table preparing his usual loaves for our supper. I waited for a moment, then entered the warm room.

"John?" I began. "Could I ask a favor of you?"

He looked up from the bread dough, noticed the expression on my face, and laid the mound of dough down on the table. "Why certainly, Michael. What can I do for you?"

I stared down at the surface of the table. "I am going to be performing one of the abbot's rituals for the first time, and I ... would you please do for me as you have done for him?"

"I had intended to." John gave me a knowing smile. "Still, I am pleased that you would ask. Come. Walk with me."

He laid a towel over the bread dough and took my arm. The air was crisp and clear as we strolled into the cloister, our cowls thrown up against the chill. The last of the snow crusted the ground around the base of the walls of the cloister garth and a few bright green shoots in Marcel's garden struggled to appear above the cold earth. It would be spring soon.

"I am frightened." I knew that, with John, there was no point in equivocating.

"Good," he said. "That is what keeps you humble."

I shook my head. "I don't fear for myself. I want to help Father Francis so very much, and I fear that I should do something wrong. There is so much that I don't understand. John, you seem to know far more about what is going on than anyone else, including, I suspect, Father Francis himself."

"It comes from doing less talking and more listening." John chuckled softly. "All the rest of you, including Francis, pay far too much heed to your own thoughts and not enough to what others are saying. I have been trying to tell Francis for years that if he tried hard enough to appear to be a saint, one day he would find that he had become one."

"But is he really a saint?"

"By whose definition?" John raised an eyebrow. "The Church's? The cardinals' and popes' who will burn a man for heresy one day, then canonize him the next? Or the frail old woman with a wasting sickness who touches the hem of his garment and is instantly healed?"

"I don't know," I replied, more confused than ever. "The latter, I suppose."

"Then, you tell me. You are the one who watched him bring a dead child back to life. Is he a saint?"

"Yes," I said. "At least he is to me."

"Then it does not matter what anyone else says."

"Oh, but it does," I protested bitterly. "If the magistrate thought he was a saint rather than a sorcerer, he would not want to burn him."

"You think not?" John raised an eyebrow. "I would say that he would want to burn Francis all the more. To Montaigne, who craves power through fear, a man like our abbot, who receives obedience freely through love, would seem to have some uncanny power at his disposal. This is a power that Montaigne does not understand and cannot possibly have. However, this is the last thing that he will admit. So, he tries to convince himself that he is a virtuous man for not having it, and that the abbot's power is diabolical."

"But how does that help Father Francis?"

"By helping you, his apprentice, to know your enemy. You are the one who must go after Montaigne. Our abbot cannot do so."

"Now I truly don't understand," I said, annoyed at my own confusion. "Father Francis is a powerful wizard."

"In many ways. However, you know something that he does not, and it is the knowledge that you possess that will free him. You know that he is a saint. He still thinks that he is a sorcerer."

"But you said yourself that you have tried to tell him."

"Ah, yes." John sighed. "And he did not hear me. He cannot."

"Are you telling me that in order to truly be a saint, you have to be totally unaware that you are one?"

John smiled and clapped his hands. "Now you are beginning to allow yourself to understand. Do you see why it must be you that rescues Francis?"

"Yes, I think so. But how do I go after Montaigne?"

"Montaigne is terrified of Francis, to the point of obsession. Why, Francis cannot wish him so much as a good morning without Montaigne accusing him of bewitchment. It is not sane. Do you realize now what a powerful weapon you wield? You know Francis even better than he knows himself. Montaigne knows nothing. He fears and you do not."

"But how do I wield this weapon?"

"You already know how. Francis has taught you. The question is, do you have the courage to wield it against Montaigne?"

"A man who is trying to destroy everything that I have come to cherish?" I replied furiously. "I should hope so."

"Perhaps. However, keep in mind that an arrow loosed in anger cannot be recalled once the temper cools."

"I know. And I will take that responsibility."

"Are you very sure?" John scrutinized me carefully, with an intensity that knew no evasion. I knew now why the English king had wanted him dead. "Think hard on it, Michael. When you conjure the blessed angels and ask your boon, you must then stand aside and let it be done according to their will, not yours. For if you unleash divine power for your own purposes and not for the glory of God, you remain nothing more than a conjurer in a black robe. Then, one day, that power will turn on you and rend you."

"I understand." I squared my shoulders and met his gaze, then faltered as the implications of what he had just said began to dawn on me. "I think."

"Good enough." John rose, drawing me up with him. "Now go and prepare. And when you are ready to do your working, I will be at your side."

Just before supper, Antonin and Fernando returned from the village with a roan mare, already saddled and bridled, tied to the back of the cart. Antonin jumped down off the cart and tied the mare to the gate as John and Fernando put the mule in the stable.

"It was as I had thought," Fernando reported as we sat down to a quick supper of bread and cheese. "Nearly all of Sainte Felice watched the soldiers drag Francis in chains through the village square."

"Where did they take him?" Juan-José asked.

"To the bishop's palace in Orleans," Fernando replied.

"At least they did not take him to Paris," I said.

"I think Montaigne wishes to keep an eye on him," Fernando went on. "He cannot help but have seen the angry crowd in Sainte Felice. Journet is outraged, as you might expect, and will rouse the rest of the district before another day passes. If Francis is harmed, there will be a revolt. Of that I have no doubt."

Dusk was falling as we waited by the gate. Antonin appeared, clad in a simple tunic and leather hose with a hooded cloak over his shoulders. At his belt hung a dagger encased in a leather sheath.

"I am armed, as you suggested," he said, pointing to the dagger. "It is not in a league with your sword, Juan-José, but it will do the job if necessary."

"Be careful," Fernando admonished.

Antonin gave him a reassuring smile. "Oh, I intend to." He embraced each of us in turn and gave me a pat on the back. "Give your angel my regards, Michael."

The sun dipped below the hills as Antonin swung up into the saddle and turned the horse's head towards the road to Orleans. He waved one final time and kicked the horse into a gallop. We watched until he had vanished around the bend.

"God's grace ride with you, Antonin," Fernando murmured.

I led the way into the kitchen, my candle quivering in my hand and throwing undulating shadows on the walls.

"We don't have enough people for this," Juan-José observed. "Besides the operator, we need four quarter men. Without Antonin, we have only three."

"I will be the fourth."

We turned and found Marcel standing in the doorway, clad once again in habit and cowl. He was pale, I noted, and walked with difficulty, but he seemed to be moved by an inner force that I had not seen in him before.

"Are you sure that you are up to it, Marcel?" Fernando asked in concern.

"Yes," Marcel stated simply.

"Then, come and be welcome." John held out his hand. Marcel hesitated for a moment, then joined the tail end of the procession through the kitchen. Fernando released the lever, and the slab slid away from the stairs. Holding my candle aloft, I led the way down into the passageway.

I clutched my sword tightly with both hands as the others lit the torches. The spirits of air, earth, fire, and water were summoned, and all, I was sure, came gleefully to watch a fledgling magus either take to the air or plummet to the ground.

Finally, all was ready. I stepped into the circle before the tiny altar, and froze. "I can't do this," I protested, so terrified that my voice emerged in a mouse-like squeak. "Somebody else with more experience needs to do it."

"Michael," Fernando said gently, "you are the only one who knows the invocations. None of the rest of us do. This particular art was Francis' own . . . and yours, since he instructed you. You must do it."

"But I don't know enough yet."

"You know enough to invoke something that tossed a duke through the air." Fernando reached out and took me by the shoulders. "Little brother, Francis believes in you. So do we. You can do it . . . you must . . . for him."

I swallowed hard and drew myself up to my full height. I was a Sacred Magician, and I would perform my magic for Father Francis—and all of the people who loved him and depended on him. His cross hung heavy on my breast, reminding me of the awesome nature of the task I was about to undertake. I clutched it for a brief moment. It burned like acid in my hand. I took a deep breath and began.

"Come, ye angels, most powerful, most strong, most benign..."

My nervousness vanished with the first puff of incense smoke. Nothing else mattered but saving Father Francis. I begged, pleaded, threatened, and cajoled, prayed and mortified myself with increasing passion and urgency until I could contain my emotion no longer. Raising my sword above my head, I cried out my final conjuration as the smoke from the thurible curled and writhed upwards towards the ceiling.

My voice echoing off the cavern walls, I fell silent, spent and trembling. The smoke continued to plume for the space of several heartbeats. Then, before my astonished gaze, the form of a man appeared within the smoke, a warrior with drawn sword and bright shield. Tongues of fire fanned out behind him.

"What would you of me?" The deep, guttural voice which issued from John's throat was so unlike his own that I could not help a shudder.

"Not for myself do I call. But for the succor of another who is as dear as a father to me. I plead, O Blessed Archangel Michael, rescue Abbot Francis from the Jackal of Orleans."

The answer came in no uncertain terms. "It will be done

according to your petition provided you do one thing, and one thing only."

"I will do anything," I cried. "Only tell me what it is."

"Wait," the voice stated flatly. "Until the will of God is fulfilled and the time of deliverance is at hand."

"But how will we know that time?" I demanded. "Give us a sign, we pray you."

"You will have your sign," the stern voice issuing from John's mouth insisted, "when the pyre rises in Sainte Felice."

I began to protest. Once the pyre was erected in the village square, it would too late.

But the angel would say no more, and John, his breathing shallow and gasping, looked like he would soon faint.

My heart heavy, I recited the License to Depart as Fernando extinguished the brazier. The presence faded and John sank to the floor with a moan. I knelt beside him until he regained enough of his strength to stand. Then, exhausted and numb, I extinguished the candles while the others dismissed the angels at the quarters.

"This cannot be," I lamented. "I have failed."

"Have you?" Juan-José said sharply as we ascended the stairs. "You insist that I trust in the power of these angels of yours. The least you can do is set a good example."

Chastened, I watched as Fernando threw the latch to close the entrance to the passageway. I now understood why a rite of magic was never discussed afterwards. In the clear light of reason, one cannot help but doubt the events which took place in the candlelit darkness. Eventually one would question whether or not they occurred at all. It was enough to drive one mad.

Had I really summoned an archangel—me, a fifteen-year-old novice monk? Or had it all been nothing but a theatrical charade? A hard lump rose in my throat and I felt tears rising to my eyes.

Juan-José was right. I would have to have faith.

—⁓—

The bishop's palace loomed before me as I steered the cart into the center of town, dodging chickens, sheep, and small children that scurried in my path. I tied up the mule and found the vaulted entrance flanked by soldiers. They eyed me suspiciously, but I was merely one cleric among many others scurrying in and out of the entryway, so they let me pass.

"I wish to see the bishop," I told the clerk seated at the huge desk.

He looked me up and down, taking in my Benedictine habit. "Have you an appointment, Brother?"

"No, I do not," I replied. "My visit is unexpected. But it is a matter of great urgency."

"It always is," the clerk muttered sullenly. "Bishop Sorel is a busy man."

"No doubt," I said in a conciliatory tone. "And I will not disturb him for long. Perhaps if you would give him a short message for me, he will agree to see me. If he does not, I will be on my way."

"And what might that message be?"

"Two words," I replied. "Sainte Felice."

"Sainte Felice?" I noticed his expression change from indifference to sudden interest. "Wait here."

He rose and entered the bishop's chambers, leaving me in the corridor. There was a nearby bench to sit upon, but I was far too nervous. I paced the colored tile floor like some tethered beast until the door creaked open.

"The bishop will see you now." The clerk stood aside as I entered.

The bishop's huge desk, littered with books, papers, and other business, dominated the room. But the bishop was not at it. He paced the floor near the roaring hearth, stopping only to look up at me as I entered.

He scowled at me as I knelt to kiss his ring. "And who might you be?"

"I am Brother Michael de Lorraine," I replied, throwing back my cowl. "From the Abbey of Sainte Felice."

"You!" He scowled into my face for a moment. "You are the one who was the cause of all this trouble."

"Yes, Excellency," I said sheepishly. "To my deep regret. That is why I am here."

He waved me impatiently into silence. "Let me guess. You wish me to release your abbot. Is that right?"

"Yes," I whispered in bewilderment, my prepared speech flapping out the window like a pigeon.

"Well, I cannot. And that is the end to it." He turned away and lumbered to his desk.

"You cannot?" I returned, suddenly angry. "Or you will not?"

He turned on me with a ferocious look. "Hold your tongue, boy. You are beginning to sound like him."

I obediently fell silent, but kept my gaze upon the bishop who, clearly agitated, began to pace the carpet again.

"Brother Michael," he finally said. "Do you really think that I relish having a saint chained up in my dungeon?"

"Even though he concealed his past from you for all these years?" I asked.

"Bother it all, I knew he wasn't who he said he was before I ordained him." Bishop Sorel heaved a sigh. "Hiding a disreputable past behind a monastic habit is a ploy as old as the Church herself. But that didn't matter. I sent him to that ruin because I felt that he was the one man who had both the cleverness and the determination to revive it. And so he did, far better than I had hoped."

I paused, then lowered my voice. "Do you believe that he is a sorcerer?"

"I don't know what he is." The bishop fell into his chair and massaged his brow. "All I know is what he has done. He has made a destitute village prosperous, prosperous enough to pay taxes to both Church and Crown. He has made your abbey into a place of pilgrimage. Where I cannot get two dozen people into the cathedral on a Sunday, he packs them into his tiny church like herring. People from Orleans to Paris have proclaimed him a saint. I have even had a formal protest from the Duke of Orleans for holding him prisoner, threatening to go to the Pope if I do not desist. By God, I would release him in a moment if I could. But I cannot. Cannot, Brother Michael. Because if I did, I would be guilty of heresy for disagreeing with the Holy Office, and I would be tied to the stake as well."

"There is yet something that can be done," I said, heeding a sudden inspiration. "Something that would not seem uncooperative to the Inquisitor."

"And what might that be?" the bishop asked suspiciously.

"Father Francis is sentenced to the pyre tomorrow morning. Is that correct?"

"It is," the bishop grunted. "That weasel Montaigne wants to erect the stake in the village of Sainte Felice. I've done my best to try to move it here to Orleans, but the duke is not being cooperative. I don't know what else to do."

"Excellency," I said softly, "you must allow the magistrate to erect the stake in the village of Sainte Felice."

The bishop glared up at me. "Have you gone mad, boy? If I allowed that, it would cause an uprising that would take all the soldiers in Orleans to quell."

"Excellency," I said in a humble tone, "forgive me. I am but a novice and unschooled in these matters, but it seems to me that if Montaigne causes a riot over attempting to burn the abbot in Sainte Felice, it would be the king's responsibility, and not yours. Surely the Holy Office could not fault you for it."

He stroked his multiple chins and studied me for a long moment. "He has taught you well, I see."

I stared at him. "Excellency?"

The bishop heaved a sigh. "Your abbot is a man unequaled in the art of persuasion. Many is the time that I would watch helplessly as he would take the words from my mouth, tie them into knots, and flog me with them until I found myself agreeing with everything he said. And all while pouring me yet another goblet of that exquisite wine."

"Excellency." I knelt down onto the carpet. "I beg you, please help him. He may be a sorcerer. He may be a saint. He may be both. But it doesn't matter. He means so much to so many people. Please, if you can do no more, do this one thing. Let Montaigne have his way."

"Oh, very well." The bishop rose ungracefully to his feet and waddled over to me. "I promise nothing, mind you. But I will do as you ask."

"Oh, thank you, Excellency." I kissed his ring so many times that the bishop pulled his hand away in embarrassment. I rose to my feet, but hesitated before turning to leave.

"Is there something else?" the bishop asked.

I nodded, pressing my lips together as I stared at the floor. "Could I see him?"

The bishop considered this. "I don't see why not," he replied. "But just for a moment. I don't want that bastard Pagnelli on my neck because of it."

Gratefully, I agreed. Bishop Sorel went to the door and

ordered two of the soldiers to escort me down to the dungeon.

I ran my hand firmly along the stone wall of the stairs in order to steady myself as I followed the guards down into the bowels of the bishop's castle. I knew all too well what the inside of a dungeon looked like, and it only served to increase my dread at what I would find. I felt as though I had returned to Hell itself, and I had to shut my ears with an effort to the moans and cries of the damned that followed my passage down the dark corridor.

The abbot's cell was the last one in the row. The guard produced a set of keys and unlocked the door. I placed my torch in the holder on the wall and entered.

Abbot Francis lay sprawled on the filthy straw—his habit torn and bloody, his thick hair matted, his hands and feet raw and oozing beneath the cruel shackles that chained him to the wall like an animal. The sight broke my heart in pieces. But there was no time for self-indulgent tears. I had only a few moments and I had to make them count.

"Father Francis?" My whispered voice echoed from the stone walls like hissing serpents as I knelt beside him and laid a hand on his shoulder. I thought for a moment that he was asleep, or lying in a faint. But at last he raised his head and looked up at me.

"Michael?" he murmured, then shook his head. "No ... a dream."

"Yes, yes." I grasped him by the shoulders and pulled him to a kneeling posture. "I persuaded the bishop to let me see you. Now, please listen. I don't have much time. We are attempting to arrange a pardon."

To my horror, the abbot shook his head. "It is no use, my dear Michael. The show is over. The juggler has stumbled and dropped his batons. I thought that I could command both the powers of this world and the next, the sacred and the profane, the godly and the ungodly. I offered up my life to the Holy Angels for this ability. But I was foolish … damned foolish, and now I must pay for my folly."

I shook my head earnestly. "Forgive me, Father Francis, but you are wrong. You have pledged them your life and it is your life they want, not your death." The words tumbled out of my mouth unbidden. "Your life is what has been a blessing to so many, to us and to the people of Sainte Felice. This is the life the angels want. Dying would be far easier."

I had no idea what I was saying. Something hovering behind me was putting words into my mouth that I didn't understand. But I continued to babble as the abbot's eyes widened in astonishment. "Dear Father Francis, you have no idea what has been happening to you. You told me yourself when I first arrived at Sainte Felice that this is not a performance, not a magical *tour de force* like the ones that so dazzled the Fratres Illuminati in Rome. And it is indeed so. You command nothing. You called upon the blessed archangels, and now it is they who command you."

He studied me for a moment. "You have been practicing the art, haven't you?"

"Yes, and I have succeeded. John has been guiding me. The Archangel Michael gave us a sign. The sign shall be seen when the pyre is erected in the village square of Sainte Felice."

The abbot frowned. "But that is absurd. The bishop would never allow it."

"He will. I managed to convince him to acquiesce to Montaigne's wishes."

"You did?" Abbot Francis thought for a moment, then looked up at me with a glimmer of hope in his pained countenance. "Very well, we will await the sign. What would you have of me?"

"Just believe in us, as we have all believed in you. You have saved all of us in some way or another. Allow us to do the same for you."

He was silent for a moment, then smiled faintly. "It shall be as you say, my young magus."

The guard rattled the bars to signal me that my time was up. I grasped the abbot's hand in both of mine and kissed it fervently. "Pray for me," I whispered.

"Without ceasing," he replied softly. I rose to my feet and turned away with an effort as the guard let me out the door. I could feel the abbot's intense gaze until the iron door slammed shut behind me.

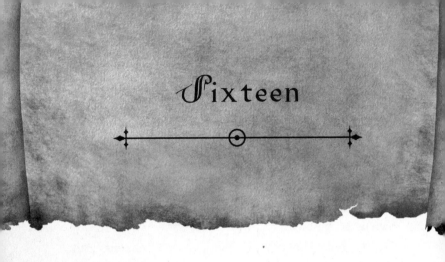

Sixteen

We arrived in the village square well before dawn, and we were not the first to gather. Already a crowd of villagers had assembled at the fountain brandishing kitchen knives, broom handles, and other makeshift weapons. Journet, gripping a stout club, moved among them, going from person to person and speaking to each one. All I could hear were angry whispers and muffled curses.

Journet caught sight of us and made his way over to greet us as we maneuvered the mule through the gathering crowd.

"I have sent runners throughout the countryside, Brother Fernando," he said. "People from as far away as Paris are coming. And I have told them to be armed with some weapon. If Montaigne so much as singes one hair on Father Francis' head, we will fight."

"Many of you could die," John warned.

Journet scoffed. "Many more of us would have died without Father Francis."

As the sky lightened even more, carriages filled with sumptuously dressed people filed up the road. More and more villagers, many whom I had never seen before, gathered, both mounted and on foot, until there was no room to breathe.

"Come with me." Journet led us through the bodies. After a moment, I stumbled against a pile of sticks and straw. I glanced up and could not help gasping. In the glowing light from the rising sun, the pyre loomed up above me, the wooden post reaching nearly to the sky. It stood only a few yards from the fountain. I clutched at the cross at my breast and breathed a silent prayer.

Would the archangel come through with a sign, or was it all over?

Drums and the clatter of hoofbeats rumbled like thunder and lightning. The angry voices grew louder. From the Orleans road, a procession of soldiers rode through the restless crowd. There had to be at least twenty of them, armed with swords and crossbows. The people fell back reluctantly as the horses passed, merging in a wave behind them and cutting off any effective retreat.

Flanked by two lines of horsemen, Abbot Francis rode on a large, black horse. His hands were tied behind him and he sat the horse with difficulty. At the sight of him, the crowd roared as with one voice, many brandishing their weapons in a show of force that the soldiers were hardly expecting. Several of them dismounted and held the angry crowd at bay with crossbows as two soldiers pulled the abbot down out of the saddle.

The drummers in the lead began beating their drums while the two soldiers led the abbot to the pyre. Giles de Montaigne, his black gown flowing behind him, followed. Four soldiers flanked him, twitching nervously as the people hurled jeers, insults, and occasionally pebbles at them.

Montaigne, his face set into a permanent scowl, did not take his gaze from the abbot's form as he walked through the village square. It took two soldiers, one on either side, to drag Abbot Francis, stumbling and slipping on the loose twigs, up onto the pyre. Finally the soldiers stood him up against the stake and tied him securely about the waist.

Montaigne gathered his robes up around his knees and climbed up onto the pyre, facing the abbot squarely.

"Jean-Phillipe Desqueroux," he intoned. "Also known as Francis Duchienne. You have been tried and found guilty of the crimes of heresy and sorcery. Have you anything to say before sentence is passed upon you?"

The crowd began to murmur and rumble. Abbot Francis, his features composed in resignation, merely shut his eyes and remained silent.

Montaigne clearly had not expected this reaction and glanced around nervously at the crowd that began to press in on the base of the pyre, waving their weapons. I was sure that, perhaps for the first time, Montaigne realized that if he lit the abbot's pyre, he would never get out of Sainte Felice alive.

His scowl deepening, Montaigne cleared his throat and

went on. "In the name of His Majesty, Louis XI, King of France, I hereby sentence you to be burnt at the stake and your ashes scattered to the four winds. And may God have mercy upon your soul."

At the sound of a single drum roll, a soldier carrying a burning brand approached the pyre. I clutched at the cross around my neck so hard my knuckles grew white. Beside me, Fernando whimpered and began to tremble. John took him firmly by the shoulders. "Have faith, dear brother," he whispered. Juan-José merely grumbled and rested his hand on the hilt of his sword.

Not caring what the villagers thought, I kissed the cross and held it aloft. "Michael!" I called over the angry din. "Mighty Archangel, show us your sign."

The soldier thrust the burning brand into the sticks at the base of the abbot's pyre. I held my breath as the flame flared briefly, then abruptly went out. The soldier swore loudly as other soldiers piled on more straw and sticks. The first soldier relit the torch and tried again. The straw steadfastly refused to ignite.

A hush fell over the crowd. Several people murmured prayers and crossed themselves. One more time, the soldier relit the torch and thrust it into the base of the pyre, keeping it in place so long that the flame crept up the torch and seared his fingers. He let go with a yell, but the flame immediately vanished. It was clear to all that the pyre simply would not catch fire.

The crowd began to roar, scream, cry, and pray. Abbot Francis opened his eyes and looked up in astonishment.

Finally, Montaigne, with a shriek of fury that echoed off the far hills, grabbed the torch from the soldier's hand. He relit it, then knelt down and thrust it into the pyre himself.

A wind blew up out of nowhere, whistling through the village square like a vengeful spirit. The torch flared and ignited the hem of Montaigne's robe. Screaming, Montaigne ran from the pyre towards the fountain, the yellow flames licking at the folds of his gown. He finally fell to the ground and one of the soldiers tossed a blanket over him.

Still, the abbot's pyre remained unlit. Marcel broke away from us and scrambled up onto the pyre, facing the crowd.

"Behold the judgment of Almighty God," he cried above the babble. "He has separated the wheat from the chaff. The innocent has been spared, and the true sinner punished by the purifying flames. Justice has been done!"

I could no longer contain my tears of joy as I kissed the cross one last time, breathing my prayer of thanks to the holy angels. Marcel stood aside and allowed Fernando and Juan-José to climb the pyre beside him. Juan-José drew his sword and sliced through the ropes that bound Abbot Francis to the stake. The abbot fell, half fainting, into Fernando's arms.

The crowd roared its approval. John and I also ran to the abbot's side as Fernando and Juan-José helped him down from the pyre. Montaigne, singed and furious, picked himself up off the ground and faced us defiantly as the soldiers flanked him, crossbows drawn against the furious mob.

Before Montaigne could utter so much as a word, another group of soldiers rode through the crowd. This time they wore livery emblazoned with the fleur-de-lis. Their captain dismounted and handed Montaigne a document from which a heavy red seal hung by a ribbon. Montaigne read it through, then crumbled it up with a snarl. He tossed it to the ground, turned, and stalked away amid the cheers of the crowd.

Ignoring Montaigne completely, the captain looked at each of us in turn. "Which of you is Abbot Duchienne?"

"I am," the abbot said.

"Then come with me, if you please," the captain replied. "I have orders from His Majesty King Louis of France to escort you to the palace at Plessis-les-Tours."

Juan-José scowled, but before he could reach for his sword, Abbot Francis laid a firm hand on his arm. "I don't think that will be necessary, my brother," the abbot said gently. "Let us see what His Majesty wants with me."

Calmly, Abbot Francis mounted a horse that had been brought for him and rode off, flanked by the liveried soldiers.

"Well, he certainly is not going anywhere without us," Juan-José declared.

"You go," Marcel said, eyeing the crowd intently. "I'll keep the cauldron stirred up here."

Quickly, Fernando fetched the mule cart and the other brothers clambered into it. I reached for the edge of the cart also, but the nervous mule brayed and fidgeted and I lost my grip. Hoards of people stampeded like a herd of cattle towards the base of the pyre, snatching bits of straw and twigs as souvenirs of the miracle, and I found myself lost in the backwash of bodies that crowded between me and the cart.

Fernando brought the mule under control and Juan-José bellowed my name. I cried out in reply, but the crowd, like a human tide, swept the cart down the road before it until I could no longer even see it much less reach it. I called out again, but my voice drowned in the shouting and babbling of the people around me.

I called out one more time, my voice shrill with despair. A horse trotted up behind me and snorted, making me jump.

"Climb up," the rider said. "We will get there faster than they will."

"Antonin!" I cried.

With a grin, he reached down and grasped my arm, pulling me up behind him. I clutched him about the waist as he maneuvered the skittish horse through the crowd.

"You have no idea how glad I am to see you," I said when we were finally heading down the road. "Father Francis has been arrested by soldiers."

"I know. I followed them here."

"But who are they, and where are they taking him?"

"They are members of the royal guard," Antonin replied grimly. "Francis has been summoned before His Majesty King Louis."

I caught my breath. "What for?"

"In order to find out if all the stories that he's heard are true."

"What happens when he finds out that they are?"

"That remains to be seen." Antonin replied. "No doubt he's heard all the lurid tales of our abbot's past. On the other hand, he might not be willing to allow his daughter's confessor and favorite saint to burn at the stake just to placate either Montaigne or an Italian Inquisitor."

"His daughter?" I echoed. "The Duchess of Orleans is the king's daughter?"

"It appears so." Antonin turned to me with a raised eyebrow. "Apparently, she sent a messenger to her father as soon as the warrant was issued. Louis knew about Francis' arrest and, even more importantly, about the riot that would ensue. But then Montaigne turned up on the royal doorstep with that Inquisitor in tow. And now Louis must decide if Francis should be spared."

"And if he does?"

"According to Her Grace, Louis has scant use for the Inquisition and desires to keep them out of France at all costs. So if Louis grants Francis a royal pardon, there is nothing that the Holy Office can do, in France at any rate."

"And if he doesn't?"

"Then our abbot will go from one pyre to another," Antonin replied softly.

I shut my eyes against the tears of despair that welled up behind my eyelids. Did I dare believe what had happened in the darkness of the Tabernacle, or had it all been a cruel delusion? Maybe there had been no archangel and no miracle. Maybe the straw on the abbot's pyre had been wet or moldy and it wouldn't have caught fire no matter what anyone did.

All I really knew for sure was that if Abbot Francis perished in the flames, my heart and soul would perish with him.

The walls and spires of the city of Tours loomed before us as we left the main road and crossed a stone bridge over the river. The procession wound around a hill towards the steep ramparts of a castle.

"That must be Plessis," Antonin commented, as we watched the soldiers head towards the massive gate.

I stared at it in distaste. "It looks more like a fortress than a palace."

"No doubt Louis thinks more of security than of comfort," Antonin said. "So he leaves the luxury to the bishop."

He reined the horse in under a tree and dismounted. Reaching into one of his saddle bags, he extracted his black habit and scapular and tossed them over his head, hiding his tunic and leather hose beneath the generous black folds. Vaulting back into the saddle, he nudged the mare into an easy canter.

We caught up with the royal guard just as the drawbridge lowered. Antonin nudged the mare behind the last horse and we followed the soldiers across the bridge into the fortress.

The soldiers halted at the gate. Abbot Francis dismounted in the grassy courtyard and we discreetly dismounted behind him. As he approached the entryway flanked by armed guards, the Duchess and her mother-in-law appeared in the doorway.

The Duchess cried out, ran towards the abbot, and flung herself at his feet. "Oh, Blessed Father." She clasped his hands in hers. "I had so feared that our guard arrived too late."

Her voice dissolved into sobs as Abbot Francis raised her to her feet. "Be comforted, my daughter." He patted her hands. "I am unhurt."

"Ah, you have arrived." The Duke emerged from the doorway. "Good. His Majesty has been pacing the floor all morning. Come."

The Duke led the way through the door and into the foyer. A crowd of soldiers, courtiers, nobles, and servants who had been waiting for a glimpse of the notorious Abbot of Sainte Felice began to press forward. Only a couple of guards held them at bay. I elbowed my way past them, caught up to Abbot Francis, and took his arm. Reaching into the folds of my habit, I brought out his pectoral cross.

"Here." I pressed it into his hand. "You might need this."

He gazed down at me for a moment with an expression too complex for me to fathom. Then he smiled and quickly slipped the chain over his head. I fell back as the soldiers surrounded him and let the tide carry me into the great hall.

King Louis stood as we entered, the ermine-trimmed hem of his mantle brushing the stone floor. He looked old and withered, with a sharp-featured face and tiny eyes. Behind him stood Fra Pagnelli, not much taller or more pleasant looking. But it didn't look as though the king was any more pleased with Pagnelli's presence than he was with ours.

Scowling, he waved the soldiers back towards the door, leaving Abbot Francis standing alone in the center of the massive room. I pushed forward, but someone behind me grabbed me firmly by the arm.

"You cannot help him," Antonin whispered in my ear as he drew me back against the wall. "It is his turn, now."

"Abbot Duchienne," Louis began, fixing the abbot with a piercing gaze. "You have put me in a very difficult situation."

"I, your Majesty?" the abbot asked, pointing to his own chest. "How so?"

Louis reached over to the table and picked up a letter bearing a large red seal. "This." He waved the parchment about emphatically. "This is a letter from His Holiness the Pope declaring your beatification. I received it on the same day I received this." He held up another document, also with a red seal. "A royal decree from the Magistrate of Orleans declaring that you are to be burnt for the crime of sorcery in the village square of Sainte Felice. I cannot help but wonder, who is this Blessed Francis Duchienne and why is my magistrate burning him at the stake?"

The abbot's mouth tightened. "Your Majesty," he began.

Louis ignored him and paced the floor in agitation.

"Upon inquiry, I learned from Cardinal de Joinville that you are a rabble rouser, a troublemaker, and an enormous pain in the clerical arse. The Grand Inquisitor over there claims that you are a dangerous heretic and a sorcerer. However, my daughter, the Duchess of Orleans, insists that you are a saint and a worker of miracles. She gave me a sample of this blessed wine of yours." Louis held aloft a crystal decanter, its contents glowing like a ruby. "The real thing, mind you, not whatever swill you gave to De Joinville, and it indeed is everything that it is reputed to be. Abbot Duchienne, what the devil is going on here?"

The abbot stepped forward and a hush fell upon the crowd gathered in the king's chambers. "Majesty," he began softly, as though he were making a deathbed confession, "you have been most gracious to grant me this audience. You deserve the truth, and I will give it to you. Know that my given name was Jean-Phillipe Desqueroux, and I was the fourth son of the Duke of Nivernais. As a youth, I had little inclination for arms, and so I was sent to the University of Paris to take a degree in Theology, to prepare for the priesthood. While there, I began the study of certain arcane subjects that the Church has forbidden to the faithful. Being of a curious and somewhat argumentative disposition, I chose to discover for myself the nature of these forbidden things. So I traveled to Rome and became Grand Master of the Fratres Illuminati, a secret order which engaged in these arcane practices."

He paused for a moment, clasping his hands together as though in prayer and pressing his fingers to his lips. The assembled company remained silent, focused on the abbot's every word as though he were delivering one of his riveting sermons. At last, he continued. "I soon began to realize the order was hopelessly corrupt, and I attempted to reform it. But by then it was too late. I was turned over to the Holy Office, tried for heresy, and condemned to the pyre. Still, God was merciful to me, poor sinner that I was. On the way to the square, the cart in which I rode overturned, dumping me into the Tiber. I was assumed dead. In actual fact, I was rescued by several Milanese peasants who aided me in returning to France. I arrived in Orleans, changed my name, and took Holy Orders as a Benedictine monk. I was finally ordained by Bishop Sorel in the Cathedral of St. Martin, and was sent by him to the Monastery of Sainte Felice, long abandoned by the Church, to revive it, which I have done to the benefit of both Church and Crown."

Only Fra Pagnelli seemed to be unmoved. The scowl on his thin face deepened, his thin lips tightened, and he thrust his hands more deeply into the sleeves of his habit. I watched him for a moment, a sudden shiver running up my spine. A more diabolical look I had never seen on a human face. He had lost this round, and he knew it.

"God forgives His prodigal sons," the abbot said, with a sidelong glance at Fra Pagnelli. "But sadly the Church often does not. There were those within the Holy Office who desired vengeance rather than justice and were not content with my repentance. They wished my death. Consequently, when the overzealous Magistrate of Orleans wrote to them concerning me, they were all too willing to come to France and assert their authority. It was under their auspices that Giles de Montaigne arrested me, chained me in the bishop's dungeon, and set up the pyre in Sainte Felice. The rest I believe you know."

Abbot Francis took a step forward and spread his hands before him in a gesture of supplication. "And so, your Majesty, I commend myself to you, a sorcerer to some, a saint to others, but in any case, a man devoted only to the service of God's people...and yours."

The abbot finally fell silent. The only sound I heard was the collective breathing of the spectators. A prickle of something—terror, excitement, I know not what—crept up my spine. Something was about to happen. I held my breath.

Whether it was a trick, an accident of nature, or the work of angels, I shall never know. But as the echo of the abbot's voice died away, the sun moved to where it shone through a small stained glass window placed high in the vaulted ceiling, sending a shaft of golden light down to the precise spot in which he stood.

I watched as a corona of brilliance surround him, glinting off his rumpled hair and torn habit. I remembered the last time I had seen him illuminated thus, the moment I became a novice monk. Then, he had been magnificent in his priestly garb, standing before the altar and wearing the golden cross that was both the symbol of his office and the source of his power. But now, even though he stood stripped of his priestly vestments, battered and bruised, with shackles still around his wrists, he was still a Sacred

Magician—part saint, part sorcerer, with the *baraka* that Juan-José told me about emanating from him like an odor of sanctity.

A gasp rose up from the assembled company. Many knelt and crossed themselves. I heard one or two sobs. Several others looked frightened and made for the door.

King Louis, however, seemed to accept the situation as he saw it. "Very well, Abbot Duchienne. Far be it from me to question the ways of the Almighty." He picked up a third document from the table, this one also carrying a heavy red wax seal, and held it out before him. "Here is your pardon. Now, go back to your monastery, make your blessed wine, and live in peace. I ask but one thing from you."

The abbot looked startled. "What would you have, Your Majesty?"

"Your blessing." Striding forward, Louis knelt at the abbot's feet. Slowly, Abbot Francis laid his left hand on the crown of the royal head and made the sign of the cross with his right.

"*In nomine Patris et Filii et Spiritus Sancti,*" he intoned. "Amen." The sun finally moved away from the window and the brilliance faded.

Louis rose to his feet. "Farewell, Abbot Duchienne."

"God keep you, Your Majesty." Abbot Francis bowed slightly, then turned and strode from the hall, with Antonin and me at his heels.

Out of the corner of my eye, I caught a glance of Fra Pagnelli's face and I shuddered. His bony features were dark with a fury that seemed decidedly unclerical, and his fists clenched and unclenched at his sides. But he could do nothing. His teeth had been pulled, at least in France. He had no choice but to go back to Rome empty-handed.

The young Duchess of Orleans pushed her way through the crowd. "Oh, Blessed Father." She knelt directly in the abbot's path, trapping him so that he could progress no farther. "I prayed to the Virgin that my father would pardon you."

I watched her for a long moment, a feeling of shame rising in my breast. Here was a young woman we all had laughed at for her simple-minded devotion—just as I had scorned my mother's similar devotion. But the duchess had been as instrumental in saving the abbot's life as I had. Perhaps even more so. Her faith in him had never wavered, as mine had.

Abbot Francis smiled, took her hands in his, and raised her to her feet, pointedly moving her out of the way. "I am grateful for your intercession, my daughter. God has truly been merciful. I must bid you farewell for now. I have abbey business to attend to."

By now we had reached the door, and Antonin and I flanked the abbot to make sure that nobody else got in the way. Fernando and Juan-José met us in the archway and I could see the mule cart standing out in the courtyard.

"Francis!" Fernando said, clutching the abbot's arm. "What happened?"

The abbot gave him a reassuring smile. "His Majesty

has decided to keep me around for a while." He handed Fernando the parchment.

Fernando scanned the parchment, Juan-José reading over his shoulder.

"A royal pardon!" Fernando exclaimed with a delighted grin while Juan-José whistled in astonishment.

"I do not think we will have to worry about Montaigne for a long time," Antonin said.

We stepped out into the courtyard and found John holding the reins of the mule. Fernando showed him the pardon. He embraced the abbot with a secretive smile, as though it were something he had known all along.

"Come, my brothers." Abbot Francis heaved a weary sigh. "I've had quite enough of dungeons and pyres for one day. Let's go home."

Antonin drew me aside. "Take the horse and ride into the village." He took the parchment from Fernando's fingers and handed it to me. "Deliver this to Montaigne and tell him that if we ever see his ugly face in Sainte Felice again, we will personally roast him on his own pyre. Now, go. Quickly!"

Bearing the precious parchment close to my heart, I mounted the horse and took off at a gallop. The chill wind whistled past my ears as I crouched low on the horse's back. I felt as though my soul, my faith, and my hope had sprouted wings. But even though I rode the horse into a lather, the sun was dipping down towards the horizon by the time I reached the village.

Montaigne's soldiers were still prowling the square,

fending off the insults and jeers of the townsfolk. I dismounted and led the horse past them towards Journet's tavern. Inside, Journet and Marcel sat near the door, eyeing Montaigne and his crossbow man, who lounged with deceptive ease by the hearth.

"Michael!" Marcel jumped to his feet as I entered, ignoring the crossbow bolt pointed at his midsection. "Thank God someone has returned. This vermin refuses to leave."

"Well, they have no choice but to leave now." I held up the parchment. "There will be no burning here, by the king's orders."

Montaigne strode forward. "Give me that." He snatched the parchment from my fingers. Marcel and I gave each other a meaningful glance as Montaigne scanned the parchment with an ever deepening scowl. "What devilry did he use to arrange this?"

"It doesn't matter," Marcel replied archly. "The king has pardoned him. So get your soldiers and your lumber out of this village."

Journet cast his gaze up to heaven and crossed himself. Montaigne, his thin lips pressed tightly together, glowered at each of us in turn. Finally, however, he had no choice but to call his soldiers and order them to dismantle the pyre. The soldiers nodded and ducked out of the door of the tavern.

"I shall make sure they do what they're told," Journet said gleefully as he followed them out the door. We heard his voice ringing like a church bell in the courtyard, announcing that the abbot had been pardoned. A cheer rose up from the villagers assembled by the fountain.

Montaigne slipped the parchment into his belt and turned towards the door. "Very well," he conceded gracelessly. "You have won ... for now."

Marcel quickly drew the dagger at his belt and pressed it against Montaigne's ribs as I plucked the parchment from his waist.

"I think that we shall take this," I said, tucking it into my own girdle. "We shouldn't want it to suddenly vanish."

"Now, get out of here," Marcel poked the point of the dagger deep into the folds of Montaigne's singed robes. "Before the rest of you gets torched as well."

Montaigne clenched his fists in frustrated fury. "Of all the diabolical impudence," he muttered. "Even on the pyre, he calls upon his foul spirits for aid."

I opened my mouth to tell him that it had been I who had summoned that aid. And yet I couldn't make the words come out. I should have been proud of my newly found magical power. But instead, a feeling of mortification engulfed me, making my stomach drop to my toes. Just how much summoning could I have done without the abbot's tutelage and the support of my brothers?

I knew that I stood at a crossroad. In order to consider myself a Sacred Magician rather than, as John had said, merely a conjurer in a black robe, I had one final test to pass—that of humility. Whatever I had done, I had only been an instrument of a far greater power. It hadn't mattered who had performed the magical rite that had summoned the angelic forces for aid—all that mattered was that the help had arrived, that everyone was safe, and that, for the moment at any rate, justice had prevailed.

"And those spirits have obeyed him, in spite of you. However, in his mercy, he has spared your worthless hide." I lifted my gaze and met Montaigne's eyes. "But if you so much as lay a hand upon any of the brothers again, he will summon them to finish the job."

Montaigne frowned darkly, his eyes glittering with the fear that John had assured me lurked beneath his hatred. "One day, you will all burn."

I saw a smile of approval tweak at the corner of Marcel's battered mouth. He turned back to Montaigne. "That may be." He gave Montaigne a stern look. "But not today, and not by you. Now, go!"

Prodded by Marcel's dagger one last time, Montaigne turned and stomped out of the door. Marcel watched the door until we could no longer hear Montaigne's furious footsteps.

"Father Francis would admonish us that 'Vengeance is mine, saith the Lord,'" I said, quoting a long-forgotten scripture.

"Maybe," Marcel conceded. "But sometimes He allows us to be instruments of that vengeance."

"Sometimes." I turned to Marcel, who met my gaze for a long moment. "Damn fool thing to do," I finally said with a faint smile. "Running off like that."

He gave me a lopsided grin. "It won't happen again."

I was about to comment when I heard the unmistakable

sound of cartwheels and the braying of a decidedly unhappy mule. Marcel and I ran out of the tavern as Fernando drove the cart into the center of the village.

If Abbot Francis was hopeful of returning to the monastery before nightfall, those hopes were surely dashed by the crowd of villagers and well-wishers who clustered around the mule cart, effectively preventing the mule from even moving. There was nothing to do but help the abbot out of the cart and escort him into Journet's tavern.

Soon, the tiny room filled to the walls with people, jostling, laughing, calling for wine and ale. A man with a concertina jumped up onto a chair and began squeezing a raucous tune. Several of the young men and damsels began to dance.

We seated the abbot on a stool by the blazing hearth and put a cup of warm wine in his hands. Antonin hovered on one side of him and I on the other. Villagers clustered about him, sitting at his feet and kissing his hands with expressions of joy and congratulations. Even the miserly cheesemonger came to pay his respects. Soon I was pleased to see that the deep lines of pain and weariness around the abbot's mouth and eyes began to smooth out and his genial smile return.

Finally, Journet himself came over and knelt beside the abbot, gazing up into his face with a strangely grave and solemn expression. "Tell me, Father Francis. Is it true what they say?"

A cold shudder rippled through me. Was Journet going to ask about the charges of sorcery? How would the abbot explain our magic to this quick-witted but unlettered man? Would Journet understand?

"What is it that they say, Emil?" the abbot asked gently.

"That you have been beatified by the Pope?"

I let my breath out in relief, but the abbot shifted uncomfortably on his stool. "It is true, Emil." He gave Journet a stern look. "However, if you plan on selling my bones as relics, you will have to wait until I am actually dead. Is that understood?"

Journet frowned in confusion, wondering if he had committed some grievous offense. But Antonin and I both dissolved into helpless laughter. Finally, Fernando wandered over to find out what was going on. "What is so funny?"

"We will tell you on the way," Antonin said, wiping his eyes with his sleeve. "Come. It is time to get Francis back to the abbey."

The stars twinkled in the black sky like a thousand candles as we bid Journet a good night and bundled the abbot into the cart. Then, with a shout, Fernando urged the reluctant mule onto the road and we rumbled up the hill towards the monastery.

About the Author

Ann Finnin has a degree in biology and works as a freelance technical writer for the healthcare industry. Ann and her husband Dave live in the hills of Tujunga, California, with a big black Lab named Hunter.